Amanda Brunker .nd
a former Miss Ireland. Glamorous and outspoken,
she's rarely out of the public eye. *Champagne Babes*
is her second novel; her first, *Champagne Kisses*, is
also published by Transworld Ireland.

Reasons to read *Champagne Kisses*:

'One of the most hilarious books I've ever read'
Patricia Scanlan

'An Irish Jackie Collins is born'
Evening Herald

'Amanda Brunker stirs up a saucy, steaming
pot-boiler spiced up with racks of totty hot
enough to self-combust'
Sunday Independent

'Light, frothy, fun. Great to pop in your bag
on the way to the beach'
News of the World

'Laugh out loud stuff. The ultimate page-turner'
Sunday World

www.rbooks.co.uk
www.transworldireland.ie

CHAMPAGNE BABES

Amanda Brunker

TRANSWORLD IRELAND

TRANSWORLD IRELAND
an imprint of The Random House Group Limited
20 Vauxhall Bridge Road, London SW1V 2SA
www.rbooks.co.uk

CHAMPAGNE BABES
A TRANSWORLD IRELAND BOOK: 9781848270503

First published in Great Britain
in 2009 by Transworld Ireland,
Transworld Ireland paperback edition published 2010

Copyright © Amanda Brunker 2009

A CIP catalogue record for this book
is available from the British Library.

Addresses for Random House Group Ltd companies outside the UK
can be found at: www.randomhouse.co.uk
The Random House Group Ltd Reg. No. 954009

Penguin Random House is committed to a sustainable future for
our business, our readers and our planet. This book is made from
Forest Stewardship Council® certified paper.

MIX
Paper from
responsible sources
FSC® C018179

Printed and bound in Great Britain by Clays Ltd, Elcograf S.p.A.

Typeset in 12/14pt Bembo by
Kestrel Data, Exeter, Devon.
2 4 6 8 10 9 7 5 3 1

To Jade Goody and all other cancer victims.
I had a scare during the writing of this book.
And I know how lucky I am.

CHAMPAGNE BABES

1

'Don't blame Michael for just being a man – he can't help being clueless. It's genetics . . .'

'Excuse me?'

'You heard me . . . Your husband is reacting no differently from any other man in his situation. You've had a baby, and that means he has to share you. Men don't like to share.'

'Oh, so that means I just have to ignore his mood swings, then . . . Sorry, but was I not the one who gave birth? Am I not allowed to be the fragile one?'

'No, you're not. You're the mother. You're the one who has to know all and understand all. And if you'd had any sense, you'd have known not to get pregnant two seconds after his whirlwind proposal.'

'Says those in glass houses! At least I married the father of my child. You don't even know the name of yours.'

As celebrations went, this was a disaster. It was my first night out on the town since the birth of my daughter Daisy, a month previously, and for some reason my best buddies Lisa and Maddie were at each other's throats and bitching at me in the crossfire. Tired, emotional and with half a bottle of Bollinger inside me, my temper was flaring. Maybe I was annoyed with my grumpy husband at home rather than the girls, but he was there and they were here, and nobody was going to boss me about on my first night out.

'Well, at least I didn't trap my man,' snarled Maddie, clearly wounded by my comments. 'One minute you're in a coma, next you're pushing Michael – who you'd barely even noticed before, may I add – and then you're marching him up the aisle. You hardly had time to find out if he was a grumpy bastard or not.'

'Fuck off, Maddie. He's a decent guy. Just because we're fighting at the moment doesn't make him a shitty person. All couples argue. Since when did he become public enemy number one? He cared for me through my coma, and nursed me back to health in the months afterwards. The man deserves a medal.'

'Oh, get off your high horse,' growled Maddie again. 'A minute ago you were cursing him. And now you're—'

'Oh, stop barking at her, Maddie,' interrupted Lisa. 'Just because you're a mother doesn't make you an authority on everything. This was supposed to be fun, remember?'

'Well, I just think Eva needs to remember her role as a mother, now. Daisy is special and she needs extra—'

Not able to contain my anger, I saw red. In a fury I grabbed my coat and bag from under the table, and screamed, 'Stuff your champagne. I don't need a lecture from you . . .' And with that I ran out of the bar, leaving the two girls dumbstruck, and pushed my hand out in front of the first taxi I saw. I needed to get away from Maddie before any more hurtful things were said. I wasn't used to getting so angry with her. Maybe it was my hormones, but I was too mad to be reasonable.

Despite the fact that I had really been looking forward to getting out and feeling like the old Eva, this wasn't the evening that I had planned in my head. I was all dressed up, but the only place for me to go was home . . .

Within seconds a car had pulled up and I gratefully slumped into the back. With the directions to the house in Terenure given, I closed my eyes and practised some breathing exercises I had learnt at yoga, hoping to steady my nerves. I hated it when there were cross words between us. It didn't happen often. I just needed to get home and sleep off this frustration. Or maybe I'd have a little nap on the way? I didn't think I had had too much to drink, but the fresh air had kinda knocked me for six. Yes, a short sleep would be good. The taxi was nice and warm, and . . . somehow exhaustion had overpowered me. I was sleepy. I was too hot. I wasn't sure where I was.

I had to open my eyes, though. Something didn't seem right.

What was that smell? Was it cigarettes, coffee and sweat? Who was touching me? It hurt. The weight on my chest made it hard to breathe.

I had to sit up.

I couldn't.

I tried to open my eyes, but they were now being

held shut. I tried to wriggle, but somebody was on top of me.

Wake up, Eva, this is serious.

The pressure on my chest was increasing. It was now almost impossible to breathe.

Focus, girl, snap awake and fight.

I didn't feel strong enough but somehow a natural instinct to defend myself kicked in.

'Je-sus Chr-ist,' I screamed through the dirty hand across my face. Panic gripped me. The realization that I was in a car with a man on top of me, and, hold on . . . this was a taxi. I was in a taxi . . . and this was the taxi driver who was crushing me. I was being pushed down on the back seat, while the man I'd trusted to get me home safe held me down with the weight of his body. One of his hands was on my face, while the other was forcing its way down my top.

I struggled, but he was so strong. His hands were rough and abrasive on my skin as I tried to free myself from his vice-like grip. The stench of stale nicotine on his fingers was as violent as the force he was using to keep me trapped.

A memory of stepping into the taxi flashed through my head. I'd hailed it after running out on the girls. The streets had been quiet. I'd been standing all alone. I'd been easy prey: I'm sure I'd looked drunk stumbling down the street. A vulnerable woman without the protection of her better judgement.

Had I noticed if it was a licensed taxi or not? I was certainly fully aware, now of what was happening to me.

Storming off in a drunken huff had not been a wise move, and I was paying the price for my diva behaviour.

Apart from grunting, my attacker didn't speak. But he did pant rhythmically with arousal.

My head was still quite hazy, but as he crushed my face and breasts I knew I was in grave danger. Was I about to become another rape statistic? Or would this animal kill me?

I didn't want to die.

I needed to think quickly. This was not a time to panic, and struggling was getting me nowhere. His face was a blur, but he felt like a big man. I would need to trick him to get free. So I stopped moving, and tried my best to steady my breath. He didn't notice at first, but then he temporarily paused – as if to reassess the situation before returning to his groping.

Still, there were no words.

I could feel the pull of the leather strap of my hand-bag on my neck. The handbag itself was lying across my stomach, which was probably protecting me from his wandering hands. If he wanted to explore my body further he would have to reposition himself and remove the bag.

What I needed was a diversion, just one lucky moment to make my escape.

I wanted to scream for help, but as his hands slipped down from pressing my eyes and latched themselves around my neck I could see very little through the steamed-up windows. Outside was dimly lit and I was clearly nowhere near the bright lights of the city centre.

What was the point of screaming? No one would hear me, and it would probably only anger him more. Worse still, he could keep me hostage in a cellar somewhere as his sex slave for the next fifty years.

If only there was some way I could hurt him. If only I had a knife or something sharp in my handbag. Desperate thoughts kept flashing through my head. I had visions of him tying me up and dumping me in a lake. Or of him beating me with a crowbar and then running me over. Maybe he'd just torch the car with me in it?

Complete terror had started to overwhelm me, when a mobile phone began to ring. It was his phone ringing from its cradle in the front. Instantly he froze, but he still said nothing.

While he retained his grip around my throat with his left hand, he started to fumble his right one out of my blouse, getting it tangled in my bag strap and nearly decapitating me in the process. With my heart almost pounding out of my chest, I tried to keep my composure.

Could this be my moment?

As the phone continued to ring his mood became panicky. It was obvious that he needed to take the call. His balance unsteady, he made wild swipes to grab the phone with his freed hand, but kept missing. Then, in a clumsy move, he knocked the phone out of its cradle on to the floor. He gasped loudly and then stretched further to retrieve it.

He strained but obviously couldn't reach it. It had stopped ringing. Had he answered it by mistake? Or had he cancelled the call?

I was just about to scream for help, when he lifted his other hand off me but held it just a couple of inches from my face. He kept stretching but still seemed unable to reach the phone. Again I thought about screaming for help, but what would have been the point? I didn't know where I was, so how could anyone rescue me?

Despite his shuffling and my deafening heartbeat, the car was extremely quiet. And as I remained still I faintly heard a voice from the phone, and so did he.

That was the first time I saw him properly. He had tightly cropped hair, a neat moustache, and a large mole on his left cheek. He couldn't have been more than thirty-five years old. As the voice from the phone continued he retreated slowly back to the front seat and gave me this evil glare. Still there were no words, but he made a signal with his hands for silence and a devilish stare that said: 'Don't fuck with me.'

In total submission I raised my two hands while I positioned my feet under me towards the door. He didn't notice in the darkness. He was now too concerned with getting to his phone.

This was my moment. It was either now or never – so I scrabbled at the door handle, unlocked it and pushed it open with one surprisingly swift and easy movement. Out of the corner of my eye I saw my captor panic. It was almost as if he half-lunged towards me but changed his mind midway. I didn't know what stopped him, and I didn't care.

As the cold damp night air refreshed my face, I could feel strength come back to my body. The alcohol haze had lifted and I was focused on my getaway. As I leapt from the taxi I could hear him bash his hands off the steering wheel. He was grunting, but he didn't scream or call out after me. And I wasn't hanging around to exchange goodbyes.

Although I took a lump out of my ankle as I scraped it on the kerb I kept moving forward with speed. Splashing through the waterlogged grass in my strappy Louboutin heels, like a rugby player in drag, I trailed my new Prada handbag that the hubby had bought me for Christmas.

I ran for about ten minutes solidly, until I found myself in a brightly lit housing estate, one of those generic property-boom nondescript mazes, and collapsed once again in exhaustion behind a black Golf Polo that sat in a sterile, uncultivated garden. Although I never looked behind me, I knew I hadn't been followed. I sensed my freedom almost immediately, as if some guardian angel was leading me away from danger.

I had no idea how long I crouched beside the car, rigid with terror. Despite being scantily clad, I could have been there anything up to an hour before I noticed the cold of the cement driveway rising up through my bones.

It wasn't until a passing fox stumbled upon me on a midnight ramble that I snapped out of my trance. It stared at me for a while, with suspicious beady eyes that seemed to question, 'What the hell are you doing out?' At first its body arched with surprise, but then the fox began to relax; no doubt it sensed that I was more scared than it was. Then, as quickly as it had appeared, it was gone, the white of its tail disappearing around the corner of the house.

Left alone once more, I noticed the state I was in.

My feet were destroyed: bloodied and torn from running to safety through bushes and fields, and over gravelled road works. My shoes were ripped, and the M that I had had tattooed on my right ankle on my honeymoon, as a sign of my love for Michael, was covered in mud and barely recognizable.

We'd been so in love the day I'd got that tattoo. We'd larked about, pretending that we were Brad and Angelina, morphing our names to Michaeva, and telling each other that we'd be for ever inseparable.

What another fine mess I had landed myself in! That M would stand for 'magnet for trouble' if, or should I say *when*, my marriage to Michael failed. Everything I touched always seemed to turn to shit.

The last eight months had been a roller coaster. People tell you the first year of marriage is the worst, but you don't really believe them. Whether I'd wanted to or not, I was beginning to now. I'd thought we would be different. Be the couple to defy the odds and make everyone else jealous. Who had I been kidding? Not me any more, that was for sure. I suppose Michael still was my Mr Wonderful, my rock, my soul mate, but for some reason the universe kept throwing us curve balls to push us off course.

Sometimes I looked at him and wondered what I'd ever seen in him. I wasn't even sure I fancied him any more, as all he ever did was annoy and irritate me. Sometimes just the way he left his dirty plates in the sink instead of placing them in the dishwasher six inches to the left would send me crazy. It wasn't exactly a major deal, but it drove me mad.

'It doesn't take much,' he'd bark at me as I banged and crashed around the kitchen. After that, we wouldn't talk for days. Neither of us would be able to back down. 'You're stubborn to the core,' my best friend Maddie always said, and she was right.

But how was I going to explain myself to Michael tonight? He hadn't been impressed that I had '*abandoned him*' with Daisy. She was only four weeks old and he was '*only a man, after all*'.

I had needed some head space, though. I hadn't wanted to become a mother so soon. It had come as a shock to me, too.

Babies were something other people worried about. I might have done an extremely grown-up thing by getting married, but I hadn't been ready to take on any extra responsibility. I wasn't even thirty-two years old yet, and little over a year ago I had been very single, and partying like it was going out of fashion.

As my best friends Parker and Maddie had started to settle down, Parker in a serious (yet currently rocky) relationship with Captain Sensible Jeff, and Maddie becoming a doting mum to Woody, I'd been stepping things up a notch with lesbian girlfriends and Jacuzzi threesomes with cocaine-snorting bad boys. Unbelievably it had taken a bang on the head from the handlebars of a Ducati 1098 to actually knock some sense into me.

I had spent three weeks in a coma, lifeless, tuning

in and out of people's conversations yet completely unable to communicate with them. Everyone had been so worried about me. My limp body had given very little hope to those around me that I'd ever pull through. I'd just been starting to get to know Michael at the time. He'd been reserved and sweet, and for some reason into me, despite my reputation as a spoilt brat.

The first time he'd kissed me I'd still been in a coma. But he hadn't taken advantage of me. I had willed him to lock lips with me. In some ways it had been like he'd breathed new energy into me with each tender smooch. He had given me the kiss of life, and been there by my bedside when I'd eventually woken up.

Along with my family he had helped nurse me back to health, so when he'd popped the question and produced a massive single solitaire diamond ring for my birthday just two months later, how could I have said no? It'd been the stuff of fairy tales. It would have been so unromantic to have looked for reasons *not* to marry Michael.

I had read *The Secret*. I'd been a convert. I had felt reborn, and positive thinking had been top of my 'To Do' list every day.

I had cheated death and that had made me feel bulletproof.

I had become a 'YES' woman. 'Yes, I'll raise money for the hospital.' 'Yes, Maddie, I can babysit for you Saturday night.' 'Yes, Michael, I don't mind you going on yet another stag party to Amsterdam this month.'

If there had been a question, the answer had been yes. But as the months went by, and life started to wear down my enthusiasm for a perfect world, my attitude had occasionally reverted back to its old diva ways.

Before the accident my only commitment had been to myself and getting home safely after a wild night out. Something I was still clearly struggling to do.

On paper I was a totally different woman, but I hadn't become a nun. Yes, I might have been knocked down, hit my head and almost died, but I hadn't had a lobotomy!

I turned the key in the front-door lock as slowly and gently as possible. It was 3.25 a.m., and most of the house lights were on. But that didn't necessarily mean Michael was awake. He wasn't the most energy-efficient person I knew, so there was still a hope that . . . fuck . . . My dishevelled head had barely passed through the door when his furious face swung around from the living room, screaming, 'What fucking time do you call this?'

With a weary heart I tried to speak, but was instantly interrupted by another crazed rant from Michael.

'Is this your idea of a joke, huh? Do you think this is acceptable, leaving me here alone with Daisy all night? I've got to go to work in about, oh, three fucking hours. You're such a selfish bitch, Eva. You really are a piece of work. I've been trying to get our baby to keep a bottle down since the moment you walked out of the house. Our little princess only fell asleep about forty minutes ago, and now I'm so angry I can't sleep. Fuck you. I've had to change her clothes and cot five times.'

He stormed off to the kitchen, huffing and cursing.

Unable to find a suitable response I just stood motionless, my brain feverishly trying to assess the situation. I heard him bang the dishwasher and fridge open and shut, and then he returned, just as angrily, with a pint glass of milk in one hand and some coloured brochures in the other. But he stopped in his tracks when he saw I hadn't moved.

'Are you stupid, or something?' His voice almost quivered with the anger, his body shook with frustration. 'Are you gonna close that fucking door so we don't wake up half the neighbourhood? Most normal people are in their beds *sleeping* right now. But then again, I forgot you're not normal, Eva – that would almost be a fate worse than death: to be *normal*.'

By now I knew the quickest way out of this was to simply close the door and remain silent. He was suffering from sleep deprivation and – still – the shock of becoming a father. Whatever I said would only set him off. So I just dropped my eyes to the floor, closed the door as smoothly as possible and wished for it all to be over.

I kept my body faced towards the hall door as long as possible, hoping that he would walk away – but he didn't. His heavy breathing was almost strong enough to knock me over. Although he was a few strides away, he felt so close in that icy house.

As we both waited for the other to react, the stony silence was broken by a weak cry from the bedroom. I swung around to look up the stairs, and then back at Michael. His temper hadn't waned. With an annoying, childlike smirk he snapped, 'Your *fucking* turn, sweetheart.' He walked back into the living room, washing his hands of all responsibility. I was too exhausted to fight with him. I wasn't going to rise to his temper. He'd eventually cool down.

As I dragged myself up the stairs to check on Daisy, smudging dirt on our cream carpet with every step, another bark came from Michael, this time not so angry. Not so harsh.

'I'm not happy,' he said with a hint of remorse. 'I was worried about you . . . It's not good enough, Eva . . . I'm really *not* happy.'

Once again, I chose not to respond.

I was not happy on so many levels, it would have been impossible for me to articulate them. The attempted rape was too much to explain to Michael tonight. I'd try and tell him about it tomorrow, when things had calmed down.

But so much had changed between us in the last few months . . . We'd been so carefree. Michael had once been the most attentive man I'd ever met. He'd leave 'I love you' notes on the fridge. Text me saucy messages like, 'Can't wait 2 C U sexy minx☺', and ALWAYS pleasure me, before himself, in bed.

The moment we found out I was pregnant, though, his mind-set changed. I didn't know quite how, but there was a definite shift in his attitude towards me: less eager. It was only really in the final months of my pregnancy, when I became really big, that I felt he became seriously distant. I would ask him if everything was OK. But I'd be dismissed every time, and told to 'Stop with the nagging. What happened to fun Eva?'

All that had started before the birth . . . Many months on, the cloud still hadn't lifted. Tonight he hadn't even noticed how muddy my clothes were, or how messy my face was. Why could he not see that I was traumatized?

By the time I got to Daisy's nursery, she was once again peaceful and calm. Settled in her baby boudoir, she looked like a china doll, all snug in her tiny cot. Surprisingly Michael had her tucked into her blankets just like the hospital had showed us. He had struggled with it before, but tonight she looked totally secure and safe. If only I could share the same inner peace she had.

She never usually cried much. Every other mother told me how their children never stopped crying when they brought them home from hospital, but Daisy wasn't a complainer.

She was so tiny lying there in her cot that it was still mind-boggling to think that she was mine. Looking at her reminded me of the first time I'd had to bath her in the hospital, and how terrified I'd felt when lifting her tiny limbs. I'd been sure that she would break. But the midwives had explained to me that, despite her delicate appearance, she was sturdy. They were right. She might look weak, but she was a toughie.

Not wanting to breathe alcohol on her, I stood back and watched her sleeping, the glow of a large lava-lamp softly lighting up her face. Even though her features were so delicate and petite, her slanted eyelids were evident. Every morning I woke up and wished that it was all a dream. I felt guilty, sick to the pit of my stomach that something I'd done had made Daisy Down's syndrome.

I hadn't known I was pregnant when we got married. I drank my way through the hen party and two-day wedding celebrations, not to mention drowning my liver further on the honeymoon. There wasn't much to do in Mauritius except eat and drink. Even newlyweds could only stomach a certain amount of sex during the day, so once it was past noon yours truly would work her way through the cocktail list thinking she was Kate Moss. As if that wasn't bad enough, I'm almost sure I got pregnant around the time of my birthday. Michael and I had been very physical, not to say pissed, for all the days leading up to and after it.

I felt I'd been punished for misbehaving.

I hadn't realized I should have looked after myself. I'd been celebrating being alive and in love. Staying sober and eating five a day had not been high on my agenda.

Of course, me being a piss-head hadn't caused Daisy's condition. In a moment of guilt I had looked it up on the internet, and been bombarded with websites full of information on DS babies, and how they had an extra chromosome. Even I could work out that booze had played no part. But somehow I wanted that to be the cause. Otherwise, what other reason could there be?

The first few days after her birth, I had felt so close to Michael, like we were living in our own bubble. He had even brought me a baby book of names into the hospital, and laughed at all the absurd ones that I had picked out. When it came to it, he wouldn't help me choose. Told me that I was to pick out her name and said that he 'didn't want the responsibility'.

While it wasn't the worst thing that could have happened, I just hadn't planned on getting pregnant that quickly. I hadn't wanted a baby so early in our marriage – now I had Daisy. We were told she only had mild Down's syndrome, but she would always be classed as different.

'Oh, special needs, poor thing,' the neighbours would mutter as I passed them in Tesco's. I wasn't sure if they were showing pity to Daisy or me. But I hated their comments.

'They don't live long, ya know,' was probably the most hurtful I heard.

The day that remark was made, Daisy had been smartly propped up in her car-seat on top of the shopping trolley, in full view of everyone. I'd been trying to show a brave face. I hadn't wanted to hide her away, she was my daughter. But secretly inside, I'd been screaming. Screaming at everyone. But no one could hear my screams.

Every time I'd looked at her back then, I'd thought how much I had drunk and how I'd abused my body. All that time she'd been growing inside me I'd damaged her, selfish cow that I was. But as I looked at her now, she just seemed like somebody else's child. She didn't resemble me, or Michael.

I went to bed still muddied and fully clothed, and sobbed till I fell asleep. Michael didn't join me.

★   ★   ★

'*What do you mean, you didn't tell Michael?*' Parker sounded extra screechy. Parker was my gay best friend. Spoilt and opinionated, he possibly wasn't the best person to be speaking to this morning, as a comforting shoulder he did not have. Despite holding the phone away from my ear, his pitch was still grating. The hangover had kicked in, not to mention the guilt of my diva strop when I'd stormed off from the gang last night. If I hadn't gotten thick about comments Maddie made about my fucked-up motherly emotions I would never have ended up alone in that taxi.

'He's your husband. The nearly-best-sex-you-ever-had, and father of your child. You know, the guy who vowed to love and protect . . .'

'OK. I get it . . . *Just shut up!*'

Momentarily the conversation went dead. Not really wanting to hear the answer I asked, 'Are you still there?'

'Mmmm, barely; well, whatever, since you've left your husband to his ignorance I suppose I'd better call around and check out the state of you. Don't leave the house. I'll be over to do my concerned-friend bit in half an hour.'

'*No*, don't, Parker, I really don't want—'

'I'm gone . . . See you in thirty.'

This time he was gone *and* on the way.

I really didn't feel up for company – well, not company that could talk.

Daisy was lying on my bed beside me. Her tiny eyes watched the morning light bouncing off the wall. She looked so content and peaceful. What did the future hold for her? And, selfishly, I wondered what it held for me. My attempt to keep a brave face about things was about to fail. I had the fear in me. Was it trauma from the attack? Or was it belated baby blues? Either way, as Michael put it, I was not happy. With my head throbbing painfully, I laid my face close to Daisy's and just watched her breathing, observing the contours of her face, and the amazing length of her eyelashes. I inhaled her smell. I would have liked to kiss her soft pink skin, but for some reason I couldn't bring myself to. She was the picture of perfection and I was disgustingly filthy.

I thought about singing her a lullaby, but then couldn't find the voice. I was a bad mother and this wasn't going well. So instead we just lay in silence, watching the light flicker on the wall.

Time would heal us, wouldn't it? Or at least heal me and my feelings of guilt.

'Oh God, you weren't kidding when you said you looked like Amy Winehouse. Wow. That really is a look . . . Listen, I bring cake and good karma. After I work my magic the world will seem like a better place. Just call me Auntie Potter and let me wave my magic wand.'

'Huh, is that some of your regurgitated banter from last night with Captain Jeff, or was that line spanking new for me?'

'Too early for spanking talk, pet, especially in your fragile state. No, I'm keeping it fresh this morning – speaking of which, why don't you take a shower while I look after my new goddaughter here?'

'I haven't managed to talk to Michael about that, yet.'

'Details, details! Now, go wash away the evil of last night. Everything will be fine here. I promise not to drop her . . .'

'*Parker!*'

'*I'm kidding* – we'll be fine. Go, cleanse yourself, and we'll catch up on the world's recession on *Sky News*. Babies love that sort of thing. That and cake.'

As Parker gently took my daughter in his arms, all paternal and glowing, I felt emotion flood over me. And without warning streams of tears just rained uncontrollably down my face. I didn't want to do this in front of Parker. Breakdowns were meant to be private affairs, and shared only with bottles of gin or strangers across bars or phone lines.

As I bolted I momentarily caught one of Parker's concerned faces. It was horrifically heartfelt-looking. The only time I'd seen him look like that before was when I'd collapsed after being released from hospital last year. We'd been out for a light lunch and he'd insisted I had a glass of bubbles. Just one, but unfortunately the alcohol went straight to my head – my damaged and mildly medicated head – and promptly dumped me to the ground. I never told anyone except the doctor what had happened. Parker's guilt was punishment enough.

But today Parker's face was filled with pity more than concern. His eyes spoke volumes, and I didn't want to hear, think or live any of it.

I was in a vortex of pain. It consumed me; every inch

of my body, including my fingertips, was beginning to ache. Stumbling out of the room, I couldn't even find the words to tell Parker about Daisy. She could need a bottle, a nappy change, a blanket to keep her warm . . . He'd have to work it out. I did . . . If only I could just figure *me* out.

As I waited for the water to warm up, a million random questions flashed through my head.

Why did Michael get so angry at me?

Would that taxi man have killed me after he'd raped me?

Should I go and make a report to the Garda?

Where was I going to send Daisy to school?

Where was Maddie? Why hadn't she phoned to see if I was OK?

My brain raced while my body began to lose the will to live. Without thinking I stepped into the shower with my clothes still on. I didn't have the energy to take them off, but it didn't matter. I'd never wear them again.

As the steaming water crashed down over me, it pushed my body to the floor. Slumped in the shower tray I sobbed. Last night Maddie had told me to get over myself and start acting like a mother. But how could she be so harsh? I had just wanted to get drunk and have a laugh – I had spent months sober, and longed to feel like the old Eva the Diva for one evening. Not Eva the wife, or reckless mother to '*that*' Down's syndrome baby. Was that so bad of me?

I knew I was being weak, but I couldn't help myself. I felt so alone. I couldn't reach out and tell anyone how

I really felt. They'd only hate me even more. So there I sat, head throbbing, heart breaking, tears streaming and clothes clinging.

After about twenty minutes I had watched the last of the dirty water from my muddied and bloody feet run clean. My fingers had now shrivelled up, but despite feeling dehydrated and hot I found the strength to strip myself and properly wash my face and hair. On reflection, Maddie had been correct. I did need to get over myself. Whether I liked it or not I had responsibilities to Daisy, Michael and myself.

I could wallow in misery for ever, but I did need to speak to someone about Daisy's condition. I needed to face my fears. It wasn't going to be easy, but then I suppose nothing worth doing ever is.

Parker was busy cradling Daisy, and clearly loving every minute of it.

'Oh, wow, you look much better,' he gushed. 'You ooze Katie Holmes just out of the shower after a run in Central Park.'

'A very fat Katie Holmes. Probably more Beth Ditto after one of her concerts.'

'Yes, surely. The two of them *are* so easily confused . . . Listen, forget about squeezing into your skinny jeans for five minutes, I've got an idea.'

'What kind of idea?'

'OK, now don't say no immediately. I want us to go away for a few days.'

'Oh, no problem. Let me grab my coat.'

'I'm serious, Eva.'

'Me, too. Don't be so stupid, Parker. That tiny creature in your possession right now is my new daughter. I can't go anywhere and leave her.'

'I never said she wouldn't be coming.'

'Ah, Jaysus, Parker, don't start stressing me out. I'm a woman on the edge, I can't . . .' Once again the emotion inside started welling up, and my eyes began to fill.

'Hey, hey, hold up there, I don't want to do that to you. I'm trying to help, here. You're tired, and your poor hormones are raging, and you need help.'

'Don't forget . . . I narrowly escaped *death* last night.' No sooner had the words left my mouth than I had a vivid flashback of me in the taxi.

Seeing my pain once more, Parker swung his spare arm around me. He wasn't a natural comforter. He was normally very self-absorbed, but for today he was pulling it out of the bag.

'Whisht now; I've a plan to make things better. You've just got to trust me.'

'But what about Michael? I can't just say to Michael—'

'I said, whisht,' interrupted Parker in one of his butch voices. 'Leave everything to me, including Michael. You just need to concentrate on getting yourself strong, and looking after this little lady. OK?'

'But . . .' Words were now failing me. Exasperated, I just sat at the end of my couch and put my head in my hands. Before I had time to let myself think, I was conscious of Parker placing Daisy in her Moses basket, and returning to me on the couch. Peeling my hands away to reveal my broken face, Parker cuddled in real close, and gave me one of his silly little smiles to make me laugh.

All he managed to extract from me was a heavy sigh, but that was good enough. As I let it out I felt a small weight lift.

'OK, listen, today is one of those bad days. You were told you would have them, but tomorrow will be another day – a better one, and the black cloud that surrounds you right now will go.'

'Do you promise?'

'Of course I do. In that hollow, haven't-got-a-clue way that only I can make promises. But that's something, right?'

He was right. Even his just saying it would get better suggested it could.

'Thank you, Parker.' My whisper was almost inaudible.

'You're welcome.'

'Listen, I'm fine now, well, I will be fine, so don't worry about the trip. I really don't need any trip.'

'Non-negotiable, my sweet.' Parker leapt in the air, dismissing any further chat on the subject. 'I'm being masterful here, so you've just got to roll with it.'

'Roll with it, eh?' My mood was softening more. 'Well, I love your confidence. I just can't wait to see how you handle Michael.'

Then, in one swift movement, he whipped his mobile from his trouser pocket, hit a few buttons and raised it to his ear. 'Michael, it's Parker here.' He wandered off into the dining room as if on some business call.

In between some muttering I could hear, 'Monday or Tuesday at the latest.'

Could he really be serious about taking a trip?

Had he forgotten the work that went into babies? We had all lived together when Maddie had had Woody, but clearly a year was enough time for a man to forget.

It seemed like a lifetime ago that Maddie had found out she was pregnant after a one-night stand in London. It had been the same weekend that I had met New York Michael, the original Michael in my life, but unlike my relationship Maddie had never seen her guy again.

Instead of fading into the distance, my New York guy had proposed to me on our first date, and filled my head with success stories about his life as an international fashion photographer. Despite my better judgement I had continued to let him pop into my life from time to time. He'd been just too goddamned sexy. And then he'd been exposed as a total fraud, left me abandoned in the street, bleeding, and caused my near-fatal accident.

Although Maddie – being a blonde, leggy bombshell – had managed to conceal her bump for about six months, the moment her secret was exposed all her modelling work had dried up, and with that her ability to pay for her apartment. She had initially moved in with her mother, but a massive row had broken out between the two of them in the late stages of Maddie's pregnancy, which had resulted in her doorstepping Parker with her suitcase in tow. He had had no choice but to let her move in. I had already taken up residence in his apartment several months previously after being filmed on CCTV snogging a very married publisher, which had caused my life to take a tumble. At the time, I had worked as a celeb reporter for another magazine, which just so happened to be owned by said publisher's best friend. The morning after the photo images made the papers, I was handed my P45 and poverty soon followed. Having been a spender rather than a saver, back-up funds soon ran out. So Parker's penthouse haven had become one busy time-share. They'd been crazy times, good times, but so much had happened since.

'Right, that's sorted, then,' beamed Parker as he swiftly returned.

'What, just like that?'

Instantly Parker switched from his grown-up alter ego and clapped his hands with excitement.

'Just like that,' he whooped.

'I suppose there's no point in putting up a fight?'

'Nope. Pick-up is tomorrow morning, so pack a few bags and bring your camera. It'll be nice to capture Daisy's first road trip.'

'*Road trip? Are you mad?*'

'Trust me, if it's good enough for Scarlett Johansson, Jonathan Rhys Meyers and Kim Cattrall, it's good enough for us. This is gonna be a road trip VIP-style. It'll be a hugely modified version of *Driving Miss Daisy*.'

'What's the plan? Are we going to play kings and queens while *Lost in Translation* – all the time looking for some *Sex and the City*?'

'Tut-tut, young lady. There'll be no sex, please, we're Irish. But I'll be bringing a little piece, or should I say an extra-large piece, of Hollywood bling to your doorstep tomorrow, so prepare to be dazzled.'

2

'OK, Michael has got Daisy. All you have to do is walk
slowly and let me direct you.'

Parker was standing behind me, steering me towards
my open front door with his hands covering my eyes.

'OK, no cheating, keep your eyes closed, until . . .
three, two, one. OK, now look.'

Almost afraid to see what had come to greet me, it
was a couple of seconds before I chanced a peek. But
nothing could have prepared me for the *beast* that stood
before us. I quickly glanced at Michael, who was already
outside, but he looked just as shocked as me.

'Eh, does Madonna realize she's missing her trailer
yet?' I questioned, aghast at the fifty-foot tour bus,
deluxe-coach thingy that was blocking up the road.

Parker just beamed with pride. 'It's on loan. It's got
double beds, plasmas, fully stocked mini-bar, a nice
man called Teddy to drive us around, and one big
surprise.'

Without missing a beat Maddie and Lisa stuck their
heads around a middle door and beckoned. 'Quick, get
in, it's totally fab!'

'Between them, surely they're two surprises?' I questioned.

'Well, technically they're more of a crowd, but let me introduce you to the real surprise.' As he pushed me towards the giant motor home all I could see was a sweet older woman smiling down at me from the steps inside.

'Hello,' she cooed. 'My name's Betty. I'll be your nanny.'

'More like life-saver,' gushed Parker feverishly.

'Excuse me, did you say nanny?'

'Yes, dear – for Daisy, isn't it? I can't wait to meet her.' Before I had a chance to respond, Betty was out of the bus and cooing over Daisy.

She was a small homely-looking woman, with that sixty-something short haircut, badger-grey. She had the look of an Irish Mrs Doubtfire, with a friendly warmth that was magnetic. Still stunned, Michael stood clueless, with Daisy dangling from his arm in her car-seat, which Betty signalled for him to hand over.

'She'll be in safe hands, Daddy. Enjoy your break and get some sleep.'

'Don't worry,' explained Parker. 'She's been working on movie sets for years, looked after everyone's kids – a total pro.'

Unable to find any words, both Michael and I stared at each other in disbelief. Realizing neither Michael nor I were quite in the same party spirit as himself, Parker chose to speed up the goodbyes by hopping on the bus and beckoning me to do the same.

'She'll be well looked after,' he shouted at Michael,

throwing the last of my bags on board. 'So kiss your wife and head back to the couch for the day. I'm sure there'll be plenty of manly sports to keep you company.'

Of course, all Michael could do was throw his eyes up to heaven. He was now so used to Parker's fanciful moments of spontaneity that he knew life was always easier if he left him – though it was normally us – to it.

Pulling me close for a kiss, Michael's tired face made me feel teary – again!

'Don't worry about anything. I'll be fine; go and enjoy your adventure, Eva.'

'But I don't want an adventure . . . Are you sure you don't want to come? You'd be more than welcome . . .'

'Enjoy Cork. I know a girls' outing when I see it. I'd only cramp your style. I need to keep an eye on the café this weekend, anyway. I wouldn't be much use as a manager if the staff could manage without me. Would I?'

'As if! Cork? Is that where we're going?'

'Kinsale is what he said. Listen, get some rest on the way, and take advantage of Nurse Betty there, and try not to go as wild as the other night.'

'About the other night, Michael . . .'

'Shh, I don't want to know. Just let's not make a habit of it, OK?'

'Of course, but I want to talk to you about the other night . . .'

'Eva, hurry up.' Parker's demands interrupted our train of thought.

'Just go. Love ya. Call me later after you have had a rest. And give Daisy a kiss for me.'

'OK, coming! Love you too, hon. Sorry about this – then again, I'm sure you're thrilled to see the back of us and have a free gaff for a few nights.'

'Don't be silly. Now run along, the hookers are due in five minutes.'

'Ha, ha, very funny. Love you.'

It felt really weird leaving him. We hadn't spent a night apart since we'd moved in together. And that had only been about three weeks after I came out of my coma. The distance would do us good, though. He was right: I needed a girlie weekend to bitch and let my hair down. Fingers crossed, he'd miss me.

It wasn't until I stepped on to the bus that I appreciated the true luxury that had been bestowed on us.

'Is this what MTV's Kimora would call true Fabulosity?' I asked, waving my arms around for effect, taking in all the bling.

'Yes, darling,' smiled my effortlessly rich, blonde best friend 'Princess Lisa', glass of bubbles already in her hand. 'Most definitely. This is life in the fast lane, so welcome aboard, sista. You're what we've been waiting for.'

I had waved goodbye and blown kisses back at Michael, but I didn't think he could see me through the tinted windows. I felt so guilty about leaving him, not telling him about my taxi abduction, just being a bit of a mental bitch full stop, but I reasoned that this trip would be the best thing for our relationship right now.

He was worn out running around after Daisy and me since the birth. I was so wrapped up in myself; I suppose I had forgotten he had needs too. Although he'd try and mask it sometimes, he wasn't always good under pressure. He needed minding, and I had been neglecting him.

Since the birth I'd never once asked him if he was OK. I hadn't thought that he deserved it, especially since I'd been the one carrying the baby around for forty weeks, not to mention having to endure the eighteen hours in labour. I had been the one doing all the puffing and panting – not him! But on reflection, he had been there with me during the whole thing: held my back when it ached, fed me fruit pastilles when I demanded them, and shouted for midwives when I was scared. He had done his best throughout, but then his best had meant nothing to me after I'd first set eyes on Daisy.

I had known immediately that she was Down's. I'd gone cold. It was as if my entire body had gone numb, protecting me from the pain that I was feeling.

My baby was beautiful, but there was no denying she was different. I wasn't sure how I was going to cope. I never once stopped to ask Michael how he was coping.

Perhaps I should? But today was not the day. I didn't think I could handle his answers today. Imagine if he rejected us. What if he said this family wasn't what he had signed up for when he'd married me?

If I didn't ask, I wouldn't have to hear his answer. Maybe I should just leave things as they were. It wasn't the right time to rock the boat. A couple of days' break would do us both the world of good. He could sleep and catch up for pints with the lads, and I . . . God, I thought, what was I doing on this bus? I loved Lisa but I didn't think I was in the right frame of mind to listen to her latest sexual conquests and most recent cosmetic procedures. She was constantly having both.

As for Maddie, ever since she'd become a mother she'd become this walking, talking, know-it-all, and right now I couldn't handle lectures, I just wanted space. And if she started another character assassination, like she had on Thursday night, I'd be off this motor home quicker than you could say, 'The wheels on the bus go round and round . . .'

Parker I could handle, because I just ignore him most of the time, but ever since he'd become a caring, supportive friend he'd totally unnerved me.

And now I'd got this woman, Betty, who'd already manhandled my child away from me. The sentiment was sweet, but I hadn't fully bonded with my daughter yet. Letting a stranger care for her at this stage wasn't going to make that situation any better.

'Penny for them?' asked Parker, in his newly acquired sympathetic tone.

'Ah, fuck it, I'm fine. Pass me a glass of whatever is going. I'm on my holliers.'

'There she is,' cheered Lisa, full of the joys of life. 'Forget the argument from Thursday, hon, let's have a laugh. Just like the old days. OK?'

'To the old days,' I saluted as Parker handed me a glass of champagne, 'and to having the best ride of our lives.'

41

★　　　★　　　★

The sound of laughter woke me from my snooze. After the initial rush of excitement and the two glasses of Mumm champagne – which Parker had chosen especially in my honour – I had done a Houdini to one of the back bedrooms and conked out for about two hours. But it was obvious the fun had started without me.

'It was just a simple injection,' pleaded the Princess, as she wiped away tears from her eyes. 'Honestly, it gave me the best sex I've ever had.'

Snapping out of my slumber I rejoined the group. 'Eh, have we not heard this line before? Were you back in rehab shagging granddads again?'

'Well, good morning, sleeping beauty! No, I was just telling the gang about my new orgasms,' explained Lisa proudly.

'What's so new about them?'

'Well, technically I've bought them . . .'

'Prostitution?'

'Noooo, I've had my G-spot enlarged.'

That statement instantly caused a ripple of oohs and aahs. Feeling a sympathy pain in my nether regions, I automatically grabbed myself and questioned with a whimper, '*You did what?*'

'I got my Grafenberg amplified,' announced Lisa, in terms to deliberately confuse us.

'In English,' cried Maddie, now scrunched up in the corner of the couch.

Only to be followed by a wounded-sounding

Parker, who had stuck his fingers in his ears, moaning, 'I don't want to hear this – I'm not the better for this topic of conversation.'

'Oh, don't be so squeamish,' said the Princess, trying to keep a straight face. 'It's only a little squirt of human collagen.'

I then watched as Lisa, Maddie and Parker fell about the place, laughing. By the number of empty bottles of champers it was clear that the guys were on a higher level than me.

I quickly caught the eye of Teddy, the driver, who was chuckling away to himself. 'Apologies for my friends . . . They're all over-sexed.'

'And under-serviced, in my case,' chuckled Maddie.

'So what's a Grafenberg, then?' I half-heartedly asked, making an effort to mix.

'He's the dude who discovered the G-spot back in the fifties. But the real genius was a gynae in Beverly Hills called Matlock, who invented this G-shot to help give you multiple orgasms.'

'How many is multiple? More than one, less than what?' asked Parker inquisitively.

'About six or seven . . .'

'You're such a liar,' blasted Maddie, with a direct dismissal. 'I've never come anywhere near that, and I've done some mileage.'

'Oh, we all know that,' I joked sharply, still feeling a tad hurt about what she'd said Thursday night. 'Just as well you left your son at his nana's. He'd be scarred for life hearing this stuff!'

'Yeah, but seriously,' she continued, trying to ignore me, 'two or three at a push. But *seven*? Is that not an assault on your body?'

'Nope: average session for me now, kids. I highly recommend it.'

Despite his earlier squeamishness Parker's interest in the conversation had returned. 'So, what? Is it like Botox for your fanny? Do you have to get a top-up every three months?'

'Exactly. I'll need a booster soon; life will be suicidal if I lose it. That's another trip to New York for me.'

Not feeling as jovial as the others, I chose not to respond to Lisa's comment. If I had nothing nice to say, after all, it was best I left quietly again, not to break up the party mood.

So I decided to leave them to it, and went back to check on Daisy. As I returned to the end cabins, I heard, 'No joke, the doctor was in and out in ten minutes – I didn't feel a thing.'

Only to be followed by Parker squealing, 'He must have been a little squirt, all right?' Followed once more by belly laughs from all three.

'Hello, mammy,' whispered the nanny as I walked into the adjoining bedroom. It was a compact one, with a double bunk and a TV – playing *Murder She Wrote* – sunk into the wall. Although an unconventional nursery, it was a safe haven for Daisy. 'Your daughter has been an angel. She's so good. We've been fed very slowly, and kept nearly all of it down. Did you get some rest?'

'Yes, thank you. Has she been asleep for long? I feel terrible about dumping her on you . . .'

'Not at all, lovee, that's why I'm here. I've been looking after babies for forty years, and she's been no problem at all. If you don't mind me asking, how have you been coping? Parker mentioned her condition had come as a bit of a shock to you.'

Her enquiry hit me like a steam train. A midwife had asked me the same thing on one of those home visits, but I had fobbed her off successfully enough by waxing lyrical about my fabulous support network. But there was something in Betty's face: a deep sincerity. She wasn't some random social worker with a routine questionnaire that needed filling out. Her questions came from the heart, and that just stopped me in my tracks.

Sitting down on the bed close to Daisy, I gazed at her for a moment, taking in her delicate features, her rose-pink lips and tiny ears, before turning to Betty and explaining my inner thoughts as if I had been granted doctor–patient confidentiality. 'I'm not sure I've adjusted. I feel like I've failed her.'

Surprisingly, tears didn't come this time. Perhaps I had run out of them.

'It's early days.' She smiled, giving me a wink of encouragement. 'If you're out and about this soon, the doctors must feel she's very strong.'

'It's kinda hard for me to say out loud, but yes, she's only got mild Down's syndrome . . . Whatever that means. It's been explained to me, and I've checked it out on the internet, but I'm still not fully sure of all the details.'

'Young Daisy here needs exactly the same thing as any other baby – love, compassion and more love.'

'And protecting,' I said sorrowfully.

'What child doesn't?'

Feeling uncomfortable with the amount of information I had already divulged, I quickly snapped out of my sharing moment, stood up and tried to change the subject. 'Listen, if you want to take a break, Betty, I'll . . .'

'Are you trying to get me fired?' she teased playfully. 'Go back to your bed now. When Daisy wakes up we'll have another bottle and some song time.'

She gave me another one of her motherly winks and gently nudged me towards the door.

'Go on with ya, now. We'll see you in a couple of hours when she's awake for a kiss and a cuddle.'

All I could manage was a short, 'OK', before leaving them to it. I wasn't needed, which felt wrong. But hey, why waste a golden opportunity?

I didn't know much about Kinsale, apart from the fact that Keith Floyd used to live there. It clearly had to be a good place to eat and drink, so who was I to rebel against the wishes of its people?

I hadn't really wanted to leave the luxury of the trailer, but in spite of myself I was beginning to enjoy the trip – and also being able to tease-text Michael with, 'After U this is the best ride! Eva'

And, after four hours on the road, stopping and starting for road works and tractors, we eventually pulled into the picturesque setting of coastal Kinsale, with its bobbing yachts in the harbour. Trust Parker to scam such a treat. God bless his movie connections. I couldn't remember whether he'd told me the bus had been booked for Cillian Murphy, or Jonathan Rhys Meyers or one of our other Hollywood A-listers, but after a 'personal crisis', I think he said, they had left the set early to return to the States. Leaving 'My Gayle', as Teddy called the Gayle Transporter, available for someone like Parker to take advantage of.

His job as a production designer allowed him many perks, including dinner dates with stars where he'd discuss locations and themes for their movies. Mind you, that would happen pre-cocktails; by the end of any of his 'celeb dates', he'd have got them pissed and be interrogating them about their love-lives and sexual practices. But getting this trailer was a major coup, and the timing was fairly spot-on. A couple of days earlier would have been even better, as then I could have avoided my near-death experience, but hey!

'Right, everyone.' Parker was clapping his hands and generally being bossy again. 'Here's the plan, people. Or should I say, let's make a plan, as I'm a little tipsy and I'm up for a couple of things. OK, one, does anyone fancy some lunch? We could go to *Fishy Fishy*? It's Eva's trip after all, and we all know she's enjoyed a little Fishy Fishy in the past!'

My mood had thawed, and I indulged Parker and his wit. If he wanted to tease me about my lesbian phase, he could. 'Ha! Ha! Keep that up and I'll be making you swim with the Fishy Fishes!'

'Or, two,' continued Parker, 'we could all take a nap, because I'm bollixed.'

'I'm for a nap,' agreed Maddie.

'Me, too,' yawned Lisa.

'OK, me, three,' smiled Parker, continuing the yawn.

'Well, I'll see you girls later, then,' I said. 'When you can stomach another drink. I'll take Daisy for a walk, and then wake you all when I get bored. OK?'

Without further encouragement, the gang pushed past me to seek refuge in the back cabins. There were weak mutterings of, 'Sure thing,' and, 'See ya later.' There was even a pathetic, 'I'll be thirty minutes – *max*!' from Lisa. But from past experience I knew they'd be out cold till about 6 p.m. at least, so that meant an entire afternoon to myself, and of course Daisy.

After some intense negotiation, I managed to secure sole custody of my daughter from Betty, and made the decision to dodge further mammy-chats and make a break for some fresh air. Amazingly there was an ice-cream shop open, so with a 99 in hand, complete with chocolate flake and raspberry sauce generously dribbled all over it, we took to walking the pier. Despite the biting wind and the slight drizzle, it was so great to get out and expose myself to the elements. Daisy was comfortably swaddled in blankets, her buggy totally protected with a new plastic rain-cover, which had never been used before, but I embraced this cold and wet January day, thankful for all it had to offer.

Straight out of a picture postcard, Kinsale was just

the distraction I needed to break free of my demons. Watching the freedom of the seagulls gliding above us made me feel so alive. The vibrant colours of the shoreline houses across the bay, and the tall masts of the sailing yachts that almost danced with gaiety – all helped to release my negative feelings.

This was just the escape I needed. The last month had been extremely claustrophobic. I'd been trapped in the house, caught between health-care workers and family and extended friends, all of them calling by and offering their twopence worth of advice. I'd wanted to tell them all to get lost. To leave us in peace and find another outlet for their pity. Instead, I had bottled up my anger, which had only bred resentment and bitterness.

Now, just soaking up the seaside smell of Kinsale managed to ease me back to a happier place in my heart. In a fitful moment of giddiness I decided that today would be a turning point for me. The cobwebs were blowing off, and it was time to think positive. Perhaps because the wind was scouring my face with a natural face peel, hurling grit and sand at me, I began to feel rejuvenated.

Yes, my back still ached, which I had convinced myself was a result of the epidural, and my eighteen stitches were still tender, though healing, but all the same I felt a renewed lust for life, and that things could only get better.

I wanted to share my new-found joy with someone, but it was too soon to wake the dipsos. I was also afraid of ringing Michael in case I woke him from one of his

Saturday snoozes and got a grumpy reply, so I decided a text would be safer. Keep it short, I thought. 'Today is a good day . . . Love U, Handsome xx'

I stared at the phone, bubbling with manic excitement. Thankfully it beeped a new message before I had a chance to get despondent. 'Love U2 xx' was Michael's response.

That was it? Love U2. Did he mean the band or me? The old Eva probably would have texted back, 'Don't strain yourself whatever you do.' But I thought, no, it's fine.

While it wasn't quite the declaration of love that I'd wanted, texts can be misinterpreted. So I texted back, 'Talk later xx,' and left it at that. After all, he was still at home with his thoughts – and the memory of our last argument – and I had moved on. Thank God for that. I just hoped that this feeling would last.

'You are never going to guess who's around the corner in the restaurant! Think; who are the most embarrassing couple in Ireland right now?'

Lisa followed Z-list celebrities as a sport, and knew everything there was to know about the antics of the wannabe famous. After the gang's big sleep we had decamped to a local hotel, which was smart yet traditionally decorated: old Ireland meets and greets rich Americans. It was perfect for us, because it offered far more than warm beer.

It was now 7.30 p.m. and hunger was almost getting the better of some of us. Although we'd had another bottle of bubbles at the bar while waiting to be seated, blood-sugar levels were at a low, and food was needed quick.

'Unless they're carrying a platter of lobster for me, I'm not bothered,' snapped Parker.

'Barks the man who ate a super-sized bag of cheesy nachos and all the blueberry muffins when no one was looking,' said Maddie bitterly. As an ageing model of thirty-four or thirty-five – it was hard to remember since she never reminded us – Maddie couldn't afford to eat many luxuries. But on get-togethers such as these, limits were off, belts were loosened, and she got extremely competitive over food.

'Hey, hey, hey, bitches,' squealed Lisa, doing her best to quash the tension, 'this is Eva's weekend, so best behaviour, please.'

'Yeah, sorry, hon,' chimed Parker and Maddie as Lisa pulled up a seat and started to reveal the drama next door.

'OK, tonight got a whole lot more exciting. The tango-tanned promotions girl slash model Nikki O'Brien is here with a certain Owen Murphy-Keane, and they're next door making out like they're in some sort of staged sex-show. Better still, I think I've also recognized a paparazzi guy and a journo that Eva introduced me to ages ago sitting in the corner watching them.'

'So what?' I blurted out, without thinking.

'Sooo – we'll be sitting right in the middle of a tabloid sting. Who knows? If we play our cards right we might even get a mention.'

'Whoah! No way.' Although I had been a reasonably

successful freelance magazine journalist before I gave birth, and I'd regularly interviewed famous people, I hated being the subject of any stories myself. I had loathed my Z-list notoriety after my 'snogging-gate' scandal.

It had been one of those scandals that shatter the rule that all publicity is good publicity. Afterwards I lost my job, my dignity, my house and the respect of my parents – it was a domino-effect that eventually saw me totally lose the run of myself, too!

Celebrity, minor or not, was not something I was comfortable with. Column inches were what Irish people as a race strived for, but I'd had a taste of it, and it wasn't to my liking.

Although Maddie had still managed to hold on to her top model status – despite being of a more mature vintage now, and taking time out to have a baby – she, too, recoiled from being a name. 'I'm a clothes-horse, not a reality star,' she'd tell us. 'People don't need to know who I'm fucking. They just need to want to fuck me!'

On the flip side, Parker was elated at the prospect of devilment – and of course about the idea of seeing Owen Murphy-Keane again. Years ago – before Parker fell in love and married one of the nicest and richest 'confirmed' bachelors in Ireland, Jeff – he'd had a flirt thing going with Owen, who, at the time, was a Dublin county hurler. Parker used to bore me at length about Owen and how he definitely believed he was fighting his tendencies. Parker's mantra had been 'He sooo wants me!'

Because Parker and Jeff were experiencing difficulties in their marriage due to Jeff's endless travelling
with work – his family's building firm had concentrated
their efforts in Dubai since the recession – Parker claimed
to be officially 'on a break'. Which, in his mind, meant
that he could rejoin 'the shagging classes'.

You see, once upon a time, a young buff Owen asked
Parker if he wanted to share a taxi home from Val's
nightclub, but, without knowing, I had jumped into
the car with them and drunkenly refused to get out.

It wasn't until Parker and myself celebrated Christmas
Eve one year with a bottle of Laurent-Perrier Rosé,
a tub of my home-made brown bread ice cream and
many flirty texts from Owen, that I believed Owen
could be bi-curious. Messages like 'Hey there handsome, I'm out later, r u?', followed by 'Will I call over
to yours after pub?' are not suitable texts to be sending
to an over-sexed gay man unless you wanna play balls!

After taking a couple of minutes to plot out a strategy,
Parker knocked back his glass of champagne, stood
up, and smoothed down his trademark black Prada
ensemble of skinny jeans and skinny shirt. Being tall
and poker thin, he was distinctive, to say the least, and
knew it.

'I wanna be bold,' declared Parker, with the broadest
smile across his face.

'How bold?' questioned Lisa, her eyes dancing with
delight.

Fighting the hunger pains, I offered, 'Tonya-
Harding-sabotage-of-Nancy-Kerrigan bold?'

'No, too gruesome,' he dismissed, almost offended.

'More like Madonna abusing her seniority and making Britney and Christina kiss her at the VMAs, and then having to tell Lourdes that she was a mommy pop star and they were the baby pop stars, and she was just kissing them to pass on her energy. That kinda naughty bold.' Although I hadn't been part of his circle for some time, I could only laugh at his remarks. They were normal. He was just being the same ole Parker, and I wasn't sure if a little part of me felt sad that I wasn't the same ole Eva.

Parker had just finished checking himself out in the reflection of a large Guinness Is Good For You mirror when a smiley hostess appeared, asking, 'Eastwick party for four?'

The gang all turned to look at each other and laughed.

'In honour of the bitches' reunion,' explained Lisa, all chuffed with herself.

Once upon a time, Parker, Maddie and yours truly used to call ourselves the Bitches of Eastwick, and enjoy champagne-fuelled Thursday night sessions. We used to start drinking Parker's rosé stash at his penthouse down the Docklands, before breaking out to town to find trouble. On reflection, we mainly concentrated our efforts on losing our single status, yet they were probably the nights that we had the most fun. Isn't it bizarre the way we fail to realize how good things are until they're over?

Those days now seemed to be a lifetime away, but I was determined to prove to myself that there was fun in the old girl yet.

'Thank you.' I smiled back at the hostess. 'That's us. I'm Eva Eastwick, and it's my birthday.'

'Are you looking for free drinks?' Parker asked, trying to work out my motivation for lying.

'Abso-fucking-lutely,' I beamed. 'And maybe some cake.'

Just as Lisa had described, Z-listers Nikki and Owen were indeed indulging in some very inappropriate tonsil-tennis, and never noticed our entrance. Parker tried not to be peeved, and the rest of us pretended to ignore his sighs and loud coughs, which made his large bushy black eyebrows wriggle with annoyance. And just as Lisa said, the newspaper hounds were patiently hovering, blending in well with their steak dinners and full glasses of wine. God bless the expenses of a busy tabloid newspaper! I had abused such luxuries down through the years. Laughing in the face of recession, journos always got to eat at the best restaurants for free.

We had only been seated a couple of minutes when a very handsome Brazilian waiter cosied up to us brandishing four sweet-looking cocktails. 'Cosmos?' he asked.

'Thank you.' I smiled, feeling thrilled with myself. My subtle hint had worked.

We made several mini-speeches, toasting each other and how wonderful we looked – clearly in my case they all had to lie. I was a size 16 in Spanx and hadn't quite accepted my extra mommy-weight yet. We then gave our individual scores out of ten for the lovers, joking that we hoped there wouldn't be an extra charge for the show, as it wasn't quite pay-per-view standard – but then who was I kidding? We were easily pleased, and so far they had scored everything from a three for Owen for a messy tackle with Nikki's hair, and a ten to Nikki for her quick, blink-and-you-miss-it move of taking a giant slug of wine before returning to her snog-athon.

But our free drinks tasted sweet. I was feeling bullet-proof. We had almost polished off the lot when the same gorgeous waiter returned, muttering, 'Sorry, emm, did you order those Cosmopolitans? You see, emm, I got the wrong table. These, yes, were another order.'

Whooping with laughter, Parker couldn't contain his giggles. 'You're not in Kansas now, my sweet.'

Aware that our giddy mood could come across as offensive, Maddie took it upon herself to explain the situation. But her damage limitation was wasted on this guy.

'We thought that they were complimentary drinks – for her birthday.' She articulated her words as best she could, over our childish giggles.

'Complimentary?' the waiter asked, clearly confused.

'Free. We thought they were free.'

'But why would they be free?' The concept seemed alien to him. Maybe it was a strictly Dublin thing.

They could have debated the point for ever, but thankfully Parker stopped it in its tracks. 'Ah, to hell with the expense, good man. Four more of your finest Cosmos, please.'

No sooner had our handsome waiter left when

I noticed Nikki and Owen disentangle themselves momentarily.

In a deliberate move for attention I demanded, '*Laugh!*'

Not understanding my tactics, the group muttered in confusion.

'*Laugh*,' I repeated, now donning a ridiculous fake smile. 'Hysterically, like we're having the best fun ever!'

As I eyeballed the star-crossed lovers the gang quickly copped on and started making painful hyena cries. Realizing we had their attention, I piped up hysterically, 'Well, why else do you think I'd be naked on a Wednesday afternoon?'

Once again, the gang fell about loudly, banging on the table and whooping with now uncontrollable laughter.

It never took much of a reason for us four to be happy. That's why we had stayed firm friends down through the years, despite our individual dramas. And now we knew we had Nikki and Owen double-barrel-bi-curious-boy's attention, we were milking it.

Taking up the baton, Parker then flung his arms in the air and screamed, 'Well, if that bitch isn't drinking from the furry cup, I'm gonna cry hetero!'

Thankfully for the rest of the diners, our gorgeous waiter returned with more Cosmos and softened our tone. Then, despite Parker's overtly flirtatious eyelash flutters and distinctive tongue clicks Owen remained totally unresponsive; much to Parker's disappointment.

It wasn't working, so he tried a softer approach. Or, should I say, he got his Eartha Kitt groove on.

So, above the chit-chat of 'Would you like your beef with sautéed or garlic potatoes?' our neighbouring tables could hear lots of Parker purring, and making smutty comments like 'I want it all', and 'Give me what you've got!' Which was, in fairness, comical but wasted on our sexy waiter – who skedaddled shortly after taking our extremely excessive food order. Not to be beaten, Parker laughed off his red card as a triviality. 'I'm just warming up,' he muttered into his drink. He was lost in his Cosmo for only a few moments before resurfacing to declare, 'Definitely single tonight. I am, you know. Jeff has now physically and emotionally left me. So tonight I'm going to find a man.'

Not believing a word, I tried to ignore his heavy statement, which made our jaws hit the table. Instead, I proposed another toast. 'To friends.' I encouraged the others to follow my lead. But the girls didn't get a look-in.

'OK!' Parker butted in. 'Here's to getting fed and getting laid – Lisa? Maddie? Would you single ladies like to join me in a bet?'

'What are you proposing, Pink Panther?' Lisa had once again dug out a golden oldie. It was a nickname Parker had earned from his glory days of being a sexy gay predator, and it suited him down to the ground. When he turned it on, he was hot stuff; it was just that none of us were quite sure if Kinsale was ready for his heat.

'Well, I propose that whoever doesn't score tonight pays for my hotel room . . .'

'Aren't you sleeping in our "beast of a trailer" as Eva keeps calling it?' Maddie had a face that almost looked insulted. 'So, basically, you're not willing to share with us, then?'

'Daisy doesn't cry, you know.' I immediately went on the defensive, too.

'All children cry . . .' snapped Parker. He was about to continue, but was hit by a pang of guilt. 'Listen, I'm not trying to get away from any of you, Daisy included. I just fancy a little male company tonight. As much as I love ya's, there's nothing that beats snuggling up to a boy's bum. Deal with it!'

'So tell me, why are you suggesting that *we* pay for your hotel room?' Lisa's tone was playful rather than tetchy. Her father, Daddy Tiswell, paid all her credit cards, and she'd never wanted for anything. Lisa treated money like men, easily gotten – and there were always plenty more to be had . . .

Despite Parker's goodwill over the last couple of days, his sensitivity was fast running out. 'I just think it would be nice for all of us to go to bed with someone tonight – other than ourselves. Considering we're in a sleepy seaside village, and, let's be honest, it's far from Blackpool with its nightclub scene, I am confident that I'll bag a man quicker than you girls.'

'As if!' snarled Maddie.

Parker looked directly at her, hoping to wake her inner slut instincts. Anyone who knew Maddie knew it didn't take much.

Lisa glanced over her shoulder, taking in the talent around the room. She let out a little sigh before declaring, 'It's slim pickings, but I'm sure there's some old retired git that I could stomach.'

Wincing at the thought of some wrinkly pensioner putting his liver-spotted hands all over me, I asked Lisa in the nicest possible way, 'Why the old blokes? You used to save yourself for gorgeous ski instructors, but now it's all crinkles.'

'They're more grateful,' she tutted, as she finished off her drink and waved it like a bell in the direction of a passing waiter, signalling for another. 'Young guys, especially good-looking fuckers, just want to be serviced. It's all about them. "*Give me a blow-job, rub my balls, blah, blah.*" There's always a battle to get any sugar back. But older guys just adore you. They want to worship your body – make you come. In my book that's a much better plan.'

Almost wanting to get in the game, I cheerfully agreed. 'Well, you can't argue with that.'

'OK, I'm in.' Maddie's eyes bulged with delight. 'Lisa?'

'Like I ever need to be given a reason to chase dick? OK, Parkey baby, get that gold card out. I think you'll be paying for a suite for me, too.'

Feeling a tad left out, I weakly asked, 'What about me?'

'Don't worry, we won't abandon you yet, but I thought you wouldn't have the energy to stay out late anyway.' Parker was speaking the truth, but I hated being the odd man out.

'Fine,' I said sharply. I was just about to launch into a moan when I noticed the Z-listers were staring right in our direction. 'OK, don't look now,' I said, 'but the snog-fest across the way has stopped, and we seem to have caught their attention again.'

Drawn like flies to shit, both Parker and Lisa spun around on their seats, only to be caught in the headlights by Nikki and Owen.

'Oh, hiya,' was the only thing Parker could think of to say. 'Nice evening for it!'

Although Owen looked a little bit startled, his new girlfriend was far from amused. She pulled a fake smile – showing no dentistry – before returning her gaze to Owen.

We were just about to embark on a bitch-fest when I saw her get up from her seat in search of a loo.

'There's your chance, big boy . . .' I said to Parker. 'Miss Nikki has left the room.'

Without hesitation he was up and gone. 'Watch this for speedy work,' he quipped over his shoulder.

Trying not to be too obvious, the three of us huddled close, attempting to gauge the body language. After about two minutes of shrugging from Owen, Parker returned.

'OK, he thinks she'll be out cold in about an hour. He reckons another couple of glasses of wine and he'll be putting her to bed.' His face beamed with a sense of accomplishment.

'And then what?' I was curious about what he thought would happen after that. 'Is he going to dump her and hit the hay with you?'

'That's the plan,' Parker tutted.

'Fuck off,' bleated Maddie. 'Do you honestly expect

us to believe that you've just pulled? That after a two-minute conversation it's a done deal?'

'What can I say? When you're good, you're good.'

'Wow. That's some move, Mr Pink. Oh, keep calm, she's back – actually, she does look a bit locked. I'd feel sorry for the bitch, but she's a total C U Next Tuesday.'

'Exactly. And ancient history in a short while, so let's just enjoy our evening, then.'

'Get him,' I mused. 'We'll have to start calling him Rohypnol breath.'

'Huh?' The gang were all equally puzzled.

'Rohypnol breath. You know? Parker just spoke to the guy and he fell for him.'

'Ohhh.'

No one seemed impressed with my lame attempt at a gag. The girls were annoyed at being outsmarted, and Parker was too busy feeling chuffed with himself.

Having a brief moment of conscience, I asked, 'So did you tell Owen about the press guys?'

'Oh no, I forgot.' Parker was now too focused on his prize. 'Who cares about the journalists, anyway? I mean, what are they going to do?'

Almost choking on my cocktail at the memory of how badly I got burnt at the hands of the red tops, I said quietly, 'You're right, hon. Sure, they can't do anything.'

Picking up on my facetious tone, Maddie quickly turned to me and giggled. 'As the saying goes, only time will tell.'

3

'"Murphy-Keane scores *on* and *off* the pitch: is he batting for both teams?" That's what it fucking says on the cover, right . . . With a picture of Owen and Nikki underneath, and then when you turn to page 3 there's another fucking picture: of me, *kissing his ear* and *grabbing his man boob*!'

Parker was hysterically screaming down the phone. It was Monday lunchtime after the weekend before, and we had stopped off in Waterford for some supplies. Of course, us girls being bone idle, it meant Parker had to be the one to cave in and finally pluck up the energy to go to the shops. But the sight of himself outing an Irish sporting hero in one of the biggest-selling newspapers had left him sorry he ever left the trailer.

'And then, wait for this,' he continued in his high-pitched screech, 'they call me a fucking barman! The fucking cheek!'

After a ten-minute rant I finally managed to talk Parker off the phone and ordered him to come back to the trailer straight away so the group could assess the damage; while telling him in no uncertain terms not to dare to return unless also brandishing fresh pastries and a carton of Actimels.

'I'm suing their asses,' declared Parker in a huff. His return could be heard from outside the trailer, and from the moment he opened the door the obscenities were flying. 'These fuckers are not going to get away with this – I mean, how the fuck? Like, what fucking right have these idiots got slandering . . .'

'Wow, slow it down, sista.' Lisa was doing her best to keep a straight face, as she delicately prised the bag of treats out of his firm grip. 'It can't really be that bad, I mean . . .'

Cutting her dead, Parker slammed the paper on the table and demanded, '*Look*.'

He was right. The evidence was damning.

It was hard to muster much solace. 'OK, so you're nibbling his ear and fondling his chest,' I began slowly. 'But it just looks playful.'

'Read what it says,' demanded Parker once more, sternly.

'OK. So *Daily Life* thinks Murphy-Keane is Owen-ing us an explanation. "We tracked him down to the gourmet village of Kinsale where the hurling legend was gorging himself on every tasty delight that caught his fancy."'

'Well, you did say he was a midnight delight,' beamed Maddie, as she grabbed a chocolate croissant off Lisa and dunked it into her coffee cup.

Parker could only hiss under his breath at Maddie; his focus wasn't going to shift from the paper. 'Look here. They give the time that Nikki goes to bed, and then, look, they say that thirty minutes later Owen pops back down to the bar to – *look here* – "pick up a staff member" and "prove himself a handful".'

'And was he?' asked Maddie, pulling a serious face.

'He was adequate,' explained Parker. 'Well, below adequate, actually. But, seriously,' he snapped back to the present, 'Jeff is back home this week. There's no way he's not going to hear about this. It'll definitely be over now.'

Afraid to confirm his fears, Maddie, Lisa and I just quietly looked at each other, pulling sympathy faces, while Parker continued to stare at the exposé that could be the final nail in the coffin for his marriage.

He had cheated, and was paying a heavy price for it.

Over the course of the relationship I had heard snippets of Jeff's complaints about Parker, and infidelity was top of his list. Although he'd always known Parker was a social butterfly when they had gotten together, I don't think he had really been aware what he was taking on when he'd asked Parker to be his life partner.

'I tried to stay faithful to Jeff, you know. But I'm just broke . . . I'm a flawed human being.'

'Parker . . .' I attempted to bring a little clarity to the situation, but he didn't want to hear anyone else's opinion.

'Eva, just don't say anything. OK? Any of you. I've finally messed up good, now. Maybe that's what I wanted all along. I think I've just been fighting it too long. I was set to self-destruct, and now I'm back on track. Jeff was merely a blip in my life story. A sweet loving intermission in the corruptness that is my life. It could never have lasted.'

Understanding that he was in wallowing mode, I begged him to take a lie-down, and said that I'd follow him in a few minutes to see how he was feeling.

If I was honest I needed him to go before I said something to offend him. He acted like a spoilt child that night, and had even been aware that the press were there; although I think we had all forgotten about them after the fifth round of Cosmos.

In my eyes he had selfishly acted like a single man when he clearly still wasn't. He had no right to feel sorry for himself. I was the only one with the monopoly on self-pity in this group, and there was no way I was going to allow him to drag out one of his old drama-queen sulks. Well, not for too long, anyway.

It had certainly put a dampener on our weekend. It had been so great to bond with the gang again, even if Parker had decided to take leave of his senses and us for an evening and late morning.

Although I hadn't forgotten my motherly duties completely, it had been such a tonic to kick back and relax, and fully get a physical and emotional release from being a new mum.

Yes, I had suffered pangs of guilt when not with her, but I had reasoned that this weekend was a one-off, because as soon as I stepped off the bus in Dublin, I'd be back to coping on my own, as Michael spent most of his time working.

With Parker taking some time out, the trailer fell silent. All that could be heard was Maddie's frantic text-messaging, no doubt checking with her mother to hear how Woody was, and if he had taken his first steps yet.

Lisa was busying herself with reading the rest of the newspaper, or, more realistically, should I say, looking at the pictures and processing the occasional headline.

With Teddy gone to find a local bookie, and Betty taking Daisy out for a stroll, I was left to my own thoughts – which inevitably led me to wonder about the lack of communication between Michael and me while I'd been away.

Every time I had spoken to him he had seemed strained, as if he was trying to rush me off the phone. Although I'd kept asking if there was a problem, he'd kept telling me that everything was fine and I shouldn't worry. So I had decided not to. I had enough on my plate. I didn't need to be conjuring up a drama or a depression when there wasn't one there in the first place. After all, I was a woman still wearing maternity clothes and *not* pregnant. My body was in a state, and not shrinking back to its original shape the way Maddie's had.

Maybe I was being paranoid, but I'm nearly sure the waitress had been giving me dirty looks at dinner the night before, as I'd kept knocking back the champers and ordering more bottles. I'm sure she thought I was Kerry Katona's long-lost twin. If I had been looking at me, I probably would have been equally disgusted. Perhaps I should invest in a personalized tee reading: 'Not Pregnant – Just Fat!'

In fairness I had been overdoing it. I had been feeling greedy because Daddy Tiswell was paying for the evening. Lisa had said, 'He's insisted on paying for the coming-out-of-retirement party.' It would have been an insult not to have taken him up on his offer.

I was obsessing about the size of my thighs in my jeans, and trying to imagine what they used to look like pre-pregnancy when Parker re-emerged from his den, looking like someone had ripped up his copy of *Men's Health* magazine.

'Was no one going to follow me in? I could have slit my wrists just for attention, and no one would have found me. I could have died in there without even wanting to. You three are bad friends.'

Understanding his ways, Lisa defused the moment with a simple line. 'Parker, we love you, darling. Now sit down, and give me a hug.' She knew it would shut him up, and it did, though only for a moment.

'But I've just got a text from Owen saying, "You have ruined my life."'

'He's just being silly. If it wasn't you, it would have been some other barman, darling.'

His face recoiled in horror as the rest of us shared a cheeky giggle.

'I'm just going to tell Jeff that I was acting as a warm-up for Eva.'

'Fuck off!' There was no way I was going to get pulled into this untruth.

'Well, Maddie, what about you? Can I say he was your fella for the night?'

'*No.*'

'Lisa?'

Lisa thought for a moment, flicked her long blonde

locks across her overly Botoxed face and sighed, 'Nah, sorry. You're on your own, love rat.'

'OK. OK. I'll just tell him straight.'

It was too good an opportunity to miss. Maddie teased, 'I didn't think that was a word in your vocabulary.'

'Wanna hear another couple, Mama Meow? Since when did you like your first chin so much that you added another two?'

Instantly fixing her posture, Maddie checked out her invisible folds in a mirror and, once reassured that he was merely being catty, returned to teasing Parker. 'Nice try. I'll let that one go – for now. So what are you going to text back to Mr Adequate? "If I had a fuck, I wouldn't give you one"?'

'Maddie, I've only one nerve left, and you're starting to get on it.'

'Girls, girls,' said Lisa, trying to quash the arguments. 'If I promise to miss you both, will you take this outside?'

'I'm not the one being a bitch here, Lisa. I've been publicly slandered.'

'No, you haven't. You've been outed.' In typical Eva style I had spoken without first consulting my brain, and Parker didn't seem amused by my honesty.

'Ohhh, some thanks I get for organizing you a weekend away. What's this? Shit-on-Parker day?'

'I'm just saying that—'

'Well, I'm just saying now, stuff the lot of you. I'm going out, and I don't know when I'll be back.'

Just as he said it, he stormed out of the trailer in a

diva tantrum. All that was missing was a fake thunder-bolt for dramatic effect.

Having seen all this before, like giggly schoolgirls we rushed to the doorstep and pulled apart the blinds. Just as we expected, he was standing outside waiting for some-one to chase him and beg him not to leave. Disgusted, he turned on his black Prada loafers and marched off into the traffic. His long beanpole legs made him look like an extra from a Monty Python sketch.

All we could do was laugh. It was cruel of us, but he would have done the same. But of course when he returned we'd respect his pain. Or at least attempt to. After all, he never made it easy for us to feel sorry for him.

An hour on and Lisa was beginning to struggle with the baby talk. There was still no sign of Parker, but both Teddy and Betty had checked in and left again. This time I think it was for a bite to eat. It had become obvious over the past few days that a mini-romance had started to blossom between them. It was really very sweet. They were like the lovable grandparents that Daisy didn't have.

Daisy wasn't close to her real grandparents yet. Both sets were still alive but she hardly saw my parents, and never visited Michael's. And Teddy and Betty were two old salt-of-the-earth types who seemed to have a common bond. Collectively we had all been willing them to hook up.

'Oh-my-God, how much shite is a woman expected to take on a Monday morning? Between Parker's crap, talk of Woody's "massive logs", and Daisy's "problems with pushing" – can we not talk about something more adult? I'll never be able to enjoy playing with a bottle of baby oil ever again. I'm scarred for life.'

Lisa had understandably reached her limit. Until I had become a mother I had hated women who discussed nothing but nappy rash and the consistency of baby poo. Now it seemed to hold an endless fascination for me.

'Sorry, hon.' I quickly realized what a boring mammy I was being, and changed the subject. 'I wonder how Parker is getting on. I hope he's OK.'

'Good enough for him,' barked Maddie, quicker than I could think where he might have gotten to.

'That's a bit mean, Maddie.' Lisa had been mother hen to him all weekend, and was still feeling protective about her wounded soldier.

'It's not at all, Lisa. He's far from stupid. He knew exactly what he was doing Saturday night. I feel sorry for that hurler guy. He was ambushed.'

'Mmmm, I suppose she's right.' It was now my turn to butt in and defuse the tension. Maddie had been going through a really bitchy phase recently, and wasn't holding back her feelings about any of us.

'Yes, but Parker hasn't exactly been a hundred per cent this last while . . .'

'Lisa, which of us has?' Maddie snarled. 'Just because at times he possesses the ability to act more pathetic does not mean we should allow him to be such a diva. He fucked up. Now's the time for him to take it on the chin.'

Afraid to say anything, I didn't speak, praying that the moment would pass. Dumbstruck Lisa did the same. As a result, an eerie, heavy silence fell. Although Maddie had that flaring-nostril thing going on, as if she could explode at any minute, she held her tongue long enough for her temper to calm.

Out of the corner of my eye I could see her facial expression soften. She was clearly going through some drama of her own, but if she wasn't prepared to share it with us, there was no point in me trying to get it out of her.

Needing an escape from the trailer and the bickering between Lisa and Maddie, I grabbed an old winter duffle coat I had brought with me. It belonged to Michael, but at least I could close all the buttons on it, and it was warm.

No sooner had I left the water's edge and made my way towards the main shopping streets than I bumped into a rejuvenated Parker.

'I've got a plan,' he beamed, as he clasped my shoulders and shook me a little too vigorously.

'And what would that be, then?'

'Mind-blowing sex . . .' He paused, as if I was supposed to congratulate him.

'Ah, yeah, genius,' I replied, giving him a sarcastic two thumbs up.

'Eva, I'm serious. When I make the effort, I can be pretty spectacular in the bedroom.'

'And?'

'Hear me out. I know you might find this impossible

to believe, but I can be a bit selfish when it comes to sex . . .'

'Really?'

'Yeah, so I've been thinking that if I step up my game a little, put more effort and thought into my welcome home for Jeff, he'll forgive me anything.'

'Gosh, Parker, I'm not sure if an enthusiastic blow-job and a bunch of flowers will be enough to save the day. What did you have in mind?'

'Well, I was on my way back to get you, so you've just saved me the trip. I've discovered a really cheesy-looking sex shop up the town, but I didn't have the courage to go in on my own. Will you come with me?'

'And what? Pick out flavoured butt-plugs for ya?'

'Well, sort of. You know that I value your opinion. Come on, please! You've already got the dodgy coat for it . . .'

'Hey, easy. I might just find the urge to flash you . . .'

'Yuck, I'd rather you didn't . . .'

'Huh, thanks a million. Well, I'd rather not, too. But come on, let's have a look, then. Who knows, I might even find something to help rescue my own marriage while I'm at it.'

'So what do you think you're looking for? I've got a couple of fun ones here. How about *Throbin Hood* or . . . *White Men Can't Hump*? Or . . . *Raiders of The Lost Arse*? It looks an oldie, but a goodie.'

I'd never really been in a sex shop before, except for

the one time I stepped into Ann Summers on O'Connell Street to avoid an ex. After five minutes of trying not to stare at the vibrators, I left with a packet of chocolate penises, which several weeks later helped a middle-aged diabetic woman on a train to Galway.

After recovering from her hypo, she confided that it was the first time she'd had a willy in her mouth in ten years. And that she never remembered one tasting so sweet before.

But, as a woman who loved shopping, this was right up there with Christmas in New York. I was a child in a candy store, and forgot all my inhibitions as I fondled and ogled the merchandise.

'Here's a couple for you,' giggled Parker. 'What about *A Tale of Two Titties* . . . or *The Texas Dildo Massacre*?'

'Ouch . . . That sounds far too painful.'

'Mmmm, what else . . . Why don't you get *Thighs Wide Open* for Michael?'

'Eh, no, I don't think so. I'm not quite back in the saddle yet. He'll only get disappointed when he realizes that the only thighs opening will be the ones on the DVD. Mine, I can tell you, will be remaining firmly shut for the foreseeable future.'

'Oh, get over yourself. You think you'd just had a baby.'

'Exactly. If he's looking for any action, he should pick himself up a copy of *Saturday Night Beaver* here, and keep it to himself. Whatever wanking he gets up to, I don't want to know about it.'

'Seriously?' Parker's face looked shocked.

'Of course I wouldn't be so naïve as to think that

Michael doesn't wank in the shower. He's been spending longer and longer in there the last few months, but I don't like the idea of him fantasizing about other women.'

'What? You feel he's cheating on you if he imagines other women when he's masturbating?'

'Eh, yeah. Just as well you're not married to me, eh? I suppose I do think of it as a form of cheating. I mean, I'm his wife, he's meant to find me sexy – obviously not in my current state. I'm not exactly at my sexiest at the moment, but surely he should be thinking of me as my former self when he comes?'

'Wow. I normally think about Javier Bardem when I'm having sex with Jeff.'

'Who? The fella from *No Country For Old Men*?'

'Yeah. Doesn't everyone imagine Hollywood stars when they're shagging?'

'No, they do not. I used to have dirty dreams about Piers Morgan and Gordon Ramsay, but I was single then. Do you think I should ask Michael if he's having it off with other women in the shower?'

'Eva, thinking about it, and actually doing it, are completely different . . .'

'Ha! Ha! You said it, naughty boy.'

'Yes, we'll get back to me in a minute, but you can't ask a man what he thinks about when he's wanking. In fact, you shouldn't ever ask a man what's he's thinking, full stop. It's like an invasion of their brain. If men can't keep their own private thoughts, I don't know . . .'

'Listen, I'm not looking to find out what's in your heads. I shudder to think what's going on inside there.

It's just that if he's jerking off to other women so soon, what hope have we got?'

'The same chance as every other couple. This is normal behaviour for a man. Don't go looking for problems. You're a hormonal mess right now. If you're not giving him any sugar, be glad he's letting you have space.'

'Mmmm, maybe you're right. He's been so good, not putting any pressure on me.'

'There you go. He's been a model husband, and deserves a gift. Here, give him *Whore of The Rings*. That looks so filthy he'll be hours in the shower washing away his thoughts.'

'And that's it? I shouldn't even mention anything to him about the length of time he takes in the shower?'

'No, definitely not.'

'But what if he's fantasizing about Angelina Jolie and not me?'

'You're as safe as houses. It's when he starts fantasizing about one of his assistant managers at Le Café that you'll have problems . . . You see, I bet you're sorry you ever brought this up. Now stop obsessing, and let's get focused on some party fun for me and Jeff. You're not the only one with issues, you know. Everyone on this planet has their own dilemma, whether major or minor. Wake up and smell the champagne, babes, you're one of the lucky ones.'

I could hear the hum as Michael's car pulled up in the driveway, and I excitedly fixed my hair to make myself look as attractive as possible.

It had kind of crept up on me, but I hated the way I looked, and felt almost nauseous when I imagined what he must think of me. I was a far cry from the size 12 I used to be, and my legs and stomach were now riddled with ugly stretchmarks. In passing, Michael had complained that maybe if I had used the expensive Clarins Tonic Oil he'd kept buying me, instead of decorating the bathroom with it, I might have been able to preserve my body a bit better.

I had chosen to ignore his comments, but they had hurt. Of course I had gotten quite lazy towards the end of my pregnancy. First thing in the morning my main priority had been to get to the toilet and pee; then by eight o'clock in the evening I'd been so tired that Michael had practically had to carry me to bed. Personal grooming had become a luxury, as even little rituals like keeping my hair brushed had exhausted me. After endless morning, noon and night-time sickness, I'd just been glad to be able to sit and eat a meal without having to throw it all up again. After spending countless hours in our en suite either peeing or vomiting, I dreaded going near the place. I hated the sight of the dodgy tiling behind the toilet pipe, and the look of the old-fashioned key in the door that didn't work. I knew every inch of that room, and despised it. Because I was avoiding the room the practice of spending an extra ten minutes every morning and evening in there spreading oil over parts of my body I could barely reach fizzled out. Occasionally I'd just throw some of the oil down the sink to make Michael believe I was using the bloody stuff.

As he walked in through the living-room door, with his usual *Irish Times* under one arm and his gorgeous old faded tan briefcase under the other, I stood with my arms outstretched and a big smile across my face. But my smile quickly slipped when I realized my love wasn't being reciprocated.

'Eh, well, that's not much of a welcome home. Any chance of a kiss for your long-lost wife?'

'Oh, sorry, let me see, it's Tuesday night and you've finally decided to come home from the party. What? Did Parker's liver give up the will to live? Did Lisa have a date with a surgeon? What was it exactly that brought you home? It couldn't have been me – could it?'

'What, no bitchy comment for Maddie? How kind of you to spare one of my mates from this evening's venom.'

'Oh, yes, very clever, Eva. Deflect everything that's directed at you. How's Daisy? Or did you leave her on the bus?'

He had only been in the house a couple of minutes, but I already knew his mood was too dark to lift before morning. Although Parker had previously been the champion at holding a bad mood the longest, Michael had the ability to surpass him on occasion.

I'm not sure if he took work problems home from Le Café, or if it was just his contempt for me that created such bad feeling. Either way, it was sometimes like sharing the house with a human, living, walking, growling piece of barbed wire.

'Well, what brought you back, then? You've been

gone four days, there's no food in the fridge, and I'm down to my last clean shirt.'

'Ah, sorry, there I was thinking you were pining after me, when in fact you were just missing your personal assistant. Cheers. My body is so weak I feel like I've been knocked down again; only, this time by a juggernaut. I've had to endure the endless questions and staring from strangers about Daisy's condition – did I not deserve a little break from the torment inside my head?'

'Grow up. Torment inside your head. You've had a baby, Eva. Women have been having babies all over the world since the beginning of time. How come I end up with the one diva that can't cope?'

'Who are you?' My heart had just sunk. Michael was being so cruel that I was barely able to recognize the man I had fallen in love with. It was like he had disappeared, eaten up by his stronger evil twin.

All he could muster was, 'I'm too tired for this bull-shit,' before collapsing on the couch and highering up the volume on the TV.

Disgusted, I just walked out of the room in total shock. There was nothing I could say that would calm his temper. I had learnt the hard way that time was the best medicine.

Somewhat lost, I wandered into the kitchen. I had just flicked on the kettle to make myself a cup of tea when he barked through, 'Is there going to be some dinner this evening – or do I have to order in again?'

Taking a deep breath, I walked through to the living

room again and forced a smile. 'Chicken or beef?' Too fed up to cook, I had spent €60 at the Spar around the corner on ready-made meals. They were really expensive ones, so if he never saw the packets in the bin, he wouldn't suspect I hadn't been slaving all day over a hot stove.

'Whatever's quick,' he grumbled, without removing his eyes from the television.

'Beef it is so,' I chirped, before removing myself back to the kitchen. Although he had temporarily riled me, I wasn't going to let him suck me back into another cycle of arguing.

My road trip with the gang had given me some clarity. Some distance from the rut that I found myself slipping into. Michael and I would have to talk, but not before his beef in black bean sauce with seasonal vegetables. Like all men he'd be more agreeable after food. Maybe even approachable.

Clearly it's not just good things that come in threes.

First, Michael hit me with the news that he was going to some two-day business conference in Munich in a fortnight, before telling me I'd have to fork out for a new car for me and Daisy myself, as 'I no longer have the funds to afford one.'

As a freelance journalist I was never exactly rolling in dosh, and since the arrival of Daisy I had been subtly refusing work to concentrate on all things Daisy. Of course, I hated doing so. A freelancer always lives in fear that the phone will stop ringing. All it takes to have you on the poverty line is a younger, prettier and more eager young hack to fill your boots. I didn't want to give magazine editors the opportunity to find such a person, but my head wasn't in the right place to concentrate on writing up interviews. Not to mention having to get tarted up to meet and greet celebrities. If anything was going to dint my already badly damaged ego, it would be facing arrogant, self-centred actors or pop stars and having to listen to them complain about how shit their lives were.

Yes, I loved my job as an ace celebrity reporter, and down through the years it had provided me with many crazy stories and even a few conquests. But as a chubby new mum, I couldn't bear to accept work and parade my fat ass around town. Thankfully, Michael had been happy to bankroll the house while I was in hiding. The question was, how long would he continue to do so? Once upon a time he had worked as a trader in New York, but now he was just general manager of Le Café, a small but busy city restaurant.

Indeed, time was running out. Dublin was a small town and everyone would now know my news. I would just have to wait till another good story broke before showing my face again. A model would soon be humiliated in a sex-tape, cocaine-snorting scandal. Or another journalist would get himself thrown out of a function and be caught cheating on his wife. I was praying for any disgraces to come to light. Anything that could deflect fellow-colleagues from discussing the disappointment I must be feeling over having a baby with Down's syndrome.

The fact that Parker had managed to embroil himself

in a gay smear story was indeed helpful in that regard, but of course I was also hoping for that one to be buried fast.

Amazingly, Parker didn't really understand just how devastating being part of a scandal could be. Although he was fretting about how Jeff would take the news of Owen Murphy-Keane, I knew he was secretly loving the attention, too.

While the news of Michael's trip and the possibility of having to drive my Mini – my old-style Mini – around with buggies and babies sticking out the windows for the foreseeable future was bad, Michael's third bombshell was the most worrying.

'I want sex, Eva.' He spoke slowly and calmly, as if asking for me to pass the salt. 'I'll rephrase that. I actually *need* sex. It's been two months now, and I'm fed up.'

Temporarily, I was speechless, but quickly found my voice.

'*You're* fed up?' I asked, fiercely aggravated by *his* dis-satisfactions. 'How kind of you to see things from my point of view, honey . . . There are plenty of things that I want *and* need – like a bigger car, for instance. But sex – are you mad in the head? I've just given birth.'

'Yeah, like over a month ago.'

'And what? Did you consult some little husbands' rule-book that says you should be sleeping with your wife again within a month of her bearing a child?'

'I've got needs, Eva. You won't even let me touch you. Do you know how horrible that is for a man?'

Disgusted at his behaviour, I threw my eyes and arms

up to heaven and laughed. 'Oh, boo hoo. Poor neglected Michael. What a selfish bitch I am withholding sex from you. After all, I only had eighteen stitches.'

'Oh, here we go again. My stitches, my back, blah, blah. You're not the first woman to have a baby, Eva. I've heard stories of women being pregnant before they left the hospital. No fear of that with you.'

'Can you hear yourself? You'd think you'd just stepped out of a Dickens novel. Women have rights these days. We can even vote. Servicing our husbands is not seen as a chore any more. Sex is supposed to be a loving and/or passionate pastime that is enjoyed by both parties.'

'You've said it. Past times is exactly what we're talking about. I'd like to bring our sex life to a more current status . . .'

'Yes, well, I don't exactly like being bullied into having sex. You're right that I don't want you touching me. You've become so distant and cruel. It's like I don't know who you are.'

'That's what a frustrated man is like, Eva. I'm a red-blooded male. Not a monster. Just a husband who wants some attention.'

A part of me felt that if we were in a movie this would be the exact moment when I pushed him to the floor and started to make love. And at the same time I wanted to slap him across the face for being so selfish. But I wasn't living in a movie, and there was an even bigger part of me that was afraid that if I smacked him he might just smack me back.

Although my blood was boiling, I gave us both a

minute to reassess the situation before asking, 'So where do we go from here?'

'That's for you to decide.' His eyes practically pierced through me with sincerity. 'You can either help solve this problem, or let it fester. I just hope you realize soon that having Daisy didn't simply happen to you. I've been forgotten along the way, too.'

'That's not true.'

'Eva, if you hear nothing else, hear this. I'm going to need sex soon, or I'm going to lose my mind. Now, why don't you sulk off to the bedroom and have a think about it. Ring Parker or whoever, and talk it through, and then come back to me. Sex, Eva. I need sex.'

4

'OK, be honest – is my left breast drooping or is it just my imagination?' Lisa was standing in my bedroom naked from the waist up. It wasn't necessarily a shock to see Lisa's cosmetically enhanced 36C boobs on display – as soon as there was ever a glance of sun she'd have the girls out to even up her tan-lines – but for her to be in my bedroom on a Friday morning asking me to inspect them was a little too close for comfort.

'Come on, Eva,' demanded Lisa in a panicked voice. 'I'm really worried about them. Do they look hideous? Tell me the truth. I've a date tonight and I don't want to look like I've had a monkey swinging on one of them.'

'Have you?' My question would have sounded ludicrous to most people, but Lisa's family owned a little capuchin monkey many moons ago, so with her the possibilities really were endless.

A wounded look on her face, she snapped back, '*No* way! Well, not unless you call Francis a monkey. I definitely think he was a little too rough with me last night.'

Francis, to put it bluntly, was a total loser, but Lisa was blind to his shortcomings. She'd met him almost two years ago, after checking herself into an exclusive rehab centre in Wicklow called Bramble Hill Retreat for Exhaustion. She had wanted to enrol as a sex addict, but changed her mind when she discovered her father was the one who was going to be dropping her off there.

Although Francis was a scruffy middle-aged alcoholic (think Bob Geldof crossed with Peter Falk as Columbo), and Lisa was the tallest, vainest, most cosmetically altered diva on the compound, the two of them hit it off immediately, and spent four weeks getting stoned and enjoying tantric sex in the bushes, while Francis further educated Lisa on the gospel according to his idol Oscar Wilde. Thankfully, Francis had commitment issues and hadn't wanted to continue a relationship outside Bramble Hill, but after a chance meeting last year at the Electric Picnic Festival and a spot of reunion nookie in a two-man tent (I'm still shocked at Lisa roughing it), they had become fuck-buddies once again. Though, after Lisa put her foot down, their relationship took a more conventional turn. These days sex was indoors in the comfort of Lisa's apartment – and only when she felt bored or lonely.

I called her cool behaviour her man-itude. I had always envied her way of dealing with men. Though I felt less jealous when I finally met Francis, as I'd rather have eaten a homeless person's shoe than had intercourse with such a rat.

'Eva, are you concentrating?'

'Sorry, hon, yes. It's just I'm not sure what to tell you.'

'Just say what you think. Do they look lopsided? I genuinely think Francis might have burst my implant. Look here, feel it.'

Not caring whether I liked it or not, Lisa abruptly grabbed my right hand and placed it on her left boob. 'Touch it – properly. See, doesn't it feel squeegee?'

'Eh, yeah, sort of . . . I suppose.'

'Here, this is what it's meant to feel like. See!' Lisa then removed my grip from her left breast to her right. 'This one is perfection.'

I could only look her in the face and laugh. 'Yes, darlin',' I chuckled. 'This is how Hitler would have wanted all breasts to feel like!'

'Yes, very funny. They cost enough, so they should be damn good. Ah, screw it, anyway. I'm just going to have to call Dr Wiseman and get him to look at it. The implants are at least sixteen years old, so they're probably due to be replaced, anyway.'

'I agree. With a name like that he is definitely the best man to figure out this dilemma; or probably any problem, for that matter. Why don't you ask him the meaning of life and why Michael Flatley keeps coming out of retirement?'

'I must say, you're sounding very perky this morning.'

Signalling towards her boobs, I chirped, 'How could I not? Even with a slightly deflated boob, your company is fantastically uplifting . . . I'm sure even Dr Wiseman would agree.'

★　　★　　★

Later that day I was in the middle of watching a distressing documentary about parents dealing with dysfunctional mentally disturbed teenagers – on one of those baby channels – when I received a phone call from an equally stressed-out Parker.

'I need you,' cried Parker down the phone. 'You've got to help me.'

After a busy week dealing with Daisy's reflux, yet another home visit from an intense young midwife who basically put the fear of God into me over my parenting skills – or lack of them – Michael's sex-demands, and this horror story of a documentary I was watching, I didn't feel like giving a cheery reply.

Not in the mood for his pathetic moans, I blasted, 'Take a ticket,' before hanging up and highering up the volume on the telly again. There was a mother in tears because her 13-year-old son had gotten so strong and violent that she actually feared for her own life when he took one of his turns. It was extremely unsuitable viewing for a woman like me in a vulnerable emotional state, but I found it fascinating. It was as if I wanted to punish myself and get into a teary state.

I was only permitted another two minutes of Shirley's story. She handed her son Damien over to the authorities for . . . what did she say? Ring. Ring . . . Did she say he hit her over the head with a frying pan? Ring. Ring. 'What do you want, Parker? I'm busy . . .'

'I need to see you . . .' His voice was full of self-pity and hopelessness.

'What's wrong now? I thought Jeff told you he was

away for another week. Is that not good? I'm sure the gossip over Owen will have calmed down by then.'

'You're not listening, Eva. I need to see you . . .'

'Why?'

'I'm sick.'

'How sick?'

'It's something that medicine cannot cure.'

'Jeez, Parker. I'm so sorry. I didn't realize. Do you want to come over to the house?'

'No. I'm in town. Can you come in and meet me?'

'OK. I'll pack up Daisy and head into you asap. Where do you wanna meet? Somewhere quiet like the Fitzwilliam Hotel?'

'Thank you . . . I don't know what to do. Hurry up. I'll see you there in twenty minutes.'

'Genital warts! You've dragged me into town to tell me you've got genital fucking warts. Was that really necessary?'

'Eva. The doctor told me you can never get rid of them.'

'You can get the bloody things burnt off . . .' My patience was stretched, and I wasn't in the mood to humour him.

'Yes, I've been iced already, but apparently they grow back. I can't believe this has happened to me . . . *Warts.*' His face was puce with anger. 'I have been with some dodgy men in my time. But I can't believe I've gotten warts from a straight guy. Could it possibly get more ugly?'

'Were you not, well, you know . . . careful?'

'No, but we didn't exactly do it . . . we were just messing and stuff.'

'Messing and stuff, hey. As Alanis Morissette would say, isn't it ironic? Or just plain bad luck?'

'There is no way I'm going to get away with this . . .' Parker was now slumping over his Mojito and looking utterly despondent.

'Did you ever think you could?'

'Probably not . . . I don't think I could have *not* told Jeff. I'd say I would have held out all of about five minutes.'

'I'm sorry, pet.'

'Ha. You're sorry? That's nothing to how much I feel sorry. I really messed up – *again*! I can't believe these bloody things came up so quick. The pain was horrific. Owen bloody Murphy-Keane has some cheek accusing me of ruining his life. Just wait till I get my hands on him. Infected people like him should come with a big tattoo across their foreheads. Is it illegal to have sex with someone and not tell them you're infected? That's got to be illegal?'

'I think it only counts for people with HIV, or something. Genital warts are hardly life-threatening, so I don't think it's worth your while going to the Gardai.'

'Well, it should be,' he huffed, before swigging back his Mojito and signalling to the barman for another. 'If only I were a poet, I could throw my misery into some great writing and release my demons. I could eventually end up on the Leaving Cert papers, and teenagers for hundreds of years to come could debate my hurt and pain.'

'Would you really want the world knowing the state of your arse? Gross. Again, let me remind you that Oscar Wilde died of syphilitic meningitis, not genital warts. No, actually, forget historical poetry, maybe living with warts could make for a good rap tune. Yeah, like: "I slept with a straight dude, I think I should have sued, he sunk me in the papers, he said I ruined his life . . . and then he gave me warts . . ."'

'Very catchy. Lovely ring to it.'

'Ha! As opposed to your ring, which I'm sure is far from lovely right now.'

'I used to be told I had a gorgeous bottom. Apparently it's one of my best features . . . Do you think I'll be left scarred?'

'Mmmm, probably only emotionally.' With the stress at home, Parker's worry over no longer having an attractive backside was a tonic. Without realizing it, he could always put a smile on my face. Even though he'd become totally self-absorbed in his own mini-dramas – completely removed from the outside world and anyone else's problems – his childlike behaviour always made me feel like a grown-up, and better able to handle my own difficulties.

As Parker continued to prattle on about himself, I watched Daisy sleeping quietly in her car-seat beside me. She was so good. No matter where I dragged her, she'd just doze with this cute half-smile across her delicate face.

As a singleton, I had hated ever being close to people in public with screaming babies. I had always said how much I'd hate to end up like that, wrangling with a snotty-nosed kid and trying to get it to shut up. I had watched Maddie juggle milk bottles, water bottles and juice bottles, and trying several types of soothers before getting Woody to accept one, in order to get a moment's peace.

I suppose I had gotten what I wished for: a quiet baby. At the time, of course, I hadn't understood that a loud baby was a perfectly healthy and normal baby. Babies were supposed to give out and complain when something was wrong. Instead, Daisy was almost silent. It would be easy to forget she was with you, at times. Yes, I'd heard of women leaving their kids on the bus before, but I'd never thought it possible. With Daisy it would be. Other women told me that my new-found forgetfulness was called 'baby-brain' but I just dismissed it as being tired and rundown. Apart from missing some sleep due to her reflux, Daisy was practically a perfect baby. Yes, she was, come to think of it. It was other people who had bigger worries than me. So what if her eyes looked different, and her ears were unusually small? She was so pretty she looked like a china doll.

I knew that would all change one day. But, for now at least, I could love her and protect her from the outside world. I was just admiring the adorable tiny bows on her white pump shoes when: 'Have you been listening to me at all?' Parker had finally discovered I had totally zoned out from his moaning.

'Eh, yeah, more or less . . .'

'So that's a plan, then?'

'What's a plan?'

'Me moving to a monastery. Jeez, girl, can I have a little focus here? Should I ring Jeff and spill my news, or just wait till he gets back tomorrow?'

'Definitely wait and tell him to his face. Don't do the cowardly thing. That's about as evil as your actual warts.'

'Yes, well, I'm in a living hell right now.' His face was masked in cartoon horror.

'Perhaps you were asking for trouble wearing Prada?'

'What?'

'Eh, earth to brain . . . *The Devil Wears Prada*.'

'Ah, no, the devil wears the guise of being a clean-living straight boy, and goes around swinging his contagious mickie at psychologically weak homos who were just looking for a little TLC.'

'So what you gonna do about it?'

'I don't know, yet . . . But keep watching this space.'

I was balancing on the edge of the bed, hoping and praying that Michael wouldn't so much as brush my feet with his, when he abruptly did just that.

He'd been out late *again*, and shuffled into the bed beside me at 11.05 p.m., stinking of booze and cigar smoke. He had texted about 8 p.m. that he was going for a 'few scoops with the lads'. His half of my chicken korma dinner had already hardened solid in the pot.

My best efforts to pretend I was asleep went unnoticed. 'Are you awake?' he asked, with an almost yobbish tone. Then his arms wrapped around my waist, with his feet curling over mine as if to entrap me. 'Eva,' he called again, shaking me this time, to have his voice heard. 'Wake up. I want to talk to you.'

Realizing I couldn't ignore his direct approach, I put on a fake yawn, rubbed my eyes and tilted my head enough towards him to make eye-contact. 'I was asleep. What's up?'

'I missed you.' He laughed as he spoke, and started poking his finger in my ear. For what, I couldn't work out, but he was finding it hilarious nonetheless.

Batting his hand away as if it was a fly, I couldn't hide my mood. 'Michael, it's late. Just go to sleep.'

'But I don't want to sleep yet. I want to play.'

'Well, find someone else to play with. I'm tired and I'm not in the mood.'

No sooner had the words left my mouth than he snapped into his alter ego, Ugly Michael. This was a personality that had been kept well hidden from me until after the honeymoon, and unfortunately had stuck around ever since.

'Fuck's sake, Eva. What has happened to you? You're like some ole wan in the bed with your Bridget Jones knickers on. You're as frigid. I'd get more warmth from cuddling a frozen pizza.'

'Well, then, go down and open the freezer,' I said childishly. 'Listen, you've barely lifted a finger with Daisy all week, so don't think you can just cosy up to me expecting sex. I'm not in the mood. Get it?'

'You're like a broken record. I'm sick of all this poor Eva crap. I've held your hand through all of this, and what do I get in return? Nothing. Fucking nothing.'

Infuriated at his comments, I switched on my bedside

lamp and sat up in the bed to retaliate. 'I didn't plan on being a nag. But I've kinda been left to most of the parenting. You keep trying to ignore your role here, but you've got to wake up. We're parents now, so just get on with it.'

'And what if I don't want to?' He stared straight into my eyes as he questioned me. He was still looking a little drunk, but the honesty in his voice was obvious.

Dumbfounded, I just sat there waiting for an answer to come to me. But nothing did. I genuinely had no clue what to say to him to help solve this matter. All I could do was stare back at him. He gazed at me. Eventually he broke the stony silence. 'Well? What words of wisdom will Eva be sharing with us tonight? I can't wait to hear this . . .'

'There's nothing I can say to you. If you don't want this . . . Daisy, me, the little family that we've made, well, there's not much I can do about that, is there?'

'No, Eva, the ball is in your court here. You've got to make things better now, or else we're in serious trouble. I'm sick of trying. Keep your precious bed. I don't want to be near you, anyway.'

His footsteps down the stairs into the living room were almost as loud as my heartbeat. I wouldn't follow him, despite thinking up a million comebacks to his demands. I wasn't going to be the martyr and put myself on a plate for him. He had been turning into a total shit lately, and this recent behaviour was not endearing. If he wanted sex, he was going about it in totally the wrong way. Call me old-fashioned, but my kind of pillow talk needs to contain a lot more wooing and fewer ultimatums.

Furiously angry, I stayed sitting upright in the bed for a further ten minutes before I had the bright idea to text-annoy him. 'Hope U & URE frozen pizza have a nice nite on da couch!' I pressed send and waited for a response.

A couple of minutes passed and I received nothing back. So I thought I'd try again. 'Ever heard of vino & a bunch of flowers as a good prelude 2 sex?' I waited again, but there was still no response. I was halfway through a third text when I decided, fuck it, and jumped out of the bed and headed downstairs to confront his lordship. I was preparing to call him every name under the sun when I stormed into the living room. He was snoring on the couch, his right hand clutching the TV remote, his left hand positioned halfway down his jeans, and his mobile phone nowhere to be seen.

Bloody typical, I thought. There was another wasted argument that Michael wouldn't even remember in the morning. The joys of married life. Only yesterday I'd asked my father if things had ever been that difficult between Mum and him when they first started living together, and he had said, 'Of course.'

But why hadn't someone told me how bad it could be? I'd demanded.

'You would never have believed me,' he'd said. 'But it's also the duty of parents never to let on how shit marriage can really be. Otherwise their children wouldn't settle down and have children of their own, and then they'd die as lonely old people.'

'Why would you be lonely?' I asked, confused as to how me or my sister having children could change my parents' social lives.

'Before you hooked up with Michael, between your travelling and partying we never saw you from one end of the year to another. Since you've had a daughter of your own, we've seen more of you than we did in the last ten years.'

He was right. Although my parents did drive me mad, it had actually been nice recently, spending more time with them. It was just a tad sad that I had to suffer an unplanned pregnancy and live with an increasingly unhappy man for all that to happen.

'I've decided to throw you a baby shower.' Maddie was standing at my front door with a cheerful, yet dribbly-nosed, Woody on her shoulders, and a heavy-looking baby bag in her hands. 'Here, grab that first,' she said, shoving Woody's stuff in my face, nappies spilling out all over the hall floor. 'We can't stop long, as my mam is taking him this afternoon. She's also taking him for the night, so that means I get to go out and play.'

'With who?' Now that I was housebound again, I couldn't help but be a little jealous.

'Never you mind, young lady . . .' She swished past me, wrestling Woody off her shoulders, grinning like a Cheshire cat.

Curious about her secret date, I slammed the door shut, throwing all her baby paraphernalia on the ground, and hurried in behind her as quickly as I could. My back had been playing up again, so the word 'hurried' should probably be replaced with 'hobbled'.

'Is it with anyone I might know?' I asked curiously.

'Maybe. Maybe not.'

'Ah, Maddie, tell me. I need a distraction, some romance. Michael is being a pig, and I'm going barking mad hanging around here all day. Cheer me up, please.'

'Really, what's up with Michael? Is he acting strange?'

'Ah, forget about Michael, I don't want to talk about him. Let's talk about you, and how fabulous it is to be a sexy, single gal out on the town. Do you really have a date? Or are you just hooking up with one of your booty calls?'

Still smirking with one of her incredibly bold faces, she threw her jacket on one of the chairs and pulled Woody away from grabbing at Daisy in her Moses basket, before starting to speak.

'It's a date, if you must know. He's tall, dark and handsome, and a really nice guy.'

'Sounds promising. When did you meet him?'

'Oh, ages ago, but I've only just seen him in a romantic light recently.'

'Does he have a name?'

'No, not yet . . . but I'll keep you posted. Listen, I wanna do a baby shower afternoon for ya.'

'Are you not supposed to do that before the baby is born? So the mammy scores loads of free pressies, and doesn't have to buy all the baby stuff?'

'Mmmm, maybe, but there's no written rule that you

can't do it after. I want to do something nice for you. Please let me. You deserve it.'

'OK. What do I have to do?'

'Nothing, except make a list of people you'd like to invite to the party. I'll do the rest . . . the food, champagne. I might even get a couple of the boys from the agency to work as naked waiters for a couple of hours, just as a little eye candy.'

'I've heard of naked chefs, but naked waiters? Is that not a little much for a kiddie party?'

'They'll only be naked from the waist up. They'll be totally ripped and gorgeous. Trust me, they're all the rage. Now get writing up your list. Between us we must know at least thirty horny bored mammies who'd be thrilled with something to do of an afternoon.'

'I'm not sure if I'm really in the mood for entertaining a whole lot of oestrogen.'

'Ah, shut up. The male models are so pumped with steroids they'll more than make up the balance. Hey, I'll even pay them a little extra so they'll flirt with you . . .'

'Ah, cheers, hon, you think I'm that unattractive you'll have to pay people to be nice to me. Lovely. You've just done wonders for my ego.'

'Ah, I didn't mean . . .'

'It doesn't matter. I know I look a frump. I'm nearly thirty-two years of age and even though I'm a size 16 in Spanx, my boobs are still the same size as a 13-year-old's. I know that I've turned into a slummy mummy, and that wearing my husband's Gap sweatshirts and American Eagle tees isn't exactly feminine, but it's just a stage in my life, and I have to keep thinking that, or else I'll crack up. OK?'

'Of course, you've just had a baby, give yourself a chance to adjust.'

'Well, I'm not adjusting as quickly as I'd like, and until then I'd appreciate a little understanding.'

I was about to career off in a mini-tantrum, when Maddie stepped over and put her arms around me.

'Shhh, it's OK. I do understand. Let's take baby steps here. You're still a big ride, OK?'

'*Big* being the operative word,' I sniffed.

I was waiting for Maddie to respond with an up-lifting comment, when I felt her grip on me loosen.

'Oh, shit,' she screamed, pushing me out of the way.

'What?' I turned around and saw what the drama was. Woody was standing at the wing-backed chair where Maddie had left her jacket, with a black biro in hand, vigorously scribbling. The seat was a cream mock-vintage design, and it was destroyed, but all I could do was laugh.

This was my life, and it was no time to get precious. I could either sink or swim. This was the time to fight and get my sanity back before it slipped away completely.

'I'm so sorry, Eva, I'm mortified. Bold Woody. That's so naughty. Look what you did to Aunty Eva's good chair.'

After my mini-fit of the giggles, I told her, 'It's fine. Honestly. Look . . .' I swapped the pen off Woody in return for Maddie's car keys, and then started scribbling on the chair myself.

'What the fuck are you doing, Eva?' Maddie gazed at me in shock.

'I'm releasing some pent-up anger, and it feels great. See, the chair is a complete mess now, and I feel much better. Thank you, Woody, for showing me the light. Why have I been trying to make everything perfect? It doesn't need to be. So what if this chair has ink all over it? So what if my baby has Down's syndrome? So what if I wear Bridget Jones knickers and eat mini-chocolate bars every time I go to the fridge for Daisy's bottles? Life's not perfect, I'm not perfect, and I never set out to be.'

Unsure if I had finally lost the plot, Maddie picked up Woody and started to make her way to the door.

'Listen, it's a bad time. I really need to take this little guy over to my mam's. I'll get someone to come over and clean up the chair. Write up that list and I'll text you later, yeah?'

As if she was running from a tornado, she upped and left without waiting for a reply, leaving me and my manic mind racing. What had got into me? I had just chased one of my best friends out of the house with my craziness. Was I losing the plot? Or, worse still, had I lost the plot?

Daisy was now starting to mooch in her basket. I checked my watch and it said 10.15 a.m. She was due a feed about half past. I'd have just enough time to squeeze in a quick cuppa before she fully woke up. There was also a packet of Cadbury's chocolate fingers hidden at the back of the press with my name on them.

My new diet could start later. Chocolate was my

friend, and made me feel happy. I'd worry about the stupid chair, and dealing with Michael, later. Right now I was going to have quality time with some yummy, scrummy chocolate, watch a little morning TV and switch off my brain. Maybe by lunchtime I might be better able to focus on how to fix my life. If not, there was a fun-pack of Milky Ways hidden in the pot cupboard that would help mend it again . . . Even if just temporarily.

'Hello, is dis Eva?' There was a man with a gruff Dublin accent at the other end of the phone.

'Mmmm, yes, this is Eva . . . Can I help you?'

'It's Dave. I'm ringin' about ure chair. Ure mate has hired me ta clean it. When's gud to call up?'

'Oh, gosh, well, whenever, ah, she didn't have to.'

'Well, it's sorted so I can call up about three-ish. Does that suit?'

'Yeah, cool. See you then.'

It's a rarity that I get blown away by the sight of a man, but when I opened the door to Dave, I couldn't help but go weak at the knees.

'Howsigoin'? I'm Dave. Here to fix ure chair.' Totally in shock, I just stood in the doorway staring at him. 'Are ya all right? Can I cum in?'

'Sorry. Of course,' I snapped out of my drooling momentarily. 'Come on in, eh, the chair is through here.'

Unsure if I was part of some set-up for *Candid Camera*, I looked outside, to check if anyone was lurking in the bushes, before shutting the front door and following the bit of rough that had brightened up my afternoon inside.

As I turned the corner I almost gasped as I saw the most gorgeous backside in front of me. There was Dave bent over my redesigned graffiti chair checking out the damage, and sticking his bum – his beautiful, perfectly shaped bum in black Snickers workman trousers – directly in my face.

'Standard biro stuff – shouldn't be a problem ta get out. I just need to get some bits from me van.' Dave quickly swung around with a cheerful cheeky grin on his face, catching me ogling his assets. He was drop-dead gorgeous and looked like a hunk who'd star in a Diet Coke break ad.

'Hope you weren't checkin' out me arse, were ya? I've let meself go recently – it's an age thing. Can't fight it, eh?' Before I had a chance to respond, he was out the front door, off to his van.

Gosh, had he flirted with me? I was nearly sure that he'd been flirting, or was it his standard repertoire with lecherous lonely housewives? I was sure he encountered them every day.

I literally had two minutes to fix my hair and move Daisy into the other room, so as not to distract his attention from yours truly, when he strode back into the living room carrying a small Hoover-type machine.

'Did ya miss me?' He chuckled, giving me a dirty Dublin wink. 'Hey, don't suppose there's a cuppa tea goin'? I've been out all day without a break. I'm parched.'

'Heavy day?'

'Ah, Jaysus, nothin' I couldn't handle, it's just there's a lotta needy women out there who need the services of Dave, and I'm only one fella. There's not always enough of me ta go around.'

'Oh, I'm sure you cope just fine,' I said in my best flirty tone. 'I'll get that cup of tea for you. Best keep your strength up. Milk, sugar?'

'Plenty of milk, please, no sugar. I'm sweet enough as it is. Wot?'

Totally bowled over by his cheeky charm – not to mention his delectable *derrière* – I almost skipped into the kitchen to put the kettle on. Well, I skipped, and then hobbled with twinges of pain from my back. It didn't matter, though. A scruffy chancer was standing in my living room and it was the most exciting thing ever. Unlike Michael, Dave was going about getting me into bed the right way. Not that I would, of course. Well, not that there was even an offer on the table any-way . . . I mean . . .

'Hey, Eva,' came the voice from the living room. 'Do ya wanna know the good news or the bad news?'

Shocked at my dirty thoughts, I slapped myself across the face before calling back to him. 'Sorry, what do you mean?'

'I said do ya wanna hear the good news or the bad news?' Dave had now walked into the kitchen, and was standing really close to me, holding a strange plastic container. 'Oh, could you fill her up, please?' he said. 'A drop of water for the machine.' He went on: 'Oh, yeah, of course. You wanna know – is that the good or the bad news? Sorry, the bad news is I didn't find any money down the back of the chair.'

'Right . . .' I let out a nervous giggle, and instantly started to blush with mortification.

'And the good news is you're my last job of the day, so I can take me time and clean up your chair just right. And I'm also on *The Afternoon Show* in twenty minutes; they've asked me to do the odd handyman slot. So we can sit down and watch that together. Huh. Happy endings, or wot?'

Unable to speak, I turned back to the kettle and busied myself with putting teabags into cups. Happy endings, he reckons . . . Could I be that bold?

5

Note to self: I must stop fantasizing about Dave. The thoughts I had been having were not healthy.

I had been lying in bed last night imagining his powerful muscular arms wrapped around my waist. His Celtic warrior tattoos peeped out from under his tight grey tee, and his narrow waist extended down to a pert bum perfectly etched through his grubby workman trousers. He was gruff and rough, definitely a league away from my normal type, but sexy as hell. I was sure he enjoyed many a happy ending with lonely women. But was that necessarily a bad thing? He'd be experienced, and would know how to keep his mouth shut.

Oh-my-God, I could never speak these thoughts. If Michael ever got wind of this he'd hit the roof. Why couldn't I be feeling this aroused about my husband? Michael was dependable and . . . well, it didn't matter what he was, he was my husband. But I couldn't fight the attraction I'd instantly felt for Dave. He was raw sex. I could imagine him throwing me about the bed. And imagine loving it.

He had stirred something in me: a passion that I had forgotten about. The last man to turn me on like that had been New York Michael. He'd been such a dirty dog: like poison candy. When we were separated I would crave him, but when we were together the fun would be short-lived, before everything turned sour.

The pregnancy, Daisy's health issues and the stress between my husband Michael and myself had put a lid on any sexual desires I had once had. But since Dave had stepped into my life, or should I say my living room, my inner minx had woken up. I could imagine myself playing naughty sex games with him. I imagined being the dominant mistress and Dave being my slave. A plaything to help me with my own version of DIY.

I had never cheated on a guy before. I'd been cheated on, but never done it myself. But the idea of cheating on my own husband was beyond bad. Could I actually deceive Michael in that way? Go behind his back for some cheap thrills? Noooo. Well, maybe just once? Surely I could blame raging hormones if I got caught? Women can get away with murder while suffering from PMT . . . Surely a bit of afternoon nookie could be allowed?

I was just moving from excitement to despair – because I'd figured no amount of leg-waxing or spray-tanning could make me attractive enough to another man – when I heard a strange convulsing noise coming from Daisy's Moses basket.

In a snap reaction, I dived towards her. She was choking on her own vomit. Just like I had been told, I always left her sleeping on her back, but she had started to bring up her last bottle and was getting into difficulties moving her head.

As quickly and gently as possible, I flipped her over and wiped her mouth and nose clear. Strangely, she felt piping hot, so as soon as she stopped coughing and choking, I stripped her down to her vest, which was still dry, cradled her close to my chest for comfort, and then tried not to panic – and kept trying until it worked.

We sat on the floor, rocking, for about twenty minutes before her temperature started to come down and the distress left her eyes. Poor pet. She was so tiny and fragile, and worse still she was totally dependent on me. I could barely look after myself, never mind her. But looking into her scared little face I found a confidence that I didn't know I had. My sister Ruth kept telling me that I'd just cope, and she was right. It was as if some mystery mammy power had surfaced and was guiding me. As the sparkle came back to Daisy's eyes, I took her upstairs to find fresh clothes. She had a wardrobe almost as full as mine now, with presents from family and friends – they ranged in size from premature baby to three years old. A part of me resented all that she had been given, because it would be wasteful to buy even more clothes for her to wear. But as a mother was it not my privilege to be able to go shopping for my daughter?

As I dressed her in a totally inappropriate pastel-pink frilly meringue dress with white tights, a delicate white knitted cardigan, white matching hat to cover up her barely there fair hair, and pale pink sequinned pumps, she looked more like she should be sitting in the window of a dolls' shop than spending most of the day sleeping. I thought about taking her to the GP's surgery up the road, but what would I tell them? My daughter was really hot, she got sick, but she's now fine? Instead, tomorrow I'd take her to the health centre. They had an open surgery between 2 p.m. and 4 p.m. where struggling mums with new babies could ask for advice.

As I returned back downstairs to clean up Daisy's Moses basket and prepare her another feed, a text beeped through from Maddie. 'Still perving about Dave?'

Trying to play my fantasy down, I texted back, 'As if!'

But she was far too cute. 'Liar, liar, Bridget Jones pants on fire!' came beeping back within seconds.

'OK. I had another dream about him . . .' It was safe to tell Maddie. We had known each other since we were eighteen, and knew all there was to know about one another.

'Was it fantastic? How's things with U and M?' Maddie texted back. I paused for a moment to think. How were things between me and my husband? 'Things shite with M. Dirty dream, Hottie McHot!!!!'

Expecting another snappy response, I waited, and waited. I had warmed Daisy's bottle, stripped her sheets from her basket and even started to feed her before another text came through. 'OK. Enjoy,' was all it said. That was it? Did she not want to know what Dave and I had done on our imaginary date? How sexy I had felt imagining that I was Daisy Lowe in Agent Provocateur? And the wild sex that came after because of it?

Clearly Maddie had enough fantasies, or realities, should I say, of her own to keep her entertained. She wasn't interested in mine this morning. Maybe she was sussing out if I had rung the number that she had given me last week? It had been extremely naughty of her to give me Dave's mobile, as she'd known I was a woman on the edge. Although I had deleted it from my messages in case Michael accidentally came across 'To make fantasies happen, call Dave . . .' I had written Dave's number down in my diary under cleaning services. Just in case. Who was I kidding?

I didn't dare ring it, though. What could I say? 'Remember me, the fat horny housewife from No. 62 Pinewood Terrace? Fancy calling over and cleaning away my cobwebs?' I had found out through previous experience that fantasies are sometimes best left as fantasies.

My best example was a wild threesome in a Jacuzzi that went horribly wrong. After being lured up to the extremely salubrious Hartley Hotel under false pretences, my date night had extended: instead of just one ex-boyfriend, aka New York Michael, it had suddenly included a previous snog – who just happened to be a girl!

Although, in my opinion, she was quite possibly the sexiest thing on two legs, and a threesome is one of those sexual practices that everyone should enjoy at least once before settling down and starting a family, my fantasy had turned into a nightmare when New York Michael had pulled out a bag of cocaine and pressurized me into snorting some.

I had witnessed drug-taking before and always managed to avoid being involved – the great thing about coke users is that they are so greedy they don't want to share their stash with anyone. But on this occasion the cocaine was there especially for me, and there was no way I could escape it.

Since I was about to indulge in a threesome I'd thought: why not go all the way and have a line of cocaine as well? So I'd taken the plunge and got my head down and released my body to all temptations. That night had become a haze, though I think I chose to blank most of it out, from sheer embarrassment. But whichever way I looked at it, it was far from classy to wake on a bench at the side of a road at six o'clock in the morning – cut and bloodied from smashed champagne bottles and glasses which had been thrown at me from New York Michael's gate-crashing jealous fiancée.

I had always wanted to be wild. I had grown up in total awe of Amanda de Cadenet and wished to be able to party hard. But the reality wasn't as glamorous. That night I had ticked many boxes off my 'Must Try Once' list . . . It was that sort of situation that had driven me into the arms of my husband Michael.

I just wished I could find another reason to go running back there.

'I think you're just imagining things. Daisy is fine. All new mums imagine symptoms.'

I was sitting in the health centre with a fossil of an old woman roughly pawing at my daughter. I had told her about Daisy's dramatic temperature changes. It had happened again a second time this morning: she had gone piping hot and started vomiting, but was fine again now. I was trying to explain to the doctor how quickly these hot flushes came and went, but she was having none of it.

'I know I'm new to this . . .' I stuttered, trying to find my inner confidence, 'but I know she *was* overheating. I didn't imagine it.'

'You don't think I know what I'm talking about?' she asked sternly.

'No, I mean, of course . . . I'm not saying you don't know what you're talking about . . .' I had now grabbed Daisy back and was cushioning her from the scary lady.

'There's nothing I haven't seen before. Babies don't overheat. You either have an overactive imagination, or your child is a freak.'

For a couple of moments I sat in shock as the old fossil busied herself with paperwork. Had she actually just called my daughter a freak? Did I imagine that? Unable to comprehend the nastiness coming from this woman in authority, I abruptly stood up and made excuses to leave.

'Excuse me . . . young lady, I'm not finished.'

Terrified that I might open my mouth and start hurling vulgarities at her, I just kept gathering up my bits and walked straight out of the door. I was totally dumbstruck at the ignorance of the woman.

Where did she get off questioning my integrity? Yes, I'm sure new mothers can overreact, but to dismiss my diagnosis out of hand was downright rude. But to call my child a freak . . . that dragon needed to be reported for malpractice, or whatever it's called. How the hell had she been allowed to practise for this long with that attitude? She needed to be stopped. I was the woman to stop her, but not today. I was too damaged by what she said, too insulted, too hurt. I'd make a call tomorrow and complain. Report her condescending ways and save other new mums from her abuse. Yes.

Although I had planned to go for a walk in the near-by park to break up the cabin fever, I couldn't bear to be in the vicinity of the clinic. All I wanted to do was flee.

So I jumped into my little Mini, grabbed a bottle of Rescue Remedy out of my handbag, and gulped down half of it to try to settle my shaking hands. The whole journey home I refused to let anyone with indicators in front of me and drove straight back for the second half of *Ellen*, a pot of tea, a giant Mars bar and three fun-packs of Hula Hoops.

Frustrated at myself for wallowing, I picked up the phone and started phoning around my pals to see who was available to meet up with. I needed a change of scenery, and an early dinner in Le Café with some of the gang was bound to cheer me up. Plus I'd get to see Michael, and hopefully we could be civil to each other. I'd have Daisy with me, so he'd have no choice but to spare me some time out of his busy working day.

After a quick ring-around I had gotten through to Lisa, and that was enough to get me out of the house. Parker accepted a quick call from me, too, in which time he conveyed his mounting stress over Jeff's impending return from Dubai and his various plans of action for humiliating Owen Murphy-Keane, before finally telling me he couldn't meet up because he was on location with a new docu-soap for Channel 4.

Although two phone calls to Maddie rang out, I left a message about what time we'd be in Le Café and forgot all about her. The timing probably wouldn't suit with Woody, so I wasn't going to apply any pressure. Besides, she'd seemed very busy lately. She still hadn't gotten around to organizing my baby shower.

The idea of rejoining the outside world made me feel better about myself immediately. After splashing on some war paint, I even plucked half a rainforest off my eyebrows and felt almost human again. Although there wasn't much in my wardrobe that made me feel attractive, I popped on my pair of beige Spanx and struggled into a pair of respectable denims. They were from the maternity range in Top Shop, but no one could see the elasticated waistband under my baggy tee and long knitted cardigan from Zara. I wasn't going to rock anyone's world with my outfit, but I wasn't going to scare them, either. In my head, I was strong again. I was sure it was merely a temporary state, but I was going to roll with it while it lasted.

Arriving at the door of Le Café with a resurrected inner diva attitude, I strutted past the random customers loitering around the menus, and propped Daisy in her car-seat up on the service counter. This was the gang's old hangout. We had spent countless wasted hours over a twelve-month period discussing hopeless relationships without even noticing what a sweet guy Michael had been to us.

Although we'd known him as the manager guy who'd occasionally throw us a free bottle of vino or the odd strawberry cheesecake on the house, hoping I'd mention his hip-happening eatery in a magazine column I used to write, it wasn't until I got stood up one evening by Maddie that I'd actually found out his name – and that he had always fancied me.

Although he was seriously overqualified for his position as manager, he was good at it, and between us we were making the bills.

'Evening,' chimed a happy face from under the counter. 'Table for two, is it?'

She was new and didn't recognize me, which was a bit of an anticlimax, but I smiled through my disappointment and asked, 'Is Michael about?'

'Sorry, Michael who?' Her faced was pained, as if I had just asked her an impossible question. How many Michaels could there be working in this place?

'Michael Logan Michael,' I replied, sounding a bit short.

'Oh, sorry, Mike. Sorry, no, he's not in at the moment.'

'But it's *Mike's* shift?' My shortness quickly shifted to tetchy.

'Yeah, emm,' her young studenty eyes rolled with the triviality of my questions now, 'he mentioned something about meeting a supplier and that he'd be back in a couple of hours.'

'Really. And how long ago was that?'

'Emm, a couple of hours ago now, I suppose. Sorry, you are?'

'His wife,' I declared assertively.

'Oh, right, well, do you want me to give him a call? Or would you like to wait and I'll get you a coffee or something?'

'Yeah, well, we were going to eat anyway, so a table for three, please, thanks . . .'

Disgusted by the lack of a welcoming committee, I shuffled to my seat, grabbing a few girlie glossies from the shelf on the wall. I looked at the newspapers on offer and decided against picking them up. I was depressed enough already without having to read about the latest missing child or gangland shooting.

As a text from Lisa beeped through saying, 'See U 5 mins,' which always meant at least a further twenty minutes, I tucked Daisy's seat safely along the booth and ordered a glass of Pinot Grigio. I deserved it. I'd also left the car at home, and got the bus in deliberately, so I could have one.

Despite trying to resist the temptation to ring Michael, I lasted about three minutes before buckling. My first attempt rang out. At my second, a winded Michael answered.

''Ello?'

'Hello, yourself.'

'Who's this?'

'It's Eva.'

'Oh, right, sorry, Eva, what do you want?'

'Charming.'

'Sorry, just a bit busy. Is everything OK?'

'Fine. Where are you?'

'I'm in work. Why?'

'No, you're not. I'm in Le Café and you're not here . . .'

There was silence on the line. 'Emm, sorry, I mean I'm out on work. Suppliers and other errands.'

Furiously mad with him, I momentarily forgot that I was in public and screamed, 'You're a lying shit!' Which of course made everyone in the café turn and stare. Not caring what anyone thought, I continued my rant, but chose to lower my volume just a couple of notches.

'Well, did I catch you out or what? You have staff for things like errands, and suppliers normally come to meet you looking for business, so don't try to kid a kidder. So where the fuck are you?'

Again there was a silence down the phone. 'Well?' I screamed once more, determined to get an answer. But I was wasting my time, the phone was quiet. I looked at my screen and it was clear. He'd obviously hung up on me. The shit . . .

As I reached for my bottle of Rescue Remedy my glass of wine arrived, so I threw the remedy back in my slightly torn and tatty Prada handbag, the one Michael had given me for Christmas, the one that I had had with me the night of my taxi abduction, and started to neck the wine. The euphoria I had felt down in Kinsale was well past. Never mind Kinsale, the sense of excitement I had felt just ten minutes ago had collapsed . . . Was this now my life? Doom, gloom and manic mood swings? Despite my best efforts to ignore the global recession that was depressing everyone else, I was now feeling quite blue.

After two sizeable gulps, I noticed neighbouring tables were still looking at me disapprovingly, so I decided to slow up a little. Would they be so critical if they knew my husband was cheating on me? Was he? I asked myself. Nah, I decided. He wouldn't have the balls. Knowing Michael, he'd probably spent the afternoon with a counsellor, pouring out his problems and telling them how shit his life was. How it was full of disappointment, and how his wife wouldn't provide him with sex. Boo fucking hoo . . .

My mood was becoming darker and darker, when an angel of light and happiness strode in. Lisa was dressed head to toe in white. For February that was brave enough, but to do it when you were going to share a meal with a baby that had a reflux and found it hard to keep down any nourishment was looking for trouble.

'Hi, gorgeous . . . oh, Jeez, what's wrong?'

Clearly my exterior was matching my interior. I didn't have to speak: Lisa could read me like a book.

'On second thoughts, don't answer that . . . I've a present to cheer you up.'

Me being childish, I snapped back, 'I don't want a present, I want—'

'Ah, ah, ah, since when have you been a woman to turn down presents? You can tell me all your worries in a minute. Open it first.' She pushed a smallish package on to the table beside me. It had a really obvious pink helium balloon attached to it, which stood tall, but I grabbed my glass of wine instead.

'O-K,' she said hesitantly. 'I'm sensing this dark mood is more than just a drama over nothing. But honestly, open it. You'll like it.'

Although I felt ready to scream, it was sweet of Lisa to buy me a gift, so I felt duty bound to at least take a look at it.

The Princess being the Princess, she had gone, as always, to the effort of extra wrapping. Her presents never came without fancy paper and decadent bows.

The neighbouring tables seemed to love the entertainment of it all. I could hear them whispering and wondering what was in the over-blinged present.

'Thank you . . .' I muttered under my breath, 'you shouldn't have. But Daisy will love the balloon, anyway.'

'Oh, before you open it . . . do you have an electric toothbrush?' Lisa looked really concerned for a moment – well, as concerned as her Botox-injected face would let her.

'Yeah, I do. Why?'

'What make is it?'

'I don't know, an Oral B, I think. Lisa, can you please sit down? People are starting to stare like you're going to propose to me . . .'

'Oh, sorry. Listen, that's perfect. Forget the questions, just open your pressie.'

Straining a fake smile for appearances, and thinking to myself that this had better be good, I quickly reattached the pretty balloon to Daisy's car-seat: she was still sleeping but would be fascinated by it when she woke up. Then I ripped off the fancy pink wrapping paper to find a box that said, 'Voted Best Sex Toy 2008 by readers of *Diva*.'

Not thinking straight, I blurted out, 'What *shite* have you got me?'

'It's called a tingletip,' she answered meekly. 'It's supposed to be a great little thing. I read about it in *Cosmopolitan* magazine; they had a review on it, and it came best in the test or something, though I'm not sure if it's won anything since 2008. Basically you replace the head of your electric toothbrush with the tingletip, and it's your own little vibrator.'

I tried to stay angry but I couldn't. Her gift was so random and out of the blue that I just had to laugh. 'Well?' she asked eagerly. 'Do you like it?'

'Lisa, it's really very kind . . .'

'You see, I know you're not really ready for proper sex with Michael yet, so I thought this might help ease some frustrations you might be having.'

'Yes, thank you, very thoughtful, but I actually use my Oral B toothbrush orally. I don't think it'd be very hygienic to use it both orally and vaginally. I can't believe I just said that . . .' I let out another giggle at such a ridiculous suggestion.

'Hey, you've had worse in your mouth,' chuckled Lisa playfully.

'Ha! You're one to talk.'

'Mmmm, I'm not talking to Francis at the minute. He's been such an asshole. I've been ringing him for three days now, and he hasn't returned any of my calls. He'd better be lying in a ditch somewhere or else I'm never talking to him again.'

Not knowing what to say in reaction to that I finished off my glass of wine as Lisa snuggled up to Daisy and started to gush over her outfit. Happy to let her, I was looking around, trying to catch someone's eye to order another glass of wine, when I spotted Michael walking through the café like a bull.

'There he is . . .' I growled with contempt as I spoke.

'Who?' Lisa popped her head up innocently and scanned the room. 'Michael? Hi, Michael.' She waved at him without realizing the situation.

'Stop it . . .' I pleaded, but it was too late. He marched over to the table like a man on a mission.

'Lisa.' His acknowledgement was cold, but not as rude as his dismissal. 'Will you leave us for a minute?'

His request baffled us both.

'Excuse me?' Lisa put her hand to her chest and looked mortally hurt.

'I said leave. I need to talk to Eva.'

Shocked, her jaw hit the table, as did mine. The two of us just looked at each other. I mouthed the words 'I'm sorry', and then she left without another word.

I was so furious with Michael I couldn't bear to look at him. I kept my focus across the café, while also trying my best not to make eye-contact with anyone else. The eyes of fellow-diners were burning into my brain. Someone was going to encounter the wrath of Eva da Diva pretty soon. I was just biting my lip and hoping that I could channel that anger at one person – i.e. Michael – and not hurl abuse at some unsuspecting person who happened to look at me sideways.

Practising my yoga heavy breathing technique, I had inhaled once and was holding when Michael blasted, 'How dare you come into my workplace and try and make me look foolish?'

'*Me*? Whoah, where did that come from?' My head was so consumed with anger it was shaking like one of those bobble-head dolls.

'I've got the staff laughing at me – jeering at me for being in trouble with the wife,' he went on. 'We had a clear-out recently, and now the place is full of new staff. They didn't need to know I was married. I didn't want anyone knowing about my private life. You've gone and ruined that now. Should you even be out this late with Daisy?'

'Eh, firstly it's only ten past six. Daisy is happy to be out, as you can see. But thanks for checking, anyway. And secondly, *Mike*, why the hell do you feel the need to keep your marital status secret from your staff? Are you bonking any of them? Or is it all of them?'

'As if! Not that I'm getting any action to keep me amused at home. I don't think I've had a drought like this since my teens.'

'Oh, you're quite the stud,' I grumbled.

Clearly he was embarrassed about me. Maybe he was having sexy fantasies about his waiting staff the way Parker had warned me. Or even shagging them. By now my panic had risen up beyond my chest, and I felt like I was drowning. I needed to get out.

Michael was still barking at me about 'respect', and saying something like, 'Have you no sense of duty?' But I could barely hear him. I needed to escape. So I left. No explanation. No instructions about Daisy. I just upped and left, and didn't look back.

I could feel the eyes of the room follow me. I didn't care. I'm not sure what Michael imagined was happening. I heard some sort of question like, 'Where do you think you're going?' But he probably thought I was heading to the toilet. I wasn't, though. A queue had formed at the entrance, and I disappeared out among them. The blast of cold air gave me a sudden feeling of freedom. The Princess was out there, furiously ranting to someone on her mobile, but she excused herself once she saw me and the state I was in.

'Are you OK?' she asked, with a worried look on her face.

All I could manage in reply was, 'I need another drink.'

I must have walked at some speed as even Lisa with her Amazonian long legs found it difficult to keep up. It was only a short trip, though. For some reason I just instinctively walked in the direction of the Westbury Hotel. This had a quiet and comfortable bar, plenty of spare seats and was always full of Americans. The Americans were great: it meant you never had to worry if someone listened in on your conversation, as you'd never see them again anyway.

But as we bulldozed through the teatime crowds across Grafton Street, Lisa kept asking me questions I couldn't answer. 'Will Daisy be OK? What did Michael say to you? Why is he acting so horrible? Are you guys OK?'

Once parked in the safety and comfort of a corner

couch, with a Cosmopolitan in front of me, I could feel my power of speech return, at first just slowly, but by the end of the glass I was at full power.

'What an asshole, Lisa. I mean, I had eighteen stitches after giving birth to Daisy, does he think they'll just evaporate overnight?'

'I dunno . . .'

'Well, I tell you this, they haven't! These days, my fanny hurts. My back hurts. I feel I have the physical strength of an 82-year-old pensioner – and not a particularly active one. I'm just totally wrecked all the time – and he fucking wants sex. He has some nerve trying to bully me . . .'

'Well, maybe . . .'

'And I'll tell you this for nothing. I know that I caught him out today. He was definitely up to no good. How dare he accuse me of trying to humiliate him? I was only trying to smooth things over. If he thinks that's humiliation, he ain't seen nothing yet.'

'Eva . . .'

'And I tell you another thing . . .'

'*Eva!*' Lisa raised her voice this time, to be heard.

'What?'

'Are you not worried about Daisy? I know you're angry, but it's not really her fault that Michael was a shit. Do you not think you should go back and get her?'

'Michael will be looking after her. She'll be fine.'

'What if he isn't? What if he's just pawned her off on some young waitress, and she's currently sitting in the dusty stockroom trying to feed Daisy now? What if he hasn't explained about her reflux?'

'OK. OK. Jeez, I just needed five minutes. Thanks for making me feel like I'm Britney Spears. Oh, gosh. You're right. What if he has pushed her in a corner? Oh-my-God, it's teatime. He'll need all his staff on the floor. What if he's put her somewhere quiet in the staffroom and asked the kitchen staff to keep an ear out for her? Fuck. She could have overheated again and be choking on her vomit. Quick.' I grabbed my stuff and swilled back the dribble at the end of my glass. 'I'm so sorry for being psycho. But I gotta go back.'

It was less than a five-minute sprint to Le Café, but I couldn't get there quick enough. I don't think it did my body any favours. I hadn't run anywhere since before my pregnancy, but I managed it and arrived at the front door surprisingly still intact.

Pushing through the tables, I desperately searched for Michael's head but couldn't see him. I glanced through the kitchen hatch: no sign; I looked up the stairs to the small seated area upstairs: still no sign. I was half-way back downstairs before I clocked him. There he was, sitting right where I had left him, with Maddie – what the hell was she doing here? Thankfully she was cradling Daisy. What a relief. Daisy was awake and looking quite content. Woody was on the couch beside Maddie, gently fussing over Daisy.

Knowing that Daisy was in safe hands, I grabbed a confused Lisa and pushed her back out of the door. 'Everybody is fine. We're not needed. Well, at least, *I'm not needed*. Let's get another drink.'

None too impressed by my decision, Lisa held her ground and stopped me in my tracks. 'What? You're just going to leave Daisy again, and go and get drunk? Do you honestly think that's going to solve anything?'

'Since when do you get to tell *me* to be the sensible one?'

'Since you've started acting like a spoilt child.'

Winded by her answer – after all, *she* had always been the ultimate spoilt brat – I could only cough and tut with the silliness.

'I'm serious for once,' she said. 'I can be the brat because I've no one dependent on me. You've a baby in there. You've got to get her. Your husband is being a total dick right now, so I wouldn't trust him as far as I could throw him. Get in there now . . . Or do I have to drag you in? Anyway, what's the story with Maddie? Was she supposed to meet us?'

'OK, I know you're right. Yeah, I asked Maddie to come in. I didn't think she would, though.'

'Well, at least Daisy wasn't abandoned in some dirty corridor with nothing but a Henry and a rancid mop and bucket for company.'

'Small mercies, eh? So what do I do now, oh wise one? Storm back in there and demand he give me my child?'

'No,' she said hesitantly, stalling for time while she thought. 'You need to, ah . . .'

'Yes?'

'Just calmly walk up to the table, tell Maddie there's been a change of plan and that you have to call by your mother or something, and take Daisy out of there.'

'What about Michael?'

'What about him? The shit doesn't deserve anything . . . OK, I don't mean that. Just be civil.'

'And what? Ignore how rude he was to you, and how badly he's been behaving to me?'

'Correct. It's called the mature approach. Or so I've heard.'

Knowing I had no other option, I walked up to their table and smiled at Maddie. 'Hi. How's she been?'

Immediately she looked uncomfortable. 'Are you OK?' she asked, darting awkward glances at Michael.

Playing confident, I flashed a fake smile. 'I'm fine. You?'

'Yeah, great. Not long here. Traffic was brutal.'

'Well, I'm sorry to break up the party, but something's come up and I've gotta take Daisy back home. Mum's having a turn about some new table she's ordered, so I promised I'd drop by. Can you hand her over?'

'Stop right there,' interrupted Michael. 'Daisy's fine where she is.' Maddie just froze, clearly afraid to get caught in the crossfire. 'The four of us are having tea, and we're having a nice time. So why don't you run off again, like the bad mother you are. We're doing just fine here.'

Dumbfounded, all I could do was turn to Lisa, hoping for some inspiration. But she looked as shocked as me.

'Excuse me? Where do you get off calling me a bad mother?'

'Sorry, did you not just run off and desert her?'

'Eh, I left her with her father. I hardly abandoned her on the steps of a police station.'

'Either way, why don't you take yourself and Lisa off

and leave us to it. Daisy is in perfectly good hands with Maddie here. You run along and have some fun.'

'I don't want fun, thank you very much, just my daughter. Now, Maddie, if you wouldn't mind . . .'

'Maddie, don't you move. Daisy's staying right where she is.'

Not happy with the escalating tension Lisa stepped closer and put her hand on Michael's shoulder. 'Michael,' she spoke calmly and with great authority, 'let's not make this any messier than it already is. Let Eva take Daisy, and you can continue to play happy families, if that's OK with Maddie?'

'Yeah, I've just ordered some food,' muttered Maddie, while doing her best to keep her head down and avoid eye-contact with me.

'Fine.' I grabbed Daisy this time, and signalled Lisa to grab her car-seat and baby bag. 'I don't think there's anything more to say here. Enjoy your food.'

Once again Lisa was finding it difficult to keep pace with me, laden down as she was with extra accessories.

'Sorry, but what just happened there?' Lisa was wheezing from all the exertion.

'I-don't-know . . .' I spoke in rhythm with my marching. 'But-it-looked-very-bloody-cosy.'

'You don't think—' Lisa stopped herself mid-sentence.

'I-don't-know-what-I'm-sure-of. But-methinks-the-can-is-now-open-and-the-worms-are-gonna-go-everywhere . . .'

6

'Apparently your big knickers could be giving you back pain.' Parker was perusing the papers and picking out the highly intellectual bits, as per usual.

'Really?' I was in the act of shoving more white towels, bibs and Babygros than I knew I had into the washing machine, and wasn't really listening to his prattling.

I still hadn't fully adapted to this whole domestic goddess role, and loading the washing machine was not the most pleasant job when day-old vomit-covered baby-clothes had already started to fester.

'It says here that experts fear that bodysculpting undies can cause long-term damage, from back problems to heart disease . . .'

'Mmmm, right now they're just causing marital strife.'

It was the lunchtime after the drama in Le Café, and Parker had called over with the papers. At first I thought he had arrived to offer me moral support, but the reality was his Channel 4 gig had wrapped early for the afternoon, or so he said, and he was simply at a loose end. Although he was acting a little odd, I didn't take much notice. Consumed with my own personal dilemmas, the usual Parker nonsense was beyond my energy levels.

'Are you incontinent, or do you think your muffin-top is just fat?'

'Excuse me?'

'Nah, you see, the weak abdominal muscles which you're squeezing into those God-awful pants can be an indication of a prolapsed womb.'

'Give me a break, I've just had a feckin' baby. I'm carrying excess baby weight, for the record. You can only call me fat when I look like this on Daisy's fourth birthday. And the only thing lapsing right now about me physically is my personal hygiene. I never get a chance to wash my hair any more. Look at the state of me. It's 11 a.m. and I still haven't had a shower yet. *And*, yesterday I didn't even have one at all . . .'

'Lovely thought . . .'

'Actually, I'm not bothered. My husband hasn't spoken to me in a week. And he leaves for a business conference in Munich at the weekend, which means another two days doing the same shite all on my own. I feel like I'm living in the Big Brother house. "It's day 3,748 in the Big Brother house and Eva is putting on the washing." But hey, I'm fine. My marriage has clearly collapsed, I'm turning into the ultimate slummy mummy, and to top it all off, the medical profession think that my daughter is a freak . . . like I'm not already sensitive enough . . . And . . .'

I didn't know what I was going to say next, but I

just stopped. I wasn't talking rationally any more. I had started to hyperventilate, and was ranting like the miserable housewife that I'd always feared I'd end up being. I could have easily gone off the deep end again, but I reeled in my voice in case stray dogs started appearing at my front door.

After straining to push the door on the washing machine shut, I took a moment to look at Parker and work out what was wrong with him. He didn't notice me. Or at least, he was trying his best not to.

It was unusual that he wasn't demanding the gories on yesterday. I had left a lengthy heartfelt message on his mobile, filling him in on what had gone down, but simply got a 'How are you?' when he'd walked through the door today. There was something definitely up, but what – and why?

'How's work?' I asked, trying to pry. After all, maybe someone else's problems would deflect attention away from mine.

Without lifting his head away from his newspaper he chirped, 'Grand. Nothing very exciting.'

For Parker that was not a standard answer. There was always a story to be shared. Some gossip that he would have to divulge or else he would burst. What could be wrong with him? Think . . . Think . . . Oh, I got it . . . How could I have forgotten? 'So Jeff got home last night . . . How did that go?'

'Fine, thanks . . .' His gaze remained transfixed by his newspaper.

'Sooo, he was cool with the warts, and your affair making the headlines?' I probably should have worded it more diplomatically, but tact wasn't high on my agenda.

Doing his damndest to ignore me, Parker ruffled his paper about and refused to lift his head. For a man in his forties he was possibly the biggest baby around.

Tetchy enough to argue with my reflection, I questioned Parker once again. 'So, he was fine with the warts and the public humiliation then, yeah? Gosh, he's very understanding.'

All I got back was a grumble from behind the newspaper. 'I don't want to talk about it.'

'What was that?'

'I said I don't want to talk about it . . . If you must know, he got back late, so we just got into bed.'

'Youuu didn't?'

'Noooo, we just fell asleep. We barely even talked.'

'Do you think he's heard anything from his family about Owen Murphy-Keane?'

'Dunno. He didn't say.'

'And what happens next? Are you going to talk about it tonight? You can't keep putting it off.'

'Ah, yes, Eva, thank you. I'm aware of that. I do actually have a conscience of my own without you nagging me . . . He came in really late. I wasn't about to start wart talk at half eleven at night. I'll . . . I'll talk to him this evening. It's just a difficult subject for me to bring up. I'm not exactly thrilled at killing my marriage, you know?'

'Mmmm, I'll say nothing.'

'Why, have you nothing nice to say? Any possible words of encouragement?'

'Well, I kinda have my own problems, ya know?'

'Don't mind the doctor, she was just a narky bitch.'

'Forget the stupid doctor, my husband Michael totally embarrassed me in front of Lisa and Maddie. He called me a bad mother . . . Have you nothing to comment on that?'

Bizarrely, Parker just stuck his head back in the paper.

'*PARKER!*' I screamed at him in true fishwife style.

'*WHAT?*' winced Parker, just as irritated as me. 'What do you want me to say? Your husband's a bollix? I wasn't there. I didn't see it.'

'And that means you've no opinions on the matter?'

'Not really, Eva. I'm sorry that he's upset you. But after that, I've nothing to offer you.'

'Fine, I won't show any interest the next time you have a drama. So tomorrow don't bother ringing me to cry about Jeff. I'll just come back with your line . . . Oh, sorry, I wasn't there.'

After a five-minute stand-off, me banging cups and pots in the dishwasher, and he huffing from behind his *Daily Mirror*, Parker started loudly coughing as a sign he was ready to talk again.

'Cough all you like,' I snapped. 'I'm not in the mood. You're such a shit sometimes . . . I'm feeling very confused right now . . . My head's in a total spin, and I don't know what to think.'

'Well, do you want to know what I think?'

'I'm not sure . . . Do I?'

'Let's go to Paris for the weekend.'

'Good luck. Remember what happened the last time we went away? Were you not happy with just contracting genital warts? What are you going for now, gonorrhoea, maybe?'

'You're wasted as a desperate housewife,' cooed Parker.

'No shit, Sherlock. Unless you want to start calling me Eva Longoria. I'd quite happily live on Wisteria Lane.'

'So, get your mum and dad to babysit Daisy and let's get the flock outta here to Paris . . . I'm sure they have hunky gardeners there, too.'

'Why Paris?'

'Cause Kylie was there yesterday, and it looks nice. See . . .' He showed me the paper and an image of Kylie wearing oversized round-rimmed shades and a Grace-Kelly-style wrapover scarf. 'Look, we can dress up like we're old movie stars, smoke thin menthol cigarettes and talk about the vulgarity of art these days while swilling on *magnums* of cheap champagne . . . What do you think?'

'Ah, that you live in fantasy land. It does sound nice, though. Humour me, then. Where would we stay?'

'Mmmm, we could stay in the George V – loads of stars go there. Or maybe that fancy place that Madonna likes, the Crillon. It's real old-worldy French style. You'd love it.'

'What about the Ritz, though? We could put loads of fake tan on you, and I could get myself a short blonde wig and we could pay homage to Diana and Dodi . . .'

'Or we could just go online and get some relatively cheap place that's central to all the bars and clubs.'

'You're being serious, then?'

'As cancer.'

'Don't say that, that's horrible.'

'Sorry, you're right. But yeah, come on. I'll need to escape Dublin and the tragedy that was my former life after tonight. I can't imagine Jeff will want to know me once the truth has been outed.'

'I think it's a bit soon to leave Daisy, though.'

'We'll only be going to Paris, not Sydney, Australia. If there was a problem you could be back within a couple of hours. Come on, whatya say, gorgeous?'

'OK, then. Fuck it. I'll ring my mum now.'

'Really?'

'Gosh, I'm not sure. We're only building up our routines . . . Ah Jeez, shag it, yeah. Daisy's only what? Five, six weeks old? My brain's not working any more. Of course, my mum will be fine with her . . . That's if she takes her.'

I take my mobile out of my cardigan pocket and ring my mum. She answers after just a few short rings.

'Hello?'

'Hi, Mum, it's Eva.'

'Everything OK, love?'

'Yes, fine, very tired, but Daisy's fine, been a bit more pukey than normal, but fine. Mmmm, I've a little favour to ask.'

'You don't need money, do you? It's just I'm doing up the guest bedroom at the moment and I've new blinds for the kitchen on order . . .'

'Mum, no, relax, I don't need money, but I need you to babysit this weekend.'

'That's no problem. When do you need me, Friday or Saturday night?'

'Actually, Friday and Saturday . . .'

'You're going out *two* nights?'

'And I suppose three days.'

'Are you being serious, Eva? I don't think your father and I could take care . . .'

'Mum, you'll be great. Daisy's no bother. Michael is in Munich, so Parker is taking me to Paris for the weekend. I really need the break.'

'Oh, Eva, I'm not sure.'

I shake my head to let Parker know that my mother's not biting, and he dramatically raises his hands to his face in horror. 'Give her money,' he mouths quietly.

'Eh, Mum, how about I pay you for the babysitting? It would help towards the blinds.'

There's a pause on the line. 'Oh, I don't think so . . . well, how much?'

I quickly look at Parker and whisper, 'How much?'

'Three hundred,' he blurts loudly, all excited now, as if he was bidding in an auction.

'Yeah, emm, three hundred euros sound OK?'

'What sort of heartless grandmother do you think I am?' There was a silence on the phone. I had no clue how to answer that question without sounding sarcastic. 'Well . . .' she continued, 'I suppose it would be nice to see Daisy this weekend . . .'

'Thanks, Mum. I'll get back to you with the details, gotta go, byeeee.'

⋆　　⋆　　⋆

'Men are bastards,' sniffed Parker. It was 1.25 a.m., and I was just about to give Daisy her last feed of the day – or night, depending on how you look at things.

'You do realize it's the middle of the night, Parker?'

'Oh.' Sob. 'Sorry.' Sob. 'Did I wake you?' Sob. Parker did not sound like he was in a good place.

'Nah, it's grand. You know you can ring at any time. I was up with Daisy anyway. So tell me something I don't know – why are men bastards?'

Instead of a tirade of abuse all I could hear down the line was whimpering and crying. Clearly his heart-to-heart with Jeff had gone disastrously badly.

'Parker – are you OK?' Although I was trying to be sympathetic, I needed his sob story like a hole in the head. Michael hadn't come home yet and had switched his mobile off. No doubt he was off painting the town red with one of his new young staff members. Probably filling them full of stories that I was just some silly stalker, and not his wife at all.

'It's *over*!' cried Parker hysterically. 'I never want to talk to him again.'

'Parker, I'm confused. What did he say about the papers, and, well, the genital warts? You did tell him, didn't you?'

'Not exactly . . .'

'Parker . . .'

'The fucker beat me to it. He was the one who gave me those hideous warts, not Owen Murphy-Keane. The fucker has been having an affair in Dubai with somebody who's apparently a lot less high maintenance than me – *he's the one who gave me the warts.* I'm so mad I feel like smashing up his Porsche and cutting up his Prada suits . . . Hello? Are you still there?'

'Yes, sorry, Parker, I'm just a bit stunned. But did you tell him about Owen?'

'Why the hell should I? I asked him could we have a chat, and he said he had something to tell me. So I let him get on with it. I never fucking thought he'd tell me this . . .'

'Where's he now?'

'He's gone back to his place in the K Club. I should have guessed he wasn't serious about us when he kept it on. I mean, we were married . . . How did he want to live out our marriage, like Woody Allen and Mia Farrow?'

'Jeez, I can't believe after all that's happened that your relationship is over because of *his* cheating. Wow. I'm stunned. And how did he tell you? Was he all remorseful, or just, like, "This is how it is, I'm leaving you"?'

'Nobody's said it's over yet.'

'What? And you think your relationship can survive his infidelity? Or yours, for that matter?'

'Listen, it's late and I've a bottle of Jack Daniel's to swallow and several hate texts to send. I'll talk to you in the morning. Sorry again for ringing so late.'

'No problem. Any time,' I dismissed sarcastically, though my tone was lost on Parker.

As I rejoined Daisy in the living room with her warmed formula, I wondered if my own marriage was also hanging in the balance. At least Parker and Jeff were being half-honest with one another. Was there a chance that Michael and I could do the same?

'Eh, sorry about last night. Listen, Paris is booked. Maddie's working, but Lisa is coming. And Jeff very kindly paid for the flights and accommodation.'

'Does he know?'

'He will when he gets the bill. Oh, I also picked out a lovely new snazzy pair of loafers while I was online.'

'Prada, I presume, darlin'?'

'Of course, and I bought us two front-row tickets to see U2 later in the year . . .'

'Excellent.'

'In New York City, baby . . . OK, gotta go. Oh, the flight is at 12.25 p.m. tomorrow, so I'll pick you up about 10 a.m. *À bientôt, mon amie.*'

9 a.m. Friday morning and I'm standing outside the front door at my mum and dad's house.

As I slipped my key in the lock I was whisked back to my teenage years. All those late nights and early mornings when I'd come stumbling home drunk, and stand at this front door, trying to pull myself together just enough to be able to walk into the hall and strut past my parents, pretending to be sober.

They'd never bought any of my performances, I'm sure. They weren't stupid. But out of fear of the repercussions, or just sheer relief that I had made it home safe – I'm not sure which – they had very rarely pulled me up about my inebriated state.

This morning, of course, I had a different performance to try and act out. I wasn't drunk – well, not
yet anyway; get me to the airport bar and I'd be on my
way with a couple of novelty vodkas – but I knew I'd
be greeted with a semi-hostile reception. Last night on
the phone I had been told by my mum without any
sugar-coating that, 'You're pushing your daughter away
from you. You haven't accepted full responsibility for
Daisy's disabilities . . . Self-indulgent trips like these
won't help the bonding process.'

It would be grief from the moment I stepped inside.
But unlike my teenage years, on this occasion I was
racked with guilt. I knew that my mother was speaking
the truth. I wasn't sure when I'd fully accept Daisy's
supposed shortcomings. She was still just this little tiny
bundle that wasn't required to do much else than what
she was already doing. Time would change that. But I
told myself that I'd take fewer self-indulgent trips in the
future, and pushed my way through the front door in a
defiant manner.

'There she is,' cooed my father from the kitchen. 'The
great explorer. Have you got your column with *Lonely
Planet* yet?' He was slumped in his favourite corner seat,
and looked his usual happy self. Just like every other
morning, he was stirring his three Shredded Wheat and
hot milk in a bowl on his lap and watching *Ireland AM*
on the kitchen portable TV.

'Yeah, I have, Da. The column is called "Escaping
from reality" . . .'

Appearing from thin air, my mother stormed into
the kitchen looking demented. Her face was puce, and

her hair looked like she had been dragged through a bush backwards.

'You may joke, young lady, but I haven't had a wink of sleep worrying about that daughter of yours. I'm beginning to question if you love her at all.'

'Jeez, Mum, that's a bit harsh. I'm just going away for two nights – not emigrating.'

'Ahhh.' She shook her head in an agitated manner and tapped her forefinger off her right temple. 'Indeed, you may only be taking a short break, as you call it. Escaping from reality, as you just said, but emotionally you're totally detached. I can see it in your eyes . . . I'm worried sick, Eva. I don't mind tellin' ya. I'm worried sick about this.'

I darted a glance at my dad for support, but he quickly snapped his eyes back to the TV. He knew which side his bread was buttered, and he wasn't going to take any chances by siding with me. All he wanted was an easy life, and going against my mother was *not* something he was going to do. Over forty-four years of marriage she had moulded him into the cowering, subservient puppy that she had always wanted. Her motto had been: if you want an opinion, I'll give it to you!

Accustomed to being shouted at, I just proceeded to off-load Daisy's belongings, spreading them across the kitchen table to make sure I had brought everything with me. Doing my best to ignore my mother's rants, I quickly emptied Daisy's baby bag. Sterilizer – check. Bottles, soothers – check. Bibs, blankets, Babygros, vests, nappies, moisturizer – check.

'OK, Mum, I think everything you'll need is here.

Oh yeah, and Vaseline and cotton-wool, too. All here – oh, and not forgetting your money.' It acted like an instant painkiller: I could see her facial muscles relax.

'Oh, well, yes, thank you. Daisy will be just fine. Didn't I raise two of you? Not to mention half the road you used to bring home with you.'

'Thanks, Mum, you're the salt of the earth.' I kissed her on the cheek and gave her a large bear-hug. She was a major pain, but her worrying and over-stressing was normal behaviour.

Reminding my mum that Daisy needed to be fed really slowly, and given sugared water if she got constipated – and to watch out for any signs of overheating – I gently kissed my daughter, who was wide-eyed and enjoying her new surroundings from her car-seat on the floor. Then I gave a peace sign to my dad, and disappeared out the door before my mother could muster up the energy for another rant.

My poor father would get it in the neck for the entire weekend, and would have to be at my mother's beck and call every hour. Although he pretend-moaned like he was this hen-pecked husband, he really loved her, and could stomach endless hours of her abuse. She was his glue, and held everything together for him.

Walking back to my car, I felt sad that Michael and I hadn't had a chance to sort things out since Wednesday night. He had been avoiding me, and I had made it easy for him. I didn't bother pestering him with phone calls or texts. I just didn't have the energy to fight any more.

By the time I got back to the house, I was sure he'd

have left. I didn't think he was leaving for Munich till later, but there was no way he'd be hanging around the house, waiting for me to bump into him. Hopefully, next week we could get things back on track. Kinsale didn't exactly do the trick, but maybe this break would be different?

Unfortunately my positive thoughts only lasted till I pushed the key into the door of my tiny car. I thought to myself what a shit he really was, making me drive his daughter around in this tin can. Lifting the key back out, the fake diamanté champagne glass on my key-ring caught my eye. It was shiny and sparkly just like I used to be. What a sweeping life shift I had made in just one year. God only knew what crap was going on in Michael's head these days. But as I fell into my driver's seat, turned on the radio and fiddled around until I came across a loud disco tune, I decided not to dwell on the dire state our marriage was in this weekend. I was sure he wouldn't be worrying about me.

If I didn't mind myself, I would slowly – or should that be speedily? – slip into a depression. I would be no good to Daisy as a crazy lady. She needed a happy mommy who would make her happy, too. Yes, this trip to Paris was going to be a mommy tonic. OK, why didn't I blast up the music and get this party started? In less than two hours I would start to feel numb to outside pressures. Parker would rant on about his own dramas and all I'd have to do would be nod sympa-thetically to humour him. I wouldn't even have to offer opinions – he'd be so worked up.

I didn't care if he'd booked us Ryanair. I didn't care

if we were staying in a hostel when we got there. I just wanted to be close to French men and drown in their smoky scent. I wanted to listen to their accents and feel like I was on holiday – a holiday from my own life.

Roll on springtime in Paris . . . Oh-my-God! I looked at my phone and checked the date. Today was 13 February. That meant tomorrow would be Valentine's Day. How had I missed that? I couldn't believe Michael had already booked himself in for a fucking work conference in Munich on our first Valentine's Day as a married couple. That was not good. That was a really, really grim sign.

I had been so shut away at home that I hadn't realized it was upon us. It was one of my favourite days of the year. I was a woman who demanded to be spoilt, and I had always believed being born Eva Valentine gave me an extra reason to celebrate the date.

Tears welled up in my eyes, but I fought them. This was a sure sign that my husband felt he had made the wrong decision by marrying me. What a coward he was for not being able to talk to me about it! Sure, our circumstances weren't ideal, but there was no looking back now.

I was just about to descend into a full-on self-indulgent crying fit, when I noticed my mother's nose peering through her net curtains in the living-room window. Shit. I smartened myself up quickly, gave her a cheeky wave and high-tailed down the road. I couldn't let her see me cry. It would just be used as ammunition against me at a later stage.

★　　　★　　　★

Maybe the stress had done it. But I had somehow miraculously shrunk a little, and managed to squeeze into a pair of size 14 jeans that I had bought when pregnant. They weren't a maternity pair, either, and the confidence boost made me feel brand new.

When Parker arrived to pick me up his eyes were bloodshot, but even he noticed a difference in my shape and whooped a flattering, 'Work it, work it, what your momma and your credit card gave you,' as I stepped into the taxi.

Strutting into Dublin Airport I had my head held high, dangling as many coordinated labels as I could find and carry. In honour of Parker, though maybe it had been a state-of-mind thing, I had dressed head-to-toe in black. Let's be honest, part of me was mourning my marriage, but with any death or ending there is always a new beginning. So, keeping that in mind, I worked my inner diva and even got a few double-takes in the process.

By 11 a.m. the Princess, Parker and I were sipping on slightly iffy Bloody Marys in the Executive Lounge. Maddie had sent me a text to wish me bon voyage and many champagne kisses in Paris. They used to be a speciality of mine . . . Oh, how I'd love to be that bold again.

'A toast,' I declared, raising my cocktail. 'Whether it's our drinks or our relationships, things seem bloody awful lately. So let's just have a blast this weekend and sod the lot of them. Huh?'

'To Paris,' chimed Lisa and Parker. 'What goes on in Paris . . .' I smiled, encouraging the others to join me, 'stays in Paris.' The three of us clinked glasses, and then instinctively looked around the room to see if there was any trouble to be had.

'Why can't you be straight?' I was lying across the couch in our decadent Errol Flynn Suite at the Hôtel Napoléon, and I was knocking back the bubbly.

Through sheer fluke Parker had managed to get one of the best suites in the hotel, even on a Valentine's weekend, because of some last-minute cancellation. From our balcony we could see the Eiffel Tower and almost touch the Arc de Triomphe. It just didn't get any more Parisian than that.

After bitching about our respective partners the entire plane trip, we had temporarily expelled our demons and were now in let's-get-drunk-and-have-fun mode, with Parker and me leagues ahead of Lisa in the getting-drunk stakes.

'I mean, if you were hetero, we could have just married each other and saved ourselves a lot of heartache. Think about it. You like Prada, I like Prada. You like champagne, I like champagne. You have loads of money, and I like spending money. You see, a marriage made in heaven.'

'Ah, indeed, Miss Valentine, tragically the problem is we both like boys, along with high fashion and, eh, Pommery.' He checked the label on the bottle of champagne we were drinking, and topped up our glasses while he was at it.

'Two youngish guys own Pommery. I had dinner with them once. Really nice guys, actually. I think one of them said he was also into flying.' As always Lisa came out with the most random of statements.

Even through my fuzzy haze I remembered something she had told me before about an old champagne-tasting trip she had taken to Reims. I vaguely remembered a story involving her flashing her boobs at the director or MD of one of the champagne houses. 'Were they the guys you flashed your boobs at?'

'No, that was at Laurent-Perrier.' Hiccup. The bubbles started to get the better of her.

Through a fit of the giggles I could see she was about to launch into another anecdote. Then I suddenly remembered her burst boob. How could I have forgotten?

'Oh, Lisa,' hiccup. I slipped on the couch and started to giggle and hiccup with her. 'Did you get your boob fixed?' Hiccup.

Without so much as a blink of an eye, Lisa lifted her top and bra and proudly exposed her breasts. It was an effortlessly swift, one-handed move that suggested we hadn't been her first reveal. 'Don't the girls look fabulous?' she questioned, before ejecting a large hiccup that made her pert breasts bounce with delight.

Fascinated by such a womanly display Parker fell to Lisa's knees and pleaded to touch them. 'Can I, pleeese? They are fantastic . . .' A stranger to subtlety, Lisa grabbed Parker's hand, just like she had grabbed mine in my bedroom, and thrust his large fingers firmly on her chest.

As if he was investigating a car-engine Parker silently

played with her breasts, being careful not to be too rough. Totally intrigued, he studied their movements as she continued to hiccup, only now she wasn't laughing so much. Being the kinky woman that she was, she was enjoying being fondled, even if it was by a gay man.

'Yes, it is a pity he's not a straight guy, Eva. He really has lovely strong hands. Take as long as you want.' She smiled at Parker. 'That's quite pleasant, what you're doing.'

Repositioning myself upright to enable me to hold my breath better and try and beat the hiccups, I also had a better view of what Parker was at, but I wasn't sure if I was comfortable with two of my best mates being so intimate with each other. There was something incredibly wrong about the whole picture. The fact that we were in Paris – the city of love – and we were all almost single, and drunk, made the situation no less icky. It was the same unease you get when you watch your parents getting frisky.

Curious as to what Parker was thinking, I sucked in a big intake of breath and quickly asked, 'Well, do you still like boys' bums?' Then I took another large breath and held it.

His reply was defiantly proud. 'Heck, yeah!' Leaving no doubt as to his sexuality. 'But boobs are lovely, too. I wish I had a pair of my own to play with. I'd say they're hours of fun on a cold night.'

As I grabbed my own pair and gave them a playful jiggle (they were slightly bigger now since Daisy – but then again, everything was bigger since giving birth) I looked up to see a waiter with a trolley of food smiling at me with the biggest grin across his face.

'*Bonjour,*' he cooed, in his sexy French accent. 'Would you require ah hand, mademoiselle?'

Of course I just froze in shock, not simply because I was caught out, but at the sheer beauty of the man. He was a Parisian vision, and had the cutest smile. Not to mention the most sexy deep, masculine voice.

Although I tried to speak, nothing but a large belch stroke hiccup erupted out of my mouth, startling Parker on the adjacent couch with Lisa's globes in hand.

Instantly the mood was broken. In other words the French waiter muttered, 'Oh, pardon,' and exited stage left like he was running for the last Metro.

As we all fell about the place laughing Parker pulled down Lisa's top and quipped, 'Typical, boobs are nothing but trouble. They've just chased off that perfect specimen of French manhood. I'm going to have to go downstairs and do something really gay now.'

'Set yourself a challenge, why don't you . . . Hey, I think he's just gotten rid of my hiccups.'

'And mine, too,' sniggered Lisa. 'We need to get him back here to see what other talents he has. Anyone up for ordering more food?'

After savaging the pommes frites and assorted sandwiches, Lisa packaged up her newly mended assets and we took to the streets, literally.

While she rabbited on about the new cosmetic surgery techniques that left her without fresh scarring, because she had had her latest breast inserted through her bellybutton, I embraced the feeling of absolute joy that I felt while walking down the Champs-Elysées. The air might be bitingly cold, but my face was toasty hot from the amount of champagne we had drunk back at the hotel. I was fairly well sozzled and loving it.

In the intense hustle and bustle of the street, I linked arms with both Parker and Lisa to keep me on course and closed my eyes to soak in every bit of the moment. Even for February the atmosphere was electric. With every pedestrian that kept brushing past, I fantasized about chance meetings. How I could just turn a corner, bump into somebody new, and how from that moment on my entire life could change. With the power of positive thinking – or drunken fantasy – I told myself that my life would change for the better very soon. I just had to want it enough. And as I strutted down the Champs-Elysées breathing in the combined smells of food, aftershave and car fumes, I convinced myself that by the time I returned home to Dublin, life would be different. Better. More fulfilling. At least hopefully less confusing and less stressful.

As I continued to step on and between the cracks I kept my eyes firmly shut, imagining that I was an important person being ushered to a VIP location. I did that occasionally, when I needed to feel better about myself. I imagined I was famous or special in some way, and every time I succeeded in doing so, it made me feel giddy. Not as giddy as at this precise moment, though. Feeling cocooned between two of my best mates, I felt incredibly protected and happy. I wanted this moment to last for ever. Sure, it was the alcohol that made me swagger more, but I didn't care. I was the hot momma Eva Valentine, walking down the Champs-Elysées, looking for trouble.

I wasn't here for long, but I sure as hell was looking for a good time!

7

'I cannot believe you're taking me to a swingers' party.'

'Eva, it's very fashionable, you know. I guarantee you there will be nobody here who's not supermodel material or a multi-millionaire.'

Lisa was almost causing static she was so sexually charged. She had managed to get us invites to an underground swingers' party at some lavish home in the suburbs of Paris, by pretending that Parker *was* the movie business in Ireland – oh, and straight. No gay men were allowed at this party. No ugly people, or poor ones, either. Strictly the rich, the physically blessed, and the free-thinking were welcome.

Of course I was trying to suppress my frantic nerves about being deemed beautiful, but what did it really matter if I was rejected for being genetically imperfect? I was an out-of-towner: I was just sightseeing, like one of those fat Americans who came to Ireland to trace their ancestors and squeezed themselves into green trousers while huffing about Trinity College looking lost. As locals, we tolerated their big asses slowing us up as we went about our business; tonight's party people would just have to do the same for me. Toleration was my buzz word for this evening. Live and let live. No matter what vile sexual perversions I saw, I'd just ignore or accept them. I'd watched enough documentaries on kinky sex to know that people mixed urine in their champagne instead of Red Bull. I'd listened to people talking about what a turn-on it was, letting small furry animals wriggle all over their privates, and we'd all heard the rumours about Michael Hutchence and how he got his kicks from asphyxiation. Nothing was going to unnerve me. Well, that was the plan.

Although I'd often thought of myself as an impressive lover, I wasn't too comfortable with kinky stuff around my own bedroom. Call me old-fashioned, but to me, one guy and one girl was the perfect recipe. Yes, I've kissed girls in the past, but I'm a big believer in keeping things simple. It's when you start throwing extra elements into the mix that it all gets too complicated. That also goes for battery-operated apparatus, too – indeed, Lisa's present was yet to be removed from its box. Of course I had tried the odd Rampant Rabbit, and even a Wacko Jacko black glove that had vibrating fingertips, but the sheer noise of the gadgets always put me off. Now that I thought of it, I had never really been able to include pornos in my lovemaking, either. Sure, what woman hasn't Googled free porn and enjoyed a little one-on-one time? But I hated the idea of competing for the limelight, and preferred to throw myself into some extra Dita Von Teese performances to distract my lovers from using them.

So I had no idea what to expect of tonight's party. After a chance meeting with some fabulously outrageous guys and gals at a bar yesterday evening, Lisa had received an SMS on her phone with the location of Club Désir.

All we knew was that everything was free. Free admission, free champagne and of course free sex.

Not that I would be partaking in any free love. I was going to be strictly a voyeur tonight; but maybe I could indulge in some champagne kisses? Surely that could be deemed innocent flirtation? After all it would be extremely rude to attend a sex party and not swap some bodily fluids . . . I was hoping if I kept repeating this in my head I might just convince myself . . . So far, I wasn't buying it.

According to our new acquaintances, Club Désir was hosted by various rich society couples who were big into the swinging scene. Tonight's orgy was courtesy of some drugs mogul – prescription pills, apparently – who had a penchant for fake breasts and rubber. Lisa felt like she had died and gone to heaven.

'Thank God I got the girls fixed. Can you imagine having a wonky boob at a gang bang?'

As we pulled up to the address, respectively our jaws hit the ground. Even our taxi man seemed impressed, and rattled away in French, occasionally blurting out a, '*Mon dieu*,' or, '*Wouaou*.' Without a word of exaggeration, it looked like some sort of castle worthy of a Harry Potter movie. It was massive, and had pointy towers either side. But instead of having a haunted feel, it was a building that spoke to you and welcomed you in.

It was magically illuminated, as were all the surrounding trees and garden statues, which even from a distance looked like copulating couples. Not much of a surprise there, though.

Just as we had been instructed, Lisa hopped out of the car, pressed the intercom and in her best sexy voice said, 'Club Désir 101,' when the voice at the other end asked, *'Bonsoir?'* As the dramatically historic-looking iron gates started to open, Lisa hopped back into the car like an excited teenager and feverishly fluffed her hair.

'I feel like a virgin bunny on her first trip to the Playboy Mansion. I wonder if it's anyone's birthday? I can do a Pammie on it and present the cake nude . . .'

Too gobsmacked to speak, Parker and I just sat in awe as we were slowly driven up the pebbled driveway, crunching the stones underneath us as we went.

The driver continued to mutter, *'Mon dieu,'* to himself, so Parker shoved fifty euro into his hand and thanked him. Then we stepped out of the car and moved towards the grand entrance, which was made slightly more grand by the two semi-naked models chained to the wall and dressed in black leather straps, which exposed their breasts like welcome gifts. It was terribly scary and thrilling; I felt we were lambs being led to the slaughter.

Lisa's enthusiasm began to rub off on me. I was in the middle of making eye-contact with one of the women to say *'Bonsoir'*, when Parker made an uncharacteristically butch move and grabbed her right breast. Totally unoffended, she began to purr at him, clearly pleased with the attention.

'Parker?' I whispered, with a gasp of mortification.

'What's wrong?' he asked, disgusted by my interruption. 'This is what you do. For one night only I'm straight: remember? And anyway, I'm really starting to get to like breasts. We've made friends.'

Inspired by Parker's forthrightness, Lisa followed his lead and stepped forward to fondle the other model's breast.

'You are beautiful,' she cooed, before kissing her new acquaintance on the cheek.

Thankfully there were no other bondage babes left for me to make a move on, so after a couple of moments of standing around like Billy no mates, I just stepped into the castle and hoped that they'd hurry up with their groping and follow me in.

Although there were many directions to head off in, I followed the most noise and arrived at a ballroom, which had a massive swimming pool in it.

Everywhere I looked breasts bounced and old men's bums in unforgiving thongs paraded about looking for sex. There were naked women lying on lilos in the water, on chaises longues beside the pool, and doing private dances for appreciative audiences. This was a den of iniquity, yet somehow I didn't feel threatened. It was like I was on a movie set, or even a virtual tour; I was watching from a distance. I was starting to get engrossed in the mating rituals of one couple – who had clearly just met each other for the first time but shared an instant attraction – when Parker pounced on my shoulders. 'Spotted any hunks yet? I've already groped four breasts, two bums and even touched tongues with the cloakroom attendant.'

'Haven't you been busy! . . . Was it a girl or a guy?'

'Girl, of course. Tonight, people, I'm crawling for bitches.'

'What? As opposed to your usual creepy crawling?'

'It was actually quite exciting, really. I've regressed to my pre-gay teenage years.'

'Where did you leave the Princess?' I asked. 'Please tell me she's not being whipped with paddles in the vaults.'

'No, but I've left her with a set of twins. True Italian stallions whose names are Romeo and Massimo. So, let's head back to her quickly, or else she'll be having all the fun without us.'

'Are they identical? I think she's always had a fantasy to do twins.'

'They're like mirror images of each other. As tall as her, dark-skinned, and, oh, they've matching pony-tails.'

'Fuck off . . .'

'No, honestly, real romance-novel heroes.'

'Jeez, happy Valentine's to her.'

'Now, now, missy. We made a vow not mention the V word tonight. Men are bastards, so much so, I'm gonna feel more tits and smack more ass. I suggest you do the same.'

'Are you serious? You've told me you're allergic to the female form. I don't want to be mopping up your vomit afterwards.'

'Nah, I think I can handle it. I like having to act

butch, though the fucking men in that library are to die for . . . Unlike the old craggy guys in here. Right, quick, let's go and find us some V love.'

I threw him a scared look, but he spun me around back towards the door and ignored my concerns. Michael hadn't bothered to ring me all that morning. I'd eventually rung him at six o'clock, hoping to wish him a Happy Valentine's, but all I'd got was his voice-mail.

I was feeling pangs of massive guilt, but the second we set eyes on Lisa all I wanted to do was touch up Massimo. Or was it Romeo? I woulda taken either – or both! Wow, the twins were hot! They left both Parker and me speechless with their beauty. Albeit an extremely cheesy lothario-type beauty. Lisa wasn't having the same problems as I was with confidence. She was the filling in an Italian salami sandwich, and looked extremely happy about it. We were just about to get to her, when the new recruits began kissing her neck from either side. I stopped Parker from interrupting, and the two of us stood and watched as she was systematically caressed, licked and kissed by the fabulous Fabio wannabes. Lisa being Lisa just swooned with the attention being lavished on her. I think her eyes were about to roll into the back of her head when she noticed Parker and me staring at her.

'Why don't you get some popcorn?' she asked drily. 'I'm just getting warmed up.'

'OK, we'll go do that, so, and we'll check in on you in a little bit. Don't do anything I wouldn't . . .' I waited for a response, but none came. This princess did not need rescuing.

Clearly, five, not three, was a crowd, so as soon as I'd ditched my coat Parker and I got our hands on some champagne and took to exploring the medieval party palace. Through the sculpted archways we found corridors that led to endless doorways, many of which we were afraid to open. Although there weren't a huge number of people floating about, no one blinked twice at Parker or me. No one knew us, but no one was suspicious of us, either.

The fact that we were there at all gave us instant membership to this elite club. No secret handshakes were required; though I'm sure Lisa was by now involved in a few special handshakes of her own. I just hoped she waited to find a room first . . .

Wandering aimlessly past courting couples in quiet corners, we somehow made our way out to the court-yard. There, amidst the classic French architecture of yellow stone walls, terracotta-tiled roofs, and potted manicured trees, was what looked like the epicentre of the party.

Just like the entrance, the courtyard was lit up with thousands of white lights, complemented by lanterns and discreet flamed heaters. Funky acid jazz music hummed in the background, and men and women, dressed in everything from cocktail wear to lingerie, swarmed in and around the steaming heated pool, their whoops of laughter peppering the atmosphere.

It was total fantasy stuff, and the pursuit of passion was infectious. I might have arrived a prude, but I couldn't help but feel turned on by the ambiance.

Everywhere I looked there were horny, happy, beautiful people. No one was being forced to do anything they didn't want. Everyone here was a consenting adult. This was unashamed entertainment. Good clean, kinky fun . . . Last night I had been a frustrated mother on the verge of a breakdown, tonight I was a diva at a sex party in Paris. I had been feeling that the old Eva might have vanished, but, wow, had she made a comeback!

Parker found a sunlounger for us to relax on, then headed off to get more champagne. Now that I had a base I was happy to sit back and take it all in. In all my previous adventures I had never witnessed exhibitionism like this. I was surrounded by wonderfully wicked people, and I couldn't think where I would rather be – this was definitely leagues better than sitting at home and feeling sorry about my lot.

Once again I'd become mesmerized by a nearby couple – who were engaging in some sort of foot-fetish, toe-sucking erotica – when this gorgeous black man started walking in my direction and smiling.

Checking to see if he was actually looking at me, I glanced over my shoulder, but there was no one there. Oh-my-God, he was definitely looking my way. As he knelt down on the ground beside my lounger I realized my face was frozen in shock. Quickly, I tried to smile and look more sultry, but my new friend had read my rigid body language.

'*Bonsoir, belle fille, mes excuses, comment allez-vous?*'

At a loss as to what exactly he was saying, in typical

tourist ignorance I pleaded, '*Je suis Irlande. Eh, no parle français, emm, je suis désolé* . . .'

'Ahh, beautiful Irish girl. Welcome to Paris.'

'Ehh, thank you.' I looked around frantically for Parker, but he was nowhere to be seen.

'Have you lost anyone?' he asked in a deep husky French accent.

'No, no, it's fine. Just thirsty, that's all.'

'Ah, no problem, champagne OK?'

'Sure . . .'

'*Bon.* One minute.'

As quick as a flash, he leapt into action and swiftly returned, brandishing a bottle of bubbly and two glasses. I barely had a chance to reposition my body in a more sexy pose. He seemed amazingly keen.

What was this guy bothering with me for? He looked like the supermodel Tyson Beckford, with the same magnificent eyes, tightly shaved head and bad-boy smirk. His broad shoulders and chunky arms flexed boldly through his tight white ribbed long-sleeved tee. He was a real-life Othello, and neither Parker nor Lisa were around to notice him hitting on me. Despite trying to play it cool, I was failing miserably. He poured me a glass of champagne, but before he had the chance to do the same for himself, I had already knocked mine back.

'Do I make you nervous?'

'Yes,' I said bashfully, before signalling for a top-up.

'Why are you so bashful? You're such a breathtaking lady.'

I tried to hold my composure but the intensity in his

dark eyes just made me blush. 'Eh, sorry, you're gonna have to ease up on the compliments. I'm Irish. We don't go in for them much.'

'Ah, yes, you prefer drinking instead.'

'Yes, we do. *Beaucoup.*'

'*Tu es si mignonne. Puis-je vous baiser?*'

'Eh, in English, please . . .'

'Ah, I just thought it would sound better in French. What I actually asked was: can I kiss you?'

As much as I would have liked to jump him there and then, I remembered my manners and hinted that he do also.

'But you don't even know my name.'

'Do I need to?'

After forgetting that I wasn't at a normal party, I snapped myself into diva mode. My confidence came back, so I made an instant decision that if I was going to survive in this fantastical world of predators, I was going to have to grow claws – or fangs, or at the very least get sassy.

Choosing the latter, I flicked my hair off my shoulders and pulled my new friend close to me. 'I've never kissed a black man before . . . Do you promise to make it special?'

'For your pleasure . . . I promise to kiss you like the beautiful woman you are.' Then, without blinking he leaned in and planted his large luscious lips on me, and cupped his strong muscular hands behind my head. He had me locked in securely, and this definitely was my pleasure.

Lost in the moment, I blanked out all my relationship

worries and parental responsibilities. I was being kissed by a god. He was quite simply one of the most stunning men I had ever seen, and now he was exploring every corner of my mouth, delighting my tongue with a sensual flicking, and tasting deliciously fragrant as well.

Feeling almost powerless in his grasp, I fought to kiss him back just as passionately as he was kissing me. The delicate eroticism from the tip of my tongue raced through my entire body, and without warning I became fully aroused.

This man had come from nowhere, and within moments had brought me to a point of pulsating arousal. I couldn't help the way I felt – I wanted sex. I wanted sex so badly; I don't think I had ever needed to make love so much in my life.

Knowing that I couldn't follow through with it, I opened my eyes to try and snap myself back to reality. As I admired his dark skin I felt like I was having some sort of out-of-body encounter. We didn't have many black men in Ireland – up until a few years ago the only black Irishmen we could lay claim to were Phil Lynott from Thin Lizzy, and JFK when he had a tan. Then again we've certainly moved on, as we now have Obama tagged as one of us.

I feared what his eyes would convince me of when he opened them. Even without the use of words I was sure he could persuade me to dishonour my vows. I tried to fight it, but my body was aching to be ravaged. I so wanted to release myself to him, to live in the moment, but I just couldn't . . .

Mustering the discipline to say no, I slowly fingered my hands across his face and gently pushed him away. 'Emm, can we stop for a minute?'

'Pardon?' He was visibly shocked at my request.

'Sorry, I just, em, can't do this.' I pulled myself further away from him and straightened myself up on the lounger. 'You're an amazing kisser, thank you. You've just made me feel very good about myself, but I'm sure you're here to have sex, and I'm sorry, I . . . I can't do it. Not tonight. But thank you . . .'

'Was my kiss not special enough?' He gave me a puppy-dog look, and tried to make me laugh. He then tickled me under my chin, which of course did provoke a giggle, but I could only shrug my shoulders and shake my head.

I still wasn't able to have sex. And if urban myths were to be believed there was no way in hell I'd be ready to handle a big black cock.

'That is a pity,' he cooed, as he kissed me once more on the cheek. 'I would have liked to make love to you – special love.'

'Maybe next time, eh?'

'Maybe . . .'

Topping up my glass of champagne once more, he made to walk away, but I grabbed his hand to stop him. 'One more kiss?' I had come here fantasizing about having champagne kisses, and now was the time to treat myself.

'*Mais oui.*' He smiled back, returning to take up position. Giving him my best sexy look, I took a mouthful of champagne, held it and leaned in close for another one of his spine-tingling kisses.

As our mouths met once again, I slowly released the champagne from my mouth into his, the bubbles popping across my tongue as they left. As he smoothly swallowed back the champagne with total ease, he continued to dance his tongue inside my mouth, teasing me playfully and leaving me weak in his arms. This man was no stranger to champagne kisses, but as I started to wish that he would drag me off to a bed and shag me senseless, I knew it was time to end this marathon snog.

I peeled myself away from him and he whispered, 'Thank you, beautiful,' and began to walk away once more.

'Sorry . . .' I blurted out, worried I'd never see him again. 'Am I allowed to ask your name?'

'Orlando.' He smiled. 'You can tell your friends that you had a champagne kiss in Paris with Orlando.'

'Yes, I shall. Well, I'm very pleased to have met you. And may I say again, Orlando, you're a bloomin' fantastic kisser . . .'

'Ha!' He laughed, taking a mini-bow. 'I'm also a great fuck.'

As I raised my glass as a toast, he disappeared off into the crowd, leaving me feeling positively radiant. OK, horny was probably the more correct term, but a wonderful wave of contentment was washing over me. He simply was one of the most divine creatures I had ever met. I reckon he wasn't lying, either, about being a great shag.

After losing sight of him, I put my hands up to my

mouth and could still feel my lips throb. It had been a long time since I had been kissed like that – if ever – and I knew that Orlando was the best thing that had happened to me in a long time. He had given me back my confidence. I felt like a desirable woman again, instead of a machine that had to service my husband.

'I have just spent the last ten minutes banging on toilet doors, looking for you. I was convinced I saw you run in there,' wheezed Parker. 'Some poor woman then answered back, "I am not Eva – come in if you please!"'

By now we had managed to locate each other back at the pool party near the front of the castle. Lisa was still nowhere to be seen, and wasn't answering her mobile.

'Where did you go? You were gone ages – did you meet your quota of boobies?'

'For the record, I returned promptly to find you deep in carnal conversation with some disgustingly hunky black man, you naughty girl, you. So I went off to see if I could find myself some fun, since you and Lisa were otherwise engaged.'

'Yes, well, I can't help it if I'm a man-magnet . . .'

'Ha! I thought you were just a spectator this evening? I leave you for five minutes and you're like a dog in heat.'

'Well, maybe this bitch is back?'

'I think we need to get you outta here before you get carried away and start stripping off like that freak over there. She tried to corner me earlier, and asked if I wanted to see her collection of strap-ons.' With utter disdain Parker pointed towards a somewhat mature woman with shapely hips and a rotund waistline, who was bursting out at the seams of her strappy latex corset and suspender outfit. She was far from supermodel material, so it was safe to say she was either bank-rolling the party, or was an escapee from a mental institution.

'Is that how you see me?' I howled with revulsion.

'Noooo, well, from a certain angle . . .'

'Fuck off. Come on, then, let's hunt around here one more time for Lisa, just in case I do feel tempted to flash my murderous big pants. Or, worse still, before I tell Rosie O'Donnell over there that nothing less than a fifteen-incher will satisfy you . . .'

After an extensive search of the property, which introduced us to bare and naked sights that I think will be etched into my brain for eternity, we finally found a disillusioned Lisa slumped in a hallway, muttering.

'Lisa, wake up!' Parker shook her, but she wasn't really responding.

'Lisa, it's me, Eva. What have you taken? Are you hurt?' I scraped the hair away from her face only to find her smiling. Thankfully all her clothes seemed to be in place, but of course there was no sign of her double dates.

'I think she's been too open-minded over the years – and her brains have finally fallen out,' teased Parker.

'Emm, or maybe someone slipped a Mickey into her drink.'

'I wish someone coulda done that to mine. All I got offered was an ole saggy fanny. Happy V Day to me. Yuck!'

'Eh, can we concentrate on Lisa for a minute? It's gonna be like *Weekend at Bernie's* trying to get her out of here. Any ideas?'

'Tuck her up in a bed and hope that she eventually makes her own way back to the hotel?'

'Try again?'

'She's a feckin' giant: we'd be more discreet carrying that suit of armour from down the hall through the lobby. We've gotta try and wake her up. I'll go get some water.'

'Don't be long. Knowing Lisa, she'll probably wake up and try and ride me.' I giggled, still glowing from my close encounter.

'Oh, that wouldn't be such a bad thing. You'd make beautiful children together.'

As he disappeared down the corridor in search of supplies, my mind started to wander to Michael and Daisy. I thought how, if Michael could see me now, he'd flip.

Rummaging in my handbag to check for my phone, I put my hand on a soother instead. There, between my cranberry lip-gloss and my dirty cash, was this little innocent pink soother with a picture of a daisy on it. It had to have been in my handbag since Kinsale. Without any warning, a flood of emotion overwhelmed me. What was I doing? I was supposed to be acting like a responsible mother, not a slag.

So what if my husband had deserted me? I needed

to be there for Daisy; I just hated the fact that he wasn't there for me, during these difficult first few months.

Cursing the evil ex-boyfriends that had sent me running into his arms, I continued searching for my phone through tear-filled eyes. This was most definitely not the Valentine's Day in Paris that young romantics dream of.

I hadn't let myself down by kissing God's gift, Orlando, but by abandoning my baby. Yes, I had. Badly.

I wished I'd been better at coping with all the demands on me: been more subservient for Michael, and more maternal for Daisy, while of course retaining the old Eva da Diva for when I got the opportunity to socialize.

Within seconds of turning my phone on, a message beeped through. Although I had left one for Michael earlier, I somehow hadn't expected to get a reply. I was terrified to open it, but I couldn't stop myself.

'I can't do this any more,' the message read. 'Eva, I'm not coming back. Sorry, but we both know it's not working. Will be in touch next week. M.'

Just like I was being knocked down again, it felt like the full weight of a motorbike had hit me in the chest. I was totally winded. There was no sarcasm . . . No sad-face symbol, just simple words that carried world-changing consequences.

Was I being dumped on Valentine's night by text? Surely he couldn't be that callous?

I felt the tears welling up again, just as Lisa found

enough energy to say: 'I need help . . . I don't feel very well.' As she pawed at me in a bewildered state, my mothering instincts came back, and I did my best to reassure her that everything would be just fine.

Like Dorothy, I just wanted to click my heels and transport myself home. Luckily for Lisa, she wouldn't remember this evening. I, on the other hand, was too sober to forget it. While she thought she needed help, all she really needed was a safe bed to sleep off whatever she had taken. If only a night's sleep could have solved my problems! I was going to need many shoulders to cry on, and possibly even a lawyer.

I just couldn't believe that this was yet another Valentine's night I was going to spend without a lover. And that this time I had a baby waiting for me at home.

'Oh–my–God! Wasn't that, like, the best party ever?'

Lisa had just woken up – and decided it was time for me to be awake too, entertaining her with conversation.

'I mean, you hear of parties like that happening in Dublin, but, honestly, come on, you'd be terrified of who you'd bump into at one, wouldn't you?'

'Mmmm.' I made a noise to acknowledge I was listening, but what I really wanted was for her to shut up. After a mammoth struggle to get her into a taxi – the driver initially hadn't wanted to let her into the car – I had stayed up, drinking the contents of the mini-bar with Parker, singing heartbreak songs, and pontificating about how Daisy and I would cope just fine without Michael.

'Like, think about it . . . If that kind of party happened in Dublin, you would bump into your bank manager, your cosmetic surgeon or, worse still, a friend of your father's . . . Yuck, yuck, yuck . . . You just couldn't relax. It wouldn't be worth it. So, did you have fun last night? Can you believe I found identical twins? And then . . .'

I was doing my best to zone out Lisa's giddy ramblings. I loved her dearly . . . just not this early in the morning.

'Are you OK?' She thumped my arm across the bed, making absolutely sure I was focusing on her.

'Yeah, I'm listening. I just didn't have as much sleep as you did.'

'Oh, was I a total disaster? I can't remember what happened after leaving the lads.'

'Well, let's just say, be grateful that Parker and myself found you – instead of anyone else. Otherwise you could still be hanging from a love swing, with a cock and balls in your mouth, praying for mercy.'

'Good morning to you, too . . .'

'I'm serious. You were collapsed in a hallway on your own. What had you taken?'

'I'm not sure. The guys gave me some sort of tab, and I just swallowed it.'

'You're mad . . .'

'Yeah, well, I thought why not go the whole way? Only problem is, it only started to kick in fully after I had left the twins. I'm feeling fine now, but I reckon I'll have a whopper of a headache later.'

'So did you get a whopper last night? Or should I say a double whopper with all the extras?'

'Ha! That would be telling . . .'

'What? Tell me . . .'

'I am a lady, and a lady never reveals her secrets.'

'Fuck off. Lady, my ass. What happened? Was it really kinky?'

'Well, considering you still don't feel able to have polite missionary-position sex, I will spare you the details of last night. It might just cause you too much pain to imagine it . . .'

'Really?'

'Uh huh.'

I thought for a minute about what she could be hinting at, before quickly blurting, 'Double entry? Please tell me you didn't try double entry?'

Trying to hide her giggles, she whispered, 'I won't tell you, then, so . . .'

'Arghh . . . That's grim. How could you let them? Are you OK down there? Surely that couldn't be good for you?'

'I haven't had a look yet . . . but I feel fine. It's not that bad, you know. It's quite pleasurable. I've only done that once before, and . . .'

'*Stop!*' I cried, sticking my fingers in my ears. 'I don't want to know. Please, forget that I asked.'

'You might learn a thing or two . . .'

'Thanks, yeah, but I feel quite queasy enough as it is, so let's not go there. Anyway, I've had enough drama of my own to process this morning.'

'Like what?'

'OK, where should I start?'

'With the gorgeous black man,' announced Parker from the doorway. His voice was as hoarse as mine, and he looked ridiculously gay in his tight black boxers and tight black tee.

'There was a black man?' Lisa whooped with glee.

'Yeah, and an up-coming divorce . . .'

'Ohhh.' Lisa's face quickly fell flat.

'Forget about that arsehole for a minute,' Parker said. 'You've plenty of time to feel melancholy. Tell her the fun stuff first.'

'Well, whatever you want, hon . . .' Lisa said.

'Nah, he's right,' I answered. 'Yes, there was a fabulous hunk of a black man by the name of Orlando. He told me to tell all my friends that I'd had champagne kisses with him in Paris.'

'Ahhh, I hope he made you feel better about yourself.'

'Yes, well, this charity case did feel temporarily fabulous, until . . .'

'Until?' questioned Lisa.

'Emm, nothing. It's fine.'

'And?' interrupted Parker as he sat down beside us at the side of the bed. 'My head is still in pain from last night, stick with Orlando Bloom for a few more minutes.'

'As in the actor?' Lisa asked, switching back to excitable teenager.

'That was his name,' I said. 'Orlando. He looked more like the dude off *Make Me a Supermodel US*.'

'Wow, that's defo up there with my twins . . .'

'Ha! Not quite. Little bit tamer than your evening, thankfully. But, yes, for all of about ten minutes I was hot stuff.'

'Tell me more.'

'That was it, I'm afraid. Just a few kisses. Parker's not letting on if he got any sugar, so apart from a personal mini-drama, and Parker nearly having to resort to putting you in a wheelbarrow and pushing you all the way home, that was it, really.'

'Gosh, sorry, guys. That tab I took was strong stuff . . . It felt amazing, though.' Lisa turned suddenly serious. 'OK. Please tell me what happened,' she demanded. 'What did Michael do? Did he ring?'

I thought about sharing, but hadn't the energy yet. 'I'll tell you later . . .' I grunted.

Parker did his best to sound fatherly and distract Lisa from quizzing me. 'I thought you didn't do drugs, and that people who did them were vile low-lifes?'

'They are. I hate cokeheads, but I was in Paris with identical twins who wanted to have sex with me. It wasn't exactly an everyday occurrence, so I went for it. Don't tell me you wouldn't have done the same.'

'Possibly not . . . But try not to indulge so much next time it's my watch. I felt like I was Tony Soprano struggling with a dead body, getting you into that car.'

'Don't be mean . . .' Lisa frowned.

'Actually, I think I would have had an easier time squeezing Tony Soprano into a pair of your skinny jeans. Talk about a stubborn mule. Come to think of it, I've even pulled muscles in my back. Not even Jeff, during his best drunken displays, is a patch on you.'

'Any word from him?' Lisa asked.

'He's off limits. I don't want to comment on that man.'

'Eh, you were the one who brought him up.' Lisa darted a look at me before throwing her eyes up to heaven.

'I had a momentary lapse. That bastard has left me infected for life – and physically scarred!'

'You can get that fixed,' nodded Lisa, trying to be helpful.

'No, you can't. The fucking wart germ stays with you for ever. There's nothing permanent in this world, though warts, it appears, are resilient buggers. These little guys will be my closest companions till the day I die.'

'I'm sure you could get your ass lasered. Or how about anal bleaching? That could help,' Lisa said.

'I'm gay, pet, not a feckin' sadomasochist. That sounds like torture.'

'No, honestly, they can do some great stuff these days. Anal bleaching is huge. All the strippers and porn stars – and a lot of gay men – go in for it.'

'Really?' Both Parker and myself winced simultaneously.

'Yeah, big time. I'm not sure about the lasering, but getting your ass bleached is just a matter of spreading on a cream. It's got something called hydroquinone in it, and it's banned in loads of countries, but it blends out the dark pigmentation to match the rest of the skin on your bum.'

'You're a mine of information; bit early in the

morning for me, though. Will definitely debate the pros and cons with you another time . . . So what's the plan?' Parker said. 'I feel so ill. I need to eat soon.'

'Me too.' My body was craving soakage, so, knowing that I could quite as easily fall back asleep, I jumped out of the bed in an attempt to muster up some energy. I only managed to step on my stiletto and hurt my foot, but at least I'd got a few steps closer to breakfast. Not to mention closer to home and holding Daisy in my arms.

'He really is a prick, Eva,' Lisa announced loudly when I let her read my message from Michael. Half the plane turned round to stare at her. Oblivious, she continued, 'I hate saying it, but there's no two ways about it. He is a prize cock.'

Delayed on the runway, the three of us were occupying ourselves by reading each other's texts. Lisa had my phone. Parker had Lisa's, and I was reading Parker's.

Ignoring her comments, I forged ahead with my own reading matter. 'I can't believe Jeff called you "a diva retard"! What's that supposed to mean?' I tried to keep a straight face, but both Lisa and I cracked up laughing. I suppose I was still in denial, which made it easier for me to cope.

'Give me that phone,' snapped Parker, failing miserably to grab it back.

For sheer entertainment I continued to tease him. '"Parker, if I had wanted to live with a bitch I would have gotten myself a dog!"' I read out. Froth almost came out of his mouth, so, out of respect for our fellow passengers, I decided to give it back to him.

Reluctantly swapping his for Lisa's phone, I had just begun to work my way through some of her disturbing sex texts from Francis, when there was a loud beep from my mobile.

Instantly Lisa looked at me and said, 'There's a message.'

Not wanting to face my fears I said, 'You read it.' Then I closed my eyes and hoped it was just a text from my mother wondering what time I'd be collecting Daisy.

Clearly not wishing to be the bearer of bad news, Lisa pushed the phone towards me and nudged me to take it.

'Just read it,' I said firmly, still with my eyes closed.

'But . . .'

'I said, just read it for me, please . . .'

'OK . . .' Her voice wavered for just a moment. 'It's from Michael. Are you sure ya still want me to read it?'

'Just get on with it.'

'OK, OK, emm, he says . . . Oh, God . . .'

'What?' screamed Parker. 'What does it say?'

'Ah, Eva, I'm so sorry . . .'

'Fuck's sake, what does it say? Just *give* it to me.' Abruptly I opened my eyes and grabbed the phone. After taking a second to focus on the words, I managed to read, 'I will be back at house to collect my clothes at 7 p.m. Please don't be there till after 8 p.m. It's for the best.'

'Best for who?' I said.

'What did he say?' questioned Parker again, with frustration. 'What's he done?'

'He said he's going to pick up his clothes from the house tonight.' My voice was laced with venom. 'And he's suggested that I not be there. Apparently it's for the best.'

I looked to both Lisa and Parker for words of wisdom, but none came. If anything, they looked more shocked than I felt. 'Can somebody please speak?' I demanded, at a loss as what to think or feel.

'Eh, sorry, pet. Wow,' Parker said. 'I didn't think he'd go through with it. I didn't realize that . . .'

'*That what?*'

'That, eh, things were *that* bad. I just thought that text last night was drunk talk.'

'So did I.' Staring at the phone again, I read the text over and over, just to make sure I wasn't missing anything. But each time it said the same thing, and each time I just felt more and more frozen. Interrupting my train of thought, one of the cabin staff announced over the intercom that the plane had just been given permission to take off, and that all mobile phones needed to be switched off immediately.

Flinging my phone into my bag on the floor, I looked across at Parker, only to see his own phone flash up a message.

Sarcastically I muttered, 'Gosh, we are a popular bunch today. I just hope your text is slightly more pleasant than mine.'

Flustered, Parker quickly opened it, but as soon as he did, he looked guilty.

'What now?' Lisa questioned.

'It's from Maddie,' said Parker, giving Lisa his phone to read.

'Don't be mean,' I moaned. 'What's wrong with her?'

'Nothing.' Lisa sounded nervous. She was a terrible liar, and could never keep secrets. 'It's nothing. It's time to switch off our phones, so, Parker, just switch it off, please.'

Furious with the entire world, I opened my belt and quickly grabbed the phone off Lisa as she tried to give it back to Parker. 'Don't try and pawn me off with . . . Oh–my–God.' My heart sank as I read Parker's text from Maddie. 'Is Eva all right? Tell her I'm sorry. I never meant to fall for Michael. Tell her I still love her. Sorry ☹'

As if all the strength had left my body, I let the phone slip out of my hand, only for Parker to dive to catch it.

Barely able to process the situation, I zoned out all the noise around me and played it over in my head. Michael and Maddie? My husband has left me for one of my best friends . . . my oldest friend. Surely not? Was it not enough of an insult for him to fall out of love with me so soon after we got married, without going and fucking my mate?

That time in Le Café they had looked so relaxed together, but how did they . . . ? Why did they . . . ?

'Eva. Are you all right, hon? You've gone very pale.' Lisa was rubbing my hands as if trying to get my circulation going again.

'Did either of you know?' I asked. While a small

part of me had read the signs, I had done my best to ignore them. I suppose I was stunned at how this could happen under my nose, and I thought it obvious to ask if I was just being stupid, or had been living in denial.

Immediately, I caught sight of Lisa squeezing Parker's hand.

'Well, did you?' I demanded angrily.

'Emm,' Parker stared at Lisa, and spoke quickly. 'Not long.'

Instantly I felt my head spin. They had known my husband and best fucking friend were sleeping together, and told me nothing. Did everyone hate me?

'Bastards,' I screamed, at the top of my voice. I started to scream again, but Lisa put her hands over my mouth to stop me.

'Oh, darlin', I'm so sorry. Please don't hate me. I couldn't bear to tell you. She promised me she'd stopped seeing him. I honestly thought it was just a one-off thing. Please, try not to get upset.'

I tried to scream again, but instead the floodgates opened and the tears returned.

'Everyone's betrayed me,' I sobbed, shaking my head. 'All of you. I hope you had a good laugh at my expense.'

'We didn't, pet, honestly. We love you.' Parker's face was pained, and looked close to tears.

'He told me he loved me. She told me she loved me. Don't fucking tell me you love me. I don't want to hear it.'

Burying my head in the tiny pillow at the side of my

seat, I sobbed and sobbed. I had been trying to hold it all together, but my world had finally collapsed.

Lisa tried to soothe me by tenderly rubbing my back, but her efforts were wasted. Nothing could help me now.

A passing member of staff stopped at our aisle and enquired if there was a problem. Lost in my pillow, I could vaguely hear Lisa tell the woman I'd gotten bad news. 'Oh, and can we order her a brandy, please? Actually, order three. I think this is going to be a long flight . . .'

8

Weeks had gone by, and amazingly life had continued.

Michael had removed most of his clothes and personal belongings from the house, and left nothing much more than a note that read, 'I did love you. I really did try.'

Every day seemed as vacant as the next, but I somehow found the strength to carry on. If it hadn't been for stress, I probably wouldn't have had any energy at all.

With both my wedding and engagement rings hidden away in the bottom of my sock drawer, my left hand looked hauntingly bare. And while men had always hurt me as they flitted through my life, it was the loss of my friends that had wounded me the most. They had always been solid for me, but since Paris I had felt utterly betrayed by them.

When they phoned, I pressed ignore. When they called to the house I hid behind the couch. It was childish, and I knew it. But I couldn't let them in – I was too afraid of the poison I'd release on them. Anger didn't come close to expressing the hurt that I felt. If I let my guard down, I couldn't be sure that I wouldn't lose the plot completely.

Without my usual support-network, I had to work extra hard to keep sane for Daisy. In the last couple of weeks she'd experienced a few minor health hiccups, but nothing too serious: colds, fevers, all the usual stuff that babies suffered with. And she was developing, too: she'd started making soft cooing noises, like a dove. I knew she needed me to be strong. Her father had let her down, and there was no way I was going to do the same.

Unfortunately I couldn't escape today. It was Mothering Sunday, and my own mother had not asked, or suggested, but *insisted* I go to lunch at my sister Ruth's house. Not leaving anything to chance, she was going to pick us up and escort Daisy and me to Ruth's place in Clontarf.

For years I had pitied my older sister Ruth for what seemed her hundred-year marriage to Joe. They had hooked up aged sixteen and now, at the age of thirty-six, they had three children, Finn (ten), Brendan (eight) and Sile (six). Contentment was Ruth's middle name, and even under intense pressure from me she claimed to have never regretted a minute of her life, and to have no problem with the idea of only ever having sex with one man.

It goes without saying she is pretty much the exact opposite of me. I had more than a few regrets about my life – actually, far too many to try and list – but I was glad she was happy. I was just pissed off that I had to go and witness her joy today. In my current state, I just wanted to be left alone to wallow and eat chocolate.

'Why aren't you dressed?' barked my mother. She was

standing at my front door, not about to put up with any depressed feelings I might have been having. Her blonde highlighted hair, just fresh out of her heated rollers and solidly cemented tall on her head, matched the rigidness of her good Sunday coat – her red one, with the over-sized cartoon buttons, and sharp shoulders that could take someone's eye out.

'Happy Mother's Day to you,' I cooed sarcastically.

'Well, why aren't you ready?'

'I don't think I'm up for this, Mum. You'd better go. I know Ruth doesn't like it when you turn up late. I'm sure the kids will be tearing the house down waiting to be fed.'

'Nonsense. Get dressed, we've plenty of time.'

'Honestly, you go; it's almost 12 o'clock already. I've a Goodfella's pepperoni in the freezer with my name on it.'

'If it wasn't for the last minute, nothing would ever get done. Now get up those stairs and make yourself somewhat respectable.'

'But, Mum . . .'

Her stern look left me with no option but to obey. With what felt like concrete shoes, I dragged myself up the stairs, grumbling, 'Well, since you offered, Daisy probably needs to be freshened up.'

Despite my initial complaints, lunch at Ruth's was refreshing. My favourite nephew, Finn, was relentless in his determination to tell me all about his new hobby: collecting vintage model cars.

After twenty minutes of pestering he marched me up

the stairs to his bedroom and talked me through each of his seventeen cars in detail: prices, make, and when and with whose money they'd each been bought.

It was hard not to melt. He was such a lovable kid: warm, bubbly and always positive about everything. In the week ahead he had a maths test and a swimming competition which he was sure he'd ace, and also there was a girl called Zoë in his choir who he was convinced was about to become his girlfriend.

His infectious smile acted like a natural Solpadeine, and helped suppress the dull, pounding headache which I had been carrying around with me every day. Which was just as well, considering Ruth's youngest, Sile, was in a particularly shrill mood.

Her frank comments about Daisy didn't help ease my stress-levels. 'Doesn't her tongue stick out a lot?' and, 'Her eyes look funny,' were, I suppose, obvious observations, and, from a six-year-old, innocent ones. But when I tried calmly to explain that Daisy was a special baby, with her own unique differences, Sile's brother Brendan made matters worse by asking, 'Is it because she doesn't have a daddy?'

Thankfully, Ruth stepped in at that point, and ushered all *High School Musical* fans to the TV room for their jelly and ice cream. Although my mother had miraculously managed to bite her own tongue and dance around the white elephant in the room, which was my newly single status, once inquisitive ears had left the kitchen she could hold her questions no more.

'Was it your partying that made him leave?'

'Had you been ignoring your wifely duties?'

'You married too soon. I told you, you should have waited.'

It was her last comment that pushed me out of my mature silence.

'No, you never did,' I screeched, completely outraged. 'You would have shoved me up the aisle with anyone, just to get your day out. I distinctly remember you telling Aunty Pat that you never thought you'd see the day, and that if you were honest, you thought nobody would ever have me! Bloody charming!'

'Well, you'd been around the block a great many times, Eva.' My mum's voice was blunt and emotionless.

'So what? I should marry the first fella that asked?'

'Isn't that what you did?'

'Yes . . . It was. And look where it got me. Now, instead of being an ole spinster, I'm fat, soon-to-be-separated, and with a special needs child – *whom I love*, so don't even go there, Mum. But that being said, I know that this is not an ideal picture, and I don't think it's going to get any prettier, any time soon.'

Silence fell at the kitchen table, except for the noise of Dad scraping the last spoonful of trifle from his bowl. As everyone turned to stare at him, he gave a sheepish apology, but I just smiled. His complete lack of interest in the discussion had actually helped break the ice.

Seeing a window of opportunity for defusing the situation, Ruth quickly instructed Joe to take Dad out to the garage and ask his advice on a problem with their lawn-mower, and then she turned her attention to Mum, asking her had she been to IKEA recently? And had she'd seen the great kitchen accessories they had on special offer?

Frustrated at being thrown off–course, our mother stood up, muttering, 'This kind of thing never happened in my day. Couples worked things out.' Then she walked in the direction of the downstairs loo.

The second she had closed the door behind her, Ruth turned to me and said, 'Get your coat and get outta here!'

'What?'

'Quick, she'll be back in two minutes. Just grab your coat and go. I'll look after Daisy for the afternoon. She's no bother compared to my three.'

'But what am I supposed to do?'

'I don't care. Just escape. Her nibs is just going to be like a dog with a bone today. She won't leave you alone till she gets some answers. So I advise you to take my offer before you run out of time. Head to the cinema, go get a massage, maybe call Parker and patch things up.'

'I'm not talking to him . . .'

'Oh, stop being so stubborn. It wasn't his fault. He just didn't want you to get hurt. Call him . . . now go.'

I hesitated briefly, but the second I heard the toilet flush I gave Daisy a kiss, grabbed my handbag and bolted towards the front door, picking my coat off the end of the stairs on the way.

With my heart pumping I ran around the corner and headed out to the coast road. I had no idea where I was going, but I felt totally energized.

Without realizing, I put my hand up to wipe a

wind-tear out of my eye and noticed I was smiling for the first time in weeks. It was nice to know I still could.

As I caught sight of the sea, I found myself stopping dead to enjoy its beauty. The way the waves crashed against the pier wall symbolized the angst and ferocity in so many areas of my life.

There was still a passion there . . . like in the waves. Now I just needed to find the storm inside me, and get it working in a positive way.

Terrified that my mother would track me down, I jumped on the first bus into town. Then going with Ruth's recommendation, I grabbed the bull by the horns and, before I could fall back into negative thoughts, texted Parker to come meet me.

Within seconds I got his answer. 'Thank U. See ya in Expresso Bar in 30 mins xox' came beeping through.

I got off the bus at Connolly Station and hopped into a taxi up to Ballsbridge. For a change it was a female driver in the front seat, a chatty woman who told me she was filling in for her brother-in-law, and taking any shifts she could get to pay for her kids' schooling.

'I've lived through plenty of recessions,' she told me. 'Me husband is a tight bollix, he'd give ya nothin'. So I keep da head down and look after number one.'

I was just about to tune out of her hubby-bashing, when she chirped up, 'Are ya famous? I'm sure I know yar face?'

'No, I'm not famous,' I answered with a minor blush in my cheeks. 'I wish. And I wish I was rich with it.'

Staring at me through her rear-view mirror, Patricia Dragonetti – as her identification read – kept repeating, 'I know you from somewhere. I'm sure of it.'

Searching for a reason she might find me familiar, I told her that I was originally from Glasnevin and that I was a journalist, and it instantly jogged her memory.

'You wrote an article on "Movies In Malta", and ya said it was the best holiday you were ever on. Didn't ya? Didn't ya write up a piece on Malta? Told us all da restaurants the actors go ta.'

'Eh, yeah, I did. Ages ago.'

'Yeah, I remember now. Ya made it sound so good I ended up going meself, with me neighbour, Rita. We had a great time. We were like two ole Shirley Valentines.'

'Ha!' I blurted loudly. My nervousness exaggerated my emotion. 'That's gas. I could do with switching my name to Shirley. My real name is Eva Valentine, and it doesn't seem to be working too well for me.'

'Ah, Jaysus, luff. Don't be saying that. You're a gorgeous young thing. I can't believe I met ya, though. We had the best holiday because of ya. Fabulous men in Malta. I never wanted to come back.'

As I stepped out of her car, handing over an extra-large tip which I couldn't really afford, I felt a small but much-needed ego boost. Now that Michael had moved on, I really had to start focusing back on my own career and making decent money again. Knowing that my writing had actually inspired someone whom I'd never met to go on holiday was exhilarating. I wasn't as unimportant as I'd imagined.

OK, so moguls like Rupert Murdoch hadn't heard the power of my voice yet, but Patricia had. It might not have been a giant step for mankind, but a small step for Eva was better than nothing.

Parker was playing humble. It must have killed him, but he swallowed all his pride and grovelled for my forgiveness. 'I'm so, so sorry. You know I couldn't bear for anyone to hurt you . . .' He stuck out his bottom lip for extra effect.

I took another large mouthful of my latte, avoiding giving him an answer.

'I said I'm sorry, Eva . . . come on . . . I'm stretching myself here. You know I'm not big on apologies.'

Snapping him a scorned look, I barked, 'Well, I'm not big on liars.'

His face softened once again. 'I'll never not tell you again.'

'Ha!' I blurted. 'What if my next husband cheats on me, too?'

'Well, it depends how many husbands you decide to have. Are we talking Patsy Kensit numbers or Elizabeth Taylor territory?'

'I missed you . . .'

'I missed you, too. A lot has happened. I've so much to tell you.'

'Oh, what, you've missed me because nobody else will listen to your endless ramblings about the world according to Parker?'

'No. Aside from the fact I could be working on a movie with George Clooney – *yessss*, you heard me right, George fucking Clooney – but apart from maybe spending some one-on-one time with the world's sexiest male, I've other news, too.'

'Well, congrats on Clooney. Forgive me for not getting too excited, though. I'm sure you've mentioned at least two other projects that Clooney's name was attached to down through the years, and neither of those came to fruition. So what's your other news?'

'Do you want the good news or the bad?'

'Emm, let me think. Considering my life is just one bad news bulletin, try me with the good.'

'Everything is sorted with me and Jeff again. So he's moved back in and we're two big loved-up bunnies.'

'And that's the good news?' My voice dripped with sarcasm. I couldn't think what was so good about their reunion. I was off all men, especially cheaters: gay as well as straight.

'No, it is, actually. Things weren't quite what they seemed . . .'

'Are they ever?'

'You see, it actually turns out that he only half-cheated on me.'

'Half?'

'Yeah, he was date-raped.'

'That's what he said, and you swallowed it?'

'OK, I agree it sounds like a cop-out . . .'

'I thought he told you he was having an affair?'

'I know, but that was a cover-up. He was embarrassed.'

'About what?'

'He's a man, Eva. We're meant to be able to protect

ourselves. He was raped, and he thought it would be easier to say he was having a relationship than admitting to being buggered against his will.'

'Mmmm, sounds like a cock-and-bull story to me.'

'Ha! Ha!'

'I wasn't trying to be funny.'

'Anyway, I believe him, and we're working through it. We're both infected now, so we might as well stick together.'

'So, if that's the good news, what the hell is the bad news?'

'OK, don't go mad, but . . . Oh, I can't tell you.'

'Excuse me?'

'Listen, it doesn't matter. Just forget I said anything. How's Daisy?'

'Daisy's fine, thanks, considering her father has run off with her mother's friend, but don't change the subject, what's the bad news? And don't annoy me. I'm walking a thin line today.'

'Right, well, the thing is . . .'

'Spit it out, Parker.'

'I've asked Maddie to come in and meet us. She should be here any minute.'

Forgetting I was in a public place, I screamed, '*What?*' It roused the interest of the entire waiting staff, and even two of the chefs the other side of their window.

'How could you, Parker? What are you trying to do?'

'Mend bridges, petal. You were friends with her before me. She wants to apologize and explain that she didn't mean to hurt you.'

'Fuck's sake. The bitch has ripped my heart out.' The tears I had suppressed had now returned. 'She's an evil bitch,' I sobbed. 'I don't want her anywhere near me. Tell her she'd better not come here. I won't be responsible for my actions.'

'Eva, calm down. I'll tell her it's too soon. She'll understand.'

'I couldn't give a flying fuck if she's cool with it. I never want to see her again. She can rot in the gutter for all I . . .'

My protests had come too late. Despite the absolute hatred I had been feeling towards Maddie over the last weeks, my blood just ran cold at the sight of her. And left my body paralysed with fear.

'Hi, Eva. Thanks for letting me come.'

Frozen to my seat, I could find no words to answer her. I just couldn't believe that she was standing in front of me. That she had the balls to confront me. She had stolen my future, not just my husband.

'Listen . . .' Maddie spoke softly as she eased herself on to the couch beside me. 'I know you hate me, but I'm sure we can get through this.'

There was so much I wanted to scream at her, but I remained stuck to the seat, my hand glued to my coffee cup.

'I know that it'll take time – and I don't want to rush you, but I just want you to know I hate myself for what has happened, and I never saw this coming . . . What happened with Michael and me just hit us like a freight-train. It was totally unexpected.'

Terrified to divert my gaze from my latte, millions

of thoughts flashed through my head: like could I claim insanity for GBH if I smashed this cup across her face?

'To be honest, I want to ask you a favour. How would you feel about Daisy coming on a short holiday with Michael, Woody and me? We were thinking of going to the sun for a week. Maybe North Africa – Morocco or Tunisia; I'd look after her like my own. I wouldn't let her come to any harm. The break would do you good, too, I'm sure. You could concentrate on getting a bit of writing done. Or maybe take a holiday yourself. What do you think?'

I could contain my bubbling anger no more. 'What do I think?' I asked in a controlled voice. 'What do you think I fucking think?'

'Listen Eva, I don't . . .'

'No, you don't get to tell me anything. First you steal my husband, which automatically cancels out our friendship. And having had the cheek to tell me how to live my life, you smile at me while trying to steal my daughter from me, too, just so you can make up the numbers to play happy families. Are you mental? Do you honestly think I'd let you anywhere near my daughter after what you've done? If you're unsure, the answer is most definitely *no*. Now, while I'm still relatively calm, I'd suggest you take your slutty ass away from me – *quickly*! Just in case I decide to do something stupid, like rip your eyes out.'

'Look, Eva . . .'

'I'll slowly count to ten, and if by that time you're still in arm-shot, I will, without hesitation, hurt you.

Do I make myself clear?' I didn't wait for her to answer. 'One . . . Two . . . Three . . .'

'OK, OK, I'm going, but think about it, yeah?'

'*Four . . . Five . . . Six.*'

'I'm going. Talk to you later, Parker.'

'*Seven . . . Eight . . .*'

By the count of ten Maddie was safely passing out on to the street, stopping just momentarily to glance back at me through the window. Instead of looking away, I gave her the best icy stare I could muster. I held it until she had walked out of sight. Then, the second she was gone, my bravado left me and I returned to the shaking mess I had been before.

Parker tried to comfort me, but I pushed him away.

'How dare you? Don't you *ever* pull something like that on me again. I swear to you, I will cut you out. I may look like an emotional wreck, but I can do cold. Just try me.'

'I'm sorry . . .'

'Not as fucking sorry as me, I can tell ya, for trusting any of ya. Do I have MUG written across my face? Do I?'

'Don't be stupid.'

'Oh, I'm stupid now. Is that how you see me? Well, I feel stupid, that's for sure . . .'

'OK, OK, I'm not going to win here . . .'

'No, you're not.'

'How about I order you one glass of bubbles, which won't affect your mammying skills for later, and we start over? What d'ya think, girlfriend?'

'You don't want to know what I think . . .'

'Oh, stop givin' out. I missed ya. Let's just have a giggle.'

'Mmmm. Can you believe she wants to take Daisy on a—'

'Ah, ah, ah. No spoiling . . .' Parker was wagging his forefinger masterfully, and flashing his cheeky grin to nip any further rant in the bud. 'If I may say, Ms Valentine, this heartbreak diet of yours is working a treat. You must have lost about a stone since I saw you last.'

'Not quite – ten pounds, though. But you're still a bitch. My hands are still shaking.'

'I know, pet, let's move on . . . *But you rock, skinny girl.*' His enthusiasm was slightly over-eager, but it was still nice that my shrinking size had been noticed. 'So what does that make you now – a size 12?'

'A comfortable size 12, to be precise.' Sniff. 'No magic knickers needed, thank you very much.'

'There she is . . . You're warming up.'

'I'm still shaking, so don't think you're off the hook just yet. Now get me that champagne before I get feisty again.'

'Yes, mam.'

Two glasses of bubbly later, my nerves had started to settle, and a quick text buzzed through on my phone.

'Aren't I popular?' I joked. 'What's the bet my mother has finally thrown a tantrum and is demanding I pick up Daisy before she reports me to social services for neglect? Or could it be Maddie, asking if she can move into my house? I wouldn't put it past the bitch.'

'Maybe it's The Script calling? They could be looking for a fit bird to star in their new video and have heard that you are smokin'!'

'OK, you're definitely trying too hard now, so just roll it back a tad.'

He motioned that his lips were sealed and he was throwing away the key, so I gave him a happy sarcastic smile and picked up my phone to read the bad news.

'"Hey gorgeous – need any spots removed?"' I read the text out loud, out of sheer disbelief.

'Who's it from?' asked Parker.

'Don't know . . . "Hey gorgeous – need any spots removed?" Oh, hang on, there's more, "Any jobs that need fixin', I'm your man . . . Dave."'

'Who's Dave?'

There was a moment of confusion before I realized. 'He's the fella who cleaned my chair. The one I was having dirty thoughts about just before my world crashed.'

'Firm bum, tattooed arms?'

'That's the one.'

'So, what? Is he looking for a handy cash job or a shag?'

I placed the phone on the table and held my head in my hands and began to laugh in a demented-woman-on-the-edge kind of way.

'Are you OK?' asked Parker, now totally freaked as to what my next emotion would possibly be.

Taking a moment to regain my composure, I removed my hands and gave Parker a broad, watery-eyed smile. 'I'm great – absolutely fine. Actually, I'm more than fine, I'm horny, and I'm about to do something I haven't done in a very long time . . .'

'Are you gonna call him?' Parker was sitting on the edge of his seat with the excitement.

'Yep. I'm gonna dial me a man.'

'Go, Eva. Will this be your first?'

'Shag? Yes, this will be my first since Daisy. And yes, that is a very scary thought, but I'm a free woman . . .'

'A sexy size 12 woman . . . He probably won't recognize you with the weight gone.'

'Yes, thank you, Parker. It's a new Eva, so why not? No one else wants me, so I'm gonna exert my new single status and throw caution to the wind.'

'You mean your knickers.'

Picking up the phone again, I pressed reply and began to compose my message. 'How about I send him something simple like "Quit the BS, fancy a shag?" Maybe it was the bubbles, but I thought myself fantastically hilarious and snorted loudly with delight.

'Lovely,' mused Parker, as he grabbed the phone from my hands. 'I think you need to be subtle yet direct. Don't interrupt me now. Piddle, paddle, poodle, OK, and . . . send. There you go.'

'Huh? What did you send?'

Parker handed me back the phone, and I read the text: 'Odd job, con job or blow-job. Which are you looking to do?'

'Oh-my-God!' I said. 'You can't have sent that!'

'Too late.' Parker beamed with pride. 'Re-lax, it just cuts out the crap. It means he knows where he stands, and so do you.'

My phone beeped again. And before Parker got a chance to grab it, I opened the message to read: 'Hot stuff. I'm good on odd jobs, but gr8 at blow-jobs!'

'Told ya!' squealed Parker, as my jaw dropped to the table. 'If he's as delectable as you say he is I'd book your booty call at once.'

'Oh, Parker, do you think I can do this?'

'Just a second ago you said you were horny. Get a grip, woman. *Do this!*'

'OK, OK, I will. Sod Michael, anyway, I'm an independent woman now, so I can do this. I even give you permission to let Maddie know what I'm up to . . . Right, then . . . "Wanna call over to play about 9 pm?" There, I've sent it.'

Parker at first didn't believe me, so after I flashed him the phone, he signalled for a high-five. 'I'm proud of you, you know. This can't be easy for you.'

'No, it's not, but I'll be fine.'

'You'll be better than fine, pet, especially after dirty Dave gets his mitts on ya!'

'Am I mad?'

'Totally, now. Oh, there he is. Prince Charming in overalls.'

Picking up the beeping phone, I closed my eyes with the fear.

'Read it . . .' bleated Parker.

Slowly I opened one eye, then the second to reveal the words, 'Pinot Grigio on me, yummy mummy. See U @ 9pm.'

'Well?' Parker was hopping on the seat. 'Are you back in the game?'

'I'm back in the game, all right. I could probably do with a coach on the sidelines to give me some pointers, though.'

'Ah, you'll be fine. It's like riding a bike. Jump on, hold on and pray that you're not rear-ended!'

To save me the wrath of my mother, Joe dropped Daisy off at the house, and in traditional fashion he muttered a lot of 'I'm sorry's as he entered the house.

'I'm sorry I was late.'

'I'm sorry if she's too hot.'

'I'm sorry if she's tired.'

He was a man who apologized for everything and nothing, and would then scuttle off into the fog without waiting for absolution. Thankfully, he was over by 6.30 p.m. and Daisy was on the wind-down for her big sleep. Or at least I hoped she was. By 7.45 p.m. she was tucked up in her cot, which gave me just enough time to hop into the bath with a large glass of wine and shave my legs and other relevant areas.

It was all going according to plan until, 'Are you OK in there? Are you having trouble opening that wine bottle? I can be your big strong man if you want me to.'

Dave had poked his cheeky face around the kitchen door and was making me nervous. I had been fumbling with the corkscrew for far too long, and it was obvious to my date I was using delaying tactics.

'No, no, I'm fine. Just making you sweat a bit.'

'I can think of better ways to work up a sweat . . .'

His forwardness made my heart stop a beat. This was fast. Far too fast for comfort.

'I'm sure you can. But first you'll be gentlemanly, and enjoy a couple of glasses of wine with me.'

'*A couple?*'

'You'd think I was knocking you back till next week . . .'

'With that talk ya might as well be . . .' Not leaving anything to chance, Dave pushed the bottle and cork-screw out of my hands, grabbed my arse with his two strong hands, and lifted me up on to the counter top. 'Now, ya mad yoke.' He flashed me another cheeky grin. 'Give us a kiss, ya big ride.'

Without waiting for a response, he grabbed either side of my face in his vice-like grip and started to kiss me vigorously. Straight in with the tongue; there was no time for manners with this fella. Not quite sure if I was enjoying his technique, I went with it regardless. He couldn't be faulted for enthusiasm, so I was prepared to forgive the stubble-chafing and tongue-poking. After all he was still incredibly hunky, and I wasn't quite sure why he was bothering with me in the first place.

With one ear still listening out for any noises from the cot upstairs, and my mind focused on trying to find a rhythm for our kissing, when he placed his hand up my skirt – at an empty space where underwear should have been – I let out the loudest yelp, as if I was being robbed.

'Get you, ya dirty thing,' chuckled Dave. 'No pants on. I like it. Very saucy.'

Finding some sort of composure, I brushed my hair

off my face and gave him the sexiest smile I could. I felt like I had a big L plate on my back, as if I was some kind of born-again virgin. I had wanted to take things slow, but it didn't look like I was going to have that option with this guy.

'Ah, there's no messin' around with me.'

'Jaysus, I'm hopin' to do a lot of messin' around with you. Now, c'mere.'

He grabbed hold of my legs, wrapped them up around his waist, darted me a cheeky smile, and teased, 'C'mere, gorgeous. I need me some lovin'.'

Lunging back in for the kiss, I surrendered myself to all possibilities, and we somehow found a compatibility. His kissing was energetic and fresh. Quite obviously minty fresh, and nothing like Michael's self-serving dirty-old-man kisses, which used to reek of pent-up anger and extreme anxiety. In our final months he couldn't just kiss me for affection's sake. His tongue was always like a sex-seeking missile, which helped greatly in driving us apart.

But kissing Dave was fun. There was no aggression, or forced lust, with this guy. He playfully started making funny squelching noises and seemed to get great craic out of tickling me and making me laugh.

Chomping his way across my chest, he lifted up my red top to reveal my still ample-sized breasts in an old red-lace bra that I had dug out from the back of my lingerie drawer. It had only been modelled once before, for Michael during a dirty dance in a hotel room in Madrid. I'd thought I was being a highly seductive sexy señorita, but he'd crushed my passion just a little by saying, 'Not bad, but I much prefer white lace on you. Red is very tacky!'

Tonight, though, for Dave, I was being unashamedly cheap. I was a separated mammy who was living on borrowed time in my big house. I knew my days were numbered before Michael tried to kick me out, so I was planning on making the most of it until he did. As my post-pregnancy boobs spilled over the top of my balcony bra, Dave's face lit up with delight. 'Ah, look at ya. I could get lost in them.'

Doing just that, he buried his face in my cleavage, and while cupping his hands around both of my breasts he mischievously blew out his lips like a horse and then giggled like a child. Eager to expose all of my flesh, it wasn't long before he had slipped my black skirt up around my thighs, gently massaging my legs as he slid his hands north.

Although I had nearly cancelled on Dave earlier for the fear of actually having sex for the first time since Daisy, I somehow was totally up for it. Dave's direct, yet unsophisticated approach allowed me to feel confident. He wasn't put off by my curvy body. If anything, he seemed to be loving it.

'You're lovely and soft,' he cooed. 'I hope my visit didn't put you to any trouble.'

'Ah, sure, I'm that silky smooth all over,' I gushed assertively. 'It's just the way I was made.'

'Really?' Dave pinched my legs to make me squeal. 'Well, I'd better make a thorough inspection, just in case.'

Then, before I had a chance to protest, Dave

removed his head from my eye-line, stuck his roguish head between my legs and began to lick the inside of my thigh. Shocked, excited and terrified, I held my breath with apprehension, but when he started to make pleasing sounds such as 'Ohhh' and 'Ahhh', I relaxed into the sinful pleasure of having my inner thighs licked by a man I barely knew. On my kitchen counter, no less!

Dave the handyman was indeed proving himself just that. After giving my body some warning, he eased his tongue on to my clitoris and gently circled it in an extremely pleasing fashion. With my body almost unfamiliar to such satisfaction, a wave of ecstasy rushed up through me and came screaming out through my mouth.

'Oh God!' I cried, without inhibition. 'Oh-my-God, that's so good!' Sticking with it, he pushed my legs further apart and pulled me closer to the edge of the worktop. In my scramble to find my balance I knocked over several spice jars behind me, and took a moment to laugh that this was definitely the kind of cooking I liked in my kitchen.

Through my slitted eyes I couldn't help but notice various details from around the room. Daisy's clothes drying on the radiator. Michael's badly put-up shelf, which always looked on the verge of collapse. And the small Graham Knuttel print that was given to Michael and me from my parents as a wedding gift.

This was still the family home, only we weren't a family any more, and I was now having the most intense oral attention I'd had in a very long time. This was exceptionally bold, but who was going to judge me?

By now my entire body had started to grind and pulsate with Dave's tongue-tantalizing tricks. Without realizing it I had started to hold the back of his head, as if to assure myself that he couldn't get away. As my fingers traced up and down through his hair, his mouth continued to devour me; this was orgasmic stuff and I was on the very edge of coming. As the intensity built up with the power of his tongue thrusting up inside me, his fingers started to wander across my clitoris and gently caressed my lips, rubbing them with such maturity and such skill that it was merely seconds before I was laughing and wriggling for freedom from the strength of the orgasm.

After managing to push his head away, a content-looking Dave flashed me a smile and asked, 'Well, did you like that?'

Drying off his face a little with my thumb, I quickly kissed him and, laughing, said, 'Do I really need to answer that?' Not wanting to waste the moment, I went on: 'Do you have any condoms?'

And without breaking his dopey gaze, he produced one from his back pocket, and joked, 'As if I'd chance missing out on an opportunity like this . . .'

After peeling my bum off the shiny worktop, we shared a quick giggle at the imprint left by my cheeks, before I slipped Dave's jeans and boxers off.

Instantly his quite authoritative cock bounced up out of his cheap white cotton Essentials boxers. It was undoubtedly larger than Michael's, though it was surrounded by the bushiest pubic hair I'd ever seen.

Feeling giddy, I joked, 'Did you ever think of putting dreads in that?'

But he wasn't fazed. 'Bend over there now if you know what's good for ya. The little family of pigmies that live down there won't bother ya.'

I couldn't help but love his humour. Dave wasn't like most of the other men I had been with. He had no agenda other than wanting to get laid and wanting to have a good time. He didn't seem impressed by my home, nor interested in who I was, or what people I knew. In the shallow world that was the Dublin social scene, even the secret shags needed to be with people worthy of column inches in the back pages of the society magazines.

With one arm supporting me as I bent over the same counter, I helped direct Dave's cock – now safely covered by his latex friend – between my cheeks and smoothly inside me. All the worrying and trauma I had put myself through had been pointless. This not only felt fine – it felt terrific.

As he slowly worked up a rhythm, I could feel his strong hands tighten around my waist and over my right shoulder. His slow groans echoed mine, and we were quickly grinding and slapping our bodies together in perfect motion – as if we had been having sex together for years.

After he moved his left hand up to cup my breast, I licked my right hand and lowered it to fondle his balls. Michael had always got off on that once my hand was suitably lubricated, and Dave, from his vocal reactions, seemed to enjoy it just as much.

Aware that I might not have done enough pelvic-floor exercises to feel tight enough for him, I discreetly slipped my fingers either side of his cock as he penetrated me, and automatically heard his gratification.

'Ohhh . . . Yeah . . . That's it . . . Ohhh . . . Nearly there . . .' I pulled my fingers closer together – as tight as I could without doing damage to myself. 'Yeah . . . Ohhh . . . Oh fuck, oh fuck, yeeeeeeeah . . .'

As his body continued to spasm behind me, I gently released my grasp and he slowly pulled back. Taking a moment to feel complete again as a woman, I tried to contain my beaming happiness just a smidgen, and swung back around to face Dave with a contented, yet diva-esque smirk. Without the breath to speak, he panted heavily as he rolled back his condom, clearly not as physically fit as he looked.

Like a proud little boy he darted me a cheeky wink as he carefully mastered tying a knot in the condom, chuffed with himself that he hadn't spilled a drop. 'Where's your jacks, then?' He chuckled. 'And I'll get rid of these fightin' soldiers.'

Pointing him in the direction of the downstairs loo, I quickly grabbed some kitchen paper, ran it under the tap, and cleaned myself up as best I could. I didn't want to come across as a prude, but didn't want to start reeking of bodily fluids, either.

By his return I had finally mastered the corkscrew, and I popped the cork on his entrance. 'Fancy that glass of wine now?'

'Nah, you're grand. Couldn't stomach that vinegar. Any beers in the house?'

'But you brought it?'

'Yeah, I know. But chicks always seem to love that shit.'

Trying not to take offence, I went to the fridge and handed him a can of Budweiser. 'Will this do?'

'Top of the range,' he said, smiling. 'Listen, I can go now if ya want me to. I won't hang around if ya want your space . . .'

Without warning, tears filled my eyes, and a large lump formed in my throat. I tried to answer him but nothing came out.

'Jaysus, luff, I didn't mean to be rude. I'd love to hang around with ya . . . Please don't cry . . . Fuck, I wasn't trying to get away from ya. Honest.'

Disgusted with myself, I fought back the snivelling and steadied my voice. 'Sorry about that; just a bit emotional at the moment. I'm just being a stupid woman . . .'

'Don't be silly, you're fine. I'm sorry, like . . . I wasn't tryin' to make ya sad. I was hopin' to make ya happy.'

'Sorry, it's just I'm not used to this bootie-call business. I wasn't sure of the etiquette. Is the evening over once you've shagged? I'm not sure of these things.'

Caught off-guard, he made it obvious that he felt uncomfortable, which only rattled my nerves further. As he searched for words to explain himself, I put my hand over his mouth and signalled for him to be silent.

'I'm very tired now.' My words were weak but steady. 'I think it's best if we end this lovely evening now, and while I thank you for calling over and offering your services, I'd be very grateful if you grabbed your coat before shutting the front door after you.'

Confused at how best to deal with the situation, he obeyed my demands and left me to my now open bottle of wine.

As I lay on the floor, crying, I noticed the time on the wall clock read 9.25 p.m. Some date that had turned out to be. Shagged and shrugged-off in less than half an hour. Even for a woman who'd lost her husband before their first anniversary, that was a most impressive record . . .

9

'I can't believe you talked me into this.'

Parker was almost hyperventilating over the number of people who were in his apartment. After much argument, I had finally persuaded him to host a Good Friday party. He had promised to give one for years, but it wasn't until he realized that I wasn't joking when I'd said I was planning to join the nuns that he'd truly felt I'd needed cheering up.

Because the Catholic Church still ruled the country, and banned the sale of alcohol that day in all the land – except, bizarrely, for those travelling on trains – the Irish seemed to have an extra horn for getting drunk on Good Friday. And since there were no pubs or clubs open, society dipsos were always looking for a decent party to attend; accompanied, of course, by the trolley-load of booze they would religiously have stocked up with the day before, Holy Thursday.

While there were always plenty of parties to choose from, this year all the coolest heads seemed to have crammed into Parker's pad. Typically, many of them hadn't been invited. And while that was indeed a compliment of sorts, Parker just saw it as an opportunity for them to steal all his worldly possessions.

'Eva, I don't like the great unwashed touching my stuff. If anybody breaks anything I'll be sending their daddies a bill.'

Delighted to be out of the house – and to have booked a secret babysitter I had met at a Down's syndrome support group I had discovered online – I was lapping up every minute of the party.

Although I was still recovering from being double-dumped, I was beginning to behave rationally again, and now only said, 'All men are bastards,' every twenty minutes or so, rather than every twenty seconds. Tonight, too, I was open to persuasion. I wanted to meet a man I could flirt with. The idea that I might leave the party with a new mobile number in my phone that would possibly lead to some heavy petting – or at the very least a phantom boyfriend I could fantasize about in the comfort of my own bed – was hugely appealing to me.

I was tired of masturbating over all the usual famous men, such as Clooney, Pitt and Guy Ritchie. I needed a new face to end my evenings with. So, after donning an old lucky pulling top, I was in feverishly good form and ready to play diva.

'You are *not* going to have sex in my spare room tonight, Eva,' explained Parker sternly. 'When you're under my roof, you live by my rules.'

I gave him the answer he thought he wanted, 'Yes, Dad.' If he was honest with himself, what he actually wanted was for my knight in shining armour to stride in, shag me senseless and then take me home, so he, Parker, didn't have to listen to me moaning any more. Without meaning to, I had made Parker my crutch again, in the absence of Michael. And while he was kind enough to tolerate all my worried-mum stuff about Daisy's drinking, sleeping and shitting patterns – along with the 'All men are bastards' rants – now that he was back with Jeff he had racier antics to enjoy.

Finding a moment away from the society rent-a-crowd, Parker, Lisa and I snuck into Parker's bedroom for a quick bitch about some of the gang. Thrilled with my new figure, I felt confident enough about myself to blast an old acquaintance of ours, Anna – called Reuters because she knew everything about everybody.

'Oh-my-God, how fat has Reuters got? Is it me, or does she look about mid-forties with all the plastic surgery? No offence, Princess . . .'

'No offence taken, Miss Skinny Mini . . .' Lisa said.

'And what about that old queen, Henry?' screamed Parker. 'Does he honestly believe dialling a Bangkok bride will blind people to the fact that he's a raving homo? There really is no fool like an old fool.'

Swigging on a bottle of Laurent-Perrier Rosé just like in old times, we then shared a poignant moment on how important our mutual friendship meant to the three of us. It went without saying that there was a great gaping hole left by the absence of Maddie, but the guys knew I couldn't entertain any talk of her, and they accepted my pain by ignoring any stories that might have included her. Although Lisa had cut

Maddie out of her life, through loyalty to me, I knew that Parker still talked to her occasionally – though I secretly hoped it was just so he could keep an ear to the ground for me.

Instead we reminisced about the time two mating pigeons had found their way into Parker's bedroom and shat all over his expensive and extremely *gay* silk sheets. And also about the time Lisa ordered a stripping policeman up to the apartment for Parker's birthday, and it had turned out to be his first cousin Gerry, not long back from an extended trip to Brazil, where he had had extensive facial surgery. The full story was he had done a bunk from Ireland around 2005 on drug-dealing charges, and the newly created Mickey Rourke look was just to throw off the gardai – and a few random fellas that might still be looking for money.

It was only after Jeff had demanded for the third time that we rejoin the party we eventually mustered up the energy to be sociable again.

By the time we re-emerged, the party had really kicked off, and Jeff was looking a tad frazzled.

'Eh, Parker, just to let you know, someone's puked on the balcony, there's a bloke who looks like a distant relative of Chewbacca snorting coke off the radiator cover in the living room, and I think there could be a gang bang happening in the en-suite loo off Eva's old room.'

Bizarrely, Parker wanted to linger in his gushy, loved-up mood, and simply chuckled, 'Ah, let them at it. Now . . . another bottle of champagne, methinks, for the champagne babes.'

Amazed at Parker's tolerance, both Lisa and I chimed, 'Yes, pleeese . . .' and skipped off in the direction of the fridge to claim our tipple.

It was on my arrival at the kitchen, the heart of any house-party, that I came across Steve. Steve was a cool enough type of guy: tall, heavy stubble, looked kind of grungy like he was a graphic designer, or in a band. He was very much my type, and amazingly seemed friendly and interested in me. What was even more *amazing* was the fact that he knew my name!

'Hi, I'm Steve. You're Eva, right?' His smooth voice sounded slightly American.

'Yeah, how do you know that? Have we met before?'

'No, you just used to date a friend of mine, Michael Johnson from New York.'

No sooner had the words left his mouth than my head went into a tail-spin. He wasn't speaking about my husband Michael, but the other scumbag that I'd once fallen in love with.

'You know that fucker?' My voice and eyes instantly grew cold.

'Emm, was there some shit with you two that I didn't hear?'

'OK, well apart from the fact that he broke my heart, he *also* caused me to run out on to a road, which led to me being knocked over by a very large motorbike, which then subsequently left me in a deep coma for several weeks. There's other details, but they're kinda the bullet points.'

'How are you now?'

'Yes, well, fine, thanks. But I could have been killed, or left brain-damaged because of that prick . . .'

'For sure,' cooed Steve.

'Oh-my-God.' Freaked, I screamed in one of my usual loud tones.

'What?' asked Steve confused.

'He used to say that. Michael . . . He always used to say "*for sure*".'

'All right. Sorry, I'll try not to say it again.'

'Listen, I'm sorry. You're not his minder. It's just there's a lot of history there.'

'For . . . I mean. I understand. Why don't we start again? Hi, my name's Steve. I used to work in America but now I'm based in Dublin, and it's a pleasure to meet you.'

Taking a moment to catch my breath, I tried to release all the anger from my body and accept the attractive man in front of me as a person in his own right.

'Genuinely, my apologies.' I fought back my resentment. 'I can't blame you for any of his mess. So, anyway, please tell me you're not a photographer, too?'

'Neither is he, really, by the way. You know he's just a lowly assistant? But, no, I'm a barrister.' Maybe it was my nerves, but I instantly laughed at the idea. Clearly used to such a reaction he calmly replied, 'I clean up good for court.'

'Wow. That sounds extremely mature for one of Michael's friends. What do you specialize in?'

'Licensing laws.'

'Fuck off!'

'No, for . . . Honestly, I look after bars and nightclubs,

trying to get them their licences. Don't worry, I won't try and close this party down. Why are you so shocked? Do you not think I'd look good in a suit?'

Thinking out loud, I blurted, 'I think you'd look even better out of one,' before swiftly knocking back another glass of bubbles.

Taking this as a green light, my new friend Steve leaned close into me and whispered, 'Let's move somewhere more intimate . . .'

Of course, in the mood I was in, I didn't need to be asked twice. Since I had been hopelessly aching for a distraction like Steve, I submissively followed him away from the group and entered the spare bedroom that Maddie had stayed in when she'd first given birth to Woody, and had had nowhere else to go.

Although the room itself brought back weird memories for me, I blocked them out. I didn't want that witch to ruin any more of my fun. She was old news as far as I was concerned.

Locking the door behind us, Steve chuckled gently and whispered again, 'Hey, I'd just hate anyone to walk in on us.'

As I sat on the bed I knew that I was in a sex situation. I knew Parker had forbidden me to get in one, but not on Daisy's life had I ever considered that I would actually have an opportunity to misbehave. Although the fact that Steve had locked the door was a little intimidating, I chose to ignore any prudish thoughts, and allowed the ole promiscuous Eva da Diva to come out.

Now that I had a few drinks in me I didn't care that the last guy I had had sex with had bolted on me after the act. He had served his purpose, after all: he'd proved I could get back in the game. Now that I had shed my fears, I wanted more. Did that make me a slut? Probably. But at least I was a slut who felt strong and womanly again, as opposed to the old frumpy Eva, who was racked with insecurities and cried every time she looked in the mirror.

Fearlessly throwing caution to the wind, I stood back up from the bed and threw Steve across it. Whooping with joy, he settled himself on his back and beckoned for me with his hands. 'Give us your best shot, babes!'

I kicked my shoes off, climbed over him on all fours and playfully snarled at him. Jokingly, he whimpered back, 'Please be gentle . . .' Bored with the chit-chat and the soft New York accent that kept reminding me of my ex, I decided that I wanted to fuck this guy's brains out and be the most amazing shag – all so he could go back to Michael, New York Michael, and tell him what a wonder chick I really was.

I wanted New York Michael to miss me, and remember what he'd lost. Clawing at Steve's body, I began unzipping and ripping clothes. Before long I had disrobed him of everything, including his socks, and realized that it was now my turn to get them off . . .

As I'd not foreseen such events, my fake tan didn't go up much further than my skirt hemline. So, with some quick thinking, I decided that since my boobs were already fairly well-promoted through my tight, low-cut top, all I needed to do was remove my G-string and hike up the skirt a little. Yep, there was no need for white bits to be uncovered, and we could be back to the party half an hour after the best shag of his life – or at least my life so far this year!!!

Imagining myself to be a porn actress being filmed, I danced and gyrated over Steve, touching myself and doing my best sexy noises to try and arouse him to the point of begging. Although he kept trying to grab me, I pushed his hands away from my body, and instead continued to tease him by stroking his dick with my breasts and allowing him to see me playing with myself.

Knowing that Parker always kept spare condoms in all his rooms for whenever he and Jeff fancied a bit of nookie, I pulled out the first drawer I saw, and found a handful of Durex waiting for us. So while I used my foot to toy with his balls, I ripped open a condom and placed it in my mouth.

Although it had been a while since I had performed such a task, I decided to try and put it on with just my lips and tongue, and Steve's face lit up. 'Can you really fucking do that?' He pounded the bed with his arms. 'This is gonna be good,' he cheered.

Bending over the head of his dick, a moment of fear hit me. What was I doing? Surely I was a bit old to be trying to impress strangers with sex party tricks that I'd learnt from a hooker Parker, Maddie and I had met at a bar in Marbella? Catching the excitement in Steve's eye, I pushed all negative thoughts aside, and continued with my charm offensive. Holding the base of his dick in my hands, I slowly eased the condom over its head, and began to work my tongue around its shaft, gently easing the sheath downwards, careful not to pierce it with my teeth.

Clearly enjoying the experience, Steve groaned as he intently watched my every move. Although I could only manage to unravel the condom halfway down his dick before I felt like I was going to gag, I distracted him by lunging up to kiss him, and rolling the rest down with my right hand.

Not breaking my gaze, I positioned myself on top of him and gently eased my body down around him. Since I was already turned on by my own naughty behaviour, the feeling of him entering me was exceptionally pleasant. He was even bigger than Dave, which was just sheer luck, as you wouldn't have guessed it from looking at him: he wasn't particularly tall. He was a little skinny, if anything. Confident that my body didn't look saggy camouflaged by my clothes, I was able to push my body as far as I could without fear that I might have too much cellulite on show.

Feeling unusually beautiful, I grunted and gyrated my body over Steve until my energy levels failed me and I collapsed on top of him with exhaustion. 'I'm sorry,' I wheezed. 'I'm fucked.'

'Not yet, you're not,' whooped Steve, as he flipped over my body, jumped behind me and took control for the first time. As he entered me, he began stroking my back in a very loving motion, and instead of being selfish in his thrusts, he seemed to try and rotate himself inside me, to help arouse me fully. This might just have been a sordid one-night stand, but I couldn't have been more pleased. If I could have safe sex with studs like

Steve and Dave, without all the relationship crap that went along with stroppy boyfriends or husbands, maybe I had found the secret of happiness?

Like most women, I couldn't come during sex without my clitoris getting a bit of action. But I was still happy when he came. It didn't take long for him once he found his stride; I was just pleased to have the contact and closeness, even if it was only temporary.

Without much effort I regained my dignity by fixing my skirt, and lay on the bed to get my composure back. Taking his place beside me, his smile was as broad as his face. And while I tried my best not to seem conceited, my smug grin must have said it all.

'Wow. You never told me you could do that . . .'

Laughing off his statement, I teased, 'There's not much I *did* get to tell you, to be fair.' But I said it without any resentment. This was simply sex for the sake of sex. I didn't expect anything else. I wasn't going to act the needy desperado. There's no way I had Lisa's man-itude, but I could happily strut my stuff back into the party and not obsess about whether Steve would ask to see me again. Yes, I definitely could . . . Well, that was the plan.

Keen to avoid any awkward silences, I made a swift decision to leave first. Kissing him dismissively on the nose, I chirped, 'Thanks for that,' and moved towards the door to leave. Steve, still lying buck naked on the bed, called after me, asking, 'Is that it? You're just going to leave me here, like this?'

'Yep. My work here is done.' And I unlocked the door and trotted out.

Terrified that my confidence would wane, I rushed back to the kitchen and poured myself a large vodka and orange. I had just managed to down most of it in one mouthful when Lisa popped her head over my shoulder. 'Where have you been?' she asked.

'Shagging.'

'Yeah, and I've been pole-dancing out on the balcony.'

'No, honestly, I have. And if I may say so, I was spectacularly fantastic.'

'Well, doesn't modesty become you, Miss Valentine? – not! Well, are you serious or what?'

'I am. With a dashing New Yorker, who . . .'

'Not another one?'

'Yep, and believe it or not he's actually a friend of Michael's as well.'

'New York Michael?'

'Eh, huh.'

'Fuck off. Where is he now?'

'Probably still in the bedroom, getting dressed. I left him in his birthday suit in Maddie's old room.'

'Ha, not just a Good Friday but a great Friday for you, eh?' Lisa said.

'Indeed, apart from feeling a tad slut-like, I'm thinking of myself as a very brave young lady who is exorcizing demons at every turn.'

'Listen, you have got to go out to the living room and check out Parker. They're actually smoking a *joint* on Parker's precious suede couch, and Parker miraculously seems to be fine with it. It's as if someone has smacked him over the head and reprogrammed his brain settings. He's a new man. Go have a look.'

As I turned the corner of the kitchen, Parker's presence in the room was obvious. In his rightful place, centre stage, he was holding court as the evening's jester. Enjoying having an audience, he had several young models and beautiful types hovering around him. They were laughing at all his jokes, their eyes transfixed by the joint that he kept waving around in his hand.

Striding up to listen to his majesty's wit and repertoire, I unintentionally interrupted him in mid-sentence only to become centre stage myself.

'Ah, ha. There she is. My best friend. My lucky charm. The wife I long to be. How are you, my petal? Having fun?'

I was just about to answer him when Lisa screamed at me from the hallway, beckoning me to come to her. Realizing she looked incredibly stressed, I made my excuses and went to see what the problem was.

As soon as I reached her, she grasped my arm tightly and dragged me off to the toilet. 'Look,' she cried hysterically. 'You're a mother . . . you must know first aid.'

There, in front of me, was Jeff on the floor, anxiously trying to shake a young blonde girl awake. She had been sick across the toilet, and her body was twitching like she was having some sort of attack.

'Has anyone phoned for an ambulance?'

'*No*,' came the response from Jeff and Lisa.

'Well, I'm calling one. I've read about too many people dying at house-parties. That girl looks in a bad way. I'm gonna ring them now.'

Rushing out to the hall, I dialled 999 on the house phone and asked for an ambulance.

Although I wanted to get off the phone once I had passed on the address, the operator insisted on telling me how to care for the girl while waiting for the paramedics to arrive.

'Put her on her side,' I shouted through to Jeff. 'Make sure her airways aren't blocked.' As the words left my mouth, I felt I had somehow stepped into an episode of *Scrubs*. Five minutes ago I had been having sex with a gorgeous man I'd just met, and now I was trying to save a young girl's life . . . It seemed farcical beyond belief.

When the girl seemed stable and breathing I handed the phone to Lisa, and dashed to tell Parker what was happening. He was still surrounded by adoring groupies, but there was no time to tiptoe around the facts. 'Parker, I need you to come to the toilet, quick. There's a girl there who's really sick.'

Convinced I was trying to wind him up Parker took another blast of his joint and asked, 'Am I bothered?' Then he chuckled at his new friends, as if he was the great comic genius Catherine Tate herself.

'Parker, there's a girl having convulsions in your toilet. She's gone blue!'

Momentarily dazed and confused, Parker's face went blank. Furious with him for being in such a hazy state, I slapped him across the face. 'I need you to focus. There's some girl who looks like she's dying on your bathroom floor. Jeff's with her now. The ambulance has been called, but there's a high chance the police will turn up, too. What are you going to do with all these people? You need to get them out now. If anyone is caught with drugs on them, you'll be the one that's screwed.'

Realizing that he'd need some time to sober up, I ran to the stereo and switched it off. I flicked the lights up full and started screaming, 'Does anyone here have any medical experience? There's someone collapsed in the toilet.'

As if I had announced the place was on fire, people started frantically grabbing coats and dashing to the door. No one seemed interested in helping.

'Anyone know any first aid? Anyone?'

Convinced my request had fallen on deaf ears, I was about to give up and go back in to the girl when a young blonde woman stuck her head in from the balcony and asked, 'What's up with everyone?'

'There's someone collapsed in the toilet. You don't happen to be a doctor or a nurse, by any chance?'

'Well, I'm a dentist, so I know the basics. Where is she?'

When we got there, Jeff had the young woman cradled in his arms, and was busy trying to wipe away a white foamy substance that she was secreting from her mouth and nose.

Lisa was saying: 'She's got this stuff coming out . . . Oh! You mean you're *here*?'

The dentist and I had just knelt down beside them on the floor when a man and a woman in ambulance kit made their way into the bathroom.

'Move aside, please,' said the man, immediately going to the young girl and opening a bag.

'Can somebody give me the exact details of what's happened here?' asked the woman.

Completely in shock, we all just moved back from the now lifeless body and stared. None of us knew quite what to say.

The man checked the girl's pulse and fitted an oxygen mask over her face, while his partner asked: 'Does anyone know this girl's name?'

Everyone stayed silent.

'Come on, someone must know her. Did anyone see her take any illegal drugs? Does anyone know her name, or who she came to the party with?'

A few of us answered, '*No*,' at the same time, which wasn't exactly greeted with an enthusiastic reception by the female paramedic.

She immediately started complaining, 'If someone doesn't speak up, we're not going to know how to treat this woman. Staying quiet could kill her. Do you really want to have a dead girl on your hands?' While she spoke, the ambulanceman disappeared, reappearing quite swiftly with a stretcher.

Until I'd stepped into the toilet, I'd never laid eyes on the girl before. She didn't even look vaguely familiar to me. And I didn't think she did to any of the others, either. Looking around the loo at Jeff, Lisa, the dentist girl and now a spaced-out-looking Parker, who had joined the gang, I realized it was a sorry bunch watching over this girl.

As the woman screamed again for information, and she and the other paramedic rolled the girl on to the stretcher, I offered my own take on things, since none of the others seemed to have the ability to speak, or even grunt for that matter.

'We don't know her. I've never seen her before . . . I . . . don't even know who she came with.' I noticed a scruffy handbag by the door. 'This might be hers,' I said. 'Perhaps it's got her name inside.'

'Could she have taken drugs?' The woman para-medic was strapping the girl in place.

Lisa, Jeff and I shared a glance. I looked at Parker, but his gaze seemed frozen on the girl on the floor.

'Yes, maybe.' The words came without me even thinking about them.

Jeff glared at me, but I chose to ignore him. 'Yes, there were a few people who seemed to have drugs. But we honestly don't know who she is. None of us gave her anything . . . Honestly.'

'Well, let's hope for your sakes she doesn't die. If she does, I'd start getting your stories straight quick. Right, do any of you want to accompany her to the hospital?'

'Do we have to?' asked Lisa.

'No, you don't,' explained the man, clearly disgusted by our lack of sympathy, as both he and the woman began carrying the girl out of Parker's flat.

'Actually, I'd like to go,' piped up the dentist. 'I don't mind staying with her; just let me grab my bag and I'll be right with you.'

'*No!* It's our party. We'll go. Won't we?' I glared at Lisa and Parker, demanding a response.

At first Jeff was the only one to respond. 'Of course we'll all go, won't we, Parker?'

'Yes, fine,' muttered Parker.

'Sorry, sure,' seconded Lisa.

As if to redeem my soul from certain hell after my naughty encounter with the American barrister, I insisted on going with the girl in the ambulance while the others hitched a taxi from the road. Helpless, I watched as the female paramedic checked the girl's vital signs, the siren wailed and the other paramedic, driving, shouted instructions to St James's hospital. My ears rang with the noise. We had a terrifying speed-dash to the hospital, and the journey seemed to be over as quickly as it had begun.

Not once did the girl respond to her treatment or even open her eyes. Throughout the journey I remained frozen in fear, just staring straight at her, trying to will her to wake up.

The second the ambulance pulled up at St James's, the back doors flew open and a team of doctors stood waiting to take her. As I followed inside, I was stopped short of the theatre and told sternly, 'Do not come any further.'

I was feeling confused when the others finally arrived, and we all huddled in between the drunks and the wounded, surrounded by half-empty Coca-Cola cans and half-eaten sandwiches. We were two hours waiting in reception before a nurse came out and told us to go home.

'We found her name in her bag, and her parents are already with her,' explained the nurse. 'There's simply no need for you to be here. Other than that, I cannot comment on Amy's current state of health. You might as well just go home.'

That night we pushed the three large couches in the living room together, and, wrapping ourselves in duvets, crawled into this new bed and took solace in each other's company. Utterly stunned by what had happened, we clung to each other like we were the last survivors on some sinking ship.

'What if she dies? What if that girl, Amy, actually dies?' Lisa asked.

We had all been thinking it, but she was the first to say it out loud.

'Well, if she dies, they'll wait till the toxicology report comes out, and if they find drugs in her system they'll start looking for the person who gave her them, I suppose . . .' Jeff's voice had an official tone to it. I could tell he was already distancing himself from the scandal.

'First thing in the morning, everyone has to help me clean this place from top-to-toe. Everything must be bleached: there can't be any traces of drugs found here or else we're fucked . . .' Parker's face looked fierce. 'Is that agreed?'

While Jeff and I weakly muttered, 'Yes,' a defiant Lisa took great offence at his remark.

'Are you serious?' she bellowed. 'There's a beautiful young woman – somebody's daughter, somebody's sister – who's lying in casualty right now, with her life hanging in the balance, and all you're worried about is saving your own ass from any scandal. That's not exactly charitable, is it?'

'Fuck charitable, Lisa. You don't have a fucking career to lose. I'm sorry, but I don't know this person. I have no idea if she was snorting coke all night. Or popping pills. Don't make me out to be the devil just because I want to distance myself from a random blonde who decided to OD in my apartment. Yes, she was in my home. But I'd never seen her before. If she wanted to die, she should have . . .'

Over-stressed, I needed to kill the argument. 'Don't be such a heartless fucker, Parker. You spent most of your evening smoking weed. Imagine if somebody had laced it with heroin or something more sinister? You could just as easily have been the person in A&E. Have some respect. She has a name, and it's Amy. Now, pray that she doesn't fucking die – but for the right reasons. Not just because you're worried about having your name dragged through the papers . . .'

The group fell silent. Of course, for fear of being tarnished, we all wished to dissociate ourselves from the girl. But then, none of us really wanted to do wrong by her, either. Not even Parker.

As we shared our memories of the evening, some good, some bad, they were all overshadowed by the tragedy of a lonely young girl, abandoned by her friends and left for dead. The harsh truth was that it could have happened to any of us. The obvious assumption was that she'd been snorting coke, but maybe her drink had been spiked. Or maybe she had thought she was snorting cocaine but had been given something stronger?

Curious as to what they'd say, I asked, 'If that had been me, would any of you have left me?'

'What do you mean?' barked Parker, still sore.

'I mean, if I had been reckless enough to do coke . . .'

'*Again?*' questioned Lisa.

'*Yes*, again. I've only done it *once*. And you can't talk, either. Remember Paris?'

Thrilled with the put-down, Parker whooped, 'Touché!' But he quickly realized that this was not the time for one-upmanship.

'So would you have left me or not?' I probably should have kept quiet, realizing I might not like the answer, but after the trauma of the night's events my insecurities were starting to get the better of me.

'Don't be so stupid, Eva,' smiled Jeff, trying to reassure me. 'None of us would have abandoned you, would we, Parker?' He nudged his partner, pushing him for a response.

'No, of course not,' Parker grumbled.

'Ah, thanks. Don't go out of your way to sound convincing, whatever you do.'

'OK, so none of us are perfect,' narked Parker. 'But it goes without saying that all of us would have stayed with you. We're not complete morons. God only knows what fuckers she came with.'

'Yeah, but she must have come with someone. And then they went off and left her. How tragic is that?' Although I felt now was an appropriate time to cry, I couldn't. I tried to force some tears, but they refused to come. Maybe it was the shock? Or perhaps it was just the total absurdity of my extreme emotions, veering from joy to horror in such a short space of time, that numbed me. Then the guilt hit.

'This is all my fault,' I said to Parker, as I suddenly realized that Amy's life now hung in the balance simply because I had wanted to have a party.

'Why is it your fault, then?' asked Parker.

'Because I'm the one who pushed you to open your house up to a bunch of strangers, many of whom we'd only ever seen in the back pages of the Sundays; and now a girl is seriously ill because of it. It's totally my fault.'

His reply was cut off by the door buzzer ringing.

Burr, burr. Burr, burr.

'I'm not answering it,' squealed Parker.

Burr, burr. Burr, burr.

Weighed down by a world of guilt, I leapt out from under the duvet and dived towards the intercom phone. 'Hello?'

'I'm looking to speak with the owner of the apartment.'

'Who's this?'

'This is Detective Patrick Lonergan, and we need to gain access to the premises. Please open up now.'

'Oh-my-God. OK. Come on up.'

I turned to the group and explained that the Gardai were on their way upstairs.

'Is she dead?' asked Jeff.

I didn't know the answer, but we would soon find out.

The night was about to get a whole lot longer.

10

Turning thirty-two would normally be cause for celebration, but not in the wake of Amy Price's death.

Three days after leaving Parker's bathroom in the arms of two angry paramedics, she had suffered numerous violent seizures, which had left her severely brain-damaged. Sadly, she'd never regained consciousness, and her final few hours had been spent in a hospital bed, attached to a life-support machine. Her family had only agreed for the ventilator to be turned off after it had been established that there was definitely no hope, and her little sister Jessica had arrived home from a school trip to Berlin to say goodbye.

Although there was a minor media ripple over the shock death of a 25-year-old who had died from a suspected cocaine overdose, the collapse of another large building firm and the discovery of a new paedophile ring dominated the news. Ireland had seen many deaths like Amy's before, and fatigue about such a tragedy had set in. She hadn't got blue blood, nor was she a model with a famous suitor.

The fact that she was just a regular girl, who had

quite clearly fallen in with the wrong crowd, made no difference to our grief. The guilt that Parker, Jeff, Lisa and I shared was immense. There had been a lot of 'what if?'s. But none of us could think of anything that would have changed the outcome.

Lisa was the one who received the most media coverage, as the society princess embroiled in a drug-scandal. Her face was flashed across 'Entertainment News' on several channels, which caused much mortification for the Tiswell family, and I'm sure plenty of heartbreak for the Prices, too.

So my thirty-second birthday was quite a subdued affair, with Parker, Jeff, Lisa and myself dining chez Valentine, oh, with, of course, Daisy sleeping silently upstairs. Collectively we were a group of comfort-eaters, and tonight was the perfect opportunity for all of us to stuff our faces in the name of grief and self-pity, under the umbrella of the minor celebration that was my birthday.

And in the absence of anyone willing to cook, the local Chinese received a hefty delivery order.

As always, my rich friends brought me expensive presents. It was their way of spoiling me. And while usually a Vivienne Westwood jacket and a Chloé hand-bag would have had me dancing on the ceiling, tonight I didn't even bother with, 'Ah, you shouldn't have.' I just went straight for, 'Thank you,' and stuffed them both down the side of the couch out of eye-shot. I felt it would be wrong for me to parade up and down the living room with my new gifts just days after a young girl had taken her last breath.

I'd wait until no one could see me being unashamedly alive and giddy. The poor girl hadn't even been buried yet. So giddiness would have to wait.

'I propose a toast.' Parker was putting on his bravest face, and didn't want the tepid party-spirit to slip any further into gloom. 'Come on . . . These are difficult times . . .' He floundered, his words falling on deaf ears, as all of us continued to stuff our faces with extra helpings of spring rolls.

'Shush, come on, let's make an effort here,' he continued. 'It's Eva's birthday no matter what. And after a somewhat shitty roller-coaster year for her, we should acknowledge that this evening could be a fresh start . . . like the beginning of a new chapter. Guys?'

We all chose to ignore him, as by now we were also trying to concentrate on the movie *Brokeback Mountain*, and fighting back tears at the injustice of being a homosexual cowboy in the sixties.

Sensing he was about to make another plea, I stopped him in his tracks to save him the hassle. 'Thank you, Parker, but let's just watch the movie. My luck isn't going to miraculously change just because I'm *officially* a year older than I was yesterday. It's a nice sentiment . . . but let's just leave it for now. Actually, instead of making toasts, I'd save your energy for a prayer.'

'What do you mean?'

'What I mean is they say bad things happen in threes; well, bad things have definitely been happening to me in multiples of three over the last few years.'

'So?'

'Well, one, my husband's just left me. And if you

remember, he proposed to me on my birthday last year. An eerie synchronicity there, don't you agree? Then, two, Amy has died. And she's certainly upped the ante on the level of horror. It doesn't get much worse than that.'

'And what?' Parker looked dazed and confused.

'Eh? Earth to Parker's brain? Something else bad is due. It could happen to you through association. I'm just saying, there's a third bad experience to come, and it could happen to anyone in this room, so beware.'

'A beautiful birthday toast, Eva,' snarled Jeff, from under his glass of champagne. 'It can only be topped I think by one further statement: Here's to us three,' Jeff signalled to Parker and Lisa respectively, 'all getting killed in our taxi on the way home tonight . . . Drink up, girls. If we're drunk enough, we might not feel a thing on our way to hell!'

The morning of Amy's funeral I got a call from an old editor friend asking me if I was interested in work. She wanted to know if I'd come on board as a regular contributor for a new women's fashion and lifestyle magazine called *YES!* that she was putting together. *Would I?* Of course, I immediately said 'Yes!' with a beaming smile. I was only off the phone two minutes when my paranoia kicked in. There was something very wrong about getting good news on the day of a funeral. Or was there?

My mind was buzzing with grim thoughts as I arrived at the church just a few minutes late, to be told by Parker, 'The detectives involved in her case are here. The one who spoke to us says there's been a breakthrough, and that we'll all be called in for another informal chat. I'm shit scared. Chat? That sounds like a fucking arrest to me. OK, so they found some hash at the apartment, but they're hardly going to charge us for that. Are they?'

'Mmmm, I dunno.'

'Well, help figure it out soon, Eva. If I'm going to be framed for murder and get sent to prison, I'm gonna need to order me a chastity belt quick . . . I'm all for a bit of somethin' with strange men, but I've read the *Sunday World* and I've seen the photos of those jail creeps. I'm not strong enough to be locked up with those scumbags. They'd eat me for breakfast.'

'If you're lucky. Now just shut up for five minutes. Live in the present and respect the funeral.'

'You're the one who was late.'

'OK, OK. And now I'm here.'

The short service was a tearjerker. Everybody sobbed through recordings of 'You're Beautiful' by James Blunt and 'Forever Young' by Rod Stewart. Again, although I hadn't known Amy it was as if someone had stuck a knife in my heart, letting all my emotions spill out. I wasn't alone. Everywhere I looked, young people filled the church. All were inconsolable, and bewildered as to how someone so young could be dead.

It was a mystery to all of us. I couldn't help measuring her death against all those ageing wrinkly rock-stars who had survived decades of drink and drug abuse, like Ozzy Osbourne, Ronnie Wood and Iggy Pop. Why had people like that outlived poor Amy?

★   ★   ★

'Ya know, I really wish I could just clone myself . . . I'd like one very diligent, hard-working, genius Eva. One super-nanny perfect mother Eva, a disco-diva party Eva, and . . .'

'You'd like more alter egos? I don't think the world is quite ready for that many Evas. That's a scary prospect,' Parker said.

'And probably just some sort of spare Eva, who loves housework, pays bills and remembers to leave out the bins and stuff.'

'Do you even fall into one of those categories?'

'Huh, the cheek! Indeed I do. I'm a capable woman who multi-tasks in her sleep . . . It's just I haven't been sleeping well lately and I seem to be getting more frazzled by the day.'

Parker and I were in a taxi to Dalkey for an art exhibition that I was covering for my new magazine, *YES!* Bono was expected to turn up – after all, he was a local – so the world and his wife would also be out in force, hunting a scoop and the possibility of a photo-opportunity.

Despite the fact that you'd regularly see Bono driving his flashy Maserati around Dublin, or shopping down Grafton Street with his kids, we all still wanted to be seen near him. Almost everyone in Ireland had a Bono story. It was as if it was our born, patriotic right to have one.

Being the worldly-wise celebrity hack – freshly out of retirement thanks to my newly acquired special-needs babysitter – I had of course met the great man.

OK, it was only one night in Valerie's nightclub, but he might just remember me. Well, maybe?

'So is the pressure really that bad at the moment?' Parker had that vacant look across his face. He was doing his supportive friend act, but he didn't really want to know the answer. He had gotten so good at doing this recently that I was sure his questions weren't even connecting with his brain. Underneath a facade of sympathy, he was sure to be wondering whether his particular choice of black Prada shoes matched his black Prada suit that evening. Or maybe fretting over his hair, or something equally as important.

Not feeling the love, I brushed off his question – his gratification was instant, if facial expressions were anything to go by – and turned the conversation back to Parker, his favourite topic. In fairness, he was a good friend, so I liked to indulge his fancy – but only a little.

'Your hair looks in really good condition, by the way.'

Parker gushed as he ran his hands through his wispy side-locks. 'Ah, thanks . . . I find fish oils are great. I've been taking them four times a day for a couple of weeks now.'

'Oh yeah? Your darling Jeff actually texted me earlier to ask if I could check for any stray grey hairs.'

'What?'

'Yeah, apparently there was so much bluey-black shit all over the bath at the K Club and his formerly white towels that he found it hard to imagine any colour residue could be left on your head.'

'The bitch.'

'Yes, he is,' I smirked. And the two of us broke out in giggles. Which did go a way to help me forget about my own stresses and work worries. For once the problem wasn't finding work. As a freelance journalist it was easy to go out of favour, but once I was employed the difficulty became finding time to get the work done around Daisy. I had never thought that life as a single mother would be easy, but the juggle had most definitely become a struggle. But of course I was managing. As my sister Ruth kept telling me, 'If you're a mother, you always do.'

Getting fixed with Jeanette, my childminder, helped, and also made me realize how little Michael had actually done around the house. With Jeanette, getting out and about was so easy, I barely knew what to do with the liberty.

Of course this freedom came at a price – it gave me time to think. Time to wonder why all the men I met treated me so badly. I knew that other women suffered heartbreak, too, but I didn't know anyone who had been cursed by two cruel men with the same name.

Instead of focusing on my work, I kept feeling confused and almost missing deadlines, all because I had been fucked over by two men called Michael. Why had I been so stupid as to believe that getting married to a man I hardly knew would be a fairy tale?

So many questions, so few answers . . . No matter how long I stared at the blank screen on my laptop, it never seemed to remedy the headaches I was giving myself, trying to understand the impossible.

Although we had arrived early, punters were already spilling out on to the road from the small art gallery door. The smokers puffed bellyfuls of Marlboro Lights into the air, while small PR blondes buzzed around frantically on mobile phones.

Once we'd managed to push our way inside, extremely warm glasses of white wine were shoved into our hands, along with a photocopied listing of the paintings and photographs on sale. So far all I could see were some hideously gruesome black splodges on canvases, but then again, I didn't have the right to be too critical, as I wasn't exactly in the market for buying.

As I had imagined, the room was filled with more hacks looking for a story than people searching for an investment. And as yet, there was no sign of Bono. Parker began ranting about the standard of Irish paintings since Francis Bacon had died. He'd read a feature about this once in the *FT*, and had since deemed himself an expert. But he suddenly stopped speaking mid-sentence about his loathing for Kevin Sharkey, and the colour ran out of his face.

'What's wrong?'

'Emm, nothing. Let's just step over here behind this fabulous sculpture.' Bumping into several disgruntled crusty arty types, he manhandled me beside some sort of melted bronze head.

'Who are you avoiding?' I tried desperately hard to search for a familiar face, but couldn't see anyone of interest. '*Nobody* puts Baby in the corner,' I joked, but his face remained sullen.

'OK.' Parker looked at me with a meaningful stare. 'We need to get you out of here. Quick . . .'

'Why?'

'Forget meeting Bono, tell your editor you got sick, or Daisy threw up or something. You've got to go.'

'What's the rush? Is it because of some old boyfriend of yours?'

Tutting with frustration, he precariously balanced his nasty glass of vino beside the melted head – which looked like it had had a few too many itself – and, while clasping my head with his two large hands, directed my gaze towards the entrance. Just like Parker, my reaction was one of complete shock. There, looking extremely cocky and overly tanned for the time of year, was David Barron of *Dubliners View*.

He was the married publisher I'd foolishly snogged two years ago at a press event at the Haven, CCTV images of our clinch making the Sunday papers. Understandably this had led to David Barron's marriage teetering on the rocks. That had been the beginning of the end for me, too. But I'd really thought the bad karma had ended after I'd woken from my coma; evidently the good things had just been a temporary blip.

While I'd been paying heavily for my mistake, David Barron's public indiscretion had led to a long-standing affair – which he had been having with his wife's best friend – being exposed. He had directed all his anger at me when the story had broken, and even made a drunken swipe at me the last time I had seen him. So, knowing I was his public enemy number one, I wasn't prepared to have a scene in this small room full of hungry gossip-mongers. Not only could my frayed nerves not take it, I couldn't afford to risk losing my new job at *YES!* with any negative press.

'OK, bright spark. Any ideas on how we're going to get past him? He's blocking up the doorway and he doesn't look like he's moving.'

Parker thought for a minute, before an imaginary light bulb flashed above his head. 'OK, let's create a distraction. How about you push someone into that glass case over there and make a run for it?'

'Eh, how about you take all your clothes off and piss in the middle of the room?'

'I'm sensing you're not gone on my idea?'

'Come on, Parker. Put that pretty small brain of yours into action for once.'

'OK, then, drastic times call for drastic measures. Follow me.' He grabbed my hand, put his head down and made a bee-line for a small door. It could easily have been a closet, but thankfully it opened on to a small stairwell stacked with empty boxes, and we quickly disappeared in there and shut the door behind us.

'Where now? Is this somebody's house or something? We can't just go mooching about here. We'll get arrested again.'

I'm not sure if it was the fear of being caught, but the two of us broke out in a fit of the giggles at the madness of the situation. We were busily trying to shush each other when a familiar voice asked, 'So is this where the real party is?'

Spooked, we turned around to see Bono and his

mates Gavin Friday, Guggi and Simon Carmody standing over us.

'Fuck me,' yelped Parker with the shock.

But all Bono and his pals did was laugh.

'Eh, I'm sorry,' mused Bono. 'I've been through many passages, but I've no desire to go through yours.'

Stunned by the presence of greatness, Parker, in a choirboy tone, directed the lads towards the door and calmly said, 'Actually the party is through there, Bono, eh, Paul, eh, Mr Hewson.'

'Thank you,' cooed Bono, as he pushed past Parker.

In a fit of bravery, I thought to hell with it, I'd ask him for a photo. The worst he could say was no.

'Eh, sorry, Bono. Is there any chance I could get a photograph with you? I work for a magazine called *YES!* Well, I've just started, and I'd be really grateful. It would make a very impressive splash for me.'

He was totally cool with this inappropriate request, simply smiling at me and saying, 'Sure. How could I say no to making a splash?'

Within seconds he had gone, and Parker and I continued to flee through an upstairs door at the top of a second stairway. When we found ourselves on the road we stood giggling at my camera, like children. The picture was amazing. Bono had pulled one of his trademark uber-slick poses, and I actually looked quite hot.

My editor was chuffed. It turned out I was the only person to get a photo with Bono: either an electrical fault or someone's mislaid cigarette butt had started a small fire, and the entire exhibition had had to be abandoned.

The headline on my piece read: OUR GIRL EVA SETS BONO ON FIRE!

Even my mother was proud. She rang me and said, 'Well done, Eva. A piece of journalism that I can actually show your grandmother, with a photograph that doesn't include you kissing the married man.'

Despite the Garda threatening that we might be summonsed back to the clink to be grilled over Amy's death, there had been no word from anyone. And although her name had slipped quietly out of the media's radar – and Lisa's name, too – I continued to think about Amy every morning, grateful that, unlike her, I had the privilege of waking up. Actually I almost thought about her more than I did about my renegade husband; maybe because a part of me was refusing to accept the divorce, deliberately ignoring the truth to fend off the pain.

Daisy's routine saved me. And now my new job had filled the lonely gaps left even by that.

After setting my alarm at 6 a.m., I had nearly always finished my writing by 8.45 a.m. when Daisy woke. And although I'd then feel like taking a nap myself, the satisfaction of having a 1,400-word feature already completed would be brilliant.

By 11 a.m. the two of us would be queuing at the checkout at Tesco's, where I would try desperately hard to avoid the other mothers' sympathy smiles. Daisy wouldn't mind: in the last month she'd discovered her hands, and now played with them delightedly, as if they were the most perfect, plump pink toys. But while she cooed and gurgled at them, other mothers would admire their own children bouncing around in the trolley, and then, noticing Daisy, give me an aggravating sympathy smile.

Slowly but surely I was beginning to let people's pity float over my head but I wasn't yet at the stage where I could totally ignore or blank it out. That was a long while off yet.

This morning I was just shaking off the attentions of an over-eager mother of two well-behaved Germanic-looking blonde toddlers, when the grumpy woman at the till barked, 'Have you another card? This has been rejected.'

'Excuse me?' I said, shocked.

Far from impressed, she just repeated herself as if I was deaf. 'I said . . . Have you another card? This has been rejected.'

'Emm, could you try it again? Emm, I have another laser card, but I don't think there's any money in the account.'

Unenthusiastically she stuck the card back in the machine again, and asked me to key in my pin code.

I did so and patiently waited . . . repeating the words, please, please, please, in my head.

My pleas were unanswered. Once again the card was rejected. My face instantly burned with embarrass-ment. I apologized to both the cashier and the tolerant woman waiting behind me.

Taking back the rejected card, I pulled another from my purse. This was my own personal account, and I had no faith that there was any money in it. But what did I have to lose? 'Eh, could you please try this one?'

Once again the cashier gave me dagger eyes that could have cut me in two. She didn't speak, merely pointed at the machine when it was time to key in my pin code.

Once again, I said the words please, please, please, in my head . . . and once again my card was refused.

'Would you like a loan of some money?' enquired the mother behind me.

'Sorry?'

'I see you're in trouble with your cards. Mine are always playing up, too. Can I loan you the money? It's no problem.'

Her kindness almost shocked me to tears, but I fought them back, and swallowed hard to remove the lump in my throat, too. 'Why, eh, thank you. That's really . . . a lovely offer, but I couldn't possibly . . . It's just a silly mix-up. But thank you very much. Very kind of you. Really, very kind.'

Turning back to the witch behind the counter, my stuttering continued. 'Eh, can I . . . can I put these aside? I just need to go to the bank. Sorry about this . . . Eh, do you know where the nearest Pass machine is?'

After what seemed like an endless amount of time, I eventually managed to release Daisy's car-seat from the trolley. Frantically thanking the woman behind again for her generosity and patience, I ran out the door of Tesco's and didn't look back. As I exited, I continued past the cashpoint. There was no point stopping, as I knew there would be no money in my personal account.

246

My first wages were only going to be lodged at the end of the week.

Over the last year, I had more or less lived off the joint account I'd shared with Michael. Why had my card been rejected? Had Michael stopped putting money into the account? He wouldn't dare, would he? He might have abandoned his daughter, but surely he wasn't heartless enough to stop supporting her financially, was he?

As soon as I got back to my depressing broken-down Mini, I started to phone him, but hung up after just one ring. What if he actually answered? I didn't think I would be able to speak to him without screaming; or, worse still, crying. Better if I texted him, I thought. Texts are emotionless. Unlike me, they stick to the point of what they're saying, and don't deafen the recipient that answers them.

Finally, through the shaking and the hyperventilating, I managed to text him the words, 'Did you stop paying money into our account?'

Seconds later he texted back, 'Yes.'

Furious, I replied, 'Why exactly?'

Just as quick he answered, 'Heard you finally got a job. Congrats, Eva! You can start paying your own way now.'

I was so angry I felt like throwing my mobile out the window. But that would have been stupid. I couldn't afford to buy a new one. I pounded my hands against my wheel in frustration until I realized I was distressing Daisy – something I hated to do, but couldn't always avoid since I was often a flaky human being.

Finally the inevitable had happened. I'd guessed he would cut me off at some stage; I just wondered who had given him a tip-off about my new gig.

Lisa took me to Chapter One for dinner, by way of an apology.

Feeling terribly guilty for blabbing my good news to Reuters, who in turn had told Maddie, she said, 'I just wanted to let her know that you were moving on, and that you were picking up the pieces of your broken marriage . . . I never thought that Michael would stop your money. I'm so sorry, truly I am.'

Of course it wasn't her fault, and I didn't hold it against her. And the fancy meal, washed down with a couple of bottles of extra-cold Veuve Clicquot courtesy of her daddy's credit card, was gratefully accepted.

A long-time favourite of ours, Chapter One was always a place we'd go if we wanted to be cheered up, or felt like celebrating.

As usual, the place was buzzing, and all the staff were there to welcome us. And without even having to ask, our coats were taken and we were both handed a glass of bubbles from the sommelier, Ian. 'Ladies, your usual.'

It was places like these that made me feel as if I was rich. As if this was a world where I belonged, too. While the reality couldn't be further from the truth, I was going to ignore the obvious and enjoy the evening for what it was: rich friend, poor friend, guilt.

Two bottles of champagne later, and the champagne babes had become well and truly piddly.

'I'm so broke I go to KFC and lick other people's fingers,' I squealed.

'Well, I'm so rich,' joked Lisa, 'the only bags under my eyes are Gucci!' Instantly her laughing stopped. It was obvious that the guilt had hit her again. 'Listen, I didn't mean to gloat, especially after what I've—'

'Ah, it's fine,' I interrupted. 'Honestly. You've only partially messed things up for me . . . I'll just have to find a very rich and *old* husband next time.'

'Ah, Eva.'

'I'm only joking. It's cool. Tonight I'm eating fillet steak, tomorrow it'll be bread and water. Them's the breaks, Princess, when you're born on the wrong side of the tracks!'

'Maybe I could give you something to help you get by? How much a week would you need?'

'Fuck off, don't be stupid. Come on, we're having fun here. Let's not get serious. I'll be fine. Me and Daisy will be fine. I'm not exactly ever going to go hungry. Now, if you want to make me happy you'll come up with a plan as to where we're going next. For tonight, my dear, I'm going to bleed your credit card dry. That is a promise . . .'

'What, until you're soggy with alcohol?'

'That's it. Let's pay the bill and find me some victims to terrorize. I've decided that Michael stopping my money was the third bad thing that was going to happen to me.'

'Really?'

'Yep. And now that's out of the way, my karma is back on the straight and narrow. So . . . let's get out there and party. I'm seeing the positives here, so let's roll with it.'

We were just at the till kissing old staffers Declan, Martin and Ian goodbye when the cheeky face of Steve, the guy I had shagged at Parker's apartment before Amy died, stuck his face around the corner, asking, 'Eva, is that you?'

'Oh . . . Hiya, how's things?' I tried to look cool, but possibly failed miserably.

'Great, thanks. I knew I recognized the voice.'

'Who's this?' asked Lisa, with a twinge of anxiety.

'Oh, sorry, I'm a friend of Eva's. We met at a party recently. I'm friendly with an old flame of hers, Michael.'

Picking up on some awkwardness, the lads excused themselves to other duties, and the three of us were left standing smiling at one another.

'Michael Logan?' asked Lisa sternly.

'No, Michael Johnson from New York. Was the accent not a giveaway?'

'So which party was this?' enquired Lisa, somewhat pissed off that Steve might be mocking her. 'Would this have been a certain party at a Docklands apartment, that everyone left when they heard a girl was critically sick?'

'Hey, listen, I didn't know what the story was until a couple of days later. I had been dumped by a certain lady,' he threw a cheeky glance at me. 'And then when I came back from, eh, using the men's room, my friend grabbed me and told me everyone had to get out. The party was over. Hey, honestly, I knew nothing about it . . . I swear!'

'Mmmm, we'll have to take your word on that, I suppose.' Lisa wanted to be mad at him, but his cheeky face refused to let her.

'Sooo, what are you two gorgeous hotties doing without a chaperone? Would you fancy some company on your travels?' Steve asked.

Totally winded, I just stood on the spot with my jaw hanging open.

Not wanting to cave in too early, Lisa asked, 'Who've you got with ya? I don't want to get stuck with the ugly mate . . .'

'Li-sa . . .' I practically spat on her with the shock.

'What? Just because you're sorted doesn't mean I'm happy to talk golf with his boring mates. Who's inside?'

'A solicitor and an accountant. How does that sound?' Steve said.

'Dull.' Lisa made a face.

'Well, I couldn't agree more. So why don't we dump these stooges and let's get a cab somewhere fun, whatya think?'

'How do we know you're not going to run off and leave us?' asked Lisa gruffly.

'Trust me, I'm not the kind of guy who likes to leave just when things are getting interesting.' He looked me square in the eye and made me blush. 'And besides,' he chirped, 'I had the best sex ever with this girl. I'm sticking around in the hope that I might just get it again!'

I wasn't quite sure what it was about Steve, but he made me feel sexy and sassy, and all the other over-excitable emotions I'd once felt pre-Daisy.

He possessed a kind of magic that brought out the best in me. Just two weeks of dating, and various groping sessions in the back of taxis later, we had started to fall truly, madly, deeply in lust.

Although I hadn't felt comfortable enough to allow him back to the house yet – I still hated myself for my sluttish episode there with disappearing Dave – our relationship, if I could call it that, was going 'steady', to use an American term. And I couldn't remember being happier, or feeling giddier with life.

I had been terrified of telling him I had a baby, full stop, but he'd barely blinked when I told him the news. 'That's cool,' he'd cooed. And then, when I'd dropped the clanger that my daughter Daisy was, in fact, a special baby with Down's syndrome, who needed extra love and attention from mommy, he'd just smiled and said, 'I can't wait to meet her; she's part of you and that alone makes her special.'

With Ireland enjoying an Indian summer, I agreed for our first outing – Steve, Daisy and me – to be out in Greystones in Wicklow. As my 'heartbreak diet' had turned into a 'new boyfriend diet', I felt I was looking trimmer than ever, and was thrilled to be able to dig out an old pair of shorts and parade the legs for all to see – but especially for Steve, of course.

Like a romantically happy family unit – one that I sadly never got to make with my husband – we leisurely wandered around the town, stopped off for a bite of lunch at an outside café, and then made our way down to the beach.

Although Steve had shown quite a paternal side of

his personality, by being attentive to Daisy's needs all morning, it was only when he asked to carry her down the beach that I got butterflies in my stomach.

'Why don't we put her buggy in my car, and I'll carry her? It wouldn't be fair to her to push it over the stones. And besides, I'd like to hold her. I don't want to let either of you go.'

With Daisy looking up into Steve's face, and smiling when he did, like lovers in a movie we found a quiet spot to sit down near the water and let it wash up over our toes. As all three of us kissed and giggled and stared meaningfully into each other's eyes, I continued to fall deeper in . . . lust? Happiness? Or could it be in love?

Maybe Steve was just my rebound guy? But I didn't care if he was just a stop-gap. He was making me so happy, and for now I was refusing to think about tomorrow, and just enjoying the here and now.

Steve and I were just in the middle of one of our smoochy kisses after he smothered too much sun cream over my nose, when I heard footsteps crunch behind us. Startled, I broke away to see Michael and Maddie towering over me.

It was bound to happen sooner or later. But I wasn't comfortable with the situation at all.

Unsure what to do I grabbed Daisy off Steve's lap while retreating away from them, screaming, 'Get away from us . . . Just leave us alone.'

Although Maddie appeared reluctant to make eye-contact, Michael stood defiantly over Steve with an evil-looking smile across his face.

'Ah, we have moved on, I see. So who's the new man, Eva?'

'Just fuck off, Michael. I don't want to see you, so just leave.'

Quickly springing to his feet, Steve moved defensively beside me, and in his best macho voice asked Michael to, 'Just do what she says.'

Michael stood his ground with a bravado that I hadn't seen him show before. 'Or else what?' he asked.

'Listen, man, I don't want to fight anyone, just tryin' to keep the peace.'

Mortified, Maddie pulled at Michael's arm to leave, but he was having none of it.

'*No*,' he blasted. 'I want to see my daughter. Eva, give her to me. I want to hold her.'

Furious at the mere suggestion of him touching her, especially when he was so pumped up and aggressive, I just screamed, 'In your fucking dreams.' Then I turned to Steve and yelled again, 'Come on. We're getting outta here. I don't want to be near these scumbags . . .'

I'm not sure if it was the angry look that I gave to Maddie that enraged him, but as I brushed past them, Michael took it upon himself to grab my arm tightly and refused to let go.

'You're not going anywhere . . . *I want to hold my daughter, now.*'

'You're going to make me drop her, Michael . . .'

He tightened his grip further, and repeated his request again. 'Then just hand her over.' His eyes were cold, just like I remembered them being during our final arguments.

By now both our respective partners had become quite concerned at the situation, with Maddie trying to talk Michael down, and Steve trying to loosen Michael's grip on my arm.

'Let her go, man. Think of your daughter. You're only going to make things worse for yourself.'

After a minor scuffle, Michael calmed down and released my arm, which was now burning from his over-zealous clasp. He had turned into some sort of animal that I despised, and actually found repulsive. It was as if the old Michael I had fallen in love with, who had once been so gentle and caring, had gone. What did Maddie see in him? Fuck her. She had completely betrayed me, too. They were welcome to each other.

He'd have to fight me all the way to gain access to Daisy now. That was if he'd even bother to ask again. It had been the first time he'd seen her since he'd left the house, and that had been at least three months ago.

Obviously being fatherly didn't come naturally to him. Otherwise, they would have had Woody on the beach with them, too. It wasn't until Steve had driven us home and I had disappeared into the toilet that I finally let my emotions get the better of me. Although I had spent most of the last year crying my eyes out, I didn't want Steve to know what a basket-case I was.

I really had spent far too much of the last year crying over Michael. It would have to stop. Right now; today. I wasn't going to let that bastard ruin one more day of my life. And it was up to me and no one else to make it happen.

11

The Tiswells' family summer house in Terryglass was a paradise haven. It had the best views of the river Shannon and I woke up each morning to the sight of happy holidaymakers in their rented cruisers whizzing past, no doubt en route to crash into unsuspecting private boats at the nearby harbours.

It was Sunday morning on the June bank holiday and I was feeling a million dollars: thoroughly relaxed, spoilt and totally chuffed that I had at least another thirty hours or so before I had to worry about returning to normality.

This had been the best Irish summer we'd seen in years, and at chez Tiswell it felt like a mini Med, except that the locals spoke the same language as we did – or at least a version of it.

Belonging to builders, the house was understandably tricked-out with music in the showers, TVs in the bathrooms, indoor saunas, and of course an outdoor hot tub; it was the ultimate party pad and I always loved being invited down. Pretending I was Sue Ellen from an episode of *Dallas*, I'd swan around the place imagining I was drunk, and occasionally throwing something at a wall for effect – of course hoping that said object would bounce, and not end up breaking anything expensive.

Although I was worrying about Daisy's hearing, as I had been told by the doctor that there was up to an 80 per cent chance of her being deaf, I put all negative thoughts out of my head and fully immersed myself in the holiday spirit.

Parker, Jeff, Lisa and some new bloke called Philip were all in entertainment mode, as of course was Steve – 'my Steve', as he was now known. Before we realized what was happening, he had slipped as easily into my friends' lives as into mine, and now we had become one big, crude, happy family.

Within a very short space of time he'd got himself up to speed on all the in-jokes. He'd learned to ignore my diva moments – which were rare, to be fair – and even had a handle on Parker, who, despite himself, had almost become more of a pal of Steve's than I was. They were closer than I would have liked at times.

Obediently, Daisy had fallen back asleep after her morning bottle, so Steve and I were enjoying some lazy time in bed. I could hear the others mooching about in the kitchen, but breakfast could wait. Our pillow-talk was proving much more fulfilling.

'Emm, listen, there's something I've been meaning to tell you.' Steve pulled a serious face, like he was addressing a courtroom.

'Oh yeah?' I sat up in the bed and fixed my hair. 'What's that, then?'

'I don't want to sound corny or anything, but you truly have made me one of the happiest guys alive.'

'OK. That's a good thing, right?'

'For sure. And up until now I've found it hard to express just how much you mean to me. And I think we need to take a major step forward in our relationship.'

In a moment of fear, I felt compelled to interrupt him. 'Please don't tell me you're about to propose. I'm still married, and my heart can't handle frights like that. I couldn't be happier either, but . . .'

'Whoah, slow down there. That's a lovely idea and all, but one step at a time, Miss Eva. Can you button that beautiful mouth of yours for one minute, please? There's something very important I want to say.'

'Sorry, I'll stop talking now.'

'Good. Cause this is difficult enough as it is.'

'Well?'

'All right, what I wanted to say was . . . I'm just gonna blurt it out now . . .'

'Well?' My impatience was getting the better of me.

'I love you, all right? There, I said it. I love you, Miss Eva Valentine. Phew, that's a relief.'

Relieved myself, I planted a big kiss on his lips and said proudly, 'I love you, too. I was hoping you'd say it first. I've been dying to say it for ages, now.'

'Well, now that this little awkward moment is out of the way, please feel free to say it as much as you like. I certainly plan on saying it a lot.'

'Ha! You're sooo kind. I love you. I love you. I love youuu.'

He pulled me across the bed and we looped the

sheets as we shared a passionate kiss. It was hard to believe that I was in an exciting new relationship after everything that had happened. I had been so sure that I was destined to end up on the scrapheap, but no, I was in love with this great guy, who seemed to love my daughter as much as he loved me. It couldn't have been sweeter. And if that wasn't enough, the sex was great, too! The long journey I had had to take to get to this point seemed to be fading away into insignificance.

As if sensing Mommy was having a special morning, Daisy slept in till 11 a.m., so by the time the three of us emerged, washed and grinning from ear to ear, papers and croissants had been bought, and all we had to do was hand Daisy to Lisa and sit down with Parker and Lisa's new boyfriend, Philip.

'You two are looking pleased with yourselves . . .' Parker was angling for information. He could tell we were extra happy.

'And what if we are? Are we not allowed to be cheery on a beautiful Sunday morning?'

'I know you, missy. What's happened? What's that Steve fella done to make you so smiley?'

I tried to fob him off with, 'You wouldn't want to know . . .' But he wasn't having any of it. Getting in on the act, Lisa whooshed Daisy through the air like a kite and cooed, 'Was Steve doing naughty things to your mommy? Was he? Was he now?' And Daisy waved her arms about in response.

'Eh, actually,' interrupted Steve, 'since you're all so interested, I told Eva I loved her.'

Collectively the group went, 'Wooooooo.'

'Yes, it's our first milestone. And I'm so glad that you're all here to share this day with us.'

Compelled to dispute his honesty, I shouted, 'Liar . . .' through a mouthful of coffee. 'That's not what you said a minute ago . . .'

'Yes, thank you, Eva, never mind what I said earlier. That was just a weak moment of nakedness. I simply didn't want to leave the bed. But now that we're up, we can all enjoy one big love-in. Agreed?'

His enthusiasm was infectious, and we all chimed in again, 'Agreed!'

After breakfast, 'the unlikely lads', as they had titled themselves, took off for a wander down the town, otherwise recognized as the two pubs and art gallery. Lisa, Daisy and myself happily smothered ourselves in Factors 4 and 50+ and talked boys; we had sufficiently exhausted my big moment with Steve, and Lisa was halfway through telling me about Philip's crazy flicking trick with his tongue, when the boys came banging back through the door.

'Relax, ladies,' squealed Parker. 'We're gonna give you both an afternoon off from the cooking. I'm gonna fire up the barbecue and we shall eat meat. Cause let's face it, we're all big fans.'

He was weighed down with a heavy-looking plastic bag of frozen stuff, which he'd obviously bought at the very Oirishy one-stop-shop stroke pub stroke restaurant stroke petrol pump; the men set about firing up the jumbo barbecue, which they seemed to find strangely difficult, considering they were wielding matches and lighters and placing them over highly flammable coals.

Twenty minutes and several scrunched-up news-papers later Parker was the only one left trying to get the coals to burn. 'Has my poof run out of puff?' I asked, hoping not to demoralize him too much.

'Yes, I hate to admit it, but this just about has me beat. I don't suppose you have any bright ideas how to get it started? Maybe you could scrape that sharp tongue of yours off some stones and make a few sparks?'

'Or maybe . . . Just give me two minutes.' I disappeared off to the garage, having had an actual spark of genius, and returned moments later yielding an extremely large leaf-blower.

'What the fuck?' Parker, along with the rest of the group, was puzzled. 'What am I suppose to do with that – burn it?'

'No. Don't be stupid. You use it to fire up the flames. I saw it once on YouTube. It worked a treat.'

Ten minutes later, Steve had the barbecue roaring away, thanks to the blower. Of course after about a minute of holding it, Parker had passed the reins to Steve, complaining, 'I never thought my wrist would be too weak for a blow-job!' He'd then turned to Lisa all macho, and said, 'Get me a beer, Princess. Daddy has done enough hard work for today, methinks!'

With the posse on the brink of starvation, some extra-flamed frozen burgers were passed about, and even if we had been handed Angus steaks cooked by Richard Corrigan they wouldn't have tasted better.

With Steve and Philip at the burping stage, and Parker and Jeff in a 'Men are such pigs' mood, a text beeped through on my phone, and strangely I got a weird vibe about it. For some peculiar reason I felt that I shouldn't look at it, but being a girl that was never going to be an option.

And there like a symbol of the devil, Michael's name flashed up on my phone. I went to put it back down, because I knew before I opened it that he was going to upset me, but I couldn't fight the urge to look.

'I'm putting the house on the market,' it read. 'The sign will go up this week. I can't imagine you'll be homeless for very long. You managed OK before I ever came along.'

His words hit me like a ton of bricks. This was so much worse than when he'd cut off my money. He wanted to kick Daisy and me out of our home, like he was some evil landlord. Just because he'd found it easy to leave didn't mean I would. I'd fight it. Surely I had some rights? Even squatters' rights?

'Everything OK?' asked Steve, all concerned.

I thought for a moment, but chose not to divulge the text. 'Ah, just work stuff.' Although my heart felt like it was being ripped out, there was no point in ruining everyone else's day. I would keep this information to myself for now . . . or at least do my best to keep it in for a while.

As calmly as I could, and donning a fake smile to ward off any curiosity from the group, I wrote back, 'Don't forget I own half. No sale can go through without my permission.'

As always, Michael's text beeped back promptly. 'Don't fight me. You'll lose. You will get your share. Then we will both be free.' Free? What did he mean by free? Was he not going to look for joint custody of Daisy? Did he never want to see her again? How come I never realized what a cold-hearted bastard he was? I had been so blind.

I quickly threw my phone into a nearby nappy bag. I couldn't bear to hold it any more. His callous words made it suddenly feel repulsive.

'Are you sure you're OK, hon?' Steve could sense that I was hiding something but I wasn't going to give away any details. We were on our holidays until tomorrow. And not even my impending eviction was going to ruin that for me.

'I'm fine. Let's just leave it. OK?'

'OK. But if there's anything I can . . .'

'There's not.'

'For sure. Hey, can I get you another drink? You look like you're running low.'

'Thank you. Oh, and I love you.'

'Love you, too.'

Although it was so weird to say it, and hear it back from Steve, it instantly cheered me up. I was getting better at hiding my emotions now – my teary moments, to be more specific – and worked hard at stopping disappointments rule my day.

From now on my motto would be: I'm responding, not reacting. And today's response would be denial. I was going to fake happy. And maybe, if I was successful enough, I might even convince myself of the fact.

It took two hours before I finally cracked. Despite my best efforts I kept snapping at everyone, and it was becoming painfully obvious to all that something was up.

'What is wrong with you? You've been a bitch all afternoon.' As always Parker got straight to the point.

'Yeah. I preferred you before you were in love,' teased Lisa.

'So did I,' whispered Steve, with puppy-dog eyes that begged to know what was wrong.

Unable to hold it in any longer, and almost fit to burst, I stood up like a mad evangelist to expel my demons. 'Michael is selling the house. I'm going to be homeless. Is everyone happy now?'

As the group's jaws collectively dropped, Steve turned to Lisa and asked, 'Can you keep an eye on Daisy, please?' Then he turned to me, scooped me off my feet and ran towards the bedroom like a rugby player trying to score a try.

Not in the mood for games, I put up a struggle, but no matter how much I protested, he refused to allow me to break free. 'Let me be your hero,' he whispered. 'You said you love me, so trust me for a minute.'

Of course I couldn't argue with him. All that women claim to want is to be swept off their feet and rescued from trouble. Now I had a real-life prince in Steve doing just that, yet there was a large part of me that simply wanted to tell him to fuck off and give me some space. What was wrong with me? Was I still programmed to self-destruct? As he continued with his white-knight impression, I fought my frustration and held my tongue, for fear of saying something that would really hurt him.

I was doing my best to balance my mood, though it wasn't easy. I was a diva by nature, and because very few of my relationships had ever worked out in the past, no one had ever stood up to me. Mentally I was walking an emotional tightrope, so I kept counting to ten, silently, in the hope that I wouldn't bite Steve's head off. And although I nearly snapped at him out of sheer irritation as he banged me off our bedroom door, I somehow managed to button my lip long enough for him to calm my frayed nerves.

Once he had plonked me on the bed, he placed his hand firmly over my mouth and asked me to listen.

'This is not the end of the world,' he said. 'You knew that it was coming. You spoke about it before.'

I tried to speak, but he kept his hand in place.

'Listen . . . Instead of seeing this as a catastrophe, why not see it as a new start? A fresh beginning, if that's not too American.' Feeling slightly less volatile, I signalled to my muzzle with my eyes, asking him to remove it. With a warm smile, he did so, and gently kissed me on the lips. 'Let me take care of my girls. I know you can't see past the anger right now, but I'm here for you and Daisy. And I really think it's time you talked to a divorce lawyer. Let me—'

Not wanting him to talk himself into a slap, I rudely interrupted his spiel. 'Can I talk, please? Thank you for being my fairy tale, all ready to rescue me, but I need to be able to vent a little. I'm not used to this attentiveness. So, please, just give me a minute . . .'

'For sure.'

'Stop fucking saying that. You know I hate it when you say that. I don't want to be reminded of any of the asshole Michaels that I've had the misfortune to know.'

'I'm sorry . . .'

'Grrrr. Stop being so nice. It's nauseating.'

Clearly hurt by my venom, he pulled back a little, before asking, 'Would you like me to leave? Should I ask one of the others to be with you?'

'Noooo, just relax for two minutes. Let me just . . . just explode for a second. I'm a woman, for God's sake. We can hold secrets for years, but when they come out, we need to be able to give out a little. That's what we do. So don't take anything I say right now personally. OK?'

'Of course . . .'

Fact was, he was crowding me, but he didn't deserve abuse. If I was being really honest with myself, I would have admitted that I still had strong feelings for my husband, Michael, and that, if anything, he was the only man that I really wanted to hug me and tell me that everything would be all right.

With my head spinning, I gave Steve a sympathy kiss and asked him if I could just have five minutes to lie down. And that I'd see him back out in the garden as soon as I'd had a little chat with myself. Reluctantly he dragged himself away, and headed towards the door. 'You still love me, don't you?' His face was by now drained of expression.

Mustering some positive energy, I smiled back. 'Sure I do. See you in a bit.' No sooner had he gone when

a massive wave of guilt hit me. I hated having a temper, but I couldn't stop myself being cruel sometimes.
Imagine getting annoyed at someone for being too
nice! I needed a lobotomy . . . Or at the very least some
anger-management classes.

As another wave of rage hit me, I grabbed a pillow,
stuffed my head underneath it and screamed till my
tonsils hurt. I'm not sure if the pillow muffled my cries,
but I did feel a whole lot better – even if everyone
outside felt worse because of it. Part of me was yelling
about the fear of the unknown – my future, in other
words. Another part was expressing the pain that I still
harboured over being dumped, and the fact that two
of the people I was closest to had abandoned me, and
shown total disregard for my feelings. Yet another part
was livid that I didn't have my phone with me so I
could scream expletives at Michael, or even better at
his mailbox.

While Steve was *nice*, we didn't have a real history
yet, so it was easy for me to brush him off like he was
insignificant. Truth was, though, he was more than
important to me. If I didn't mess things up, he could be
my lifeline to hold on to during the rocky times that lay
ahead. I would have to apologize to him immediately.
Before he recognized my horrible diva traits for what
they were – the rantings of a spoilt brat – and decided
he would be better off with a less volatile woman. Ten
chewed fingernails later, I re-emerged into the garden
to see the group acting normally, as if nothing had
happened.

'Ah, there she is,' acknowledged Jeff. 'Do you

fancy the last burger? Parker has been trying to scoff it, claiming chef's rights, but I thought you might be hungry.'

'Thanks, Jeff. I'm actually starving.'

And with a quick hug from Steve, and a few knowing smiles from Lisa and Parker, my eviction drama was forgotten and put to the back of everyone's minds.

They all tried their best to distract me that night, with Lisa even appearing from the kitchen wearing nothing on top but strips of rashers across her chest. Dancing around the final burning embers of the barbecue she teased, 'Smoky bacon, anyone?' At which we all fell about the place laughing.

Maybe the outlook wasn't so bad after all. With the country in recession it would take ages to sell the house, and by then who knows? I could be screaming to make that 'fresh start' with Steve.

Poor Steve. Thank God he was just a man and couldn't read my mind. The words that I'd said weren't half as hurtful as those that I had quietly thought. I'd be a fool not to try and make a go of things with him. I'd just have to be careful to do it for the right reasons. And not just out of desperation.

What a difference a day makes. That morning I had almost burst with joy when he'd told me he loved me, and then after one simple text my whole world had been thrown up in the air, and fallen back down around me in pieces.

When I returned to Dublin tomorrow I could start wondering if I really loved Steve. Or if I simply loved the idea of being in love. Tonight, though, I would just hold my tongue and stop messing with other people's heads.

A girl could only handle so many disappointments in one day.

Sure enough, a Savills signpost arrived in my front garden by Wednesday. The words 'For Sale' cut me like a knife each time I looked at them.

There was something so real about it. I couldn't vocalize to Steve how painful it was for me. He just kept repeating all the positives connected with the sale, but I didn't want to be positive. I wanted to immerse myself in the sadness of it all for a bit. My marriage and my one-time dream was reaching an end: surely I could be allowed to wallow? Just for a few private moments . . .

But it was Friday afternoon when I finally cracked. The mere sight of the bloody thing through my living-room window sent me into such a rage that I ran out the door with a sweeping-brush and started battering it with all the power I could muster. Like some mad ole wan, I bashed the 'For Sale' sign like it had attacked me. But no matter how hard I tried to topple it, it continued to stand tall and proud.

My palms burning from the wooden handle, I abandoned the sweeping-brush, and tried a simple hands-on approach. I jumped up on my garden wall and swung out at the signpost like I was some caged and deranged monkey that had taken to violence after a long spell in quarantine. I was going to, errrrr, move . . . this fucking . . . signpost . . . ahhh, if it was . . . the last thing . . . I . . . ahhh, did . . . Ah ha!

After one final tug the signpost crashed to the ground, and I danced a victory dance on it, but that somehow wasn't gratifying enough. Although it lay limply on the grass underneath my feet, it still annoyed me. I felt it was looking at me and laughing. The only solution was to burn it.

So back into the house I went, waving at Monica from two houses down, who was wearing one of her many concerned and nosy expressions, and returned two minutes later armed with a box of matches and a bottle of Sambucca.

'Afternoon, Monica. Don't mind me, I'm just tidying up the garden.'

As always she took a step back as if to pretend she hadn't been staring, and I continued with my demolition.

By now there was almost smoke bellowing out my nostrils I was so pumped up, and without caution I threw off the cap from the bottle and vigorously splashed the Sambucca all over the signpost. With the bottle empty I took several matches out of the box and struck them alight. 'Take that, you bastard,' I said, as I flung the matches on to the alcohol-covered signpost.

Instantly it exploded in flames, and like a child from *Lord of the Flies* I whooped with joy at the destruction.

Unfortunately as soon as the booze burnt off, my signpost bonfire ceased to exist, with the evil words 'For Sale' still sneering up at me.

Just like Parker and his barbecue, I was quite clearly useless at igniting a fire, so with a defeated sigh I dragged myself back into the house, slammed the door behind me and set about admitting defeat.

By 7.35 p.m. I had received a text from Michael asking, 'What have you done with the sign?'

Annoyed that he had interrupted my viewing of *Coronation Street*, I blasted back, 'House cold. Chopped up and used for firewood.'

Immediately he replied, 'Don't fight me, Eva. You won't win.'

Of course that was like a red rag to a bull, so I texted back, 'Don't push it, or else I'll turn this house into a pigsty and no one will want to set foot in the place.'

Maybe it was because I was frustrated that he didn't text back and continue the argument. Or maybe I was just turning into a lush? But within the space of an hour I had polished off an entire bottle of Moët that had been at the back of the fridge, leaving me with a goo for more.

The following morning I woke with a massive headache after Steve texted to say he'd be calling over about 10 a.m. to 'Pick up his girls'. I had forgotten we had planned having a family day at the zoo, and I knew if I didn't find some painkillers quick, this trip could end up becoming extremely unpleasant for everyone.

As I pushed back the curtains on my bedroom window, my eye was immediately drawn to the 'For Sale' sign, which was once again vertical, and just where it had been before. If the grass hadn't been a tad singed, I wouldn't even have believed my moment of madness had ever happened.

Of course I just laughed, and went off to check on Daisy and raid the medicine drawer for drugs.

Predictably the monkey house meant monkey business from Steve. Inspired by their primitive ways, he felt compelled to drag his knuckles off the ground and leap from cage to cage, trying to keep a smile on my face. It was working, but it took as much concentrated effort from me as from him. Unfortunately my headache hadn't left me yet, but laughter did seem the best medicine. And until it had its effect, I faked it . . . Hey, it wasn't the first time, and it certainly wouldn't be the last.

'Are you sure you're a barrister? Cause I'm really starting to doubt your credentials for the job.'

'Why? Aren't barristers allowed to be devilishly handsome, and possess great wit and charm?'

'And there I thought you were about to crawl into one of those cages and start mating with the locals . . .'

'Well, I'd much rather show my banana to you than any of those hairy ladies. Fancy getting primal? I'm happy to go bareback if you are.'

'Ha! I'm sure you are. Come here and give us a kiss, anyway. You can feck off if you think I'm getting any of my pink bits out as a side-show for you or these monkeys.'

So there, in the monkey house in Dublin Zoo, surrounded by at least twenty screaming kids banging on the windows, we kissed like old lovers. His lips seemed to complement mine, and his tongue didn't invade my mouth, but instead filled it with love. It was hard to believe that a kiss could stop me in time. But it did.

Whatever his magic was, he transported me from my cranky place and swept me off my feet again. I really would have to stop questioning my emotions and run with this guy. I was nearly sure I did love him. Despite all the resistance I put up, I couldn't help myself but fall deeper in comfort – I mean love – with him. The anger and frustration caused by Michael wasn't healthy. I needed to let go faster than I was. A man who kissed me this way deserved to be loved back. And not treated with complacency.

'Thank you.' I stared straight into his eyes and squeezed his hand as I spoke.

'For what?' His eyes danced as he waited to be praised.

'For your expert monkey impression . . .'

'And?'

'That great kiss . . . And I'm sorry if I've been a little odd. I'm just feeling the pressure a bit with the house.'

'That's OK. I love you, and I'm gonna make you love me, too.'

'*I do love you,*' I protested.

'Well, let's just say I'll make you love me more. You just need more time. I'm aware of that. I've just reached the truly, madly, stalker-stage a little sooner than you, but that's OK. I know you'll catch up.' As we kissed again, amid the hustle and bustle of lunchtime monkey madness, I realized that although fairy tales didn't exist, happiness could. And despite all those years I'd spent slagging off the merits of a nice guy, versus a bastard, I was finally letting my soft and gooey side fall for kindness.

Maybe it was age? Or maybe I was just feeling desperate? Either way, this was beginning to feel real . . . solid . . . and, I suppose, normal. Poor Steve should be careful what he wished for. If he wasn't careful I'd revert back to wearing scummy tracksuits, sporting hairy legs and breaking wind in bed. On second thoughts, I was nowhere near that comfortable yet. I'd test him with wearing no make-up in the mornings, and see if he didn't go running for the hills. And if he managed to stick around for a second bowl of Crunchy Nut Cornflakes over breakfast, I'll know I'd nabbed myself a keeper . . .

After 189 new images on the camera, which covered various poses of Daisy in front of rhinos, Daisy in front of sea lions and Daisy, Mommy and Steve feeding the ducks – courtesy of passing Japanese students – we were back at the house and getting ready for a night on the town.

After much coercion, my mum had agreed to collect Daisy and keep her for the night, with the strict condition that I'd be over to hers by 10.30 a.m. so that she'd be free to go to 11 o'clock Mass. After much flirting by Mum, I managed to secure both herself and Daisy safely in the car, and waved them down the road. From the second my mum had laid eyes on Steve she had fallen in love with him. 'A barrister,' she'd gushed. 'And what an accent! Why couldn't you have found him first and married him instead of that other bastard . . .'

While I couldn't agree with her more, her infatuation

irritated the hell out of me, and the fact that Steve played up to the attention she showered on him bugged me even more.

But I knew that I was being unreasonable, so I forced it to the back of my mind, and picked up the flirting where my mother had left off. 'You certainly have a way with the Valentine ladies,' I gushed on my return. 'She's so excited she'll probably go back and rape my father, now. And that man has got high blood pressure. I just hope his heart can take it . . .'

'Well, I'm glad that my charm is working on some-one. It gives me hope that I can melt your ice-maiden heart . . . You've been proving quite the challenge, Miss Eva.'

'Don't say that.'

'It's true. I'm not sure if I'm making headway or not. Some moments I feel like I'm being allowed in, and then the rest of the time I feel like you put up this barrier and I have to try to scale the Great Wall of China.'

'Well, I'm sorry. No, truly I am. Can I make it up to you? I'd really like to make it up to youuu.' I purred for extra effect.

'Oh yeah? Give me your best shot, then.'

'Well, it's just I was thinking how well you looked in your suit.'

'Yeah?'

'But I was also thinking that . . . well, that you might look even better out of it.' As I spoke, I deliberately used the same words I had when we'd first met, and slipped his beige linen jacket off his shoulders and on to the floor. Then I began pulling his casual tee up over his head.

'OK, this is promising,' cooed Steve as his tee popped off his head.

'And I was also thinking that these trousers of yours are a little too creased already, so maybe . . .' I unbuttoned his trousers and pulled down the zip so they fell to the floor with a dull thud from the keys and the wallet in his pockets.

'OK, my little sex kitten, what next?'

'Well, we could take this to the bedroom?'

'Or maybe I could just pop you on the countertop here and we could christen the kitchen?'

'*No!*' I screamed without even thinking.

'Fair enough. It was only a suggestion. I didn't realize you had such an aversion to sex in kitchens . . . I'll make a mental note to self.'

'Sorry . . . I didn't mean to sound so forceful . . . It's just I'd really like to take you somewhere where I don't prepare Daisy's formula – so I could really enjoy ravaging your body.'

'Why didn't you say? Lead me to your den of choice, and let the ravaging begin!'

As I took Steve by the hand, who was now wearing nothing but a pair of cotton boxer shorts which bulged from his arousal, I made a determined effort to erase the image of me having sex with handyman Dave on that same worktop.

Memories of that evening still made me feel cheap and nasty. And the mere suggestion of re-creating that situation had freaked me out. I knew by the way Steve held my hand that he was suspicious about my reaction. So I would have to be extra enthusiastic to distract him, and make sure this evening stayed on course for fun, and didn't turn into a big heart-to-heart on why I was such a broken and flawed character.

Steve had tried to get me to open up my heart to him a few times recently, but I just couldn't face it. I was still a big believer in burying the pain. If it stayed hidden long enough, it just might disappear.

Quickly deciding that having sex in the bed would be far too dull, I made the swift decision to pull Steve on to the landing floor, and pinned his arms down by their wrists.

'Now, sir . . . there's no way you can argue your way out of this fix. I, the defendant, have reasonable doubt that you have been a very naughty boy. And it is my duty to punish you for such behaviour.'

'Yes, yes, I have been very naughty. I want to repent all my sins . . .'

'Ha! Easy does it. I was aiming for an authority figure, not a feckin' nun or priest.'

'Oh, sorry, ma lady. Or Your Honour.'

'That's better.'

'Listen, a minute ago you were up on your own charges.'

'What?'

'Forget it. Pretend I said nothing . . . Where were we? Something about me being a naughty boy? I'm sure I was promised some ravaging?'

'Indeed. Now shut up and stop talking.'

As I moved my left hand off his wrist and on to his

mouth to gag him, I began to kiss around his belly, which was incredibly taut and firm, and, to my great satisfaction, unblemished by hair. As I danced my tongue down towards the edge of his boxers, my flow was interrupted by a loud ringing coming from my house phone in the hall.

Muffled by my hand, Steve urged me to 'Eve it!' So after a momentary pause, I rejoined where I had left off and started to lift the top of his boxers with my tongue.

About a minute later, just when things were beginning to get interesting, the phone rang again, and Steve screamed once more through my hands, 'Ruck off!'

'Should I get it?' I asked, worried that it might be my mother having a problem.

'Noooo.'

'But it could be about Daisy. I'm sorry.'

Leaving a very disappointed and light-headed Steve at the top of the stairs, I ran down and grabbed the phone, only to hear a delighted-sounding Parker at the other end of the line. 'Hiya. What took you so long?'

Speechless, I just let out a heavy sigh and cast my gaze back up to Steve, who was now sitting up and scratching his head with bemusement.

'Well, hello to you too, missus. I'm in great form, thanks for asking.'

'Parker,' I could see Steve's eyes rolling into the back of his head, 'Steve and I were kinda in the middle of something.'

'Ah, big deal. You two are always shagging. Are you not bored of it yet?'

'Eh, no. Sorry, did you ring up to enquire about my sexual habits, or was there something else I could help you with this evening?'

'Oops, we are tetchy. Well, actually, I suggest you put some clothes on quick.'

'Why?'

'Cause I'm walking up your driveway as we speak. Hello?' Through the stained glass in the front door I could see a figure waving. 'Yes, that's me the other side. So you've got approximately thirty seconds to make yourself decent, and then if you haven't opened up, I'll use the spare keys you gave me for safe keeping. Thirty . . . twenty-nine . . . twenty-eight.' I hung up the phone and ran into the kitchen to grab Steve's clothes, and threw them back up the stairs to him. Although he didn't reply I could hear the frustration in his breathing but chose to ignore it. The moment would pass, and he'd be down laughing and joking with Parker in a matter of minutes.

It turned out Parker had just bought himself a vintage Aston Martin and was so hyper he had to show it off to all of us. Lisa had already been doorstepped in the same fashion, while enjoying some carnal pleasures with old regular Francis, and now I was the next pal on Parker's list who needed to show him some attention. Needless to say, Steve, being just a boy at heart, quickly cheered up once Parker offered to take him for a spin.

'Can I, really?' His eyes lit up like he'd just met Santa. And then the two of them were gone, and I was left standing in front of the hall mirror reapplying my make-up, realizing that I wasn't the only person or object that could give Steve a horn.

Eventually the born-again children arrived back, grinning from ear to ear. Butched-up Parker started spewing macho terms like 'Great bit of poke in her' and 'Whatta machine! Better than sex!'

At which a thoughtful Steve turned around to me and gushed, 'Well, it comes a close second when it's *instead* of sex . . .'

In a bizarre twist to events, Steve and I had gone to Café en Seine for a few drinks after our meal, instead of Ron Blacks as planned. It was a decision that Steve immediately regretted the second we walked through the door. Why? Because as soon as we got inside we bumped into Steve's old mate and my ex-fella, Michael. New York Michael, as he used to be known.

He'd once been extremely significant in my life. And although he was just another guy now, in the lengthening list of men who had broken my heart, he looked so well that I couldn't help but lust after him like old times. I wasn't sure if I was trying to prove something to myself – like did I still have that old diva allure? But without thinking it through, I began to flirt like I was a single woman without any responsibilities.

'What do you think you are doing?' questioned Steve, his face puce with anger. With the shock of seeing Michael, I had knocked back several Cosmos in quick succession, and was now suitably plastered. I had also started dancing suggestively in front of Michael in a bid to show him what he was missing, which understandably wasn't going down well with Steve.

What I hadn't realized until our chance reunion was that since Steve and I had properly started dating, he had refused to accept any further phone calls from his old New York mate, and tensions were running high between them both.

Although any sober person – or, should I say, any decent human being – would have taken their amazing boyfriend away from such a stressful situation, I, on the other hand, pretended to give a shit about their friendship. I insisted that Steve hang around to, 'Work through your issues. It's not healthy to hold grudges.' Needless to say, at first yours truly just wanted to spice up the evening by making Michael jealous; but as the evil vodka started to work its magic, I turned into the old Eva the diva, and made a complete fool of myself.

'They call it danshing, Shteve. Youuu should try it shometime. Great *air-obic* exshershize, apparently.' .

'Eh, excuse me, but have you forgotten you're now going steady with me?'

'Ohhh, lighten up . . . I'm jusht 'aving fun.'

'That's my point, you look like you're having a little too much fun with your *ex*-boyfriend for my liking. Call me possessive, but I'd kinda prefer if you didn't continue your dirty dance with Michael. I'm finding it kinda embarrassing.'

'Shince when did *you* become my father?'

'Excuse me?'

'Youuu're not my husband. Youuu don't get tooo tell me what to do.'

'Eva, you're drunk, so I'll just ignore your hurtful comments. Let's just go. You've had enough already.'

As Steve tried to manoeuvre me away from the group, I instantly became more stroppy.

'Taaaake your hanshe off me,' I slurred. 'I shaid I wash 'aving fun. Now jusht leave me alone, pleashe.'

Furious, he took one look at me, glared angrily at Michael, and stormed off in the direction of the door.

In my stupidity I whooped with laughter, which I'm sure he heard as he left, and carried on flirting with Michael, who was clearly loving having wound-up his ole pal.

'You're still as crazy as ever, Eva. I missed you.'

'Youuu're full of shit,' I blasted, spilling some of my drink on Michael's shirt. 'But youuu're shtill cute. So kish me.'

Laughing off my intoxicated state, he looked to the door to see if there was any sign of his former friend before pulling me closer into his now damp chest.

'But what about Steve, then?'

'Fuck Shteve.'

'That's one of my best mates you're dissing.'

I took a drunken moment to assess his statement, before staring into his eyes and asking, 'Dooo you not find me attractive any more?'

'For sure, I think you're still a big ride,' he teased in his worst Oirish accent. 'And I'd love to take you up the back lane and shag your brains out.'

'You were alwaysh sho ro-mantic,' I gushed, while once again spilling some more of my drink over his now very stained white linen shirt.

'So are you gonna dump the loser, or wot?'

'Dat's not very nice.'

'Listen, Eva, you're either up for it or you're not. Don't act the prick-tease with me just to wind up Steve. He's left the building, so it's now up to you as to what happens next. Do you wanna revisit the old times? Or do you wanna run off after Nancy boy and play happy families?'

'I . . . emm, I . . .'

'Well?'

'I jusht need to use the . . .' I pointed downstairs while trying to suppress a belch.

I wasn't exactly in control of my speech or actions, but Michael didn't seem fazed.

'I'll order another beer while I'm waiting. Go do whatever you must, and we'll head off when you get back.'

With a wink and an inebriated smile, I grabbed my bag off the floor and headed in the direction of the toilet.

I'm not sure how long he waited for me, if he did at all. Because instead of running off and making one of the most foolish mistakes of my life, I just about managed to find the safety of a toilet, locked myself in, and didn't leave until some kind member of female staff woke me while doing her final checks of the night, and then went one further and offered to personally drive me home.

I vaguely remember her offering to put me to bed, before I stuffed a €50 note into her hand – which I most definitely couldn't afford – and thanked her from 'da bottom of my 'art!'

As always, Eva Valentine, classy to the end . . .

12

'Marry me! I don't think you realize how much you mean to me. So let's just do it, what do you say?'

For a Monday morning, this was a fairly weighty question, and not one I was too enamoured with.

'Hello, Eva, are you there?' Steve's voice reeked of desperation, which, again, turned me off him even more. 'Eva?'

'Yessss, I'm here. Steve . . . I just . . . Jeez, like what am I meant to say to that?'

'Well, *yes* might be nice!'

'Have we not discussed this before? I'm already feckin' married. There are laws about doing it twice. And anyway, we've barely known each other a wet weekend. Most normal people date for a few years, and *then* think about getting engaged.'

'So, what if we do things a little bit quicker? OK, so you're still officially married, but wouldn't it be nice if you were going about wearing a beautiful engagement ring that I'd bought you? I feel a little shopping trip to Tiffany's coming on.'

'The only shopping trip I'm making is to Lidl's later

for washing powder. Cop yourself on, Steve. You have not thought this through. This is irrational behaviour. Not even if George Clooney asked me the same question could I consider it. I'm already married. I already have a very nice engagement ring that I don't wear, and I really don't want another one, thank you . . . Now, I'm sorry for being harsh, but this is too much at 7.46 on a Monday morning. If you knew me at all, you'd have waited at least till past noon to ask me anything.'

'I've been awake all night thinking about it.'

'Listen . . .' Realizing I was trampling all over his heart, I softened my voice to try and calm the tension which I had helped create. 'Steve, I'm sorry, it's just that I thought you knew I had no intention of getting married again. Where has this come from, all of a sudden? The last time I saw you, you were storming out the front door of Café en Seine.'

I waited for an answer, but all I could hear was Steve's heavy breathing.

'I can't argue with you, Eva. People pay me to debate, but I can't do it with you.'

'I don't want to argue with you, hon, I just want an easy life.'

'You wanted Michael last Saturday . . .'

'Ahhh . . .' The penny finally dropped for me. This was a jealousy proposal. 'So, this is your knee-jerk reaction? Asking me to marry you. Do you not think it's a little excessive?'

'This played out much better in my head,' explained Steve, now sounding pissed off. 'Then again, I do have a problem with putting you on a pedestal.'

'Do you? I mean, what's that supposed to mean?'

'Yes, I do.'

'Ohhh.'

'Yes, Eva, I somehow forget what a bitch you can be sometimes. But not for long. You always seem to kick me back into touch.'

With growing resentment on Steve's end of the phone line, and sheer terror on mine, I pretended that I could hear Daisy upstairs crying, and told him, 'I'll call you back in an hour or so.'

I could almost hear his ego whimpering as, humiliated and wounded, he whispered, 'Fine, but only if you really want to . . .'

Without wasting a minute, I dialled Parker's number, and although it rang only three times, he couldn't pick it up quick enough for me.

'The fool asked me to marry him.' My abrupt tone instantly sent my pink pal giddy.

'Who might that be? Mister April Fool? A fool with gold, or would that be just your old fool?'

'*Steve*, for fuck's sake. He wants to go shopping in Tiffany's! Bless him . . .'

'Doesn't he know you have numerous convictions for crimes against fashion? And that bigamy might just lock you up for life . . .'

'The mentaller is jealous.'

'Over what?'

'My flirting with New York Michael in Café en Seine on Saturday night.'

'Mmmm, I'm not sure who's the bigger fool in this situation, you or him.'

'Yes, I agree that was probably not one of my brightest moves . . .'

'Really? Do you not think?'

'Shut up. There's still certain men that you have a weakness for, too.'

'Speaking of which, Owen Murphy-Keane texted me the other day, saying that if I wanted to make it up to him I could buy him a pint in Toners.'

'Jeez, there is another fool.'

'Agreed. But a very cute one.'

'Parker, focus, what am I supposed to do about Steve? Can you talk to him?'

'And say what? Don't ever ask my friend to marry you again or else that's thirty-five minutes on the naughty step! Sorry, Eva, you're on your own with this one. Clearly your feminine charms are proving too much for the poor guy. Have you any spare tricks you can teach me? Jeff spends more time in the gym than working up a sweat with me these days.'

'Parker!!! I need help. Has my boyfriend gone nuts, or have I?'

'Easy, now. Quite clearly the pair of you have gone a little fruit 'n' nut, so let's just calm things down a little. Do you love him?'

'I don't want to get married again.'

'I didn't ask that. I asked did you love him?'

'Emm, I think so – or, at least, I thought so. But I'm not sure I even like him at the moment.'

'OK, that's understandable, but he's a good guy, Eva. Yes, he's obviously been dropping absinthe into his cocoa, but think about what you'd be losing if you chucked him.'

'I'm not the hapless vulnerable desperado I used to be, Parker. I'm working again, and . . .'

'And you're a single mum who's about to be turfed out of her home.'

'You have a point.'

'Come on, Eva, he's a good guy. Just set him straight that you're happy with how things are going, and that there's no need to rush the relationship. Don't do your usual and tell him to fuck off, and then hate yourself for it. Be nice to the chap. He's clearly besotted with ya . . . The fool!'

Real, heartfelt apologies are not easy. The words may be simple, yet I have always had a massive struggle with them passing my lips. But with my back against the wall with the Steve situation, I had no choice but to eat humble pie.

I had treated him appallingly, and pushed him to the brink of madness. So, leaving Daisy with her minder Jeanette, and with my tail firmly between my legs, I arrived up to Steve's apartment in Ballsbridge with a single red rose in one hand and a bottle of Moët in the other. Although I had keys to let myself in, I thought it best only to gain access to the building, and then surprise him with a knock at the door.

I must have spent five minutes fixing my hair and my outfit in front of Apartment 34, practising my 'I love you's and my 'I'm sorry's, before I mustered up the courage to ring the bell, but the second he actually did open the door, I felt like somebody had shone a big spotlight on me, and I had been transported to centre stage at *X Factor*!

Doing his best not to look surprised, Steve remained stony-faced as he waited for me to speak. And so there we stood staring at each other; the two of us paused in shock, both waiting for the other to break the silence.

As the discomfort factor reached a ten, I finally spluttered the words, 'I'm . . . sorry.'

Steve's face stayed cold. And his lips stayed closed.

'For . . . what happened in Café en Seine. For not calling you . . . For being . . . a bitch when you called earlier.'

Although I felt like I had thrown myself at his mercy, he didn't flinch, clearly feeling that he needed me to sweat a little longer.

'Steve, don't leave me hanging. Please, I meant it.'

'Meant what, exactly? That you'd rather be a lonely old spinster in a refuge for abandoned women than marry me? That you'd like to see me humiliated in front of an old friend, by deciding you'd rather shag him than me . . . What is it that you truly mean, Eva? Because I'm confused.'

Realizing that this wasn't going to be as straight-forward as I had hoped, I quickly decided I would have to up the apology or prepare to kiss this guy goodbye for good.

'You have every right to be angry with me.' I stared at the TV behind him as I spoke. 'I don't deserve you, and eh . . . I don't want to lose you.'

'And?'

My eyes immediately flicked back to his, at his totally dismissive response. 'Steve, can I come in? I don't really want to do this in your hallway.'

'For surrrr,' he purred, subtly trying to wind me up.

It was only when I walked into the living room and saw an open bottle of red wine and two glasses that I realized Steve was not quite the lonely man I'd thought he would be.

Placing my champagne and pathetic red rose on the coffee table beside the evidence, I looked towards the kitchen for signs of life.

'Sit down and make yourself comfortable, Eva,' instructed Steve in a sarcastic tone. 'I'm not sure where my friend has gone, but I'm sure they'll return promptly.'

'Eh, am I interrupting?' I asked with suspicion, not really wanting to hear Steve's answer.

'I don't know, Eva. Are you interrupting?'

'Steve, let's not argue. I've been a bitch all right. I'm sorry. I really am, but please let's just erase the last couple of days and get back on track. Can we?'

'Can we what?' asked the voice walking from the kitchen. It was Michael, New York Michael, and he was wearing the biggest grin across his face, and munching on popcorn.

'What the hell are you doing here?' While my brain had worked overtime trying to figure out if the extra wine glass was for another woman – or even Parker – never once did I suspect that it could be for Michael.

'That's not a very nice welcome, Eva. You were much more friendly to me on Saturday . . .'

I darted a look at Steve, but he just blanked me,

strolled up to Michael and grabbed a large handful of popcorn. They looked like brothers in arms.

'Well, what's wrong with your face? You look like you've been sucking on lemons . . .' Michael said.

Choosing to ignore his taunts, I grabbed Steve's arm and asked if we could step into the bedroom for a moment alone. Rebuffing me, he just shook his head and sat back down in front of his glass of wine, saying, 'No, thanks. I'd rather not, if that's OK with you.'

Frozen to the spot, I could feel my heart begin to pound out of my chest. My face blushed red with embarrassment, and my hands and eyes started to twitch as panic set in.

'Are you feeling all right?' asked Michael, in a knowingly comical tone. 'You're lookin' a tad fidgety.'

'Well, thank you for your analysis, doctor. Eh, listen, Steve, can we just have a word for one—'

'*No*, Eva! Say whatever it is here in front of Michael. We've no secrets, do we, Michael?'

'No, Steve, we've no secrets . . . Some popcorn, Eva?'

Blanking Michael, I looked at Steve, but it was clear that he didn't want anything to do with me. Obviously Michael had told him every detail from Saturday night. I couldn't blame him for being angry; I couldn't even justify my actions to myself. So what was the point in trying to lie my way out of it with him?

Feeling like I'd just stepped into a horror movie, I did what any self-respecting teen–scream queen would do, and ran, not even answering Michael. I wasn't sure if I wanted to vomit or cry, but I fled the apartment like I was being chased by a swarm of bees, and didn't stop running through stairs and doorways till I arrived back out into the fresh air, and buckled on a nearby cycle rail.

Bastards, I thought. Both of those guys had messed with my heart. Yet at the end of the day, men being men, they'd stuck together. I was ten minutes cursing them till I realized that I'd created the tragedy myself.

Once again, my self-destruct valve had been set to ten!

I couldn't understand how Steve could have changed so dramatically, though. He was the guy who had claimed he wanted to love, cherish and protect me. He had apparently loved me from the start, and while I could see how he'd be pissed off with me, not wanting to have any communication at all was very out of character. Surely I hadn't behaved that badly – had I? I'd just been a stupid drunk. I hadn't *actually* cheated on him . . . Maybe he just needed time?

How wrong could a woman be? Three months and five days later there'd still been no word from Steve. I'd even heard a rumour he'd gone back to New York.

In that time Daisy had had a minor operation on her ears, which I'm sure made a difference, as she became so much more alert afterwards. On the work front, I had been promoted, even though two freelancers had been let go from *YES!* And my house had had two more unfruitful viewings; partly due to my clever placement of broken-down toilet paper, which I first vigorously washed and then splashed around the overflow drain in the back garden. I would tell viewers, 'It seems to surface regularly,' and they'd soon make their excuses and leave.

Despite a few attempts by me at making contact with Steve, I'd been rebuffed, and so, after some far-from-gentle coaxing from Lisa, I was back on the town, and back on a man-hunt. Whether I wanted a man or not!

For the occasion, Lisa had even bought me a new dress. A stunning fringed one, Charleston-style, in ruby red. It was meant to ignite passion in men, so they would be on fire to flirt with me. Lisa called it a 'magic dress'. But I was beginning to see it as a curse. We had returned to the scene of my last man-disaster, Café en Seine, and things weren't going to plan.

'Stop laughing at me.'

'I'm sorry,' chuckled Lisa. 'It's just that every time I look at you, you're screaming, "*Don't touch me!*"'

'This fucking dress is driving me mad. Instead of getting hooked on to anyone decent, like James Bond over there, I keep attracting the losers.'

'That baldy fella looked nice,' she teased.

'Maybe to fellow-junkies; so much for my magic dress. Magnetic and bewitching powers to freaks and geeks only! Oh, and a couple of harmless nice guys who looked like they had been hooked by a she-devil and couldn't wait to get away from me. They almost tore half the fringing off the back trying to make their escape, as if I was some sort of gold-digger trying to snare them. I really should start wearing a sign that reads, "Been married – getting the divorce – don't fancy doing it again, thanks!"'

'I agree. That would make for a very fetching neck-lace. Very Britney Spears – only in reverse!'

'Emm, at least it would be less gross than one of your pearl necklaces that you keep telling me about. That Francis fella of yours is one sick dog!'

'Yes, but he's my sick dog, and I love him for it.'

'Seedy soul mates, eh? Maybe I will find the one. If Francis can manage to hold on to you, there really is hope for all of us.'

'You've just got to start living by my philosophy. Equal partnerships don't work. When you've too much in common, life becomes dull and boring. Find your-self someone radically different from you. Like, in Francis's case, he's deep and poetic, and I'm shallow and plastic . . .'

'Ah, Jeez, Lisa . . .'

'No, it's true. I find his inner beauty fascinating.'

'And what about his outer, less attractive features?'

'He's a gorgeous cock and a wicked mind. Sometimes I find his appearance repulsive, but that's why they in-vented champagne, darling, and that's why Daddy bought me my beautiful apartment.'

'What, so you can get plastered and shag ugly old men?'

'Well, it works for me.'

'And Francis, obviously. You're both mental.'

'And happy with it, thank you. Now let's concen-trate on snaring you James Bond over there. Quick, don't look, but he's coming this way. Stick your bum out and pray that he gets caught . . . Here he comes, one, two, three . . . go!'

Based on Lisa's call, I eagerly parachuted my bum backwards, only to feel the cold splash of a drink drench my back.

'Fuck's sake!' cried the voice from behind. It mirrored my own inner voice.

Turning to try and assess the damage, I was even more pained when I realized that I hadn't actually bumped into James Bond, but instead another unsuspecting random bloke who looked extremely pissed off at having half his pint spilled.

'Watch where you stick that fat arse of yours,' screamed the angry stranger.

'Excuse me? Who are you calling fat?'

'You, you stupid cow. I've lost my pint over you sticking your fat arse in my face.'

I was dazed with the shock. Lisa managed a lame, 'Get lost – ya dickhead,' before stepping backwards and cracking up laughing into her vodka and slimline.

In a typically aggressive Oirish way the stranger then started complaining, 'Is someone gonna get me a fresh pint, or wot?' But before I could manage to find any words, my James Bond stepped out of the shadows and called Mr Angry aside.

In a very Dub accent my James Bond asked, 'What ya drinkin there, pal? Carlsberg, is it? Come on over to the bar, I'll sort ya out.'

'Wow! He's a regular real-life hero, isn't he?' Lisa had now sorted out her fit of the giggles and was intrigued by my knight in navy pinstripes.

'Quick, fix me up. This tan I'm wearing isn't waterproof. Has it gone everywhere?'

'Well, I can almost make out a map of Europe on your back . . .'

'Fuck off!'

'Ha! Only kidding. Your tan is fine. The dress is just a little soggy. It'll dry. Quick, I think he's coming back.'

'Shut up, less of your quick, quick. Look what happened the last time . . .'

'Shh! Hiya, thank you for saving us.' Lisa manoeuvred her hand past me to touch James Bond on the shoulder.

As I turned to face him, I was met by his big brown eyes. He looked like something straight out of a TV ad selling chocolates. 'Are you OK?' he asked. His voice had quite dramatically changed, and didn't sound at all like it had previously.

'Eh, yeah, fine now, thanks to you. Sorry, are you some sort of mimic? Or am I hearing things?'

'What, you mean: which is my real voice?'

'Well, yeah, kinda!'

'Sorry, I slip into character every now and again. I don't even realize I do it. Did I do it with your friend there?'

'Yes, you did. You sounded a very convincing inner-city Dub there. Are you an actor?'

'Hi, sorry, I'm Lisa, and this is Eva . . .' The Princess butted in. 'Are you famous?' Her voice was all girlie. 'Should we know you, or is that a little rude?'

'Not rude at all. My name is Gavin Richards.' He smiled. 'Yes, I am an actor. Though it's a little weird saying that. It's all very new to me.'

'Really?' I fluttered my eyelashes and swung my body around more to get him to look at me rather than Lisa. After all, she'd just been bragging about her soul mate. I was still on the lookout for mine.

'Eh, well, I'm actually a painter, though I'm just home from LA after making four movies there. None of them have been released yet, so there's no reason in the world why you should know me.'

'Sounds like a line,' cooed Lisa, retracting back from him slightly.

'Li-sa! Sorry, please don't mind my friend. She's quite a cynical person.'

'Look, I understand. I wouldn't believe me, either. This is my first time even wearing a suit. I feel like a fraud. My publicist couriered me a whole new wardrobe yesterday and told me to wear the stuff. I'm not too sure if it's me or not. What do you think?' He stared into my eyes as he spoke, turning my hardened toffee core into a dreamy gooey caramel centre.

'Very smart.'

'Smart?' He almost sounded offended.

'Slick . . . Yeah, definitely very slick over smart.'

'All right, slick is better. Never really been one for smartness. It's almost an unwritten rule that artists never dress smart. It's seen as a commercial sell-out.'

'And isn't making movies in Tinseltown the same thing?'

'Pretty much.' His eyes dropped to the ground as if embarrassed.

'Hey, don't worry, we won't hold it against you. I'm

a poorly paid writer and she's unemployed, so we're not ones to judge.'

'A writer, eh?' His eyes shot up with interest. 'Creative . . . I like that.'

'Well, I just write for a magazine at the moment. But one day I'd like to try my hand at writing a novel.'

'Have you anything in mind?'

'A few ideas, but nothing concrete yet. It's more a fictional fantasy than anything else.'

'It's always good to have a plan to work towards . . .'

'Even if you don't follow it?'

'Ha! You know me already. Can I buy you girls a drink? There's no point in me being an unknown Hollywood star without being able to flash about some cash.'

'Two Cosmos so, since you're a Robert Redford in the making,' Lisa said.

'Eh, didn't think I looked like Robert Redford, not that I'd complain or anything. But I wouldn't even say this hair is strawberry blond. More muddied beige.'

'No, I meant he was a painter before he became an actor. Just one of my pieces of useless information. Forget I mentioned it,' Lisa said.

'Two Cosmos it is, then. And try not to get yourselves into any more trouble while I'm at the bar. I'd hate for someone else to have to come to your rescue and steal my spot.'

'Ha! I'm sure you're safe enough,' I joked.

'OK. Back in five . . .'

With our new friend Gavin Richards moving towards the bar, the two of us smiled at each other knowingly.

'He is cute, isn't he?' I asked, already knowing the answer.

'Very.'

'Do you think he's full of shit?'

'Maybe not. Painter to actor. It's original, if nothing else. And if it's a lie, it's a creative one.'

'So what do I do now?'

'Nothing. Keep your fat arse neatly in and do your best not to snag anyone else.'

'Easier said than done.'

'Well, you've done enough fishing for the moment. What do you want to do about hooking up with Parker and Jeff? We're supposed to be meeting them down the road in . . . eh, approximately five minutes. I could make myself scarce if you like?'

'*No way!* Bit soon for that.'

'Well, just give me the nod if you want me to get lost. What should I text Parker?'

'Nothing for the moment. Let's just play this by ear for another few minutes and see where it goes.'

'Talking about me?' asked Gavin Richards as he returned with our two delicious-looking cocktails.

'Well, you painter/actor types would just be insulted if we didn't,' teased Lisa.

'Probably. Did you start any wars while I was gone? I was thinking, I haven't played an action hero yet, and was hoping to get a bit of practice in.'

'Ha! Don't encourage us. We're like magnets for dramas. Thanks for the drink. Lisa and I were just talking about soul mates before you arrived. She's already found hers, of course, but do you believe in them?'

Lisa flashed me a look that said 'witch', but I just smirked back at her. After all, she'd thought he was just shooting a line when he'd talked about his pending fame, and she wasn't exactly in the market for a new fella. And in Lisa's case, Gavin Richards would be nothing more than *another* fella in her life.

I know I accumulated new men too, but then I never held on to them for very long. New York Michael was the only man who kept randomly popping back into my life, but that was more of a haunting than anything else. And Steve? I had found it hard to accept that it was completely over, especially since we had gotten to the 'I love you' stage. But I suppose I was embarrassed about what I had done to Steve, so that made it easier for me to blank him out.

'Eh, soul mates . . . Can't say I've found mine – yet,' Gavin said.

'Ah ha. So you believe in the idea that you could have a soul mate?' I said.

'You mean floating about in the solar system somewhere?'

'I was thinking a little closer to home, really.'

'More like here in Café en Seine,' added Lisa.

Gavin only paused momentarily before pulling on his charm hat. 'Maybe you could be my soul mate, Eva?' His chocolately brown eyes almost turned me to mush. 'If even for just here and now . . .' he added, ruining the moment just a smidgen.

'Wow!' I said sarcastically. 'We've only just met, have made a meaningful connection, and I already know that the affair is over as soon as my Cosmo is.'

'Much tidier than my last three break-ups,' smiled Gavin.

'Mine, too . . . Cheers.'

And just like I'd said, the moment we'd knocked back our drinks he kissed me on the cheek and told me, 'This was one of my most beautiful romances ever. I'll never forget you.' And then he was gone.

I must have lapped the bar three times before we left, hoping to catch one more glimpse of him, but with no success. It was as if he was some sort of dating guardian angel, trying to give me hope in mankind.

Maybe he had been nothing more than a longed-for figment of my imagination. My vulnerable and unstable mind, needing him desperately, had magicked up this Gavin Richards character for me. I even Googled his name on my phone, but again he was nowhere to be found.

He might have been nothing more than a phantom gentleman, but his message had been delivered.

Lisa and I arrived down to meet Parker and Jeff and a few of their circle of straight friends. I didn't finish the night with any phone numbers, but I did fall home about four hours later after a fun night, with a renewed sense of hope.

Maybe the dress was magic. While it might not survive another outing, my fire had been restored, and slowly but surely a more mature Eva was evolving.

Ha! That was probably a bit of a stretch. Let's just say I had become a happier and more content Eva, if nothing else.

★   ★   ★

'Eva, it's Maddie.'

Her caller ID was blocked. I never would have answered if I'd known it was her. Though, strangely enough, I liked the sound of her voice.

'Please don't hang up,' she pleaded. 'I just need to talk to you, please?'

'If you're ringing to say you're sorry for running off with my husband, I've heard it all before. You're welcome to him.'

'I'm not.'

'You're not sorry? Charming.'

'That's not why I'm ringing, Eva.'

'And don't bother asking to take Daisy again, cause it's not going to . . .'

'Eva, please shut up for a second. It's Woody, he's in hospital and he's had an accident. I know this seems weird, but you're the only one I want to talk to about this. I've missed you so much. Please? Please talk to me?'

Unsure how I felt, I simply asked, 'What happened?'

'Michael was supposed to be minding him – they went for a walk to the park – Michael says he was just reading the paper when he noticed him floating in the pond. I mean, he was supposed to be minding him while I was at the hairdresser's. What the fuck was he doing reading a fucking paper? He was supposed to be minding my baby, and now we're at Crumlin Hospital and they're saying he could be brain-damaged. What am I going to do, Eva? I don't know where else to turn . . .'

'OK, OK, slow down. What have the doctors said?'

'They're saying too much. I can't understand anything.'

'Is he still breathing?'

'Yes.'

'OK, that's a start. Where's Michael now?'

'I don't know. I screamed at him, telling him he was a useless piece of shit, and I don't know where he went. I don't fucking care, either.'

'Where's your folks?'

'My dad's on one of his trips to Thailand, and Mam's in Cork. I've left a message on her phone, but I haven't heard back from her yet. What am I going to do, Eva? I couldn't cope if he . . .'

Her voice trailed off to tears, and she sounded all alone and heartbroken. While I had wished to hear her miserable night after night as I cried into my pillow, wallowing in self-pity, the idea that Woody could die also had me on the verge of sobbing. 'Maddie, try not to get yourself worked up. You need to be in control right now. Give me half an hour, I'll drop Daisy off at my mum's and I'll meet you at the hospital . . . Don't worry, he'll be fine. He's a tough little character.'

'Eva, I couldn't go on if he was to . . .' Her tears returned, just thinking the worst. It was horrible to hear her so distressed. As a mother now myself I couldn't bear to think of anything so dreadful happening to Maddie. I'd just have to sweep aside all our issues for the moment. There was too much history between us not to.

'Maddie, I'll be half an hour. I'll find you. Now stay strong.' I put down the phone. I carried Daisy to the car and rang my mum. Thankfully she was in, and when I arrived at her house she even lifted Daisy out, without me having to get out of the car.

Although I was trying not to get upset, I could feel my throat swelling with the panic. Thoughts of Amy kept flashing through my head. By the time I burst into the corridor that Maddie was on, my heart was almost exploding out of my ears.

All the hate that I had harboured towards her, all the anger, just disappeared the moment I saw her bent over on a seat, her head in her hands, sobbing and rocking. She didn't even realize I was there until I put my hand on her shoulder and called her name.

The second she saw me, she leapt up, throwing her arms enthusiastically around my neck. And although I initially resisted reciprocating the affection, I soon hugged her back like old times.

Who could have forecast that it would have been in the cold, clinical corridor of a children's hospital that I would find my old friend again? And despite the strong stench of antibacterial cleaning agents, she still had that same distinctive Issey Miyake smell that she'd always had.

'I'm sorry, Eva, I'm so sorry. I just didn't know where else to turn. Thank you for coming in. I'm losing him. I just know he's going to d–i–e.'

'Come on, girl, pull yourself together. You need to be strong for Woody.'

I looked around to see if there was anyone in authority to speak to, but this particular corridor was empty, as if shut off from the rest of the hospital.

'They just told me to wait here,' whimpered Maddie, her face still beautiful, even though her eyes were puffy and bloodshot.

Maybe it was being a mother that allowed all my hate to wash away, but as we sat down on two lonely creaky plastic chairs, it was gone. We simply held hands and sat in silence, waiting.

Waiting for news of Woody.

Waiting on news of Michael, too.

For the first time since our fallout, both Maddie and I saw eye to eye on the fact that Michael – our Michael – was a selfish bastard who thought of no one other than himself.

I wanted to start bitching about him, but toned down my first question to, 'Any word from Michael?'

'No.' Her voice was weak from all the crying. 'He just sent a text to say he's not able to face the hospital, and that it wasn't his fault.'

'What bullshit!' I blurted out loudly, before lowering my voice again. 'What's his problem with hospitals? He used to visit me every night when I was in a coma. He never had a problem with hospitals before.'

'A lot has happened since you last saw him,' snapped Maddie protectively. 'Both his mum and dad died within a couple of weeks of each other during the summer. His mum had a heart-attack, and then his dad had the same. Though we think it was more a broken heart than anything . . .'

'Oh . . .'

'They both made it to hospital before they died. I suppose he's scarred.'

'Fuck that, Maddie. He failed to watch over Woody properly. Over a toddler. How can you defend him?'

'I don't know . . . I just . . . I don't know what to think right now.'

'Miss Lord?' A doctor holding a clipboard pushed through the swing doors opposite us and looked surprisingly upbeat.

'*Yes?*' Maddie stood to attention. 'That's me.'

'Miss Lord, we've good news. Young Woody has woken up, is breathing normally and is calling for his mummy. We can't allow him to go anywhere just yet, as we'll need to keep him in a day or two under observation, but he looks set to make a full recovery. Do you want to come through now?'

'Oh-my-God. Thank you so much. Can I bring my friend in?'

'Not just yet.' The doctor gave me a smile, but her tone suggested she wasn't going to be swayed.

Understanding that Maddie would be gone a while, I suggested that I head off, to give her time and space to be with Woody. And that if she needed anything, she should just give me a shout.

We kissed. We hugged. We parted on good terms. I then went and collected Daisy and hugged her for hours, probably far too tightly, until it was bedtime for both of us.

I had never really bonded with Michael's parents, as we had only met a handful of times, so I didn't feel very sad about their loss. It was Daisy I felt sorry for. They were her grandparents after all. And I only had one photograph of them with her, taken at the hospital when she'd been born. Now there would never be another.

Three weeks later, I had still received no text or phone call from Maddie.

She no longer needed me, and so I was sidelined once more. Parker was the one who told me that Woody was back at home with her and Michael, and of course that just made me feel bitter towards them both all over again.

I found it hard to stomach that Maddie could allow Michael to continue to share her life with Woody after failing to keep her baby, her precious son, safe from danger.

Cursing Michael's bones, I found solace in the fact that I would never have trusted him enough to put Daisy in the same danger. I'd always doubted he really cared for her. And then he hadn't even seen fit to inform me about his parents' death – Daisy's grandparents' death. He clearly didn't even recognize her as family.

It was a bitter pill. But I was gradually getting better able to swallow it every day.

13

'Please don't make me eat or drink again. My lunch is still stuck in my throat.'

'You mean your foot! You landed me in it big time this afternoon. I'm not going to hear the last of Jeff's moaning till he's back on that plane to Dubai.'

'How was I supposed to know you hadn't told him about our plans to go to New York? It was his credit card that paid for the U2 tickets after all.'

'Yeah, months ago. We were fighting at the time.'

'Over your warts.'

'Shut up. I was just hoping to break it to him gently.'

'Listen, he gave you warts . . .'

'*Eva*, shh. Hello, everyone. Thank you all for making it. Jeff will be thrilled when he realizes how many friends he has. Now, if you can all hang on here – Eva, you too – and try and stay quiet. I'll go and fetch the birthday boy. And don't forget to yell "*Surprise!*"'

It was Jeff's fortieth birthday, and Parker's first stab at organizing a surprise party. It had been the biggest secret he'd ever kept; he'd even shocked himself at how devious he had managed to be.

The four of us (Lisa, Parker, Jeff and me) had checked into Thatcher's Thatch, an extremely camp boutique hotel in Wicklow run by two small men in tight-fitting trousers and matching taches, who had an obvious fancy for strong women – such as ole Maggie Thatcher, hence the name! The four of us had spent a champagne-swilling afternoon in Granny's Grave, the hotel's imaginatively titled bar, where once upon a time someone's granny had drunk herself to death, or so the story went!

While us girlies would have been quite content to stick to a liquid lunch and watch our figures, the proprietors had insisted we try a sample menu after Lisa mentioned that I was a features writer for *YES!* I think her intention had been to score some free champers rather than the free homemade stew we got, with its extra helpings of hugely filling brown bread, along with a platter of pâtés and cheeses, and the restaurant's signature starter of Hillary Clinton pie. (According to the menu this contained: 'Determined wild salmon that swam uphill through white water.')

Needless to say, the four of us were back in our respective rooms – Doris Day's Den and Bette Davis's Bedstead – by 6 p.m., nursing early hangovers and swollen stomachs. And in Parker's case an extra headache over the fact that I had let the cat out of the bag that he and I would be heading to New York in December to catch U2 play at Madison Square Garden.

Something Jeff had clearly thought he was going to be taken to himself. Oops!

Unfortunately, by 7.30 p.m. Parker rousted me back out of my Doris cot to help him check on the Pink Palace Party Room, while the Princess spent an extra few precious minutes preening her newly coiffed locks. In a fit of madness earlier that week, she had foolishly chopped her hair into a short Victoria Beckhamesque do. But no matter how much hair gel she used to create 'texture' she still looked more like a man than our two hosts Bill and Ben could ever have dreamt of doing!

With Jeff safely tucked up in bed watching a *Breakfast at Tiffany's* DVD, Parker and myself ushered all of our mutual friends – plus a few new faces that we didn't recognize, but didn't care about because they made up numbers – into the party room.

Like frustrated and naughty teenagers, the gang sniggered and started being noisy. Some of them threatened to smoke. Some acted out well-known comedy sketches, screaming, 'Hello, I'm on my mobile!' Some even took to singing Kylie numbers, while the others kept shhing each other and breaking out into fits of giggles. The atmosphere was teetering on disruptive, when the double doors that we'd been told to keep watch on swung open and everyone screamed, the way they'd been told to: 'Surprise!'

It would have been perfect if it had been Parker and Jeff stepping through the doors. But instead it was just a waiter with a tray of glasses, who looked mortified and quickly scurried away, with several horny ole lads following him in search of some devilment.

It was a further ten minutes before the stars of the evening showed up, and of course by then all the assembled guests had forgotten their duty and relaxed into the complimentary bubbly.

Needless to say, Parker was furious that everyone had missed their cue to yell, 'Surprise', but Jeff didn't care. He was suitably happy with the turnout and his presents, which included a valuable Louis le Brocquy painting which one of his builder mates had apparently 'acquired' in a rent row with a chef.

Of course I forgot that I had been complaining about being full, and helped Jeff eat the top two rows of pink cup cakes that made up his Barbara Cartland-inspired birthday cake-arrangement.

By 2 a.m. I had started to feel ill again and I did my usual Houdini. As I snuck off to bed I left Jeff and Parker dancing to Geri Halliwell's version of 'It's Raining Men', and Lisa in a pleasant but very real argument with a drag queen, trying to prove that she was indeed a 'cockless woman', and not a man pretending to be a woman. I'd known it was time to make a break for it when Lisa had blasted, 'Grab my crotch, then!' And I hadn't hung around to hear the response.

As I walked through the lobby on my way to the lifts, I noticed an old friend of Parker's, Alistair George, sitting by himself sipping on a brandy. Another creative type, he was a legend in the theatre for his stage production and his gift for wooing big-name actors to perform in Ireland.

'Not enjoying the party, Alistair? Not like you to step out of the limelight.'

'Even by my standards things got too gay in there. I just needed a little space. Care to join me for a night-cap?'

'Promise not to sing "Ooh Aah . . . Just A Little Bit" to me?'

'Promise. I tell you, I bailed after the second round of "I Am What I Am", and took my bony old gay ass out here for a breather.'

After several double Baileys on ice, my stomach had settled, and Alistair had turned the conversation to every girl's favourite topic – men!

We were having great fun slagging off all the bastards in my thirty-two and his forty-seven years, when Alistair suddenly dropped a clanger.

'Will you marry me, Eva?'

'No problem, Al. Would you like a big white wedding or just a registry-office job? Though I must warn you, you're not the first man to ask me to marry them. I'm a woman with a past.'

'Aren't we all, sweetie. But seriously, would you?'

'How drunk are you?'

'Drunk. But not too drunk to understand my request. I need a wife, Eva. We've known each other many years now. Would it be so bad to share my large home in Dalkey, overlooking the sea, with me?'

'It would be idyllic, Al, simply charming. But what's this really about? Why do you need a beard?'

'Simply because my mother is threatening to sell the family home, and divide it up between her animal charities, if I don't fulfil my father's dying wish for me to be married. The old bat is half-dead herself, but she's been half-dead for ten years now, and still holds enough marbles that if she wants to change her will, her solicitor can't stop her. Now, do you see my predicament?'

'Gosh, you are in a pickle, Mr George. Do you think she's serious? Surely your own mother wouldn't turf you out of the family home?'

'My mother is about four feet tall, and has the same stick-like frame as me. What she lacks in physical presence, she makes up for in emotional manipulation. She's a wilful woman. Even after all these years, she still can't accept my lifestyle choices, and wants me to make a public display of straightness. To hell with the mental anguish on my part.'

'Wow! That's some pressure, all right. Could you not just take an ole pillow to the ole witch?'

'Don't think I haven't thought about it.'

'Ouch! Sorry, I shouldn't talk like that.'

'Believe me, there's nothing you could say that I haven't already considered in my head. This has been hanging over me for two years now, and D-Day is coming. I've got till the end of the year before she signs it all away.'

'Really?'

'Yep. That's just under three months. Any suggestions?'

'Jeez, Al, I'd really love to help you out. But wouldn't you be better off picking up some illegal lap dancer or something, who is actually looking for a husband because she wants to stay in the country? Surely, there's plenty who'd jump at the offer?'

'Yeah, and then they'd rob me of my house and home. I need someone I can trust, Eva.'

'You need more time, as well.'

'Why?'

'Well, the last time I did it, it took a minimum of three months to organize. It's too short a notice, Al. Can you not just pull on her heart strings and get her to drop the nonsense?'

'She's what you call old school, Eva. And bending is not a word in her vocabulary.'

'Why don't you stage a fake wedding? Get one of Parker's actor mates to dress up as a priest, draw up some fake papers and stage the fucking thing. I'll play your bride, no problem. I know all the vows off by heart . . .'

'Would you really do it?'

'Sure.'

'You'd also need to live in the house, though.'

'Well, how about you buy Daisy and me an extra wardrobe to keep in the house, and we'll make a point of visiting from time to time. How does that sound?'

'Like the makings of a fabulous plan, young lady. Or should I call you Mrs George?'

'Hey, the deal is off if you start calling me that. That makes me feel like an old woman. If I didn't take my first husband's name, I'm certainly not taking yours.'

'My God, Eva, you really are a genius.'

'Good stuff. Problem solved, I'm off to bed.'

'Are we not going to go back inside and make our announcement?'

'Off ya go. Tell them your beautiful bride-to-be has been struck down with one of her frequent headaches, and that they should start the celebrations without me.'

Giving him a hug, I knocked back the last dribble of watery Baileys in my glass and made towards the lift.

'You could do worse,' called Alistair after me.

'I know. I have already. As I said earlier, I am a woman with a past . . . Night night.'

My entrance to the breakfast room was greeted with a rapturous round of applause.

'Congratulations, Eva.'

'There's the woman herself.'

'Here comes the bride!'

Despite feeling like I had dreamt Alistair's mad plan, or at least *my* crazy plan, my welcome in the restaurant left me with no doubts. I hadn't imagined it.

Although I wasn't about to become a bigamist for real – I wasn't sure if pretending to get married was fraudulent or not – I did feel a little excited at the prospect. I couldn't explain it, even to myself, but it was impossible not to get caught up in the thrill of it.

Initially I tried to play the whole thing down, as it was totally detracting from Jeff's milestone event, but the birthday boy grabbed my hand and said, 'Don't worry, honey. It's OK. Enjoy the moment.'

Barely able to enjoy a glass of orange juice, I spoke to all the queens, who formed a queue to congratulate me and thank me, and give offers of advice when it came to picking out the dress. The hot topic seemed to be whether I could pull off a white one or not. Most thought I should. The rest suggested splashes of red or black to tie in with the scarlet woman slash winter theme.

By the end of breakfast, the group had decided, on my behalf, that New Year's Eve would be the perfect night to host the wedding, and that Daisy would play a role as Alistair's long-lost daughter.

Conning a ninety-year-old witch might not have been the cleverest of my ideas, but it certainly was proving to be one of the most devious and inventive I had ever been involved in. And the more we discussed designs by Vera Wang and hair by Alan Boyce, the more excited I became.

By lunchtime the entire plan had been hatched.

There'd be a marquee in the garden overlooking the sea at Dalkey.

Synan O'Mahony would do the dress, and all the flowers would be white.

A Cork actor, Gavin O'Connor, had agreed to do the ceremony, as long as Parker promised that he could sing with the band afterwards, and he got the second dance with the bride – which, of course, I thought was extremely sweet.

The fact that it was all a con didn't faze me. I was caught up in the romance of my newest whirlwind engagement. Even though I was only going to pretend to marry a rich gay man, that didn't take the sheen off it for me. I was back at the centre of attention again, and loving every single second.

★   ★   ★

'You're like cocaine to a sniffer dog. Why is it men with their lights on always seem to come mooching around you?' Lisa asked.

'It's a strange one, all right. Though, like sniffer dogs, the men that I attract seem to have the most fun finding me, but when they do they just wag their tails for a few minutes, and then fuck off to the next challenge.'

'You're being a bit harsh on yourself there . . . Or maybe you're right . . . I'm not about to argue with you. Now, hurry up and give us a look at the next one.'

Lisa and I were spending the afternoon in disguise while searching for wedding dresses. Lisa looked even more like a drag act with her extra-long Paris Hilton ponytail, while I was also camping it up with a blonde Raquel Welch 'human-hair' wig.

Although I had possibly tried on every wedding gown in Ireland first time round – hence the need for some sort of camouflage – I sought inspiration once again. I didn't know what I wanted. All I knew was that I'd be open to anything that didn't look like the halter-neck, mermaid style that my mother had bullied me into getting for my original wedding.

Knowing that I looked good, I stepped out from behind the cubicle curtain, feeling like a screen diva, and asking, 'What ya think?' It was very Grace Kelly. Long sleeves of white lace, and a neat heart-shaped bodice, which tapered out to a fuller skirt from the waist.

'Oh-my-God . . .' Lisa nearly spat out her complimentary glass of champagne with the excitement.

'You've found it. I fucking love it. Is that the cheap one or the expensive one?'

'The cheap one. I couldn't dream of wasting Daisy's inheritance on a dress.'

'Eva, have you lost sight of the fact that this is only a pantomime? This is not a real marriage. It's just pretend.'

'I know that . . .' I squealed. I was a little irritated at her suggestion that I was getting carried away with the whole thing – which of course I was. I mean, what woman in my situation wouldn't?

'Easy, Bridezilla. No need to snap my head off. Just trying to keep you grounded.'

'I don't want to stay grounded. Now, what do you think of the dress?'

'It's a twenty out of ten. Just like your mood . . . It's off the scale!'

'Sorry, hon, don't mind me, it's just my mind has been racing.'

'No shit!'

'It's just I've been thinking a lot about this over the last couple of weeks. And I think I could make it work.'

'Excuse me? Earth to Eva . . . This is not a real marriage. And secondly, the dude is gay. You already have a gay husband, Parker. Who is feeling a little left out over the whole thing. When was the last time you spoke to him?'

'I'll call him.'

'When was the last time you did?'

'Emm, over a week ago.'

'You're a cruel witch, Eva Valentine. Don't sweep

him aside for your new gay boyfriend. Cause he'll be the one to pick up all the pieces when this goes wrong.'

'What's going to go wrong?'

'God only knows. But you can be damn sure something will. And I can't promise to be there. I've already delayed my skiing trip to make the wedding . . . I'm disgusted I have to miss the New Year's Day naked ski race. That's a long-established Tiswell tradition. So there'd better be some straight men at this thing. Cause I'll need to be getting laid!'

'Can we focus on meeee for a minute, please? It's not every day a girl gets married.'

'No, just every year, in your case!'

'Green is *so* not your colour, Lisa.'

'Sorry, I'm back now. Yes, the dress is totally fab. Lace becomes you. Actually marriage becomes you, Miss Valentine. Here, take your glass of bubbles. I propose a toast.'

'This should be good . . .'

'To Eva Valentine. Blessed with a name belonging to lovers . . .'

'And martyrs . . .'

'Oh, that you are, just not a very silent one,' Lisa said.

'Ha!'

'Yes, Valentine is a lover, and martyr to all causes – especially gay ones. With a heart so big that she would go to any lengths to keep middle-aged men off the streets. Especially ones with big—'

'Houses. Big houses . . .'

'That's what I was going to say. You've a filthy mind,

Miss Valentine, and I love ya. I look forward to all your weddings in the future.'

'Cheers to you, girlfriend,' I said.

'Cheers to me and my . . .'

'Big house? Big heart? Big . . .' I suggested.

'Hey, easy. My *big*-busted bessie mate. Thank you for all your support . . .' Lisa finished her champagne.

'You're welcome. Cheers.'

'Cheers, yourself. Can we go for a real drink now that you've found your perfect dress? I think this cheap muck is starting to cut the lining of my throat.'

'Ahhh, poor you. OK then, chief bridesmaid, where would you like to take me to celebrate?'

'Well, would you like to go gay and be around your adopted people? Or shall we go straight and hit that new champagne bar on Dawson Street?'

'I'll have plenty of time to hang with the gays, so let's go straight. Me likey some decent champagne, please . . .'

A bottle of Moët later and I had completely forgotten about my second marriage. A busload of Scottish rugby supporters had lost their way, and found themselves, in full kilt and long socks uniform, down at our very girlie champagne bar.

Being typically Scottish, a small group of them broke the ice with a brash introduction. 'Wot about ye? Aren't ya two fine-looking hens? Can we be your cock-erels?'

Of course, neither Lisa nor I was offended by their approach, and retaliated with, 'Show us your cocks, then?'

The next five minutes involved an overwhelmingly ugly and hairy display of manly flesh, as each burly bloke – and even their two small baldy friends – queued up to lift their kilts at us. Only two men out of the eighteen who stood in front of us had wisely covered their manhood with pants. And unfortunately for us, it was the two small fellas. I got the feeling, even through my alcohol haze, that they'd be emotionally scarring us for ever!

Old and young they came, stood and flashed. Some rushed through their act like they'd be beaten up by the class bully if they didn't do it. Others giggled, while three particularly brazen ones took centre stage in front of our table, raised their kilts with purpose and waved at us in their own unique way . . .

Instead of diverting our gaze, the two of us just sat with our eyes wide open, appreciating a presentation that had clearly been perfected over years of away games. Boldly baring their mickies, the three men swung into a routine that any baton-twirling cheerleader would have been proud of. They swung east, and swung west, before pointing north again and pulsating. It was a mini-porn performance, worthy of a Cirque du Soleil badge, and it was so captivating that the whole room looked on – in jealousy, or maybe shock? – at us girls and our front-row seats.

If it hadn't been for the champagne we probably would have felt intimidated, considering the amount of testosterone in the room, but these rugger-buggers had met their match and we were loving the show.

As a highly charged bride-to-be and an over-sexed

chief bridesmaid, we had more than lost our way off the yellow brick road, and it was only when a large crowd of fellow kilt-wearers had gathered that I started to feel that maybe clapping and throwing euro coins at the lads wasn't the wisest thing for two single ladies to do. In a moment of clarity I managed to drag Lisa away from her whooping and cheering, by telling her that my mother had texted to say that Daisy was sick.

Of course it was a lie, and the fact that I could have jinxed Daisy by saying that she was ill made me feel sick. I wanted to retch. Thankfully, the street was too busy with shoppers for me to vomit in comfort, so my guilt soon passed and the imminent danger was avoided. I had removed us from an obvious rape scenario, though it took Lisa the full walk to the Shelbourne Hotel before she forgave me.

'Those guys could have won medals for their penis precision pageantry . . .' she sniped.

'Their what?'

'They had talented penises . . . and you're mean!' Lisa knew she was being stupid, but she couldn't help herself. She was a sucker, in every sense of the word, for a sizeable dick. And if it could do tricks, well . . . her vagina overruled her mind and became the controlling organ in her body. 'Ahhh, fuck ya . . . I hate it when you're right,' she said finally.

'And?'

'Thank you, Eva, for saving us from a certain *spit roast.*'

'You're welcome, Miss *Woo-hoo.* I mean, where

did you learn to wolf whistle like that? You were privately educated, madam. Know your social standing, please!'

'Jeez, that could have turned into something out of *The Accused* . . . You know the film with Jodie Foster?'

'Exactly. That would have made for some more interesting headlines, eh? CCTV GIRL CAUGHT AGAIN – THIS TIME WITH EVERYONE'S HUSBANDS!'

'More like, BIGAMIST BITCH TOASTS ANOTHER MARRIAGE BY GIVING GROUP RATE ON HIGHLAND FLINGS!'

'Oh, stop it.'

'Or how about EVA WARMS UP . . .'

'I said *stop it*! I'm not that big a slapper. I'm feeling a little unstable now, so please be nice to me for a minute.'

'Excuse me?'

'I'm serious . . . I'm just having a moment. Please, just go easy.'

'Fair enough, I thought we were having a laugh?'

'We were, and now I'm having a mini-panic-attack, so just drop it, please.'

'Don't you get grouchy with me, Eva. I didn't start this. Where's your sense of humour gone?'

'Down the pan like my morals, most likely . . . What am I doing, Lisa? I think I'm starting to lose my mind. I don't know why I agreed to this wedding. If my mother found out what I was doing she'd kill me. At first it just seemed harmless, but now, with the dress and New

Year's fast approaching, it's started to dig up a lot of deeply buried emotions. I've been trying to suppress a lot of pain, and now it's as if it's all rushing to the surface.

Doing her big-sister bit, Lisa grabbed my shoulders and squared herself in front of me.

'Hey, hey.' She shook me into focus. 'Go easy on yourself. Don't be drowning in self-pity. I can understand that you've been sucked into this whole farce, but don't let it get to you. OK, so the last couple of years have been somewhat traumatic in parts, between the accident and Daisy . . .'

Defensively I pushed her hands off me when I heard her mention my daughter. 'I'm very proud of Daisy. Don't—'

'Whoah!' she interrupted. 'I meant the shock of getting pregnant, that's all, and then all the business with Maddie and Michael. It's been a busy couple of years for you; that's all I meant. Just try not to let it all swamp you. Now, come on. It's just the booze talking. We were supposed to be celebrating.' She smiled and signalled towards the Shelbourne.

Still wounded, I whimpered, 'I forgot what we were celebrating.'

'Well, it's still a little early, but why don't we celebrate the closing of a dodgy year and fresh beginnings?'

'It's only November.'

'So?'

'It's not that easy, Lisa.'

Despite her best efforts, Lisa realized she was fighting a losing battle. Fed up with my moaning, she finally snapped. 'Huh. You're not the only one who's had problems, Eva.'

'Emm, what problems do you have, Princess?'

'Oh, because I'm rich I don't get to have heartache?'

'Well, what the fuck *do* you have to worry about, then? You never worry about money, like most normal people. If something drops, you lift it. If something creases, you flatten it. If a bloke passes you, you fuck him! Sounds like a charmed existence to me.'

'Are you finished?' Her face was almost growling, it looked so fierce.

'Sorry, did I leave something out?'

'OK, I'm trying to hold on to the fact that you're in a bad place right now. And you don't mean to be cruel. But I think you're forgetting that I have feelings, too.'

'Oh, this ought to be good. Why should I feel sorry for you, then?'

'You think my life is so perfect then, do ya?'

'Well, isn't it?'

'OK, well, let's see. I've a cunt of a sister who hates me. My father, who I love dearly, is cheating on my mother, who of course he's supposed to love dearly. I've never had a serious partner who's loved me, so I keep myself busy with losers, and call them fuck-buddies. And pretend to all my friends that I'm fine with that. Oh, and if that wasn't enough, I've got . . .'

Lisa had a scared look on her face.

'Got what?' I asked gently.

'I've got cancer, Eva. I've just started chemotherapy for cervical cancer. That's why I cut my hair short. It's the done thing.'

'Oh–my–God, I didn't know. I'm so sorry.'

'Me, too,' she snapped angrily.

Suddenly I felt so foolish. 'Listen, Lisa, why didn't you tell me?'

'Why? Cause poor ole Eva is the only one who's allowed to have problems. It's always poor Eva this, poor Eva that. I'm not allowed to have problems, am I, Eva? I'm rich, so that means everything must be rosy in my world.'

'That's not fair.'

Lisa took a moment to settle her nerves. Unlike me, she was doing her best to act calm. 'When was the last time you asked me if I was all right?'

'Eh . . .'

'Exactly. You don't. Sure, you've had your own issues to deal with, and I've always tried to be there and support you, but I'm a fucking human being, too, Eva. Things are not always perfect just because I've got my lipstick on. Sometimes it would be nice if someone could take care of me for a change. I can't always be the strong one . . .'

And then, for the first time ever, Lisa crumpled to the ground and wept. I had never seen her cry before. She had always been so strong. Her man–itude, as I called it, had allowed me to lean on her. I had become so self-absorbed that I'd rarely questioned how my closest friends felt, or were doing.

Almost seven feet high in her Chanel boots, Lisa must have looked like a collapsed dinosaur in front of the Shelbourne Hotel as she clung to the railings and sobbed. I didn't know what to do. I tried to encourage her to stand up, but she wouldn't move. I tried to ask her to stop crying, but she wouldn't. So I stopped worrying about people staring, and sat on the pavement beside her. I might not have been there for her before, but this was as good a time as any to start. So I cuddled her on the street as she cried. Held her hand, and rubbed her back, as she released years of pent-up emotion that she had never allowed herself to deal with.

Suddenly I didn't feel so hard done by. Lisa was right: I had everything to look forward to next year. Work was going well. I didn't know where I would end up living, but I was never going to be on the streets. And then there was my little doll, Daisy. Despite being abandoned by her father, she was thriving: crawling, gurgling, turning into a proper little girl. Why was it that I always saw the negative in every situation?

I didn't rush Lisa again. We must have sat on the ground for at least twenty minutes before she stopped crying. I didn't care what socialites had seen us on their way in and out of the salubrious setting of the Shelbourne Hotel, and neither did Lisa. We both knew that underneath their facades, they'd all have their own problems. After all, money wasn't a Band-Aid that healed everything. While it clearly hadn't mended a broken heart, I was still hoping it could fund a cure for cancer . . .

14

'Do you not think my sister looks older than my mother?' I asked Parker.

'Shh – she had a tough life working the streets of Paris as a whore, and of course your mother did have you young!'

'How young, exactly? What is she? Sixteen or seventeen years older than me?'

'We're conning a 90-year-old biddy, not the FBI, now stop stressing,' Parker hissed. 'If you keep frowning like that you'll end up looking more like the fucking grandmother of the bride!'

'Yeah, and what happened to her?'

'Oh, she slipped on the wrapping paper off the box of After Eights I sent her. She broke her hip and right elbow, and won't be able to make the rehearsal or the wedding.'

'Funny, that.'

'Not really. There were also five hundred euros in with the chocolates as part of her participation fee. Considering her accident, I don't think I can really ask for that money back . . .'

'Emm, I suppose it would be rude.'

'Hey, don't make me out to be a cold fish . . . I've had a lot to organize here,' Parker fussed. 'She was meant to be the only surviving grandparent. I blew most of my budget on the priest and the band. All I could afford was a sister, mother and grandmother for you. I decided that your father had run off with his Thai girlfriend to run a beach bar, never to be heard of again.'

'Is he a pimp?'

'Maybe. That could work, too.'

'Charming. What a lovely family you've created for me.'

It was the rehearsal dinner at the Four Seasons Hotel, the night before the wedding. Because Alistair's mother couldn't last too long outside her care home, everyone had congregated directly at the hotel for dinner, with a small room booked for the two families to socialize.

This was my first time to meet everyone – my own fake family included – and despite a few curious expressions from Alistair's aunties and cousins, his mother Agatha seemed to be swallowing the whole thing, hook, line and sinker.

But although I normally had every faith in Parker's ability to organize an event, by 6.30 p.m. most of his actors were looking decidedly drunk on the free wine, and were starting to get a tad loose in their improv.

I could only smile as my new mother Maisy (to rhyme with Daisy) informed Alistair's Aunt Greta that, 'Eva was such a great daughter. I always suffered with bunions. Even as a child she used to file down my feet for me!'

And when the priest, Father Russell Crowe, told the story of how I was '*more than a handful*, back when I confirmed her' he emphasized, with a naughty tone, the more than a *handful* bit. I was convinced that some-one would twig that this was a set-up. But they didn't. And try as the actors did to sabotage the nuptials, the evening continued on course, and finished up with Parker spinning Agatha around in her wheelchair while singing 'We Are Family' by Sister Sledge.

By the time the last of the George family had been poured into taxis, the actors had managed to portray me as a lover of donkeys, showering and lost causes. Thankfully all word-play and double-entendres were lost on the older George folk, and the stage had been set for a flawless wedding day. Or so we hoped!

After Parker had briefed all the special extras about their timings and duties the following day, and had ordered them home and banned them from drinking any further alcohol that night, Alistair, Parker, Jeff and I retired to the bar for a post-mortem. Lisa had bailed out early, unfortunately. She'd had chemotherapy the day before, and was still feeling very sickly. Despite her best intentions, she couldn't manage any of the meal, and left shortly after making her chief-bridesmaid speech. (Shamefully, I hadn't asked her to speak at my real wedding to Michael. Maddie had been given that duty, and fucked it up by laughing and telling cringe-making stories of how we used to 'pull men in the old days!')

But at this wedding rehearsal Lisa had spoken from the heart. She'd even had some of the actors in tears when she'd said, 'Eva makes me want to be a better person. She's turned her life around since Daisy came into her world. She's the greatest mom imaginable, and the greatest friend anyone could wish for. Not just Alistair, but everyone here today, is extremely blessed to know this woman.'

Although we had been surrounded by booze all evening, none of us principal characters had been able to drink much, for fear of putting a foot wrong. So as a treat Alistair ordered two bottles of vintage Dom Pérignon, and we all got stuck in to some serious bitching.

But after a couple of hours of stories like 'Did you see the look on Eva's face when the sister told your mother that Eva was the most tested woman in Ireland? And that Alistair had no reason to fear STDs? It was price-less!' I felt compelled to take a walk to clear my head.

Although it was all just make-believe, the whole charade had made me remember my own real wedding. And what my real husband and family had thought of me. I recalled how my own mother had told Michael's mom that she'd never thought I'd amount to much. And that the wedding rehearsal was the first time she'd looked at me in twenty-five years and felt proud.

I also remembered how Michael had looked at me with such warmth in his eyes, and told me that he wanted to be my partner for life, and always walk by my side, not in front of me, nor behind me. I had really believed him. Up until I had given birth to Daisy, the wedding had undoubtedly been the most memorable moment of my life. It had rocked me to the core, and

I had wondered at the time what I'd done to deserve such love.

The reality was that Michael hadn't meant it . . . Or that he had been a great actor and had wanted to believe it . . . Or . . . Who knows? Emotionally, the past year had been one to erase. A year to close the book on, with lessons learnt, and meteoric mistakes made – hopefully never to be repeated.

I had walked in the direction of the toilet, but took refuge on a chair opposite the Ladies', after seeing several excitable women rush in laughing about spotting one of the lads from Boyzone.

Normally I'd have been straight in to earwig in on the details, but I couldn't face giddy women and their tales of rubbing shoulders with celebrity now . . . What I really needed was some fresh air and space to walk off my mood, but it was too cold for that. My flimsy Christmas-cracker red Lipsy dress wasn't quite warm enough to protect me from the winter elements. So I sat opposite the Ladies', watching the women, old and young, file in and out. They were all dripping in diamonds and expensive watches, all blonde or highlighted, all tangoed to one inch of their lives, all looking happy . . . They were everything that I was not.

I was a brunette, always had been. I didn't own expensive jewellery. Yes, I had kept my engagement ring. But it had felt wrong wearing it for this false wedding, so I'd replaced it with a fake diamanté ring that had cost me €28 in Oasis. After all, why should the ring be real, when nothing else was?

While all the women dashed about merrily, I couldn't even muster up a fake smile when we made eye-contact. I was spent! I felt like the walls of my world were crashing in on me. My life had become a joke. But somehow I wasn't the one getting the last – or first – laugh . . .

Drifting into a zombie state of melancholy, I was distracted from my trance by the sound of my name being called. 'Eva? Are you OK? It's me, Maddie . . .'

Without the energy for sarcasm I looked up to meet her gaze, and was met with a familiar smile. She looked as gorgeous as ever, if a little full in the face. 'Are you OK, hon?' she asked again, searching my eyes for some sort of response.

'Yeah, grand. Just taking five minutes to myself.'

'Are you with Parker and Lisa? We're at a wedding, but Michael went missing, so I just came out to have a look for him. You didn't see him, did you?'

In my head I wanted to yell, '*Fuck off*', but instead I just shook my head silently.

I was about to go, when Maddie mumbled under her breath, 'I can't believe he went off and left me . . .'

'Did you say you can't believe he went and left you? Are you totally dumb? He's a lying, cheating scumbag . . . Of course he's going to go off and leave you, too, Maddie. That's what scumbags do.'

'Grow up,' blasted Maddie, well able for any of my venom. 'You can't be bitter all your life, Eva. I know you're still in love with him, but you're really going to have to pick up the pieces of your life and move on.'

Almost choking at the ridiculousness of her

suggestion, I leapt from my chair and stood over her, shaking with anger. I still loved her, so it didn't take much for me to get angry. There were many words I could have used to express my hurt, but bitter didn't come close to describing my feelings towards herself and Michael. 'I . . . could not . . . I do not . . . not even in my fingernails, have any love for that bastard.'

'Fair enough . . . Then why are you still so angry?'

'Because I'm angry with *you*. There's a big gaping hole in my life since you're gone, and I hate you for that. Is that good enough for you?'

'Eva, I'm . . .'

'Yeah, we're all sorry,' I interrupted. 'But that doesn't change anything, does it? Now, don't let me hold you up, go find my *dick* of a husband and enjoy the rest of your night . . .'

'Eva, there's so much I need to tell you . . .'

'And I have no interest in hearing any of it, so fuck off and . . . just . . . leave me alone.' I went to turn around and flee, but Maddie's next statement stopped me in my tracks.

'I'm pregnant,' she blurted.

'I'm pregnant with Michael's baby. You deserve to know.'

My first reaction was to laugh. So I did. My two hands automatically rose to my face, and I laughed into them like a naughty schoolgirl.

'What's so funny?' asked Maddie, confused by my reaction.

'I don't know, exactly.' It was true. There was no

rational explanation why the news had made me laugh, but it had.

'It's not funny, Eva. I'm serious. I'm eleven weeks pregnant.'

'Bully for you, Maddie. But you don't get to tell me what I can find funny. I couldn't care less what you get up to now. Have twenty kids, and see if I care.'

'You just said you did care a minute ago.'

'I said I missed you. I didn't say that I wanted anything to do with you any more. There's a difference.'

'Well, I've missed you, too. And I still worry about you. That's why I organized Dave.'

'Dave who? What do you mean?'

'Handyman Dave. I paid him to flirt with you.'

'You did *what*?'

'I paid him. He's a gigolo. It's no big deal. I didn't want you to be lonely.'

'Get away from me.'

'What?'

'Get away from me. You make me sick.'

'I felt guilty, Eva. I was doing you a favour, if you recall?'

'You stole my husband, so you paid some other fool to shag me instead. Nice work. I hope you had a great laugh at my expense.'

'It wasn't like that, Eva.'

'And what was it like, exactly? You paid a man-whore to fuck me, while you fucked *my* husband. Just get away from me. This is too much right now. I hate you, Maddie. Please, just get out of my face.'

Now, more than ever, I needed air. So I ran out

through the double doors, past the smokers, and straight into a drunken Michael, who was slobbering all over a young redhead in a tight black dress.

'Michael!'

He didn't register who I was immediately, but after a couple of moments his eyes focused properly, and a big smile crossed his face.

'Evaaaaa! Wowww! Aren't youuu lookin' hot to-night!'

'You never change, do you, Michael?'

'Excushe me?'

'Your pregnant girlfriend is inside fretting about where you are. Meanwhile, you're out here trying to pick up a cheap tart.'

'Hey!' cried the young redhead. 'Who are you call-ing cheap?'

'Sorry.' I looked the young girl in the eye, and realized that she was just an innocent victim in this whole mess. 'I'd advise you to stay well clear of this guy. He's a nasty piece of work.'

Clearly bolstered by alcohol and Michael's bullshit, the young woman sized up to me and asked, 'And what gives you the right to interfere?'

'Well, let's just say I'm his wife. Is that good enough for you?'

Looking at the two of us like we were deranged, she muttered, 'I don't need this shit!' Then she ran off in the direction of the Ice Bar.

'Tanks for dat!' slurred Michael, as he turned back to me with one of his menacing looks. 'I liked herrr.'

'Don't worry, you once liked me, but you soon got over that!'

'Always da funny girl, Eva. Sch-mart bitch!'

We spent the next twenty minutes talking – for the first time really talking. We shared details that we'd never have been able to offer up while sober.

Michael got a great laugh out of my fake wedding story, and went on to open up for the first time. He sobbed about his parents dying, and told me about the nervous breakdown which had led to him moving to Ireland and working in Le Café, and how it had affected him over the last two years. Although he didn't like the changes it had made to his personality, he claimed that he couldn't do anything about them. And that he was glad I was out of his life, because now he wouldn't be able to hurt me on a day-to-day basis any more.

When he asked me why I had never been more curious about his nervous breakdown, I laughed it off, telling him that I'd had enough of them myself, every time each of the men in my life had let me down. But he wasn't happy with that reply. For some reason, after all that had happened, he felt he needed to share. He really had never opened up this way before. He spoke about his trading job in New York, and how he'd had a severe psychotic episode after being brutally sacked during a Wall Street bloodletting.

I froze in shock as he revealed the story of how he was called to personnel, terminated, handed his personal belongings by security guards and evicted from the building – all within the space of twenty minutes.

As if that hadn't been traumatic enough, he spoke about how he was offered no severance pay – because he hadn't been there long enough – which had left him unable to pay his huge credit card bills and led him to sofa-surf until his friends let him know that they wanted their space back. Like all good Irish mammies, his mum had come to his rescue and bailed him out, paying off all his bills with her life savings. Her one condition was that he return home with her. Although she seemingly tried her best with Michael, he explained that his mental state had continued to deteriorate. It had led to a short stay in a locked ward, shocking him badly enough to make him stick to the strong meds he was prescribed.

While the doctors had apparently described him as one of their success stories, Michael laughed drunkenly, 'Ash you clearly found out, they wash wrong!'

Sick of listening to this poor-Michael saga, I was about to walk off when he said, 'And then I met you. The gorgeous, shcatty, in-your-fash, and eternally opti-mishtic, Miss Eva.'

His words stopped me in my tracks.

He spoke about how he hated the job at Le Café, but that his mother had forced him to take it.

He told me how he had thought I was his salvation. How he had thought that sharing his life with a force of nature like me would pull him out of his misery and distract him from the way he'd messed up his glamor-ous life in New York.

'I wash sho sure dat you were de one, dat I didn't let a liddle thing like ure motorbike acshident get in the way. I loved youuu. And then you got *fucking preg-nant!*'

As he rambled on, cursing the fact that I hadn't given him enough attention, I realized that I'd been wrong to blame myself for getting fat and unattractive. Michael was just one of those men who would always resent their women for sharing their affections with anyone – even their own child.

As I stood in shock, watching the man I had once loved drunkenly act out years of turmoil, he confirmed the sixty-four-million-dollar question: 'It washn't ure fault. I fucked dish marriage up.'

I couldn't believe what I was hearing. All this time I had blamed myself and fretted over what I had done wrong, and then, in this one chance meeting, Michael had given me total absolution.

Finally, I could see that Daisy and I were better off without him. He might be my baby's daddy, but I felt that I'd had a narrow escape, and that Daisy and I were going to be more than fine – now that we didn't have to live out a life overshadowed by his issues.

When I quizzed him on Maddie's pregnancy, he claimed that she had trapped him, and that he had no desire to become a father again; though he admitted that he hadn't even been a proper one to Daisy to start with.

He spoke about how he was beginning to be repulsed by the same changes in Maddie's body that he'd seen in mine, and I couldn't help but feel pity for my former friend.

I was sure that he was about to tell me that his

relationship with Maddie was over when I heard her calling out his name. '*Michael*. What are you doing out here? You've been gone nearly an hour.'

Realizing that it wasn't my place to interfere again, I simply gave him a knowing smile, kissed him on the cheek, and disappeared further into the smokers, allowing him and Maddie their space.

With a stupid dumb grin on his face, he acknowledged his girlfriend and then mimicked her excitable girlie voice with a high-pitched scream. Almost immediately she thrust his hand on her belly, keeping him up-to-date with her impending motherhood.

Maddie was so busy looking down at her tiny, practically non-existent bump that she missed Michael's frozen expression. I didn't, though. It was obvious that their relationship was a time-bomb, just like mine had been. It was merely a matter of time before Maddie would be back in touch, heart-broken and full of apologies.

Of course I'd be there for her. Just like I had when Woody had had his accident, because that's what you do for a friend. Even those rare dumb-model friends who think they can walk off with your husband. Yes, maybe one day Maddie and me could be friends again. Could Michael perhaps find a way to be part of Daisy's life again, too? Well, maybe the dawning of a new year was making me misty, but I did feel a renewed sense of self-worth. I shouldn't have needed reassurance that the break-up of the marriage wasn't my fault, but Michael had finally laid all my fears to rest.

He probably wouldn't remember any of it in the

morning, but he had cheered me up no end, and released me from the burden of being someone's unloved wife.

He wasn't capable of loving me, or anyone, but somehow his words made me feel free for the first time in years, and positive about the future.

When I returned to the table, both Parker and Jeff were locked in a romantic gaze, and my fake husband-to-be was enjoying the company of a very handsome man who looked vaguely familiar from Jeff's birthday.

Learning from old diva behaviour, as I went to retrieve my coat from the cloakroom I quietly asked one of the waitresses to grab my bag from under the table. There was no need for goodbyes tonight. Tomorrow was the beginning of the end. It would mark the closing of a bad year, but that was fine, I was ready for a fresh start.

However unconventional it might be . . .

It was 8 a.m., and Parker was standing over me in my bedroom, smiling like he'd won the Lotto.

'Morning, Mrs George. Are you ready to embrace your big day?'

'Eh, how did you . . . ?'

'My key. Now, Daisy is already being fed by Jeff downstairs. So hurry up and have a shower. It's not fashionable to be late for fake weddings. Your future mother-in-law might die or something before you make the ceremony . . .'

I could barely see through my sleepy eyes, but what I did focus on was Parker's silly grin. 'You're a bit happy with yourself . . .'

'I was up with the cock this morning,' laughed Parker, as he disappeared back out the door. 'Fierce noisy, he was . . .'

I lay in the bed another five minutes just looking at my wedding dress hanging up on the back of my wardrobe. As Lisa had said, it was perfect. Sophisticated and womanly, I felt it reflected how I'd grown as a person. I'm sure others would argue that point, but today other people's opinions about me didn't count. I was helping someone other than myself, and it felt good.

As Alistair had said, I could do worse than a gay husband. Although I had given up on making lists or resolutions, I was determined to make a list of them today. As part of my transitional therapy from obsessing about what I had done, I'd have to concentrate more now on what I wanted to do . . .

Yes, a 'To Do' list was what I needed, with ten new plans – well, maybe five new ideas for better living. What would they be, though? I didn't smoke. I no longer hid chocolate biscuits in my writing desk for desperate moments, and I didn't get that many opportunities to drink myself stupid any more. Honestly, what would a list of resolutions be without the inclusion, or exclusion at least, of alcohol, fags or food? Well, I suppose it might end up being more attainable . . . Since my over-indulging had stopped, maybe I was getting saner. Ha! As if!

By the time I had showered and shaved – there was no need for waxing, since there wasn't exactly going to be a *wedding night* – I had come up with my five New Year's resolutions.

1: Do ten sit-ups, press-ups and star-jumps every morning and evening.

2: Start reading again, instead of spending hours on Facebook.

3: Try to spend quality time with Mum and Sis, instead of merely depending on them for babysitting.

4: Do an evening course. Maybe drawing or yoga or fashion design?

5: Try something new. Either a bungee jump. Or getting a law changed, or writing that infamous book I keep talking about.

As I wrote my five resolutions on the back of a spare wedding invite, I could hear my hairdresser, Alan, laughing behind me.

'You're some crazy bitch, Eva,' he teased me, while teasing my hair. 'You're either going to read a book or write one . . . Or bring your mam for lunch, or take the government to court. Nice simple strategies you've got there, chicken.'

'Ha! Well, have you any other suggestions for me?'

'Yeah, how about easing up on the weddings next year? Resolutions are meant to be about giving up stuff, aren't they?'

'Touché.' He was right. The most obvious resolution of the year had been staring me in the face, but I hadn't seen it.

'OK then, smarty pants. No. 6 is *no more* marriages.' I scribbled furiously in a cartoon fashion to emphasize my point. 'Oh, and No. 7 is no more shameless plugging of friends' businesses in *YES!* I mean, that's just an abuse of my power and—'

'Hey, steady on there, chicken, let's not carried away. You marry whomever the fuck ya like, and keep them cheques sailin' in . . . You can be a princess as many times as you want . . . Whatever keeps you smilin'.'

'Oh, I've got one,' interrupted Parker as he stormed back into the room. 'How about No. 8: go back to dating women again . . . Ha! Don't look at me like that. You've clearly run out of men if you're now marrying the fellas on my bus. And let's face it, you spend so much time giving out about them that you'd probably be better off with a woman. You have your baby now so you're sorted. You've said it yourself, living with a woman would be a lot less hassle.'

'Oh-my-God! I just remembered.'

'What?' cried Parker.

'Maddie's having a baby.'

'Our Maddie?'

'*Yes*, our Maddie. Well, she's not ours any more . . . Herself and Michael were at the Four Seasons last night. First she tells me she's pregnant, and then I bump into him and he's trying to score some young wan out at the smoking area.'

'Wow! He really is a cad. What a legend!'

'Eh, excuse me. What a prick, you mean.'

'Of course, but he really is a hetero stud, though – isn't he? I mean, talk about spreading the love. He's a total shit, but you've got to admire his stamina.'

'Hmmm, there was a time when I just would have

liked his legs broken, but we actually had a nice chat last night and—'

'Chat? You chatted? Now, that guy really does have magic powers.'

'Yes, actually, and he helped me feel good about myself.'

'Wow, there's a first in a long time. I'm so happy for you, pet.'

'Emm, poor Maddie, though. I felt like I wanted to slap her and hug her at the same time. That was weird.'

'Oh, and we're lovin' the weird here,' cooed my hairdresser, as he tugged my hair over his back-combing.

'Weird is good,' chimed Parker, giving my shoulder a squeeze.

'Exactly. This will make for a great interview with Oprah.'

'O-prah?'

'Yeah. When I'm on to promote my book . . . The one I'm going to write next year. See here – resolution No. 5.'

'Sure, you can tell her about your bungee jump and your press-ups while you're at it,' laughed Parker. 'She loves all that crap. Right, I'm bored. I've a Hollywood ending to organize. You're only one part of it, sweetness.'

'Charming . . . Then again, I'm only the bride . . .'

'Indeed. Now, how much longer do you think you'll be?'

'Forty minutes . . .'

'Ten minutes . . .' My hairdresser and I spoke at the same time.

Realizing that we both had unrealistic times in our head, we settled at twenty minutes. And Parker bounced back out of the room to boss some other unsuspecting soul, with Alan the hairdresser singing, 'Bounce, bounce, Tigger!'

By noon, everyone was in position for the ceremony. The marquee in the garden looked fab, yet not too camp. All the actors were in place, with even a replacement nana, who had agreed to turn up and play the Alzheimer's card, which relieved her from needing to know any details about the happy couple. She just wanted a day out, and three simple words, 'I can't remember . . .', were there to save her from any sticky situation.

Lisa looked healthier than she had the previous day, and seemed confident now she had an extremely protective Francis by her side. There was also a surprise appearance from newlyweds Betty and Teddy, from our Kinsale road trip earlier that year. Apparently they had become inseparable after first meeting on our deluxe coach, and had just returned from Cape Town, where they had spent two long weeks resting by a pool. Before that they'd worked for a week as painters for the Niall Mellon Township Trust on a building project in a shanty town.

Tanned and happy, they took charge of Daisy, who looked extremely pleased to be in their company. The stage was now set for an idyllic afternoon, and with a smile on my face I began to walk up the short aisle with Parker as my surrogate father.

With disposable cameras flashing from my family's side, and faces of mostly shock from the Georges', I continued to rehearse Alistair's full name. I had to avoid saying 'Timotei' instead of 'Timothy'. It was harder than you might think – after seeing what the hairdresser had done to his head.

As he took my hand from Parker's, Alistair kept mouthing the words 'thank you' to me, fighting back some pent-up emotion of his own. All I could do to snap him out of his teary mood was to give him an early peck on the cheek, to which the assembled crowd appropriately aahed. I also told him to, 'Act butch, or else you'll be packing your bags and moving in with the Simon Community in the morning!'

The service went perfectly until driver Teddy tried to escort Alistair's best lady, Rita – his overweight chocolate-brown Labrador – up the shiny temporary floor-tiles of the marquee. With the special job of ring-bearer, she was expected to make the walk, but despite all of Teddy's best efforts to drag her up the aisle by the neck – much to Alistair's horror – Teddy ended up throwing down the lead and removing the rings from around her collar, after a mystery voice moaned, 'Bloody stupid idea . . .'

Amazingly, our priest for the fake marriage was taking his role very seriously, and while I think he had stolen most of his quotes from *Four Weddings and a Funeral*, he expertly talked us through the whole awkward, 'Is there anyone in this tent who can think of any unlawful impediment why Eva Louise Patricia Valentine cannot marry Alistair Sinclair Timothy Franklyn George here today?' There was a deathly silence, before laughter rippled from Alistair's drama-group troupe. But some eyebrow-raising from the priest quickly settled the hecklers down.

Thankfully Alistair's mother seemed too deaf to notice any background noise, and so Father Russell Crowe quickly quoted from *Gladiator* under his breath and powered on to the 'I do's. Speeding through the words like we were up against the clock, Alistair was in the process of slipping a gold band that looked like it had fallen out of a barnbrack cake on my finger, when out of nowhere a large seagull flew into the decorated marquee and started bashing into the tall flower-arrangements before finally perching himself on the large harp beside us. This was much to the annoyance of the harpist, who cried, 'Get off my Venus, devil vermin of the sea!'

It was then that Rita, who had seemed happy enough to be tied to a nearby table in sight of the wedding party, suddenly found the courage to tackle the shiny floor and skated across in our direction, all the while barking her head off and dragging a high-topped table behind her.

Needless to say, Rita's awakening, teamed with the toppling of the table and the arrival of the 'devil vermin of the sea', had half the room screaming with terror, and the others screaming with joy! Dutifully Parker flung into action by grabbing Rita, and semi-silenced her – well, thankfully, she was an old girl, and she seemed relieved at the intervention. Sadly, after her third bark she had become almost hoarse from the exertion, and despite her bravado had clearly hurt her paw after charging into someone's leg. Bizarrely, the seagull barely flinched. Standing proud and solid on his perch he surveyed the marquee, eyeballing each row as if counting the guests.

The disgruntled harpist kept crying, 'It's the devil . . . It's surely the devil . . .' And I suddenly noticed Alistair's mother through the mayhem; she had a big smile across her tiny face.

Alistair himself had refused to let go of my hand through all of this. I'm sure his reasoning was that we were so close, it was best to ignore the crisis until we were home and dry. I managed to pull away from him and stepped over to Mrs George in her wheelchair, and asked her if everything was OK.

'That's his father,' she mumbled. 'Alistair's father.'

'The seagull?'

Lifting her hand, which was painfully twisted with arthritis, she pointed towards the bird, which was now looking straight at us. 'He always wanted to go out to sea . . . And be free like a bird . . .'

I was at a loss as to what to say, so I simply smiled back at her, and in the least condescending tone I could muster replied, 'Well, isn't it nice that he could make it?' Then I returned to Alistair and explained: 'She thinks the seagull is your father. Whatever you do, don't let the harpist bash it.'

Taking command of the panic around him, the priest shushed everyone back to calmness, and ordered them to retake their seats.

'We are all the Lord's children,' he explained. 'Let

us continue with our prayers, and welcome all of God's creatures into our ceremony. Even gatecrashers like this fellow . . . Well, then, again, we're clearly the gate-crashers in this instance, as he is the only true local. Anyway, where were we?'

Fumbling through his Bible for inspiration, he soon got the service back on track. But Alistair's mother Agatha never moved her eyes from the seagull. The other thing she didn't let go of was her smile.

Steaming ahead through the nervous laughter, which was just starting to subside, Alistair was halfway through his 'I, Alistair Sinclair Timothy . . .' when the seagull let out a big squawk, took a large poop down the side of the harp, and flew off back out through the entrance of the marquee.

His nostrils flared, almost grief-stricken, Alistair looked at me and said, 'That was definitely my father. The fucker always found ways to shit on me!'

I stifled my own laughter, but Mrs George let hers free and whooped with joy, while the harpist gave an equally loud yelp of utter despair.

Not wanting to waste any more time, the priest rushed through his lines. 'And with the power invested in me . . . yes, yes, OK, I now pronounce you man, or should I say, husband and wife. Alistair, you may kiss your bride.'

With most people keeping one eye out in case the seagull decided to make a return, there wasn't quite the cheer that I had expected. But Alistair hugged me so tightly with gratitude that I was convinced he'd bruised a rib. After all, our mission had been completed. Yes, there had been extra excitement involved, but then again, none of us had expected the ceremony to be dull.

Then there was a much-needed champagne and canapé reception in the house, which allowed everyone to calm down and the caterers to convert the marquee from car-crash to a romantic dining scene. By 4 p.m., Alistair and myself were making our grand entrance back into the place, this time to rapturous applause.

'Ladies and gentlemen, girls and gals,' laughed Parker, 'can you please welcome the lord and new lady of the manor, Alistair and Eva George . . .'

Throwing caution to the winds, the queens stood on their seats and cheered and whistled like we were parading at Gay Pride. The party atmosphere was evidently contagious, with even Alistair's stiff cousins joining in the fun.

We took our places at the top table beside Mrs George and my own fake mum, who was playing a blinder, and beamed with very convincing joy. 'You look beautiful,' she whispered. 'You've made me very proud . . .'

Passing off the totally surreal moment with a 'Thank you, Mum,' I grabbed her glass of white wine and knocked it back. 'Happy New Year to us all,' I shouted. A few faces around the table threw me funny looks, but I reasoned, 'Well, it's the New Year already in Sydney . . . so that's good enough for me!'

Within moments Parker had stood up to start his speech. In my opinion it was a very wise move to get it out of the way, because going by previous outings when he had allowed himself to get too drunk slash emotional slash judgemental, I feared for the safety of Mrs George. Yes, it was my marital right to hate her, the mother-in-law, and while in reality she might be an ole boot, on the flip side she was also a decrepit old woman.

'Thank you, everyone, for coming,' Parker began gingerly. 'Your presence here this evening has made this experience most memorable for the special couple. And I know we'll all enjoy many happy evenings watching the wedding video, specifically the split-second when our resident seagull shat on Fionnula's harp . . . Father Russell Crowe also deserves another round of applause . . . for his wonderfully unique and *thought-provoking* ceremony. It was the first time, anyway, that I've ever heard a marriage being likened to going into battle with the Romans. I won't forget it in a hurry. But while this year could be described by many as their *annus horribilis . . .'*

'*Steady on,*' cried many from the crowd. Parker paused just a moment before continuing his speech, like a man on a mission. But at that moment, I somehow sensed what was coming next and could feel the tears well up in my eyes.

'Especially by our beautiful bride tonight, Eva.' Waiting for the oohs and aahs to die down, Parker continued to speak from the heart, not a piece of paper, knowing he had everyone's attention.

'I'm keeping it brief, you'll be glad to hear, but I wanted to tell you all a little about my best friend, Eva. In the last two years she's been publicly slandered, fired, dumped, and given birth to a beautiful baby girl . . . who will have many challenges of her own . . . But she won't be alone, will she, Eva?'

I couldn't speak, so I just shook my head in reply.

'And then two of her best friends dumped on her again, and also tried to make her homeless. And all the while she was dealing with the trauma of seeing a young woman die in her arms. Some of you may have heard on the news about a young woman called Amy Price who died earlier this year. Well, that happened at my apartment. And Eva was the woman who called the ambulance and escorted her to hospital . . . Anyway, I love this woman. She is an inspiration to me, for the way she learns from her mistakes, picks herself up and battles on. For the patience and generosity she has for others. She is 110 per cent fabulous. Which is about one or two per cent more fabulous than me, *and that's seriously fabulous!*'

Mortified, I signalled for him to wrap up his speech, and as soon as he had listed off obligatory thanks to all the family members, he raced over and knelt beside me, questioning, 'What the hell did I say wrong, now?'

'I'm none of those things,' I explained over my shoulder. 'I'm not worthy. I feel like such a stupid woman most of the time. Why would you say such nice things about me and make me cry?'

'Because I meant them. You are a wonderful mum, and friend. And you do bring out the best in people. You're like everyone's favourite girl-next-door, only better-looking. Now stop blubbing. You look like one of those Hollywood brats preparing for a mugshot.

Mischa Barton, eat your heart out. You've mascara everywhere.'

'OK, listen, I'm going up to the house for a while. Let them start the dinner without me. Tell Alistair I want to check on Daisy, anyway.'

Weaving my way back out through all the tables, I excused myself as wanting to use the loo to anyone who asked. I was just about to go inside the house, when I saw a tall man in a snazzy mustard tartan blazer sniffing around the side of the marquee, looking incredibly suspicious.

'Eh, can I help you?' I asked, in an emotionally drained, fearless tone.

'Sorry, yeah, hi, I'm late. I'm looking for . . . Hey, I know you . . . You're that girl from . . . eh, Café en Seine . . . Ha! Remember me: Gavin Richards? I was your soul mate for an evening . . .'

'Oh-my-God, yes, I do. But it was more like one cocktail . . . What are you doing here?'

'I'm making a new film with a guy called Parker, and he invited me down.'

'Parker?'

'Yeah, do you know him? He's actually set me up on a blind date. I was meant to be here about three o'clock but I got delayed. Wow! You look stunning, by the way. What a shame you're already taken. I would have loved to be set up on a proper date with you . . .'

'Hold on a second. You're here for a blind date, set up by Parker. Are you gay?'

'Most definitely not, no offence to anyone who is, though . . .'

'So you're straight?'

'Absolutely. Angelina Jolie, yes; Brad Pitt, most certainly no . . .'

'And you've no idea who your date is?'

'Nope. Apparently she's totally out of my league, but Parker seems to think she's easy around celebration times like New Year's, so he reckons I'm on to a sure thing.'

'Does he, now? And did he tell you anything else?'

'Just that I was to wear a silly jacket, because she tends to ignore subtlety, and that under no circumstances was I to ever use the words "for sure"! Fairly cryptic stuff. So anyway, how are you? I didn't get the impression you were engaged when we met. Was this some sort of shotgun thing?'

'Ha! You're right, I wasn't. And I'm not . . . well, even though I have been.'

'Huh?'

'Sorry, yes, it's all very confusing. I know what, why don't you go inside and grab a bottle of champagne off the waiters? Forget about Parker for a minute, and meet me back out here.'

'Should you not . . . ?'

'No, I'll only get stuck. You'll be fine. And don't worry, no one will laugh at that jacket except me, they're a very colourful bunch inside.'

Giving me an enthusiastic thumbs up, Gavin disappeared inside the marquee, leaving me to do a mini-victory-dance outside. I couldn't believe it. Delivering James Bond on New Year's Eve was the best wedding present imaginable. Out of his league, eh? I liked it. As for being easy, my bessie bud clearly knew me too well. I'd have to rap him over the knuckles for that one at a later date. Right now, I had to concentrate on my New Year's resolution No. 9: starting the year off in the arms of a man I'd like to still be holding the following New Year's Eve.

I was staring out at the sea, admiring the beautiful coastline of Dalkey and the orangey sun that warmed up the sky, when a seagull, presumably the same one that had hijacked the ceremony earlier, walked across my path.

Dizzy with the excitement of seeing Gavin again, and unable to contain it, I started talking to the bird like a human.

'Good craic today, eh? You certainly made an impression inside. It was the highlight of the mother's day, that's for sure.'

'Squawk.'

'I can't believe I've got a date for tonight, can you?'

'Squawk.'

'And he's a Hollywood actor. How cool is that? And he fancies—'

Suddenly, without provocation, I stopped myself from talking further. No one had interrupted me – not even the seagull – but for some reason I realized that I was perpetuating all my old mistakes. Would I never learn? Just like the Eva of old, I was making plans for a bloke I barely knew. Talk about a repeat offender . . .

I'm not sure if the correct term was having an epiphany, but it was as if someone had flicked a switch in my brain, and I suddenly saw the light. Firstly, why the hell should I assume that this Mr Smooth was my Mr Right? And secondly, how could I think I could make it work with a Hollywood actor, when I had a young daughter with special needs to consider?

Hearing voices coming from the marquee, it was my instinct to run around the back of it and hide. I didn't know why I wanted to run away, but I just did it without thinking. I needed to stop myself from jumping feet-first into another relationship, or easy sex situation.

Yes, Gavin Richards seemed lovely. But then initially so had both the Michaels and Steve, and all the other cute guys that had caught my eye over the previous year . . .

Like a fugitive, I was frozen in fear, holding on to the edge of the marquee with knuckles white enough to match my dress. And by now both Parker and Gavin were calling my name. 'Eva. Where are you?'

While in a physical sense I knew exactly where I was, on another level I felt like the ground had just been swept up from under me. Despite all my best intentions and planning, I was as clueless as ever.

As my mind furiously tried to figure out an escape plan, out of nowhere a voice behind me screamed, '*Boo!*' With my nerves already frayed, I almost jumped out of my skin with the fright. It was Gavin. He was holding an open bottle of Moët in his hands and laughing. Then again, why wouldn't he be, with an easy shag already organized for him?

Quickly noticing my distress, he put his arms around

me comfortingly and asked, 'What's happened? Are you OK?'

But I couldn't answer him. Everything felt wrong . . . I needed to get away, and see if Daisy was OK. So I pulled away from him, but somehow my left shoe was caught, and with the strength that I used to release myself, I ended up spinning backwards and crashing towards the ground.

Within seconds I was horizontal, knocking my head off a steel keg on the way. The last thing I remembered hearing was screams. They were probably mine. Within a few flashes all light had gone and I could see nothing . . .

In the distance I could hear muggy voices rushing about. But I was too tired to reply. I felt at peace and I wanted to sleep.

In what seemed like just a few moments later, I opened my eyes to find myself in a bed, surrounded by a roomful of my friends, fussing and stressing.

At first I couldn't speak, but eventually found the energy to ask, 'What happened?'

Parker did his best to push everyone off the bed. 'Give her space, people,' he demanded. 'Now, pet, you fell and hit your head. How do you feel? Do you recognize me?'

Although my head felt slightly sore, I decided to have a little fun with my worried pal.

'I think I do . . .' I mumbled. 'I remember you. You were taking me to the wizard and you were looking for a heart. And you . . .' I sat up in the bed and looked at Jeff. 'You were looking for a brain . . . And you,' I looked at Gavin, 'you were looking for a ride!'

'Ha! Ha! Very funny, Ms Valentine. Everyone can stop worrying: she's back and as feisty as ever.'

After Parker, Alistair and Jeff had dropped kisses on my forehead, the three of them headed back to the party, pulling a few strays with them on the way, which just left a tired Lisa and a slightly bamboozled-looking Gavin Richards.

Sitting down on the bed beside me, Lisa asked, 'Is it OK if I go now? I'm shattered.' She winked in the direction of Gavin. 'Nurse Richards behind me looks ready to practise his hero skills on you. If you're feeling faint I'm sure he'll be able to revive you with a little mouth-to-mouth.'

For the first time, I could really see the sickness in her face. Her strong features looked frail, and in a strange twist of events I felt like the powerful one.

Grabbing her with my two hands, I pulled her close and whispered, 'I love you. This will all work out. We're going to beat this, do you hear me?'

Reciprocating my hug, she whispered back in a shaky voice, 'Thank you. I love you, too.' Then she joined Francis at the door, and disappeared out.

'And then there were two,' smirked Gavin, as he slowly edged towards my bedside. 'You gave us all a fright, young lady.'

'Sorry about that.'

'Well, in a way it was a good thing for me. I got to learn all sorts of interesting facts about you.'

'Really? Like what?'

'Well, that you're extremely accident-prone. Ya love bangin' your head, apparently. Mad for it!'

'Ha! Yes, it's been known to happen. Mmm, do you know where my daughter is?'

'Yeah, I think she's just down the hall with the nanny. Parker mentioned it. I think she's asleep.'

'OK. Listen, do you mind giving me a minute to get myself together? I think I might slip into something more comfortable.'

'This is probably not a good time to offer you a hand with slipping it off, so I'll take myself downstairs and let you do whatever you ladies need to do.'

'Will you be hanging around?'

Smiling from the doorway, he effortlessly pulled a James Bond pose and laughed, 'I'm not going anywhere, I'm on a promise,' before slinking out of sight.

I quickly threw off my dress, which was now covered in muck, found my case of clothes, and slipped into a sexy little black dress and heels. Then I went in search of Daisy. I needed to see her. I needed to smell her sweet baby smell. Just like Gavin had said, I found her down the hall, quietly sleeping in a giant king-size bed, surrounded by pillows to keep her snug and safe.

'She's been a dream to care for,' explained Betty, who was sitting in a grand old chair beside the bed with a fat book in her hands. 'Are you OK? I heard you took a tumble.'

'I'm fine, thank you, Betty. I was about to make a familiar mistake, and then fate knocked some sense into me.'

With a knowing look, Betty asked, 'Are you talking about your handsome suitor?'

'Ha! Yes, but I'm feeling more sensible now.'

'Well, lovee, let me give you one bit of advice if I can. Don't give up on love. My first husband died six months after we got married and I was made a widow aged twenty. I was six months pregnant with a honeymoon baby, and I thought my world had caved in. I felt I would never be able to love my child because she would be a constant reminder of the man I had lost. How wrong I was. I fell in and out of love with many men during my life, and now I have been blessed again with Teddy, a wonderful man. But I always had my Megan. No matter what men came or went I always had the solid love of my child, and to this day she remains my most cherished gift.'

'Children are a gift.'

'I believe so, lovee.'

'Thank you, Betty, for everything. Daisy really is the most important person to me, and will remain so no matter what lunatics I meet.'

'But you're allowed to have fun as well, mammy. Daisy would want that for you.'

'You're always a rock of good sense, Betty.'

'Ha! Well, I'd class myself a street angel and a house devil. No one's ever perfect, lovee, so don't beat yourself up trying to be.'

'So what now?'

'I suggest you take yourself back down to the party with your lovely new frock on and wow that new gentleman friend of yours. Sometimes you need to believe in fairy tales to create your happy ending . . .'

I planted a gentle kiss on Daisy's cheek, and circled the bed to give Betty a thank-you hug. 'Yes, Mam. Positive thinking for me. My fresh start begins now.'

'Now go back out there, and take control of your destiny.'

'Ha! I'm going. I'll see you in a bit. I'll fill you in on my progress.'

Throwing me a knowing smile Betty laughed, 'Indeed. To be continued . . .'

'Agreed. This will definitely need to be continued . . .'

Acknowledgements

Hello there, and welcome to my acknowledgements.

This is the corner of the book where I try and remember all the people who have helped me along the way. So, fingers crossed that I don't forget anyone.

If you're standing in a bookshop reading this and trying to work out what sort of person the author is, well, let me tell you proudly that I'm someone who feels well loved.

On the other hand, if you're flicking to see if you're name-checked, wait your turn because there's no one who deserves a bigger thank you than my editor on *Champagne Babes* and previously on *Champagne Kisses*, Francesca Liversidge.

Although I'll be working with a new editor, Lauren Hadden – and I'm looking forward to doing so on home turf in Ireland – I can't begin to explain the depth of my gratitude to you, Francesca, for discovering me and believing in my work. Any night you fancy being a disco diva, just give me the nod and we'll hit the dance floor in Renards – again!

A big thank you also to my agent Ita O'Driscoll for

putting the deal together with Transworld Ireland – which we did on the side of a mountain in Killarney, in the rain I recall, and for entertaining all my endless requests and enquires.

To all other writers still lingering in slush piles: keep the faith, that's how I was found. It sounds corny, but it could happen to you, too ☺ 📱

Speaking of writers, thank you to Patricia Scanlan, Claudia Carroll and Anita Notaro for welcoming me with open arms to their world. You girls rock.

To the Irish critics, all I can say is *wow*! Thank you for getting me. Your praise helped sell *Champagne Kisses* around the world, and for that I am truly humbled.

And to all the Irish press and media, thank you for letting me endlessly flog my ass. I know I'm shameless, but I do try my best to keep it fresh – a little advice I picked up from my old friend Blathnaid Ni Chofaigh. Ha! Ha!

To everyone who bought *Champagne Kisses* and told me that they laughed and cried, thank you from the bottom of my heart. It made all those long nights and short weekends worth it.

Of course, I can't forget Bono for his part in helping to launch Amanda Brunker the author. It was such an amazing moment watching you arrive to my book launch, proudly holding a copy of *Champagne Kisses*. Thank you for all your support and encouragement through the years. Though if you don't slip a book into Oprah's hands quickly, I might have to bash ya!

To all the gang at the *Sunday World*, thanks a million. And apologies for boring you endlessly with novel updates. My thanks especially to Neil Leslie and Colm MacGinty for just being deadly.

Oh, and thank you to Gavin McClelland for giving me Gavin Richards. I hope you like.

To all my friends who don't see me that often because I'm such a nerd now, thank you for being a constant source of inspiration, but especially Joan who remembers all the wild nights that I forgot. If you had not been sober most of the late 90s and early 00s, I might never have been able to piece together my youth.

A big shout out to Eoin McHugh at Transworld Ireland, all the gang at Transworld UK and to Simon and Gill, Helen and Declan for their work putting the book together and promoting me. Your patience was invaluable.

If you're like me and read the acknowledgments first before the book, I need to be careful how I express my gratitude to the next two very special women: Aine Ryan and Olivia Williams. Thank you for sharing your touching stories of motherhood with me. I hope you are happy with how I handled this book. Your approval would mean a lot to me.

And of course, I couldn't forget the legend that is James Harris who introduced us all. You're a super guy, and I know you're going through a rough time of it at the minute, so I've asked Anna Nolan to light a candle for ya.

Last but not least, the biggest thank you goes to my family. Once again Betty and Moira, thank you for writing this book for me. OK, you didn't *actually* write it (God forbid, I can hear you both shriek!), but every

Amanda Brunker

time you watched over the boys, I was able to step back into my fictional world and lose myself for a few hours – bliss . . . And not forgetting Carol, too the three of you have done a great job rearing the lads while I'm busy. Though if you could hurry up and get them both out of nappies, and have them sleeping through the night for me, that would be fantastic!

Thanks also to my dad for providing me with great material for the next book, and to Norman for always promoting me. I hope I haven't let you down . . .

Well done to my sis Linda in LA for finally bringing a little girl into the world. At last I have a justified reason to hoard all my shoes!

But my final thank you goes to Philip for always supporting me, even when you do feel neglected. I'm sorry we don't get to take holidays, or do date-things like most couples, and I'm aware that I'm a bad partner.

I do love you though, very much. Thank you for being a great dad and for not giving up on me.

CHAMPAGNE KISSES
by Amanda Brunker

Like any great diva, Eva Valentine is a flawed character. Spoilt, stubborn and sassy, she exudes lioness confidence when in the company of her fellow bitches Maddie and Parker, and hungers for sex like others desire chocolate.

Eva is a woman who would kiss your girlfriend as quick as she'd steal your husband, but underneath this hard-nosed facade she's just a regular girl who craves normality, and a love that she can call her own.

After CCTV images of a clumsy clinch with her very *married* boss make headlines in the Sunday papers, her whole world begins to crumble. Eva must come to terms with the harsh consequences of her reckless actions, but don't think for a second that this would ever stop her fun. In Europe's most expensive capital, beautiful people can always find rich friends to fly them to fabulous parties in London or glamorous holidays in Marbella.

'Fresh, funny, frothy and fabulous'
Claudia Carroll

9781848270022

CHAMPAGNE SECRETS
by Amanda Brunker

Eva the Diva is back! And she's going
undercover . . .

After capturing a bust up on an airplane between
a group of footballers' wives on her camera phone,
Eva is offered the chance of a lifetime – a new job
as an undercover TV reporter. Her exciting new
career means moving with her little daughter Daisy
to London and keeping the exact nature of her work
secret from her colleagues at the TV production
company. Even the new man in her life
doesn't know what she's up to . . .

It's not all high glamour in the big city though – as a
single mum in a new town, Eva needs support. So she
moves in with her aunt's large brood, where the rough
and tumble of family life is a stark contrast to the
celebrity restaurants and nightclubs she visits in her
quest to uncover all sorts of WAG drama.

But as the intrigue deepens and Eva is forced to tell
more and more lies to hold her cover, will her secret
prove to be her downfall? And will there ever be a
real Mr Right? One thing's for sure; there'll be lots
of naughty fun and games along the way . . .

9781848270510

Coming in June 2010 from Transworld Ireland . . .